SEASONS OF THE FLESH
A NOVEL

RICHARD ALAN BUNCH

ISBN 978-1-4958-0972-9

Published February 2016

INFINITY PUBLISHING
1094 New DeHaven Street, Suite 100
West Conshohocken, PA 19428-2713
Toll-free (877) BUY BOOK
Local Phone (610) 941-9999
Fax (610) 941-9959
Info@buybooksontheweb.com
www.buybooksontheweb.com

For whatever we lose (like a you or a me)
it's always ourselves we find in the sea
—e.e. cummings

Like all things built of love, the past is whispers.
—William Logan

CHAPTER 1

N̲o one wanted to talk about what happened in the Lake District. No one. It was a hushed topic period. So they drove beneath clouds and velvet green fields sharply outlined by intricately pieced together stone fences that set themselves against purple shaded mountains. Such color contrasted with hay-colored roadside weeds that blew in the Yorkshire breezes. Even an old-fashioned train that spewed thick white smoke had passed over them just east of Penrith's curving, somber streets.

A day later they had crossed the Solway Firth and absorbed the poetic charms of Dumfries in Kirkcudbright in bonnie Scotland, a land, too, of contrasting yellows and drab greens, reds, and solemn grays. How they had loved Robert Burns, especially Enid Brown, whose love of literature was unbounded. She had squeezed Fleming's arm with a moving gesture as they had viewed the Burns Mausoleum in St. Michael's Kirkyard, especially in respect of Burn's love for Jean Armour. But Paris Brandon, a philosophy student, was poetically sensitive as well. There were unspoken understandings between him and Enid. In another way, his heart was beginning to open like a full-blown lotus for the blue-eyed Blythe Pierce who now sat beside him as the miles went by almost sleepily.

Having returned to England, they wound their way south to Lake Ullswater. Fleming had filmed the scene: the changing light and plays of shade, exquisitely over the silver-tinted lake under a gentle breeze. They now came upon Lake Windermere where they planned to spend the night. They rented a place overlooking Windermere not far from Bowness Pier. Blythe opened the window overlooking the lake:

"Magnificent," she said, "almost sunset. Sunsets should be exquisite."

1

"A good place to get a rise," said Fleming as he hung up his coat. Both he and Paris were approximately the same height. Often people thought they were brothers, even twins, but there were sufficient differences. Paris was the taller of the two; blue-eyed; a bit more pensive; foolishly sentimental; philosophical, poetical. Fleming was crude; given to crass remarks; at times too realistic; at others capable of amazing insight; a bit of an aesthete; sensuous, perhaps poetical, even spiritual, but more rebellious than his philosophical friend.

Enid was fair, blond, clear-complexioned, gaiety unbounded; capable of profound poetical thoughts; at times childishly naïve; at times foolishly demanding and overly self-assertive. By contrast, Blythe was a brunette, hypersensitive, poetic, less light-hearted, bitchy, politically a champion of causes, a strong person much as in a valley hidden in mists in old Chinese paintings.

"A rise?"

"Yes, in my pants," replied Fleming. There was a crashed silence. Blythe stared at the ceiling.

"What a grossout…"

"It is a nice view," suggested Paris who took off his olive green coat with the second button missing.

"Ah, yes, Windermere," said Fleming, "a fine place to lock loins and…"

"And gross each other out," Blythe interrupted. Fleming only smiled. Blythe gave Paris a soft-baked look.

"Let's go to the lake," Enid suggested, giving her eyes to Paris.

"Yes. You and I, my dear," said Paris, giving her him arm.

"Excuse us," he nodded at Fleming and Blythe.

After they left, Blythe said to Fleming: "You don't have to be gross."

"Maybe I want to. The world is gross, ugly. I merely reflect the world."

"Maybe so, my love, but you might just reflect if when they're not around. You and I lock loins. Tonight, eh?"

She smiled with a long cigarette balanced between her long, elegant fingers.

"I'll lock loins all right. I'll eat you alive. Suck the juices and lick away any problems you might have."

"All right. But don't drink beer. It gives you gas. And your…"

"All right. All right. I know. Dmitri and Chad back at the manor have already told me about my gas…"

"Well, you are one of the golden hogs, the studs of Room 33, Erehwon Manor. You gotta be cool. You have a reputation as being the wild bunch on campus," she said with obvious pride which concealed a way of depending on externals. He, too, felt an obligation to play this image, compelling as it was, as images go.

"Studs we are ma'am. Let's go to work," he said as he kissed her long and she, quivering like a maple leaf in a late September wind, trembled and kissed with all the feverishness of the passions. She had surrendered to him months before and was very much his lover. But that was all. Sex was superb. She got horny and called; it was the same with him. But Fleming was not as sensitively involved as was she. Often he ruthlessly took what she gave. He could accept the her in himself and she could not accept the he in herself, at least with Fleming. Soon they were on the bed and loving every dappled moment of it, especially when he would nibble on her with a humming sound. Her slender body was angular, willowy which only served to accentuate a fined sensuousness. Fleming ate it up. Although he was interested in other women, Blythe was his best lover. There were only two water bubbles in this: her asthma and her fear of pregnancy. Asthma attacks grossed him out; her fear of pregnancy was due to her refusal to use contraceptive devices. This made him angry whenever it was brought up. They argued over it. But Blythe had her way.

He now could hear her gasping, culminating, scratching him deeply, tossing her exquisite dark hair back and forth, outlined against the white pillow case. "Oh…" she repeated, breathless. "Oh, Fleming…you are… so good. Oh my God…" Fleming smiled. It was indeed a pleasure to bring pleasure to a woman. To feel a lovely heartbeat, panting, murmuring was the supreme delight of life. After several minutes, she lit a cigarette as sweat dried on her body and her dark eyes, deep and penetrating, peered at him over the sheets.

"Lovely," she said, as he wiped his forehead. He smiled. Just then, of all times, she began wheezing.

3

"Damn it, Blythe. Where's the atomizer?" She pointed to the bureau drawers. He fetched it; she began breathing it. After awhile, the wheezing stopped. This really irritated "Love 'em and leave 'em" Fleming as he was known.

"Why do you smoke when you have asthma?"

"Fleming. Let's forget it. We've been over this before," she said quietly.

"It's a pain in the ass if you ask me," he muttered.

"You're quick to anger, aren't you?"

"Of course. Everytime we go to bed this happens…"

"I'm sorry it inconveniences you…" He gave her a semi-serious look.

"You don't have to apologize. Apologies are phony somehow. It's just something you can't help, I guess," he said. "It just grosses me out. Locking loins is great but the aftermath…is…"

"Is what?"

"It undoes it. Like drinking a well-aged wine out of a styrofoam cup. It is aesthetically gross."

"You have your nerve, Fleming. You grossout people all the time with your gross remarks. Then you get pissed off because I have asthma. You can be a son of a bitch at times…" she said, very angry now, as she lit up another cigarette.

"Put that out."

"I will not."

"A defiant Aries," as he rose from the bed and dressed.

"A Scorpio grossout," she mocked.

"Let's cut it or I'll lay my horns on you again. Saddle 'n Sirloin. One Brown steak easy over."

Blythe sat up and sulked. She was passionate as she was sensitive. She rose and dressed and hung up her weekend wardrobe in the closet. Fleming stepped out on the porch that overlooked the lake through the lovely oaks. Blythe smoked her cigarette and sulked. Fleming was hell, she thought, but she had grown to care for him in spite of his antics. Onto the porch she strolled. He did not turn.

"Peaceful, isn't it?" she said after awhile.

"Yes, God's eyes are winking in that lake. That is why the lake smiles so."

"Oh?" replied Blythe a bit off guard. For the longest moments, as long as moments will stretch, she listened to the breeze that rustled the trees and lapped its tongue across the lawn.

"What does the wind say?" he asked.

"The wind says: words of love must by action be told."

He turned to her.

"The wind says: only love that is meant, can be," he replied.

"Fleming. I care for you," she said. He smiled.

"I have lust for you, my dear," he shot back, his auburn hair deepening with the shifts in late afternoon sunlight.

"Must you be so gross," she replied. "That's just a front."

"I don't need your analysis. People need to be grossed out once in a while. Everything is so tame, so lame. I love to short-circuit everyday awareness. Words must go. Hammers in time: eternity's sunrise."

"You see you hide behind a mask of words. And when you let it all down, you're really a beautiful person. Then you don't gross anyone out."

Fleming returned to his staring at Lake Windermere.

"Blythe, Aries is a ram. A symbol. You're too pushy. Lay off."

She fell silent and watched him with a love that was best articulated as a kind of concern. But it was only one-way. Fleming was bored by such romance.

"Scorpio stings. You demand everyone take your…"

"Cut it. Cut the strings!" he said.

Just then they heard the back door slam. Paris and Enid had returned. Enid returned to the front room.

"You enjoy the lake?" asked Blythe, adjusting her gold earrings that contrasted with her long, black hair.

"Oh, yes. So beautiful up here. Wordsworth Country," said Enid as she sat down, her blond curls hanging gingerly over her shoulders.

"Yes. Wordsworth and Dorothy. You see why they went on walking tours. Coleridge: a marvelous metaphysically-intoxicated genius. Stirs the deepest bones of a poet," declared Enid who wrote poetry herself.

Paris packed his pipe on the couch. Fleming returned and sat across from Paris, who noticed the disturbed sheets. Fleming eyed him. Paris retuned the look with a smile and lit up his pipe. Soon a wreath of purplish-blue smoke curled like a lounging cat about his head and neck.

"Lovely country, isn't it, Fleming?"

Fleming glanced at Blythe.

"Lovely indeed," replied Fleming. Blythe glanced at Enid whose look was disconcerted, almost apprehensive.

"Mind if I smoke a joint?" asked Fleming. Blythe frowned.

"Where did you get that?" she said, eyeing the cigarette between his fingers.

"No," said Paris, "go ahead."

Enid gave Paris a frown. So did Blythe.

"San Francisco. Where else?" replied Fleming who now lit his grass and deeply inhaled and held it. Blythe was becoming angry. Paris' large blue eyes rolled over to Enid as they searched her face. She was not happy about the situation. She started to say something but Paris shook his head.

"Let's get some dinner," Blythe suggested. Enid rose.

"Fish and chips all right with you?" Blythe asked, eyeing both Paris and Fleming whose bodies said "yes." They left. As they walked away from the cottage, Blythe said:

"I'm sorry he's this way. It has been a trying day."

"What's the matter?" she said, gesturing in the direction of the cottage.

"He got mad because I criticized his gross remarks," she said with exasperated hand movements.

"Does he smoke pot all the time?" asked Enid.

"No, just when he's trying to be an ass," she replied as they walked along. Paris smiled at Fleming across from him.

"What's up?" he asked after studying his friend.

"Fussing. She thinks I'm too gross." Paris puffed some more on his pipe, eyeing the orange glow under the crust of burnt tobacco in the bowl.

"Too gross for whom?" he finally said.

"For you all. And her," he replied, unbuttoning his shirt and taking another long puff, as he lay his head against the couch and began to stare at the ceiling. There was a long silence, then Paris spoke:

"She'll outgrow it or you will," he said, low.

Fleming laughed a silly laugh then lit up and inhaled deeply. In a few moments, he said:

"You know. I hear the lake laughing. The lake has a beautiful voice. One helluva beautiful voice. Bet you thought lakes had no voices. That's a mistake. Way we usually see things is all a mistake. We might even outgrow our scientific mythology someday. God I hope so. We haven't even heard the lake's laughter and whispers. That's how stupid we are. Totally unaware of anything. The lake laughs so profoundly," he said as he laughed at the floral designs in red, green, pink on the ceiling.

CHAPTER 2

When Blythe and Enid returned, they were ready to eat. The fish and chips wafted through the air as salivating juices were activated. Paris rose and sat at the table with Blythe and Enid. But Fleming was high and he remained lying on the couch.

"Fleming, come eat," said Blythe.

"I have no room for anything. I'm already full," he replied.

"Fleming, please eat," pleaded Blythe, finally.

"No, my love, my emptiness is fullness. Your love is my fullness, the richness of my sin," replied Fleming. Blythe ate her meal and was becoming quite angry.

After the meal, Paris and Enid left for a long walk. Blythe was determined not to stay there with Fleming acting like an ass. She decided to wander around the lake and leave Fleming to his musings. Fleming could be quite insensitive and Blythe's care for him had been stepped on multiple times.

Sun had set. Twilight merged with dusk. Darkness rolled in on padded feet and Blythe was angry and hurt at the same moment. Soon the moon had risen and on the ripples the moon's reflections danced. She adored this country. It was a shame she could not enjoy it, thanks to Fleming's behavior. The mountains were set in the moonlight and the hotels and restaurants nestled quietly in their shadows and their lights. Many sailboats were moored on the lake and with sails furled for the night, there were also tiny landing docks. She headed for Bowness

Pier and against dark massive shadows of the trees on the lake shone the white, double-decked Swan, its full name the Swan Barrow, whose keel had been laid in 1938. It was used as a tour boat from Bowness to Ambleside and back, each trip about an hour or more at a cost of half a pound and three pence.

She moved gracefully just like a swan through the deep blue waters of Windermere. Blythe was fascinated by swans, even black swans although most were white. She admired their long necks that stretched for a morsel or two. But often she had dreams of swans who wore leis of hibiscus and orchids around their necks, leis of aloha and remembrance all woven into the poetry of dreams. And at times the swans would wear not leis but necklaces of cowrie shells and make a certain melodious song as if out of great suffering and sorrow yet only exquisite music poured forth from them.

Onto the dock she strolled. As she neared the bow of the Swan, she felt a wave of utter loneliness, of being all alone in a world she did not feel at home in, of an anger-turned-melancholy, even despair. She stopped and gazed at the moon's reflection as it danced on the waters near the sleek and trim Swan. Then she climbed onto the Swan which was moored with heavy mortal coils wound about thick log posts on the dock. No one seemed to be around in the darkness and moonlight. Up the ladder she went to the observation deck and stood there, toying and playing with the life preserver. That damn Fleming, she thought, he's such an ass at times....men are such bastards, she thought, as she stared out over the proud prow of the Swan. I want somebody so bad...I yearn to touch the stars...to feel the galaxies in my veins...to love and to be loved in this ice-age of efficiency and shallowness.

She did not hear a light thump behind her. She only stared at the trees in the dark images in her mind.

Another thump occurred. This time she heard it but dismissed as the washing of the waves against the Swan's hull. And before she knew, even before she felt, the stars fell out of the skies of her mind and a hand smelling of faint wood alcohol swept across her as if she were trying to slap herself sober. All of a sudden, she was there, her long black hair lay against the deck, her arms fighting off these phantoms until she could no longer be false to herself that this was at the very least an unplanned night tour. The bandage her fingers felt crossed his temples, touched, yearned, and she began to whimper. She felt like a sheath, opening and closing, in the midnight striking of blue matches. Melancholy laughed, despair giggled, yearning showed his yellow teeth. Had he escaped from prison? He did not let up but relentlessly pursued, pumped, and thrust until despair promised melancholy in the next round. Oh Paris, oh Fleming, she whimpered, oh how lovely heaven and earth, springtime mating, oh Fleming, oh...oh...you're not Fleming. No you're not. You're not Paris either. Oh yes you are. Oh, Paris. You are not me. Me. Me. Me. You're the death of me. Open the gates of hell: oh Fleming, sweet, sweet Fleming, you bastard. Musk smells, bandage smells, and wood alcohol smells. His head kept bobbing throbbing, bandaged. Blythe had been caught unawares. The whole experience unzipped like a sparkler hitting water. It had not been difficult: she did not know what was happening or if she did, she rationalized it away. Nothing dawned until everything, including her rationalizations, had set, long after she had heard the footsteps and the running feet on the dock and watched the stars twinkle above her as she viewed the full expanse of sky without using one neck muscle. It would not be for a few weeks that the full impact of their encounter would make itself manifest.

CHAPTER 3

The next morning was not a typical morning in Cumberland. It was overcast but tourists flocked early to the landing stations to latch onto excursion and pleasure craft that would dot Windermere long before noon. Paris awoke first, got up, and flung open the curtains. The great rush of light almost blinded Fleming's closed lids and he quickly rolled over.

"What the hell are you doing?"

"Trying to show you the light," Paris softly replied as was his manner.

"Thanks. You don't have to blind me for life, do you?"

In a moment he propped himself on an elbow and looked out.

"Hell, the sun isn't even out yet. You think we should go down to the lake now? To avoid the tourists I mean?"

"No," said Paris. The tourists will be there early or late. We'll get on board, don't worry. Only costs ten shillings."

"That's not bad for two hours. In fact, that's pretty good compared to American prices."

"Anything's cheap compared to them. Anyway, breakfast will be ready the lady said around eight-thirty or nine."

"What's for breakfast?" asked Fleming, looking at his watch.

"The same all over England probably. Eggs, bacon, toast, jam, and maybe some tea," said Paris facetiously.

"I guesso. I wonder how Blythe slept last night. There's more to that than meets the eye. I just feel it. It's all too suspicious how she wouldn't tell us anything about what happened."

"I know that has worried me too. In fact, I had trouble getting to sleep I was thinking about it so much," Paris said, with a serious look on his face.

"We shouldn't let it bother us," said Fleming.

"I know. We worry ourselves to death about things that usually don't happen."

"That's true. Still I do care about her."

"Does she know it," asked Paris.

"I don't know."

"You better get on the ball and tell her."

"That's easier said than done," replied Fleming as he pulled on his pants and began looking for his shoe. "You seen my shoe?"

"No. It might be under the bed or in the closet by accident," suggested Paris as he took his toilet kit and went down to the bathroom.

"Be back in a minute," he said.

Fleming was down on all fours. Pulling up the bedspread, he found his shoe. He went to the mirror and felt his whiskers that had not been shaved for awhile. He combed his hair to one side and pulled out a cigarette, lit it, and began puffing. He looked up to the upper staircase to Enid and Blythe's room. He went up and knocked. Enid, looking fresh, opened the door. Blythe was still in bed.

"Good morning," said Enid sweetly. "Where's Paris? Isn't he up yet?"

"Yes. He's washing right now. How's Blythe?"

"Oh, she's a little tired I'm afraid. Aren't you, Blythe?"

"Hmmmmm," she mumbled as she turned her head toward Fleming.

"Oh...hello Fleming," she mumbled.

"How goes it, Blythe?"

"Just fine I guess," she said, yawning in his face.

"Well, let's go. Today's the big day. You haven't forgotten, have you?"

"Forgotten what?"

"The boat trip…across Windermere."

"Oh, no, I haven't forgotten. Look, I'm kinda tired, if you don't mind."

"Don't tell me you aren't going."

"I didn't say that. I'm just tired, that's all." Enid sat in a chair by the window as Fleming sat on her bed talking to Blythe.

Outside, the day became briefly sunnier and birds began to sing.

"Oh, all right. I'll go but I don't really feel like it."

She got up and pulled down her nightgown so Fleming could not see what he had seen time and again before.

"Could you leave now so I can dress?" she said, addressing him like a noble would address a valet. Fleming made a low, sweeping bow and went out. She began talking as she brushed her hair.

"Boy, am I bushed," she said.

"It must be this mountain climate," said Enid.

"Must be," remarked Blythe.

"It's such a nice day outside," said Enid gazing out the window.

"Yes it is."

"Blythe, Fleming was sure nice this morning."

"I know. He's nice until he gets a few drinks in him then he's a holy terror."

"I hope he doesn't drink, today."

"Don't set your hopes too high, honey. Fleming is not one to have faith in for very long. He'll probably drink like a fish."

"I hope not," said Enid. This infuriated Blythe's simmering temper.

"Gee, Enid. Do you have to keep hoping? Fleming is the way he is, a cross between an angel and a fool. That's it…"

At that moment, she realized what she had done and saw in the mirror Enid's eyes watering.

"Sorry about that Enid," she said patting her on the back. "It's just that Fleming is as Fleming does. Nothing to do with you. Why don't we get ready to go to breakfast then on to the lake."

Enid nodded as she dried her eyes.

After breakfast, they went down to the nearest launch station to pay for a ticket aboard the Swan Barrow from Bowness to Ambleside. They were soon on board and at first climbed up to the observation deck but as the ship was released from her moorings they realized it was quite windy. They decided to go to the lower deck where the wind was not so swift and watch the lake from there. Fleming ordered a beer; Paris ordered tea; and so did Enid and Blythe. The beauty of Lake Windermere and the surrounding hills was captivating.

"This is so beautiful," said Enid.

"If you can't be inspired here, you're probably dead," suggested Paris. Enid smiled and nodded. Blythe seemed far away even though she nodded in agreement.

Fleming enjoyed his beer and also appreciated the beauty of not only the lake but the countryside. The Swan was sleek and quiet since it had moved through these waters for so many years.

Blythe recognized where she had been the night before. Along one part of the ship nearest the wall, it looked like a streak of blood. She frowned when she saw it. What had happened? When did it happen? She continued to pretend to gaze at the hills when, in reality, her thoughts were far away, very far away.

The next day they drove to the Cumbrian town of Cockermouth to see where Wordsworth was born. Enid loved poems about nature and this was something that Wordsworth wrote about in astonishing detail. Once in Cockermouth, they found the home was closed on Sunday. So they left only after taking in the breathtaking views of the area around Cockermouth.

"I love looking out across the Irish Sea," said Blythe.

"I do, too," replied Paris.

"It's very romantic," observed Enid.

"It's just another sea to me," remarked Fleming who seemed a bit bored by all the talk.

"I remember in high school reading Wordsworth for the first time. In class we read a poem called "I Wandered Lonely as a Cloud" and I loved it and never forgot it," said Enid who seemed for a moment lost in thought.

"What was it about?" asked Fleming.

"About how the poet went hiking and around the side of a bay he is enraptured by thousands of daffodils."

"By daffodils?"

"That's right. Daffodils."

"He must have really been bored," commented Fleming.

"He *loved* nature, Fleming. He really did," said Blythe with a slight emphasis in her voice.

"'Ten thousand saw I at a glance,

Tossing their heads in sprightly dance'" quoted Enid. "And then he ends with a recollection of them," she continued.

> *"'For oft, when on my couch I lie*
> *In vacant or in pensive mood,*
> *They flash upon that inward eye,*
> *Which is the bliss of solitude:'"*

"I've forgotten the final lines," said Enid.

Then Paris spoke:

> *"'And then my heart with pleasure fills,*
> *And dances with the daffodils.'"*

"You know that stuff?" asked Fleming in a slight disbelief.

"It's a lovely poem," he said.

"Yes, indeed it is, Fleming," said Blythe with a kind of delight at Paris' knowledge of a nature poem.

"Hmmmmppp," said Fleming with a scowl.

After awhile, they decided to go to Dumfries in Scotland since Enid loved the poetry of that Scottish bard, Robert Burns. As they made their way into Scotland, Fleming asked:

"Does he write about daffodils, too?"

"Actually, he writes poems about nature too, poems that can often be turned into songs."

"Yes, we sing one you know every New Years," offered Paris.

"Yes, while you're drinking. It's called "Auld Lang Syne," said Blythe.

"Oh, that one. That's a good one. A good song," remarked Fleming as he looked out the window at the Scottish landscape.

"Looks like a lovely town," said Blythe.

"Indeed," said Paris, starting to fill his pipe bowl with a sweet-smelling tobacco. They got out of the car and began to wonder where the Burns Mausoleum was. It did not take them long since they went into a small restaurant and ate some fish and chips and sipped some pints of bitter.

"Ah, I love this stuff," said Fleming. "Newcastle- on-Tyne beer. Now that is beer."

"They don't call it 'Lunatic Brew' for nothing," observed Paris.

They were able to get directions from their waiter whose name was Nike. They paid their bill and went by the Bank of Scotland and some churches until they arrived at the Mausoleum which had bars around it. This was the resting place of Robbie Burns, the great Scottish poet. Blythe, Paris and especially Enid were in literary heaven; Fleming was more curious than ecstatic but he liked what he had heard about "Auld Lang Syne" and that Burns liked to drink.

"Sounds like my kinda writer," remarked Fleming.

"Some of my favorite poems are by Burns," gushed Enid who now quoted:

> 'And moldering now in silent dust
> The heart that loved me dearly!
> But still within my bosom's core
> Shall live my Highland Mary.'

"You must really like him," commented Fleming.

"He's outstanding with unforgettable songs and poetic lines," said Blythe.

"I really like his love songs," mused Paris.

"Like what?" asked Fleming.

"One I've always liked is called 'A Red, Red Rose'" said Paris.

"Pure delight," enthused Enid.

"Can you quote some?" asked Fleming.

"Yeah. Let's see. Here's some I remember:

> 'Till all the seas go dry, my Dear
> And the rocks melt with the sun!
> O I will love thee still, my Dear
> While the sands of life shall run.'

"So lovely," commented Blythe. "Just lovely."

"Another one," said Paris, "is the one my dad the engineer who really likes poetry, is called 'To A Mouse'. He particularly loves these lines so much he wrote them in hand in his yearbook. They go like this:

> The best-laid schemes of mice and men
> Often go astray
> And leave us nothing but grief and pain
> For promised joy!

"Wow," gushed Blythe, "that says it all."

"It sure does," observed Fleming.

CHAPTER 4

T he next day dawned bright and they all put their bags in Fleming's car. They would soon pass through Lancashire headed east into the Midlands, stopping here and there to refresh the unreformed Fleming at a pub.

"I thought you had changed, Fleming," remarked Enid as he tipped a bottle of ale to his lips.

"Not yet. Not as long as I've some shillings in my pocket," retorted Fleming.

Blythe was fuming.

"Can we go now? I'd like to get some sleep before I sit in boredom tomorrow."

Then she leaned over to Paris in the back seat.

"How far are we from Nottingham?"

"Can't be more than a few miles," said Paris, observing the map Blythe held.

"Let's see, we are here…" said Enid, pointing at the map.

"And Professor Arsse is there," declared Fleming, pointing into his ale bottle.

"Shhhh," said Blythe, looking crossly at him.

"A few miles west. Let's see that would mean we ought to hit Grantham in about an hour. Fleming? Fleming!" she said as the eloquent rogue lowered his bottle.

"What?!"

"Let's go," said Blythe.

"All right, I'm almost finished." He took a long, last swallow.

"Can we go now? We're not far from home."

"Soon as I toss this bottle away." He tossed it out the window into a bush.

"You could've put it in to garbage can," Paris said.

"Oh hell. I haven't got time."

He started the car and they were off again, gliding by fields and more fields and soon entered Nottingham. The city clattered with the stop and go of buses and trucks. Crowds were on every street corner. Through the teeming streets they drove and came to the edge of what was once Sherwood Forest, the very forest of Robin Hood and his merry men.

"Just a half hour and time will land us on the moon—Erehwon Manor," said Blythe.

"Let's hurry. We may get a bite to eat if Skip is feeling good," said Fleming.

"Who is Skip?" Blythe naïvely asked.

"The cook's dog." Blythe laughed, not knowing how to react.

Paris grinned and Blythe lit up another cigarette. Then Enid studied the map of England. Paris began adjusting film in his camera so he could shoot another day. Fleming's face in the rearview mirror showed a half-shaved chin wet with ale, hair combed to one side, and a delicious defiance on his lips.

"Yo, ho, ho, and a bottle of hump," he sang, knowing how mad Blythe would get when was in a frivolous mood.

"Stop it, Fleming," she said trying to be sophisticated and with deliberate dramatic flourish snuffed her half-smoked cigarette on the car ashtray.

"Why, don't you like to sing, Blythe? How about that old favorite 'Come and sit on my face if you love me.' Now that's one helluva song. Or how about 'Mary Ann Barnes, Queen of all the Acrobats.' I'm sorry, " he said, glancing at Blythe. "I have grossed you out, my dear. Your taste in music needs improvement."

"Come and sit on my face if you love me—"

"Damn it, Fleming" Blythe interrupted. Enid and Paris sat in staring silence, watching the poet and ribald crooner conduct a merry chase along the corridors of conscience.

Soon they were passing through Grantham, Lincolnshire with its tall statue of Isaac Newton. It was dusk and the streets were bare. Shops had closed long ago, except for the South China Café at the end of town. The village square was vacant except for an old man and his Irish Setter sitting on a park bench. Fleming steered past the Blue Bull pub, on past more shops and stores. Then they came to a stop in front of an overpass. Coast was clear and they passed beneath the concrete snake structure and wound past low, sloping fields with waving grasses and hedges that followed the road levels. The Gregory Arms pub appeared on the right and the black iron gates leading to Erehwon Manor were open wide on the left. Fleming down shifted, turned and gained speed beyond the gate. It was like driving into an agrarian heaven, a remnant of a mediaeval past. They crossed the cement bridge that spanned the river which cut diagonally across the estate. Manor lights glimmered faintly in the mists which usually thickened into pea soup before morning. Fleming veered sharply to the left and the little car made a trying effort to squeeze into the bullring. On the right was Jocko's truck on which were inscribed these words: "You can lick our chops but you can't beat our meat." They slowed past Foo Kee's minivan on which were printed words in Chinese few understood. Fleming found a spot to park and they climbed out. The sun, which did not set until around nine-thirty, still lingered behind the mists of early evening. They headed in the direction of the kitchen.

"I guess everyone's eaten by now," said Paris, carrying his light bag and a coat on his arm.

"Probably," said Fleming, trotting to the window of the dining hall. The place looks deserted. You'd never think anyone lived here."

"This is a ghost town," murmured Paris. Enid walked by his side. They entered the bullring door adjacent to the dining hall doors. Voices could be heard and music played faintly: "Catch me if you c-a-a-a-n, catch me if you can." The elevator, as was usual, was at the very top of the manor and Fleming pressed the button impatiently. As they waited for the elevator, down the encircling staircase trotted another student, Duci, whose incessant giggling almost invariably sparked Fleming to imitate her.

"Hi," she said with a giggle.

"Tehehe yourself," replied Fleming, slightly irritated.

"Guess what…tehehe…I've decided to switch majors from astrophysics to aeronautical engineering…tehehe." Fleming was exasperated.

"What a grossout," he lamented, pursing his lips together. "Yeah, sure, I'm glad you're going to learn how to fly jets for Chrissake."

"Don't you think that's…tehehe… a great switch?" asked Duci, quizzically.

"Yeah, you turn me off, honey. Why don't you fly a kite for right now."

Duci walked away, still giggling.

Finally, with a sudden lurch the elevator reluctantly descended. Fleming pulled back the iron, accordion-like gate and they got in. He pressed the up button but the elevator did not move.

"Close the gate tighter," said Paris. Fleming did and the well-worn elevator carried its burden to the top floor.

"We'll help you girls get your stuff in," said Paris. They helped Enid and Blythe unload their belongings. While he helped Blythe with her overnight bags, Paris passed one of Blythe's roommates, Luwanna Panse, whose facial expression seldom changed. Paris said hello but she just kept reading her book on the Egyptian dynasties in bed. Blythe wanted to change clothes and relax so Paris left to unload his and Fleming's bags. As soon as he had gone, Luwanna decided to speak.

"Where've you been this weekend, Blythe?"

"Lake District, Luwanna. It was simply gorgeous."

Interested now, Luwanna decided to leave the Nile and venture out of her cubicle to talk with Blythe.

"What did you do up there?"

"Went for a boat ride and visited Scotland," said Blythe slipping off her clothes and putting on some comfortable pants. Luwanna sat on the edge of Blythe's bed and watched her before her mirror.

"Was it cold?"

"Not in July, Luwanna. But there certainly were a lot of tourists." Then she broke off. "I'm going to have to shampoo my hair. It's all dirty and straight." But Luwanna was undeterred.

"Who were you with?"

"Paris. Why?"

"Just wondering." After a pause, Luwanna continued: "He didn't make a pass, did he?" Blythe looked over at her.

"Why, no, Luwanna. Paris is a friend. We're just friends."

"Oh," she said with a sigh, "I thought he would try something funny on you."

"What makes you think he would make a pass in the first place?"

"You know how men are…" she replied with a wink.

"No, tell me. What *are* they like?"

"Why they always want to go to bed with us girls," said Luwanna whose mother was a porn star.

Just then Enid knocked and unobtrusively came in.

"Hi Luwanna," said Enid. Luwanna nodded.

"Luwanna here has been telling me all about men," said Blythe brushing her hair.

"Oh really," said Enid almost catty.

"I can tell you a lot about men. They're always trying to get you in bed."

"Really now," said Blythe, looking at her hair in the mirror. "How do you know?"

"Oh, I just know," said Luwanna, over-possessing her secret.

"How do you 'just know' something? Tell me, Luwanna, have you ever been to bed with a man?"

Luwanna shook her head.

"You haven't. Gee, that's too bad. It's quite an experience. You ought to try it sometime." Luwanna put her hand over her wide open mouth.

Enid glanced quizzically at Blythe but did not ask.

"I must go now," said Luwanna, excusing herself after a shocking revelation.

"Yes. And I must go breed now, Luwanna. Have fun."

A shocked gasp came from Luwanna's cubicle.

"Enid," whispered Blythe, "I'm just teasing her."

"I get you," said Enid with a wink. Then, with a louder voice, Blythe said, "Must go see Fleming since he loves my ass."

Another shocked gasp and Enid smiled at a delighted Blythe.

"See you later Luwanna. I must deliver my luscious loins and throbbing thighs to my lover now."

The shocked gasps became faint and finally silent. Blythe peered into her cubicle and Luwanna had fainted. Quickly she began to revive her. Enid fanned her face and Blythe called for and got some smelling salts. The revived Luwanna was dazed at the phrases Blythe had expressed but was soon returned to her reading. Blythe went to Fleming's room 33, home of the golden hogs as they were known. She just wanted to shampoo her hair.

Blythe dashed downstairs, passed the creaking door, into a long hall leading to the "palatial" estate, that is, room 33 of the golden hogs. She knocked as someone who knew all the nicknames of the golden hogs.

"Who goes there?" boomed a gruff voice. It was, as he was nicknamed, "St. Peter."

"Just me, the shy little kitten."

St. Peter's paunch greeted her at the door.

"Oh, we thought you were Merry in heat," taking a long swallow of rotgut. He had not shaved for days and the booze soaked his sprouted stubble.

Undaunted, Blythe went in as Peter slammed the door and retired to his cubicle. Past the cubicle, she strolled until she curved into Fleming's cubicle. Pinup girls dotted his walls, a chest of drawers besieged with papers sat next to the wall, and a boda bag hung over a nail.

"Hi Fleming," she said.

"Come in, my darling," he said with his undershirt hanging over his pants. "You wanna a drink?"

"No thanks."

Just then St. Peter's wall-sized clock rang the hours.

"What in the hell is that," bellowed Fleming.

"My grandfather's clock," retorted Peter.

"Can't you keep it quiet? Why the hell do we have to listen to that infernal thing anyway?" Then tauntingly, he added: "What are you trying to do Peter, purge us?"

"Might be," said Peter who flew like an arrow onto his bed. "Don't worry, everyone gets used to it. They always did at the home campus."

Fleming then spoke to Blythe.

"He brings the damned thing all the way to England so he can get up on time."

"He could've just brought an alarm clock, couldn't he?"

"He's impractical. He'd never get rid of that thing. Sentimental value, you know."

Zee, Jocko, Sparky, and Paris were scattered to the British winds. St. Peter was already snoring as the door opened to let in Everette Lardace, "Ev" for short.

"Is that you, Lard?"

"Don't call me Lard," he said, barely able to pronounce words since his mouth was full of food.

"Cookies?" asked Fleming. "Where did you get them?"

"The pantry. What do you care?" said Ev, feeding his face.

"I thought you might have ransacked the sheep for some Shepherd's pie," said Fleming sarcastically.

"F-u-nn-ny" he smirked while gleefully licking his fingers.

"What are you eating now," said the infrequently-awakened Peter.

"Go back to bed, Pete. Can't a man eat around here without everybody" (smack, smack) "getting on his back?"

They heard his grubby paws gouging their way into a potato chip bag then the resounding crunches of his thick molars. Peter put his head under his pillow. Fleming momentarily explored Blythe as a diversion.

"Where's Zee tonight," said Fleming while rubbing Blythe's back.

"Went drinking. I think at the Welby Arms," said Peter whose ears pierced pillow feathers.

"Paris took off right after he dropped his bags in his cubicle," Fleming said.

"Wonder why," remarked Blythe, leaning on him with a kiss. Over the cookie-crunching and potato chip-devouring melody of Everette Lardace, music filtered up from the commons room. "Under my thumb, girl…" Between songs they heard a shrill church-like chorus resound: "Wonderful, Counselor, the Mighty God, the Everlasting Father, the Prince of Peace."

"What the hell is that church stuff?" asked Everette as he opened a bottle of Pinot Noir to wash his crackers down.

"They're rehearsing, Lardass, for the Christmas program. That's the university—"

"Don't call me Lardass, Fleming. Gets my blood pressure up," interrupted the double-jowled Tombstonian.

"I've never seen anybody eat as much as you do," said Fleming, changing the subject.

"Just don't call me Lardass. Reminds me of my mother," said Ev as he ripped into a candy bar.

"Ah, I'm so sorry, Lard," said Fleming. "Be sure not to neglect your stomach now."

"Don't worry, Fleming, negligence always kisses misfortune," tenderly patting his monstrous paunch.

"Yes, it's criminally negligent of you to intentionally forget your stomach pangs," taunted Fleming.

"Thanks, Fleming, for your legal advice. I prefer your cookies to your damned locus delicti slander if you don't mind." There was silence.

"Words are not confined to place, Lard. Just proceed with your eating."

Everette did. He finished the wine, cleaned the cracker box bare, stuffed candy bars into his stomach, and chomped away at a juicy apple *and* its core.

Just then Enid knocked at the door. In a flash sleepy Peter rolled out of bed and answered it.

"Who goes there?"

"It's me, Peter. Enid. May I come in?"

With the air of a Buckingham Palace guard, Peter slowly opened the door.

"You may."

"Is Paris here?"

"No. He left a little while ago." Then he turned and strolled to Fleming's cubicle and peeked at him through the curtain edge.

"Fleming?"

"Yes," said Fleming caught unawares.

"When will Paris be back?"

"Should be here soon. It's getting late," said Fleming who glanced at his watch on the arm he draped around Blythe. Peter looked at Enid.

"Would you like to stay? I have some wine. Paris should be home soon. He went drinking at the Welby Arms."

"I'll wait but I don't need the wine, thank you."

"All right. If you'll excuse me, I'll take a nap," yawned Peter, already heading to his cubicle. Enid sat on Paris' unmade bed; the blankets were tossed carelessly from side to side. Above his bureau was a small framed picture of Jesus and his drawers were half-closed and books piled haphazardly on top of the bureau. Papers were more or less stacked on top of his desk and pens laid beneath the sheets in open disarray. A tall vase sat on the edge of his bureau with two long daffodils proudly sticking their necks out. They looked somewhat fresh. The room was dark now and except for the lights on in Fleming, Peter, and Paris' cubicles and she could hear the searing whiz of the Lincolnshire wind.

She did not want to disturb any lovemaking between Fleming and Blythe. She and Blythe always reserved their confidential remarks until late at night when most of the manor was sound asleep and then they would talk over a small candle about the day's events. Faint music seethed like quiet fingers from the commons room below and the bass rhythms echoed and vibrated through two levels of Erehwon Manor. Everette was reading in his cubicle but was unusually quiet. He respected Enid with the affection of a puppy for its master. Almost at times, Everette was a child, repulsively infantile with an anemic concern for others. Enid was nice to everyone; she was social yet loved the slow often quiet walks about the manor's well-manicured lawns. Paris and she once strolled to the bridge that spanned the river that wound its way through this landed estate. Paris remembered how she looked with one strand of golden brown hay next to her smooth, clear roseate cheeks. She was gorgeous like an unaffected model. Her teeth smooth, white, the zephyr lightly blew her blond curls this way and that. She reclined on Paris' bed, gazing at the daffodils. The wind died. In a moment, a moment before decision and action, the sound of crunching, scraping gravel, hot engines, steaming motors ruptured the silence.

The bullring below hummed with shouts and songs. Just then Peter's clock tolled an ear-knifing ten bells. Blythe could hardly believe her ears. She sat up, and taking a quick stare around the cubicle, quickly went to the middle window overlooking the dimly-lit bullring below.

"Now the party starts," grunted Fleming.

"Guesso," said Everette, as he got up to go to the john. As he walked, the wood floor shuddered beneath his immense weight. Down the hall they could hear sounds of records playing. Peter had buried his head in his pillow and seemed not to hear a thing, including the tolling bell outside, not to mention his own clock. Soon the music became louder and "Oh, sweet pea, wontcha be my girl" eased upward through the floors. Tonight there was no rehearsal of Handel's *Messiah*; it was party time. Far off, faint light spread like a pianist's fingers from the dying sun. "Good day sunshine" carried the air and ten minutes passed, and soon the staircase door creaked open and quickly slammed.

"Hey, happy birthday, Jocko," said Sparky, slapping him on the back. Jocko was noticeably weaving, his red hair wet like someone had sprayed him with beer. The door to the giant east wing swung open and Enid streaked to Paris' cubicle, afraid.

"It's a shit face at Erehwon Manor," shouted Jocko who was high, still giving the impression of drunkenness. He burst through Peter's curtain.

"Chrissake St. Peter. Why the hell you sleep all the time?" He went to Peter's bed and pulled away the pillow, waking the guardian of the golden hogs. He yawned then said:

"What's up, Jocko. You're birthday, huh? Well, here my boy, here's a drink to sober you up." Peter whipped out two glasses, poured bourbon into them and gave one to Jocko.

"Here's to you. Here's to New Years in the Bronx."

"Hell I'm from Bloomington, not the Bronx," asserted Jocko, his face flushed. Drink dribbled down to where it drenched Peter's stubble. Sparky switched on the big lights and the room lit up like a liner on a dark sea. Sparky stuck his head in.

"How about let's making it a threesome." At that, Peter pulled out another glass, this one a little larger and poured it full. He handed it to Sparky.

"I'm seeing blind," grunted Jocko. "God, three pints of bitter, four bloody worthingtons. And, hell, let's see—what was it Sparky?" Sparky, much more sober, looked him square in the eye.

"What? Oh. And two bottles of that, whatcha call it, oh, yes, lunatic brew, brown ale."

"Yeah," murmured Jocko. Peter had the habit of getting quite drunk just watching himself and others drink.

"Say, you seen Paris Brandon," asked Peter.

"Sure. Where the hell is he, Sparky"

"Downstairs at the dance. Having a shindig tonight," said Sparky almost matter-of-factly. The door opened as huge Everette Lardace tromped through. He did not close the door and from the open door leading to the washing machine which operated as a clothes disposal there came the song "catch me if you can."

Jocko laid down his drink and went to the open floor common to all the cubicles. He began sliding across the floor, his thin pants rubbing like a scorched iron.

"I'm Ty Cobb!"

Sparky was just queasy enough to follow suit and he too slid across the floor, sliding presumably into third base.

"I'm Babe Ruth!"

"I'm Ty Cobb!" said Jocko. "I live in a shoe. Look for me in there too." Both slid from one corner to the other. Everette had left the bathroom door open and his perfume was not appreciated. Peter quickly closed the door.

"Good God, Lard, if you're going to fumigate the place, tell us in advance so we can cheek it outa here, all right."

"Yeah, sure," replied Everette rolling over on his side, his stomach protruding ominously beneath his tight-fitting T-shirt.

Moments flew and Jocko did enough slides to have gone nine innings. He stopped, and stood there, trying to catch his breath.

"Ty Cobb's tired man." Sparky watched while Peter laid back, stretching into a comfortable recline. Fleming listened and talked low to Blythe as Jocko went from cubicle to cubicle, soon to discover Enid Brown.

"Well, Enid. What the hell you doing in here?" he asked, standing slightly stooped.

"I'm waiting for Paris," she said quickly then added "Have you seen him?"

"Oh, sure," said Jocko, leaning against the frame of the cubicle door. "He's downstairs, but can I pinch hit for him?"

"No thanks," she said. Jocko did not move yet. He stood there, his hair combed low to the left. He seemed to study her, admiring her, from afar. Then he sat next to her, settling himself on the bed and propping his legs on an open bureau drawer. Sparky presumably went to the party that was going on down in the commons room, a party floating on wine and beer, among other things. Quickly he leaned over and kissed her; she turned away and stood up.

"I told you I'm waiting for Paris. Don't you understand?"

Jocko smiled a weird smile, one that was due to embarrassment as well as confidence.

"Sure I understand. But tell me. Why are you so fond of Paris? Why?"

"He's my type."

"And I'm not," asserted Jocko hotly.

"I didn't say that."

"But you implied…"

"I didn't mean to imply anything. Paris is simply my, what you might call, an ideal, my friend. We talk close."

"Why don't you and I talk close?" he asked in a very low whisper, leaning over to kiss her as she pressed against the wall.

"Please don't," she said, turning away from his face. He kissed her anyway and she pushed him back onto the bed and, in a flash, ran into Fleming's cubicle. Momentarily Jocko raced then stopped short and swung open Fleming's curtain.

"Sober up, Jocko. It's been a long, hard night. Take a shower or something. It'll cool you off." Jocko grimaced like a child caught stealing cookies from a cookie jar.

"I guesso. You're right." He stood there in front of Blythe, Enid, and Fleming. His face went pale, and youthful facial lines were pulled back sharply.

"You look sick, Jocko," said Fleming. Just then Jocko made a quick exit and went to the window next to the bathroom. He threw open the white-framed lattice, hung out his head, and began to throw up, or, as he liked to say, bird. Lemon meringue pie, chopped green beans, half-digested carrots dribbed down the side of Erehwon. Looking up from nausea, he saw in the next window down none other than Sparky looking pale as a green moon on a summer's eve.

"Hey, Sparky. You sick?"

"Hell yes. Christ. That damn beer."

"Nothing but sewer water, I tell you. Hell I gave up that cow piss the first day here," said Jocko, sending a multi-colored stream to the earth below.

"How goes it, Sparky!" he said as he went whooaa," which was the sound he made when birding.

"Just great, Jocko. All we get in this whole damn world…is that birding feeling, nausea," he said, letting loose with shepherd's pie, beer, crushed cookies and pineapple, and stewed tomatoes.

"Hey, I gotta great idea," shouted Jocko.

"What's that?"

"Let's count to three and bird at the same time."

"Okay."

"One, two, three whooaa." Two streams of undigested food spilled in half lumps to the earth.

"Ayeee. One good bird deserves another."

"I'll drink to that."

"Haven't birded like this in a long time."

"Aye, laddy," said Sparky, "one bird on the ground ain't worth two in your gut."

"A hand in the bush is worth two in the bird." And they howled with laughter.

"There goes my minimum adult daily requirements" shouted Jocko as wet, heavy half-digested curry splattered to the earth below. "There goes vitamin B1, Niacin, riboflavin, not to mention that fortifier, shepherd's pie. That damn beer, how tin-like it tastes. Grosses me out."

"I'm strong on wonderful bread, helps build strong birds in fifteen ways."

"Yeah, sure shows up in bread of wonder, the bread of good birders everywhere."

And they laughed until there was nothing left to bird.

"Guess I'm all out," murmured Sparky, getting down from the john.

"Me too. I'm glad I didn't have asparagus. That's really a gross out. Doesn't digest easily you know." Then Sparky waved his hand like a moderator does to get silence from her audience.

"I feel another bird coming on. It has that gross feeling that it's steak or whatever that meat was we had tonight."

"It was cheap hamburger," replied Jocko.

"Here goes. It's coming." And Sparky let out with another long bird and sure enough ground beef hit the ground.

"You know they used to do this all the time in ancient Rome."

"Really?"

"Hell yes. When they wanted to lose weight they'd just bird their eyes out."

"Bitchin'. It's a good way to diet by birding your diet."

"Yeah. Martin Luther, you know the reformer, he was the one who thought the pope was a jackass playing bagpipes. Well, he lived on a diet of Worms."

"Really now?"

Then there was a pause between them, silence oozing over them, then Jocko spoke.

"My head feels drained of life. What a sweat."

"Yeah, took the hell outa me. Forehead's all sweaty to hell you know."

"I guess I'll wash my mouth."

"Me too."

Both heads pulled in like a turtle's into a shell. Sparky came down the winding stairs and passed the middle john. He opened the door as if to enter, but quickly jumped back, closing the door where Ev had been. Jocko looked in the small mirror over the sink between running open lips through the water in his cupped hand. Sparky strolled through the corridor to where Jocko stood.

"Feeling better?" Jocko turned and slanted his eyes at Sparky, still running water through his lips. He nodded then took a mouthful, swished it around, then spit it out in the sink. As he wiped his mouth, he checked his teeth in the mirror. He stood in his undershirt, barefooted. Sparky had on his cap with a long brim, standing there waiting for a comment from Jocko. Jocko looked at him.

"There. Nothing like getting rid of cow piss, is there?"

"Nope. But whoever hit that can left an atom bomb in there. I'm afraid it was Lard. You get so you know the who's who of the john circuit. If you ask me, he just dumped a load to send off to Cuba."

"I guess it was him. He always hits the can before waking us up in the wee hours to blow up the world. Just imagine was a great weapon he'd be against our enemies. Just throw ole Lard at them. He'd kill them with such a gross smell. That would teach them a lesson in…western technology."

"Call it Yankee ingenuity. Ah, yes, I can see it now. While the Russians or Chinese parade missiles, tanks, and satellites in Red Square, we parade a three hundred and fifty pound lard ass from Tombstone whose secret weapon is the john-john inspired by shepherd's pie and strong curry."

"That's true too," said Jocko, towel in hand, heading for the door to the third floor east wing. Sparky followed. Entering, they saw Peter's light off as it usually was. He was sacked out. Just then twelve bells struck on the clock, piercing the silence. Sparky then went into his cubicle and flopped on the bed. Jocko went to Fleming's cubicle. Blythe and Fleming rested quietly side by side.

"Damn clock anyway," said Jocko. Fleming smiled as Blythe cuddled next to him with her eyes closed. Jocko paused there.

"Where did Enid go?" Fleming raised his head slightly.

"Downstairs. She got tired of waiting for Paris up here."

"I hope she wasn't too grossed out. I mean—"

"She was. But she'll forget it, Jocko. Apologize if you want to."

"I just feel bad about the whole thing. I guess I'll see her tomorrow."

"Sure," said Fleming.

Jocko went into his cubicle, turned on his lamp, and began perusing a copy from the *London Supplement*. As a journalism student, he was very interested in style, content, and format of British papers. Sparky lay face down on his bed and soon began to snore faintly. Light was out in Everette's cubicle; apparently he set his frame to rest after such a workout. The room was dark except for Jocko and Fleming's lamps and in silent moments music from the commons room floated up. "Black is black, I want my baby back" followed by "Your Bird Can Sing."

The music increased in volume as the door momentarily opened. It was Zee Ferguson. Saying not a word, he swiftly passed by all the cubicles, and, in a moment, all ears could hear, the puffing and heavy breathing of someone exercising. It was Zee lifting his weights.

"What happened tonight, Zee?" asked Jocko.

"Never mind," he said, puffing between straining muscles.

36

"Was it Enid again?" No answer. Then Jocko replied to his own question.

"If it was, Enid likes Paris. And besides, she almost engaged to that guy in Asia now." The puffing ceased.

"Look, Jocko, I'll ask for your wisdom if I want it. And so far, it sounds like insanity to me."

"But—"

"No buts about it. How in the hell did you know it was her anyway?"

"Oh, Paris told me. Said you were hustling everything wearing a skirt," said the all-informing journalist Jocko.

"That liar. A guy can't even hustle, I mean, can't even enjoy himself around here."

"There are other chicks. But I'm a cynic…when it comes to chicks anyway."

"Sure, there are, always others I mean. I'll find them."

He returned to the spot in front of his cubicle, a ritual place, and proceeded to do weight lifts. Moments passed when Enid and Paris came in. Before he realized what was happening, Zee did not see either Paris or Enid as they rounded the cubicle corridor into the main part of the wing right in front of him.

"Hi Zee," said Paris. Zee slowly looked up.

"Oh, hi," he said. "Got to do my exercises for the night you know."

He continued with his dumbells as Paris rubbed his chin thoughtfully. Enid went into his cubicle.

"Who was it tonight Zee?"

There was silence. Zee sat up, looking at Paris Brandon's muscular frame and his hair combed loosely to one side.

"Who was who?" Paris twisted his lips, knowingly.

"Now Zee you don't often lift weights unless some girl has decided you are not for her. If you don't want to say—"

"It was Grace, yes, Grace that's who…Grace Rubens."

Just then Sparky, overhearing the conversation, sat up and said: "That's close."

Zee was really embarrassed now.

"Shut up, Sparky."

Paris laughed and walked into his cubicle, shaking his head. Sparky emitted peals of laughter and dozens of snickers.

"Just get off my back, Sparky."

Sparky immediately shut his face. Paris stretched out on the bed and Blythe leaned into him. Zee gathered his robe and slippers, a half-used bar of soap and towel and quickly decided to get of the frying pan and into the tub. His Saturday night baths were notoriously routine and tonight the warm soapy water would soothe away the aches of day and predatory fiasco of the night. Gingerly he left.

As the door opened, there emanated a dull, steady monotone rhythm from the commons room below. Words were indistinct, blurred, just rhythm perspired upward. Fortunately, the wind blew eastward, taking Everette's rotten-egg limburger cheese odor from the portals. But it lingered, discouraging any who responded to the urgings of nature to venture into that john. Paris put his arm around Enid who snuggled into him. She could feel the long fingers of his hand press against her, his warm palms rubbing her back into a whimsically circular motion. He reached and switched off the lamp. Now only Fleming's cubicle light was on; apparently Everette had decided to go to sleep. Enid stretched her elegant neck and kissed Paris long. But Paris' thoughts were elsewhere. Fleming was unusually quiet and Paris thought about it during Enid's kiss. As she raised her head, staring at the ceiling, he said:

"Fleming."

After a slight pause, Fleming replied:

"Yeah?"

"Just wondering what you were up to."

"I'm okay, Paris." Another pause then Fleming spoke.

"How did things go today?"

"Fine. As usual. The council, the one we elected, is trying to set up restrictions on our weekends. You know that."

"Yeah. Heard about it today," said Fleming as Blythe began to nibble on his ear, her hair falling in his eyes.

"Seems they have a prude for president. Thinks he's king."

"Oh, yeah, Barff. That's right. John Barff. What the hell is he trying to do anyway?"

"Put the Manor on trial."

"Why does he think he's so damn powerful? What's eating him, Paris?" No answer as Enid placed another juicy kiss on him.

"Paris?" called Fleming.

"Just a minute, honey," he whispered to Enid who began kissing his knuckles.

"Go on, Fleming."

"I just wondered, I mean why does he think he's so hot anyway?"

Paris thought a moment.

"Well, Fleming, it's like this. You give a little bureaucrat a thimbleful of authority, and depending on how power-hungry they are, and I mean really power-hungry, they stretch it until is covers the globe. Power makes little people into big people. See what I mean?"

"Yes. Should've know that. Why did they choose him anyway?"

"His father."

"His father?"

"Plenty of dough. Hell yes. Money talks big. Money is power for those who feel like abusing it. Simple as that."

"And he wants to curb our weekends?"

"That's what it sounds like. And all the boozing he does, out on that spare mattress too. Christ you give the power-hungry a drop of power and they will, by God they will, play dramatic with you and walk on you as if you didn't exist. He thinks he's a Prometheus giving the human race his leadership. And to think we helped elect him. Hell we didn't even know him at that get-acquainted picnic last spring."

"No. Well I'll be," said a pensive Fleming. "What he needs is someone to sit on his face." Blythe slapped him, saying:

"Fleming, please don't get cross again. Besides we can't get rid of Barff until next quarter so why worry about it? And you of all people—why you booze it up all the time yourself."

"Thank you, Blythe. What are you offering? A Marxist revisionist program so can satisfy your hedonistic desires?"

"No, Fleming. I just don't think you should worry about it."

"Hell Blythe, we won't even be able to take off weekends, you know to go to London. And you said yourself you'd like to go to Cardiff. Well, what if—"

"It's only an if—" and with that she kissed him long and heavy. Fleming broke her embrace long enough to say:

"Paris, I'll talk about it later. Right now I'm engaged as you no doubt hear…"

Fleming went back to his prone position for love-making; Blythe gave all she could. But Enid and Paris had quite a conversation going.

"I saw you with Vicki tonight at the dance. You like her?"

"Oh sure," said Paris jokingly.

"Do you really?"

"I said sure."

"How sure?"

"Of Vicki?" asked Paris. She had sat up and crossed her arms in the position of query and demand.

"She's a nice girl, I guess." Enid just sat there almost strangely, her blue eyes dancing like ribbons in a summer breeze.

"You do like her though."

Paris sensed her alarm and decided to tease, his eyes twinkling.

"Oh sure. She looks great in those short skirts."

Enid slanted her eyes at him, indignant lips curled to one side.

"She does, eh?"

"Sure. Besides you are Ted's girl, aren't you?" Enid looked down into her lap, then at the floor, and finally toward his face but not into his eyes. His eyes were plaid swirls of mockery and compassion.

"Well," she said, pausing. "Yes, I guess I am. But like you said to me once— you remember that day—he's in Asia or back in the States, I don't know which. You see, he hasn't written me in over a month and a half."

"I thought he loved you so much."

"He does…but—"

"But what?"

"But he just hasn't written, that's all."

"Distance and time corrode love. Just remember that, Enid. Proximity. That's the magic word. How can love grow with an ocean between two people?"

"That's true. You can only hope," she said with a heavy sigh. "We'll manage, I hope," she murmured faintly. She leaned into him, needing someone to rest her head on. Paris surrounded her with his strong, taut yet gentle arms and kissed her lovingly on her temple. Soft moments passed like a light, faint scent of twisted, tasty spearmint. Her flesh was soft, squeezable and she put her hand firmly in his, lovingly, caressingly as their eyes reached out with an undefinable longing for one another. Her warm lips pressed his, deeply, a meaningful touch here and there told her she was his, he hers.

"Your kiss is like a breeze in fair April, you know that?"

Enid smiled at him.

"Yes, Paris, yes. How can I match your description?"

She thought a moment. "Ah, yes, your kiss, my darling, is like soft feathers of a mother robin. It tastes like ice cream dotted with chocolate chips."

"That's good, Enid. I just love to say things like that, don't you? You never hear things like that," said Paris, lifting his head slightly to peer into her eyes. Her look always seemed on the verge of a cute, sweet smile. Then she did smile.

"We never hear very much that is ours. I mean we always listen to construction crews, skyscrapers being built, you know what I mean?"

"Sure," he said, smiling, "but I would to listen to your heart beating. In my arms. Like it is right now. Warmly, steadily. Life gushes sometimes and then it winds like a slow, meandering river. It oozes over you when hearts beat as one."

"Ah, yes. You are inspiring. With you at my side, I could write a thousand tales of love."

"Tongue to tongue, breast to breast, we can love until the end of the world."

"A fitting epilogue to the day's circling into night," Enid murmured, caught in the warmth of his arms. Ted was out of sight and definitely out of mind.

Fast moments that sweep down ravines on autumn's earth, stirring the leaves, passed and soon the bell tolled the hours.

"Two already, I see," said Enid. "Paris. Paris. I must go to bed."

Paris did not move but was almost asleep.

"Stay here, Enid," he mumbled low. She leaned over and kissed him again. He put his arms around and hugged her tightly, her blue eyes closed yet searching for she knew not what. As she rose, her eyes softly opened.

"I must go. It's so late already."

"Only two in the morning. Do you mean to tell me—"

"Shhh. You'll wake up the whole wing."

The room now was almost dark; the wind outside rushed against the panes like the beatings of tiny fingers that wanted to come in. He began to whisper.

"Why must you go now? No one will know the difference."

"No," she said, shaking her head. He searched her eyes and saw a struggle in their depths. Her sweater kept getting hair on his Pendleton shirt and laid there picking off long strands of blond hair.

"Sure is hairy. What is that? Lamb's wool?"

"Either that or cashmere. I really don't know," she said. There was a strong silence between them. He stared into her eyes; she avoided their stare and pretended to look for more sweater hairs on his Pendleton.

"You want to stay, don't you?" She closed her eyes tightly then turned her head away.

"Please Paris." She paused again and pulled down the vase holding the daffodils. Quietly she sniffed their faint fragrance, staring into space. He kept staring although not as intensely now, her blond curls curling about her ears, her small pointed nose sticking into the petals.

"I love daffodils. Where did you get them?"

"In that mustard field, you know one next to that castle foundation. Down the driveway before you get to the river."

"Hmmmm," she murmured low.

"I don't know how they ever grow there."

"You'd think all the mustard would strangle them. But they don't. They seem to get along together. Anyway."

She sniffed again the pliable yellow petals.

"Just a faint—" Then she sniffed deeply "ah you can't really beat the smell of a sweet flower. Carnations are my favorite."

She put the vase above her on his bureau drawers.

"What's your favorite flower, Paris?"

He thought a moment, his eyes beginning to twinkle, and a faint dimple growing on his cheek.

"My favorite flowers are rosebuds. The ones that appear when, oh when you and I take walks and it gets cold at night. Even summer nights can get cold in Britain, you know. And when I see your cheeks lit up with a flushing, I mean blushing red, why those are my favorite flowers."

She smiled broadly, her teeth white and perfectly straight. Her lips were thin and her heart was quick to respond. She leaned over him, a new of seriousness on her face, pausing, and then she kissed him long and hard. This time she meant it more than the previous times. He smothered her tenderly in his arms, turning off the small lamp that had only partially lit the cubicle. Darkness set in as they stretched out on the bed. Entwined like seaweed, he could hear her slow breathing and their lips pressing.

"You know how I feel about you," he whispered.

She did not say anything but kissed his lips long into the resounding and piercing darkness of the night. Two cubicles down, Fleming switched off his light while he and Blythe lay in a slumberous embrace.

They dozed about two hours and in the faint light of streaked summer morning skies, sparrows flitted from tree to tree. Jocko had wrapped a blanket around Peter's clock to prevent it from waking him and the whole east wing during the night. But outside and inside a tower or, as some called it a "turret," one lone bell tolled the hours regularly. It now rang a mute four bells and gradually, ever so slowly, Blythe woke, her lids heavy from sleep. Paris breathed heavily, head on arm, lips partially opened.

She tried to pull her arm loose that went through the arch of his neck but she could not do it without waking him. She relaxed. Moments glided away like sands through an hour glass. As he turned over, she slipped out her arm, ready to softly depart. But one quick lurch of her body woke him. He did not even blink; he only stared for a moment. She leaned down next to him.

"I've got to go. It's four already. Paris looked at her strangely like he had not heard a word. Then he blinked and grasped her arm, saying nothing.

"Paris. I do."

He shook his head, lips drawn into the corners of his mouth.

"It's too early," he softly whispered.

"I must go, Paris. I'll come up later this morning, all right?"

"Why now?"

"Now's the best time for anything. Nothing gets done unless it is done now. I must go, Paris. Let me leave you like this—softly."

His grasp on her arm loosened and he took her by the hand. They squeezed hands. It was a squeeze of meaning not simply for the sake of touch.

"I love you, Enid," he whispered, pulling her ear to his lips. The expression on her face deepened and she smiled faintly. She bent her head slightly and kissed him silently a long-short moment, then slowly she rose, hairs from her sweater dangling from the attraction of his Pendleton shirt. Reluctantly, he dropped her hand, and she left quietly as a church mouse on Christmas Eve. Paris sat up, rubbing his fingers through his hair. He looked at the clock which read four-fifteen and he rose and unbuttoned his shirt and hung it on the small hanger-space provided. He then strolled outside the cubicle, amid the snores of all the others, and leaned over the water heater to peer out the window. The morning

44

was fresh with the blinding pink sun streaks thrown through the trees surrounding the graveled bullring. He ambled to the other window, the one on the far right and he could see past the evergreens on the right side of the lawn far down the driveway the breaking mists that enshrouded the Erehwon manorial estate like weeping children of the night. Paris Brandon was fascinated with mists, the deep impenetrable mists that lured with the lure of a Celtic imagination. Fleming did not care much about mists; he was usually too busy with Heinecken or Carlsburg beer to care much about them. But he did stare often at Paris as they walked on brisk morning roads when he stared off into them, curling about the elm and fir, wetting the fur on a rabbit huddling for warmth or even making an itinerant owl blink twice when reappearing in the Lincolnshire area. In his sock feet, he moved imperceptibly toward Fleming's cubicle curtain. With one finger, he pulled it to one side. Fleming was alone. He thought a moment then entered. All he had to do was touch Fleming's shoulder and he awoke.

"What is it?"

"Shhhh."

"Almost four-thirty."

"Oh."

"You wanna take a walk?"

Fleming rubbed his eyes slightly. He nodded almost strenuously. He flipped the covers down past his knees and sat up. Paris stood there, leaning against the wall. Fleming pulled on his pants, slipped on his tennis shoes, grabbed his heavy plaid coat and pub hat. Paris slipped on shoes and his heavy coat and they tiptoed down the corridor, past the john, and down a long hall to swinging doors that led to some stairs. They soon came to the bullring door and quietly opened it and left. Dawn had broken quietly and the far-away singing of birds as quietly pervaded the atmosphere.

CHAPTER 5

No one stirred except the walkers at dawn. The world of people slept oblivious to the beauty of dawn. Somehow dawn did not figure in their lives, although most were awake at the time of sunset.

Paris looked at mists as portents of bad dreams or, at other times, as a disappearance of all he could perceive in the present which receded in a mist. History was resurrected at the slightest suggestion. He could see King Henry V on a steed leading his knights at Crécy or Agincourt or Henry Bolingbroke landing with his men at Ravenspurn on the Humber River. History became the present as long as memory made a mist of the present.

Fleming simply thought it was good exercise to ground oneself in an early morning walk to sleep better later. Paris spoke low:

"I see our loves left before dawn."

"Sure did. Shitty bushes. Don't want to be caught in the rack. Not in daylight," he said, referring to Blythe's departure. They walked awhile, chatting idly. Then Paris asked:

"You in love with her?"

"I don't think so. Sometimes maybe."

"You sound unsure."

"I am. She's a good chick. She is. But everything is up in the air these days. We make space capsules for our breathing. But she's a good bush. Good drinker," boasted Fleming, obviously proud.

"Just a good drinker?"

"Sometimes. Say, what are you driving at?" he asked, somewhat defensive by being reminded of the uncertainty of his relationship.

"Nothing in particular. Just wondering," he said as he pulled his collar high against a gusty breeze.

"How are things with you and Enid?"

"Close. Close," said Paris.

"How close?"

"Too damn close for this act. I'll have to make the next performance. Wasn't made for this cast of mind. It hurts because there's no ground. She has a prior commitment," said Paris, braving the wind and mist-gazing.

"Commitments. Bullshit. A prior commitment has little to do with present situations. You know that, Paris. They can be traps to sap our enjoyment of the present. Sometimes they are torts of the mind. No remedy at law," he said with a seriousness that offset his usual mocking tones.

"I know. Let the buyer beware," retorted Paris, "I'm aware of the situation. Now to convince the mind of the situational reality. Right?"

"Perhaps. I would just let it flow as it will. Don't play games with someone you really love. Because games are friendly fictions that hide the refusal to call a spade a spade."

Paris looked at him in wonderment:

"I knew you had a head somewhere. Thanks."

Fleming turned to look at the river. It was pleasant to greet the dawn. Especially on a bridge since it somehow connected dawn to sunset. Some mallards quacked among themselves as they stroked in and out of the tules that bordered the river.

"Sure is quiet out here with no one awake except those mallards," said Fleming making conversation.

"It is nice to be out here. Like this. Live to greet the dawn and you shall see many. No one around. The only peace ducks have is when everyone else is asleep," said Paris with a sigh. He pushed his collar high and scanned the waters that shimmied and shook in the early morning dance of dawn. The wind blew his face with its newly-grown shadow of whiskers. A long silence came between them like an invisible glass that allowed each to see out but no one to see in. The silence kept them awake to the heart, the privacy of mind, a well interiorized where one can toss his bucket and replenish himself for barbs and arrows that pierce the days. It was possible to be deep even though most lived on the surface area of their volumes. Most wished to deny any depth to man since it was associated with idealism or wishful or sentimental feeling. Man was a nothing but. No more. Man was not capable of stimulus or creativity; he was merely a response to a conditioned reflex. But for Paris, man was not man unless he did more than merely respond to stimuli of the environment.

"Tell me," he said finally, "do you think that if prior commitments are, as you say, torts of the mind, do you think the situation is the total reality?"

"Yes, more or less. Hell what a conversation. Me heap big philosopher now."

Paris was put off by Fleming's antics. So he said with an air of persistence. "I'm serious."

Fleming looked at him with a resolution to continue seriously. It was not his habit to take too much too seriously. He reasoned thus: if you do, you die all the time. And life was more than dying all the time or so he figured.

"All right. Shoot."

"Does the situation dominate?" persisted Paris.

"Of course."

"Even if you make a previous commitment?" asked Paris, his eyes serious with intent.

"Of course. What's wrong with that? Commitments confine. They do. Who wants to be confined? I sure as hell don't," stated Fleming flatly. He continually adjusted his pub hat to accommodate the faint glow of the far-off sun.

"Yes. I agree. They do confine. But they also intensify."

"What are you doing? Justifying Enid's commitment to that guy back in the States?" queried Fleming who did not always understand his friend. Fleming retied his tennis shoe. Some sparrows began to sing.

"No. But I respect it."

"Why respect it? Hell he's probably screwing up a storm over there. You know how it is in the military. Screwing and drilling. And the idea is to find the right cavity."

Paris smiled quietly and then his smile broadened to a grin.

"I don't know that for a fact. You can't presume to accuse," protested Paris.

"I'm not accusing. Just probability. That's all. Why lose out over here by worrying about who's doing what over there? Tell me that!" exclaimed Fleming, readying himself for a hearty discussion.

"So we just operate on cynical assumptions, right? If he's in the military, he must be screwing someone, right?" offered Paris. Fleming took off his pub hat and pretended to catch the wind in it. It was like talk; it did not catch the wind either. The wind just blew where it went.

"What's your problem? You trying to justify pursing your Daphne? Enid's the kind that would turn into a laurel. What a price that would be," he said with his usual boast. Paris stared at the mallards. They ate tiny organisms among the reeds and tules. They seemed at home with themselves. If humans could only be that way, he thought. Fleming's boisterous comic airs were not appealing. It was frustrating to want to be serious when everyone else wanted to play around.

"Fleming, do you want to talk or don't you?" Fleming's face turned sober again.

"All right. Shoot," he said, sitting with one leg on the bridge. Paris turned to face him squarely, his hair tossed gently into his eyes.

"Are all commitments confining merely?" he asked with renewed earnestness.

"Yes. Of course they are. How many times do I have to tell you? Hmm? As there are crosses in genetics and at altars, there are double crosses when you live for commitments or promises or pie in the sky. You become tied down. Like a prisoner with a ball and chain," he said, spinning his hat on his finger almost impatiently. The sun now offered a slight glare off the river into the corners of their eyes. Sparrow songs now became an orchestrated movement beneath the pink-streaked skies and azure tints that peered through well above the mist-kissed rolling fields.

Paris spoke low: "What is your alternative?"

"Just don't make any commitments. I mean you do to a certain extent. What kind of job you work. Where you go to school or get trained. What military branch you're in. But a previous commitment like Enid's are prosaic at best. It prevents her from enjoying herself now. She's tied to sweet nothings whispered by the past. No fun now. And that's a shame if you ask me, Paris. A good man like you must eat the dregs. I know you are fond of her. But her commitment prevents her from interacting on any meaningful level now."

Paris cleared his throat like Chanticleer ready to prance for Pertelote in the *Canterbury Tales*.

"What do you mean by meaning-full?" asked Paris.

"We have spoken seriously and deeply about things most dear to her. In that way, we have a meaningful relationship."

Fleming shrugged and stood in dismay.

"Okay. What's your problem?" he retorted.

"If there is any, I'd like to know why commitments do not impress you."

Fleming looked puzzled.

"What is this? A cross examination? I've already told you. They're a ball and chain," he said with a slight flush in his cheeks.

Paris realized he was upsetting Fleming so he did not say anything for several minutes. By that time, his temperature had cooled enough to re-open the conversation, this time on a gentler note. By now, Fleming was scanning the fields behind them toward the field where sheep grazed. Paris, too, scanned for a few moments. The morning was a cup of beauty; sparrows sang a trinity of notes; the sun gradually rose and yawned, ready to journey across the sky. Then Paris opened:

"Tell me, Fleming. Why do people commit themselves?"

Fleming felt a lighter tone and responded:

"I don't know. Maybe they have limited horizons. Or maybe they haven't been around. Like a global affair," he said with attempted puns. Paris smiled a faint smile.

"Come on. Be serious with me. Why do you think?"

"Hell if I know. Maybe they are narrow. Too narrow. You know there are infinite possibilities," he replied with greater control in response to Paris' prodding.

"Of course. But infinite possibility is a sport illusion plays. It screws the mind. You can't live forever in infinite possibility. If you did, you'd go mad. You really would," he replied with an earnest face.

Suddenly Fleming sensed in vibrations that came between them of the utter seriousness of the conversation. He had been putting it off, playing with it like a cat with a ball of yarn. But he almost shuddered at this realization of the depth of personal involvement there arose in a mere question. It dawned on him, almost gradually, that people were the questions they posed.

"Yes. Perhaps one would go mad if left to infinite choices. But there is freedom without having to choose, right?" queried Fleming, becoming sober. "Like I said, you have to commit yourself to some extent. Job. School.

"Yes. But what about committing yourself to something that is forever. Eternal even," asked Paris.

Fleming took off his pub hat and spun it on his finger as he thought. Then he tried to catch the wind. He could not. Thought tried to catch the wind too but the wind was always invisible and could not be caught unless it became stale.

Fleming peered at Paris out of the corner of his eye with a chagrined look.

"You mean like God?" Paris nodded.

"I thought so. God is an error of man. When will you believe that? He's been gone a long time now. I mean it's almost embarrassing to even mention his name. Nietzsche, the German saint, killed him with his pen. Been a long time now. Forget the error and the myth. Be a physician if you wish to play God. But don't conjure up those memories. But you, Paris, must forget all those false consolations and other false securities."

"I certainly agree with you," replied Paris, "but one thing bothers me."

"And what is that?"

"I think there is something eternal. Eternal in all of us. Somehow. It's not finished yet. Maybe just maybe man was..."

"Was what?"

"Was an error…"

"In what way?"

"Man is in error in that he forgot the kingdom was within." Fleming gave out a cynical cackle.

"That's nonsense. How can you believe that crap?" stated Fleming with a flat out denial. Paris was in a trance-like state.

"What?" Fleming said in disbelief at his friend.

"You heard me. All the universes."

Fleming frowned impatiently but respected his friend's opinion which he privately thought was thoroughly rotten. Paris knew the knitted brows of the problematic forehead, how problems wrote their lines on a person's head as they grew old. But he was himself problematic since he reflected so much as his capacity allowed. Silence intervened. Paris thought how easy it was to be a naysayer and laugh at anything and everything that reason could not rationally approach. Fleming thought how the morning had been spoiled but, in a sense, had made him sharpen his thoughts so that he knew his edge on such matters.

"Let's go. Let's go somewhere," said Fleming. "Thought breathes better with action."

They left and slowly circled the fields that became more visible as the mists burned off. But they knew the mists would return for each had their turn with the land.

CHAPTER 6

"The angel of the Lord said to him,
'How can you ask my name? It is a
name of wonder.'" Judges 13:18

The morning had risen above the trees next to the bullring. Birds sang everywhere. A song of summer added zest and warmth to the dew-soaked earth. Voices were heard within and they realized breakfast was on. Girls came with hair freshly-combed; others came in curlers. The men slept in for the most part, although Paris and Fleming sat a table with two other guys who had somehow shown the courage to rise in the early morning. A lecture was an hour away. Professor Arsse was lecturing on "How to Live Like Ants Do." Presumably Arsse knew whereof he spoke. He had studied biology as a minor in college; ants were of major interest to him. They were amazed when, a few minutes later, Everette Lardace appeared for breakfast. It was his custom not to rise for breakfast since he would compensate for his lack at lunch and dinner. But apparently he was ready now. He sat with Fleming and Paris who looked at each other knowingly as Ev sat down placing a heavy strain on the antique chairs that filled the dining hall. He unrolled his cloth napkin (which everyone placed in cubby holes outside the hall) and tucked it into his shirt collar. Licking his lips, he surveyed the eggs, sausage, pancakes, French fries, and fruit set on the table. It was customary to have potatoes at least three meals a day. The cook's dog, Skip, would add a tail hair here and there to each table's pitcher of orange juice for a little added spice to the meal. Next to him were Duci and Luwanna. The food was passed to him and he piled his plate high with French fries, six eggs, ten pancakes, a dozen sausages, and a gigantic decanter (his own) of orange juice. Just watching him was amusing for Duci originally from Hong Kong. She was always amazed at how westerners never got enough of anything. If it was not one thing, it was another. She liked American students but they did not take too well to foreigners who giggled as much as she did. Most girls did not major in economics nor was she secretly in pursuit of a college-educated husband. Instead she just giggled alot and was imitated by every one of the golden hogs of Room 33, that is, all except Everette. He was usually eating and thus left little room for laughter.

It was her luck that Ev's act of piling food caught her humor and swung it around until she giggled uproariously. Fleming eyed Paris as they ate, pretending not to notice Duci's antics. Students at other tables momentarily ceased conversations to stare at Duci who continued to giggle. Not much ever bothered Ev, but this morning the ceaseless laughter began to interrupt his digestive tract. He continued eating despite the constant heheheheh that sounded like a couple making love on rusty bed springs. Even Luwanna, customarily wrapped in the hypersensitive arms of her ego, began to smile a smile that looked like she was in pain. It was as if the Marquis de Sade was whipping her bare back. Needless to say, Ev was quite antsy at the smiles and laughter. He was becoming embarrassed at the situation but decided a thick hide was better than none and there might not be much food for lunch so he had better eat what he could right now. His fork plunged with avidity into the pancake stack and cut a forkful. It was delicious. Eating, for Ev, was a way of life. If ever you had any anxiety, just eat. It would not guarantee the anxiety would go away, but at least you could do something pleasurable in the meantime. And besides, it was something a person could do three or four times a day. Such rationalizing accounted for Ev's grandiose figure. Paris was concerned with the faulty logic and groundless justification for Ev's physique. Fleming just perforated, or attempted to perforate, the excess layers of fat tissue with his barbs. Peter not only kept the hours but, like Paris, concerned himself with Ev's problem.

It was with severe restraint that Fleming kept quiet at the table. A temptation for satire was severely strong at that point but Fleming was thinking. You could tell he was. He didn't have to say anything but you knew, just knew, he was taking arrows out of his quiver only later to arch his bow. Duci finally quieted down and Luwanna began to eat. What began the second session was Ev's obvious lack of manners, or so they thought. Trying to eat fast, he did not get all of his food into his gaping orifice. Striving to get everything, he got nothing. Laboring to be laboring, he only busied himself. He missed the point as well as the food. Syrup dribbled down his chin onto his double chin. His napkin served to catch food that spilled out of his mouth. Portions of pancakes, pieces of potato spilled with ketchup and orange juice onto his napkin and the table around his plate looked like a littered beach resort.

Fleming almost burst his silence. He eyed Paris seriously. "What a grossout," he said. Duci began another laughing session. It sounded like a menagerie. Luwanna began to smile painfully and was herself quite embarrassed by the situation. She constantly adjusted her bra strap lest Ev might desire to continue his breakfast in another direction. By the time this laughter reached a climax, it was time for Arsse's lecture on the ants and the others began strolling out of the dining hall. Some went to retrieve notebooks which they would fill with salient lecture notes; others simply went to hear what the professor had to say. Fleming and Paris finished their meal and sat and chatted awhile. Fleming was certainly aware of Ev's ongoing concern with food. Ev still ate voraciously. It did not cease to amaze Paris that Ev's stomach made such demands on him.

Aside from Ev, Fleming kept his eyes on Joan Bradshaw across the hall. Vivacious and buxom, she was a model of style and friendliness. When she smiled, her eyes would close as if to ward off the pain her hypersensitivity attracted. She was aware that men were attracted to her body. That was usually the first step in attraction. However, she wanted them not simply to be attracted by the fullness of her breasts or by her slender but firm legs. She wanted mind. Rapport. And there was always frustration. She held herself as over an abyss. Unable to support herself emotionally, she sought support in others. Her emotions continually overpowered her. She exalted her feelings of sympathy, despair, depression; yet she deplored the very feelings she exalted. And round and round she went. Not knowing when to get off, she continually got on. She became a victim of her fantasies of finding the right person who would straighten an often meandering channel. Like most of the other men, Fleming was attracted to her body; Paris was attracted to her mind. Those attracted to her body wanted to taste her breasts that seldom sagged; those attracted to her mind primarily wished to understand why her body was so central to her being. Fleming got up from the table and ventured to hers and sat with her as others dashed to class. Paris strolled to the elevator and waited. Ev began to finish his last stack of pancakes. Luwanna and Duci had left minutes before. Soon the hall was empty except for Fleming and Joan at one table and Ev finishing breakfast and the kitchen staff jabbering to the sound of forks, spoons, knives and dishes with an occasional bark from Skip. Ev finally finished and went to the lecture. By now most of the manor was wide awake and actively engaged.

Half-way up the elevator, Paris decided to go the top floor to see Enid. Peter and Sparky woke early enough to take the minivan into Grantham to do their laundry. Zee forgot breakfast but took off to play crochet on the cricket field with others who had decided to forego Arsse's lecture on ants. Jocko was the only one to remain in room 33 fast asleep. A gentle breeze from the windows caused a slight rush in his cubicle curtain. He did not hear the door open and shut quietly or even the footsteps that slowly paused at each cubicle.

Each curtain rose as it male content was intensely examined. As is sometimes the case in sleep, you can feel someone's presence in that land between dream and reality; Jocko felt someone in the room but dreamed on in a state of light sleep. He was currently dreaming that he was on safari in Africa, hunting lion. They had found one and he loaded his high-powered rifle, raised it to his shoulder, took careful and cautious aim at the lion when all of a sudden he felt himself as a spaghetti strand torn between the Africa of dream and the present reality of a hand warm but nervous softly stroking his warm stomach. It took several moments for him to realize something quite distracted his aim as someone kept pulling his arm so he could not shoot straight and pretty soon the lion would duck into tall foliage and disappear into the deeps of the jungle not to be seen again. Easily fingers began to play with his flesh and massage taut muscles that could flex into action at a threat's notice. He looked high and low as the lion became restless and seemed to pass in and out of sight, only identified by an occasional roar to tell of his whereabouts. Three times he appeared and disappeared like a drowning person rises to the surface for the last time. Africa began to fall to pieces like a puzzle that falls on the floor. He began to surface even from light sleep since light often lies deeper than surfaces might suggest.

He began to shake as he realized the safari had only just begun. Her eyes were persistent, rushed on by a craving for this redhead just awakening to find desire staring into his eyes. Nothing was said. Only for a moment did he think of someone else coming in the room. But he forgot that and began to peel himself like a banana and she was now panting with her drooping breasts pointing straight at him with desire and desire and desire. She craved with muscles pulled tense, holding herself on him and the muscles of her mouth contorted into lines ablaze with craving for him.

Their private universe rotated and revolved with penetration to the mystery of what it meant to hold flesh as being divine as her nipples glowed like sun and moon. And round and round they went caught in the wheels of their motion, She had been aiming for him for quite awhile until he appeared in just the light she had been aiming for. The entire hunting act had been staged before in her mind every morning when she swept the floor but he was hers now and she cherished everything that united them in embrace.

Just then a door slammed and the ride was over for now. Hot had to cool. That was the nature of things. Sometimes the coolness was forced and artificial but the wisdom of the body flowed into a quietude beneath a dawn sky. This was rushed as an intruder came to interrupt the course of nature. In moments, they were re-composed. She went about her dusting in the cubicles, still breathing heavily and adjusting her hair. He merely lay in bed reading a book when Paris strolled in and quietly closed the door. At Jocko's cubicle he stopped.

"Good morning. You the only one here? I see Peter's gone." Jocko looked up.

"No. The maid's in here. You go to lecture?"

"No," replied Paris. "Where is everybody?"

"I don't know. I woke up and everybody's gone. I seriously doubt if they're in class," said Jocko, thumbing a history of Scotland. "Where've you been?"

"Breakfast. But then I went to see if Enid was in. Shot the bull with Blythe since Enid had gone to class."

Paris noticed the maid who was humming two cubicles down. Just then she popped her face out from the curtain. Her cheeks were rosy and she busied herself with an aura of duty to dusting.

"She sure works hard," Paris commented.

"Who?" said Jocko, almost surprised by his reference to her.

"Efi," said Paris.

"Oh. Yes. Her," said Jocko with emphasis and a face straight with seriousness as if making a nationwide announcement.

Paris went on to his cubicle and sang:

"Ours is time of memory
Ours a time of song
Drink and sing a merry lay
Catch a maid, make a maid
In the hay of May."

Hearing this ditty, Efi threw herself even more into her work to seal her eardrums which caused her hands to perspire a little more. Paris continued now with his guitar:

"Our songs are songs shepherds sing:
Tom beneath pastoral limb
John a-tooting to starry night;
Jim a song of memory,
Pat a song of love,
Dick a song of joy.
Ours is time of memory
Time that turneth faithfully."

When the last vibration of string ceased, Paris leaned his guitar against the wall and began to peruse assignments for the week. Much reading to do. Dust mop in hand, Efi tiptoed to Jocko's cubicle and threw him a kiss. He smiled. She then left to dust other rooms.

Downstairs in the dining hall, Ev finished his meal and took his plates to the kitchen window. The kitchen staff girls giggled and teased whenever he was around. Ev thought it was due to his good looks. They, however, were laughing at him. They had never seen such an incredible hulk.

Just after he had left, Fleming and Joan decided to leave. They went the door that led to the bullring, strolled beyond the buildings, and entered fresh fields drying in the sun. To Fleming, she looked beautiful with her shapely legs, full breasts, lipstick a coral pink she teased him at every step. The idea was, of course, that you did not notice such aspects since a platonic relationship was all that she professed. It was somewhat difficult to disguise sexual attraction behind the veil of philosophy in the company of such a sweet nymph. Fleming was ready for philosophy but did not care for it with shapely legs acting as a continuous lure for feeling. Of course he would go along with the idea of philosophizing but it was her form more than anything else that attracted him. As she walked just ahead of him through some blueberry bushes, he grew to adore her form every moment. Now he knew that passion always played musical beds and there was nothing to compare with the fire inside. It was Catullus gazing at Lesbia with passionate eyes! Beauty, he thought, beauty is poetry in love with perception. Ah, to forget Blythe and find romance with Joan Bradshaw! Ah, he could fantasize it now: cranberry juice-marooned lips, breasts aflame with passion, and legs open to the nature of now in azured arms of Paradise! He was a man for all forms. And this form tickled the eye-ribs of poetry.

She led him to a glen almost a hundred and fifty yards from the manor. By now, he was drunk with passion; like Saul, he needed a David to play the harp and soothe the agitation of his soul. She made a place for him beneath a willow tree and together they sat. She smiled that smile that hid her bright yet sad eyes and gently played with his hair. If ecstasy means to be beside oneself, Fleming was. His eyes filled with her; they became glued to her every move. What hell it was to discuss philosophy at a time like this. But this, this moment was for fools. Even beauty could awe the provocative thoughts of philosophy. For long moments they sat with silence for a companion, their eyes growing with wonder and novelty.

"I have always been a child of wonder," she began as she looked into his eyes.

"And that's not all," he said. "You're also a child of beauty, an Aphrodite of the soul," he said until he realized what he was saying. He had not intended to pour forth his thoughts still elevated by the function of fantasy.

"I did not know you were a poet," she said, almost shyly.

"Happens now and then," replied Fleming with a grin.

"I see it does. Well, as I was saying, I have always been a child of wonder."

"Must be nice," he said, not intending to interrupt. At that she sat up.

"I thought you wanted to talk."

"Oh. I do. I do. Believe me I do. Please continue." She sat back, her figure gleaming in his eyes. His head was in a spin. Just to be was a form of wonder. And to be with her was even more so. He had difficulty restraining himself. The steeds of passion and impatience were running away without reason's reigns.

"Well, as I was saying, I have always been a child of wonder," she said for the third time. It always takes a trinity to get wonder across, he thought. And it seems to me to define in a clear mind what wonder might be.

Fleming gazed at her almost disbelieving his ears. She really had philosophy in mind. It frustrated him to think that women, intellectual ones at least, always wanted to sit and discuss things. He wondered why she was so intensely and passionately interested in wonder.

"Do you have any ideas?" she asked.

"About wonder? Not particularly. Although I wonder why you want to discuss it." She laughed a horse laugh.

"That *is* a good question. But to be really honest, I don't know. I wonder."

He smiled.

"I wonder why we have to discuss wonder. Why not let it be? Why define it? Maybe wonder would cease to mean anything to us if we simply went around defining it."

"Maybe so. But words do mean something, especially if they are attached to action. Words alone scare me. They really do. I get frightened with vacuous words. Even if they are only attached umbilically, I admire words attached to action," she said, leaning on her elbow and gazing at the daisies awakening to the sun of day.

"Certainly. I agree. Suit the action with your words. And there's little action in mere philosophical discussion. Don't you agree? And don't you agree that one should specialize in his field? And if it happens to be love, he should get the action going on in the field?"

A grin slowly came on her face.

"If love is your field, action's the game," she said with a wisely and knowing look. He was in like Flint, he thought. This was easier than he thought it might be. What an easy lay; he did not have to accompany himself with a guitar, mandolin, lyre, or even an aolian harp. However, Joan was wiser than he thought. The lines came in an astounding array, careened over one another as a stream cascades toward the sea, but his lines, although nibbled, were not convincing. His hands were ready to make and record the time. But, as a current often catches itself in a swirling eddy and circles around several times and only then may flow directly to the sea, her thought current plunged into an eddy. She knew Fleming only too well. That too was a pause for wonder. Why did he feel love so early in the game? Was it love at all? Sure she wanted him but not this way. Did a romantic setting determine love? She did not think so even as his fingers crossed her breasts in a playful pinch and pluck. Obviously he desired her body and that both appealed to and repelled her. Ambivalence was her name. Off came her blouse. It was now. If only she could not have such thoughts. She was, in a sense, condemned to have a mind as well as a luscious body. Fleming ruled well. The sun streaked into her neck. She felt his hungry lips kissing her, pausing here and there for long moments, with a nibble, a bite gently placed. She felt her breathing become rapid and her mind became a pond whose mud bottom has been disturbed. The muddy mind did not make for coherent philosophy for philosophy is best when breathing is calm and the mind clear. Although she enjoyed being with him, she also felt an impulse to resist as his hands toured the hills and valleys of her shapely form. It was this split between stop and go that caused her go to stop. Her muscles tightened into a rigid pose. Rigidity meant refusal. It came as a surprise to him who was already lost in the boundless wonder of exploration; he had been oblivious to her thoughts that jousted with one another. At first, he pretended not to notice but her continued stiffness caused him to pause even as she turned her back to his fond embraces. He actually thought this was a jest on her part. Something was amiss. It was almost an embarrassment. After all, things were going smoothly.

"What's up," he said after several minutes of deep freeze.

"Nothing."

"Nothing? That's close," he said, sitting up.

"What is it?" he asked again.

She was feeling awful about it. She was hot inside, aflame but she did not know what to do. Above all, she was afraid he would get angry and mad with her for putting on the brakes but she had to. It was almost as if she should salvage self-respect this first time together with him. She didn't even know him. Yet she was set on one track and could play only in that field. It was amazing how expectations (based on past reviews) could become a habit.

"I feel awful," she said after awhile.

"About what," he barked.

"About doing this."

"Look, my dear, nothing is healthier than sex, right? You know it and I know it. Every psychiatrist will tell you that," he said with an amateurish authoritativeness. She smiled the smile that hid her eyes as if to keep out the bright glare of the present. It would be easy to simply spread herself open and let him try small bites into her. The whole affair engendered some recent unpleasant memories. Stateside, she had slept with four lovers until when she became pregnant, none of them even claimed her as a friend, much less as a bed partner. Yet it was so much fun. Fleming was getting mad. All his plans were receding like an ebb tide. The air was pouring out of his ego like a balloon. Such a cessation of pleasure was bound to provoke his anger which vetoed his previous stimulation; he went limp in one direction, erect in another.

"Why? Just tell me why."

"I don't know. Maybe some time when I'm up to it. I don't even know you, Fleming. I know you think I'm a prude. But I'd really like to get to know you and you me."

Fleming buried his head in his hands. Boy was he pissed. You could tell it meant a lot to him being this close to Joan whom everyone desired.

"Talk about a party pooper," he began with abuse. This only made her sadder. Why was it so strange to really want to know someone? Was friendship so foolish? She had gone to bed with others without even knowing their names. All that mattered was to be with someone who stimulated her and gave her a secure feeling. But the abortion had taught her a lesson. When she was in a crisis, no one helped her. Her lovers who professed love for her were in love with loving, but had no idea of what love even meant. To them, love was having sex. She had thus seen for herself that sex did not necessarily mean love at all. Their relationship, whatever that was, was an abortion in itself. It was like cheating in a game of poker. When someone else began to cheat, you were the first to cry "foul play!"

"I'm not a party pooper, Fleming. I only just wanted—"

"Cut the cock and bull," he said, his anger increasing. By now, his words were poisoned arrows. If he did not get his way, he would curse anyone and everyone. What would the guys think? At least no one had seen them leave. That was a relief. Otherwise, he would be teased for the rest of his stay in Britain. That thought made him feel better. Still the blame was thrust upon her for not completing the job.

"Fleming," she whispered, feeling bad as she did so.

"What is it, you bitch?"

That was enough. She had had it. Fleming had said the ill-timed name, one she had heard in previous months when blame was laid by all quarters at her door. Slowly she had been getting dressed. As she finished buttoning the final button, her look was one of anger restrained by her own needs as a woman. With determined precision and pride mustered by an act of courage to affirm the dignity of being human, she fought back.

"Don't ever call me 'bitch.' I've heard that name before and I hate it."

"Cut it," he said with a punctured vanity, little realizing how he now underestimated her position. She was not going to be interrupted.

"I said don't call me 'bitch'. Men think that's all we are, namely holes to fill. I'm not just a hole." Fleming began to look up to her standing there in the sun.

"I didn't say you were a hole."

"No. But you acted as if I were. You get mad when your desires are thwarted. Everything is you. You this, you that. All because I wanted to get to know you. Simply that. I'll let you wallow in your fantasies, your sexual conquests. Go and fantasize. There are some you will always have. I love to make love too. But I've been hurt by others just like you. Everything's fine until something unexpected happens. Then poof: they're gone. I know. I've been through it before. Someday, maybe someday, we'll grow up." Initially ready for accented rage, Fleming's face passed from rage to hurt to secret respect.

He did not realize her words stemmed from deep-rooted past misery. It would have been far easier for her to be bitter toward the entire male species. Bitterness was mitigated by far-reaching understanding. Compassion tempered hate. In her eyes, Fleming was a little boy. But she could not and would not tolerate further abuse. The abuse was intended to mollify his own hurt. An easy task, he had not realized he was treading tender loins with his remarks.

He rose. Her face softened but retained a dash of defiance in case he continued to abuse her with words. With matchless pressure, he restrained his tongue. Even Fleming knew an Achilles heel when he perceived it. He had found his and hers.

There was still time to amend his relation. It was her game from here to the next round. Although that thought bothered him, mingled desire and respect offset a stubborn refusal to go along with her desire to get to know him. They strolled through the fields arm in arm as the sun rose to high noon. As they strolled along, what residue of rage there was in him cooled. True, he desired her, and it would be less than honest to say he did not, for the lure of novelty was strong enough be lure anyone out of his own pasture into greener ones though several fences separated such grazing grounds. At the same time, he came to view her in the light of a challenge that commanded respect. It was somehow different from all the other lays he had strummed into position on previous occasions. He had not traveled on foot for a long but such labor, despite the fact that Fleming worshipped convenience, did not seem to be a labor at all. In fact, just being with her in the fields did not allow him to think of the labor of walking, even though he knew new brain cells were created with each step. He was, so to speak, absorbed in reflections of her and the impact dawn really had on him.

Her case was different. Of course she thought much about Fleming. But more than that, she enjoyed just being with someone. She forgot any hurt she had suffered and hoped he did too. The butterflies that flitted over the wheat-colored fields that extended into the distance to merge with the sky in the direction of Nottingham fascinated her by the moment. Sometimes she would try to catch one of the butterflies but always they eluded her. Often she would pause to sniff a flower growing taller than the others then they would pass on. In the distance, they could see Erehwon Manor set off as a castle with its limestone walls glinting in the sun. As they came to a bend, a cow sat there chewing its cud. It did not move as they approached but eyed them warily, still chewing. Now and then it swished away flies that hopped about on its rump. The cow diverted Fleming's thoughts away from himself. They stood and observed the cow.

"How would you like to chew all day long?" he asked. She smiled a happy smile.

"Looks content, doesn't she?" was her reply. "No, I don't think so."

"You would have no problems. You could just sit in a field all day."

She gave him a cursory glance then almost inaudibly chuckled at his suggestion.

"And chew my cud, eh?" she said as if to complete his statement.

"Sure. Why not?" he said, seating himself on a clump of grass.

She stood for a moment then decided to sit down next to him.

"Well, I really don't know. Maybe because I'm not a cow." He chuckled as did she.

"Have you ever thought what it would it would be like to be a cow?"

"Not really. I can't imagine anyone wanting to be a cow. That is, unless they did not like themselves. I mean as they were in the first place," she replied. She was fascinated by this bend in their conversation and listened intently as his interest grew.

"What if you were a cow? And the cow was you." Absurdity had the magic charm of producing an incredulous smile on every generation.

"What do you mean?"

"What if you and the cow were really the same?" he said with obvious awareness of the absurdity of his question. Half of his charm was his flair for the absurd. It was said of him that he lived the crazy life inspired by the song "Viva la Vida loca."

"Well maybe we are. How do you like being with a cow?" she said. It was a psychological gambit. The sacrifice would come any moment. She would play with this as long as she could.

"That's a lot of bull, my dear. You did not answer directly," he replied.

"One does not directly approach the absurd. Meaningless. To me, anyway. How does one answer the question: 'What if you and the cow were really the same?' That is an improper proposition," she said with the air of a school teacher correcting the grammar of a child.

"That's a bullshit proposition concerning my proposition. Who asked for the almighty aid of linguistic analysis?" he exclaimed with a cutting edge to his teeth. Her laughter went on for moments.

"But you must admit that to ask such a question is indeed absurd."

"Of course it is. But that does not mean that it cannot be asked. We are defined by the questions we ask. Questions pinpoint concerns."

"Then your concerns are absurd," she exclaimed with the glee of victory

"Not so, my dear. Not so," he said. He was prepared for newer propositions.

"Just awhile back you wished to discuss wonder, right? To even ask what wonder is, is somewhat absurd. This was your question. Does wonder even need to be questioned? It simply *is*. Here. There. Everywhere. What is so absurd about asking if the cow is us? And then to discuss wonder as a concept? The wonder is that we can ask questions that are apparently absurd. To restrict questions is a denial of freedom. I hope we will always have the courage to ask absurd questions. But remember to question is to articulate even such odd times as the absurd. Before that comes around, and it will as long as men cultivate time to think, remember also that as far as memory can dip into awe, wonder is there, without a doubt. Just there. Before any questions."

While all this was going on, the cow continually chewed with a look of an octogenarian who enjoyed good times in the past. The cow would not be propositioned with logic or rhetoric; she just sat there enjoying the wonder of being in the sun. Cows are like that. Joan was satisfied with his words but not with his original proposition.

"Still. You have not answered your question about the cows and us, have you?" she persisted. A grin rolled on his face.

"That is true."

"Then logically you have not solved your proposition," she persisted with logic. A look came on his face that was a blend of light and shade much as the sun fades and reappears like alternating currents when clouds blot the sky.

"That is not the point, my dear. Not it at all. The point is that one can only articulate out of his experience of being there. Wonder is sheer being there, right? Okay, the point is this: not every proposition can be solved. Sometimes it is merely a symbol. In this case it is a symbol. I did not vaguely entertain the notion such a proposition could be logically answered. When logic becomes a substitute for life, you are caught up in the analytical mind. Just remember that. Simply to even suggest such a proposition is all that is needed. The freedom to ask or even suggest. Life does not always have logical solutions. I don't care who you are or what you do."

Joan's face lit up. It was as if someone had raised a curtain and in the twinkling of an eye she could see more. A faint glow cast about her cheeks and a smile warmed her heart as she rose and gave him her hand and he helped her to her feet so that she could stand and enjoy the day just like anyone else. They walked away from the cow that casually looked their way with wisdom. She had learned more from a cow today than many of the learned lectures in the world. Fleming was nice to get to know.

CHAPTER 7

To the manor they returned. Sounds from the commons room radiated throughout; the clatter of eating utensils were heard from the kitchen. They had missed lunch and an afternoon lecture was being given. Professor Pitts was lecturing on "Irrelevance: Fact or Fiction" in the chapel below. Fleming kissed Joan long as if to suck forth her soul. That she was moved by departure was certain. A closeness, however cautiously hesitant, had grown into the texture of their relationship. They parted. He strolled through the door that squeaked with an air of enjoyment. He felt fine. Into room 33 he strolled. It was quiet. Peter was gone; Jocko's light was out; Sparky had gone to the lecture. One light beamed in a convex glow up the far wall of Paris' cubicle. In a leisurely manner, Paris was reading on his bed. Surprised, he gave Fleming an inquisitive glance, then said: "Welcome to Erehwon."

Fleming grinned. "You look happy. What's your story?"

"No story."

"Bull."

"No. Really. No story."

Paris put down his book and studied the features of Fleming's face. There was an uncommon serenity about the eyes and mouth. A radiance colored his complexion with a glow about the temples. Paris gave him a skeptical regard, hinting that Fleming was hiding something. Fleming was. Paris was undaunted; he was naturally, almost pagan-like, a father confessor image, especially when Fleming felt a disgraceful note concerning one of his many women. It was a comfort to confess. Confession, at its best, was an unburdening of the cares of the world. Jocko did not, in contrast, confess to Paris; he simply took a shower as he was right now. But Fleming felt no real need to confess at this moment. Paris sensed this. And with good sense, he did not press persistence too far. All he said was:

"I have a feeling, my friend, that you did not get laid."

Fleming gave him a look of mingled surprise and hurt. His friend had known him too many years, had weathered every wench, every drink, every complaint, every satire and parody in which his friend engaged.

"What makes you think so?" he said as his defenses became raised.

"I don't know. I just have a feeling. You usually come in boasting. Today you didn't. Something real happened. It wasn't the usual lay." Fleming could not face the judgment of Paris.

"I don't want to talk about it."

With a wide smile, Paris lay there with a nod of understanding.

He vanished into his own cubicle, a rare act for Fleming. This was atypical. And with that Paris continued to read for awhile as Fleming quietly lounged in his cubicle, thinking about what had happened. What a day it had been, how different. Her reaction to initial seduction had made him a promissory note, a note Fleming did not care to sign. Yet he had actually enjoyed her company. Just talking to her. Unusual. As he lay there thinking, he wanted to tell someone about her but a familiar face like Paris' was too entrenched in the expectations of his tales of seduction. But Paris was not so entrenched. He could change, chameleon-like, when he wished without having to abandon principles that characterized him. Slowly Fleming wandered to the western windows and felt an afternoon breeze from the heart of the Midlands. Air smelled like hay and flowers. Paris soon rose and strolled to the center of the room. He leaned out of one of the windows and took a deep breath. Fleming twitched his mustache.

"Great day out, isn't it?" Paris began. Fleming frowned. He could not stand a phony approach to what concerned someone. Paris was making small talk. People made small talk when they often did not have anything substantial to say. Such conversations, when Fleming was not drinking, annoyed him. They annoyed him like nettles sting hiking legs. The weather was not on Paris' mind but he thought to play along with him.

"Sure is a great day. Everything's in bloom," he replied as he watched a frown pass over Paris' face. Clouds passed in front of the sun and darkened the land for long minutes.

"This is bloomin' bull. Now cut it."

"*You* cut it," snapped Fleming. "What bullshit. The weather?"

"All right. All right. I give up," he said with a shrug as he held his arms up in the air. He turned to go back to his cubicle. Fleming paused, then said:

"Hey. Wait. We need not argue," he said as Paris turned and returned to the window.

"I agree. Arguments slay friends by the thousands. Why should we? We've been friends too long," said Paris.

Fleming's face softened. Paris meant much to him.

"All right, what's the problem?" asked Fleming.

Paris placed his hands on his hips and began to pace the floor.

"No problem. None at all. I just thought we could talk. I was wondering what was up," he said. Fleming grinned.

"It *has* been a different day. It really has. Joan Bradshaw and I. We went out. To the fields and haystacks."

Paris was amused; his eyes began to twinkle, cavalier eyes that laughed and danced.

"To the fields and haystacks?" he replied.

"Why not? Love happens in haystacks too."

"Depends on the field," quipped Paris.

"You bastard. You think I only lust after women?" declared Fleming, pleading innocent.

"My dear fellow. Your name is lust incorporated. I've known you for nearly ten years. And in all that time you haven't changed a bit. If there's a hole somewhere, you will find it. Like I say, depends on the field."

Fleming felt hurt by his friend's accusatory tone. It was hard to erase a bad reputation. A person's good name was their private treasure.

"I plead innocent this time. We didn't do much in that sphere. We talked. Talked and walked. And enjoyed each other's company. We really did."

Paris seemed doubtful but was willing to concede that Fleming had been persuaded onto a different tract.

"I thought so. Just had a feeling you did not get laid. I could tell. You were not your usual self," commented Paris. Fleming seemed relieved to convince him of his innocence.

"What about Blythe?" asked Paris.

"What about her?" Fleming curtly replied. He did not want to hear her name. Paris had touched an exposed nerve, a sensitive spot, an Achilles tendon.

"You like her too, don't you?"

"Of course," he said, conceding only a fraction of intention to Paris' queries. "And I like Jane and Mary and Susan, too. So what."

"And Betty," added Fleming.

"That's right," remarked Paris.

"What're you driving at?" said Fleming who was obviously upset by the cross-examination his friend offered.

"Only this. You once told me not to play games with women. Now, who is playing games? You, Fleming, you. Or don't you recognize the games you play?" queried Paris with an earnest face and a smirk on his lips. He leaned on the window sill now with intent eyes piercing Fleming's whole demeanor. Fleming sat on the table with his back against the wall, licking his mustache and would periodically stroke his chin.

"I guess you are right," replied Fleming. "The truth is on your side. You know me well, my friend. I don't need a conscience; I have you around," he said with baited sarcasm. He rose and strolled over to the mirror and looked into it. Tanned complexion and a head full of ideas, he was rigorous without being brawny.

"You laugh at me for loving many women. Man is nothing without either love or women. But I'll tell you one thing: you never know the enchantment of a real woman until you've been through hell and bed with her. You sit her up with all sincerity. I do not doubt your sincerity.

But I am who I am. Fleming. I raise heaven and hell at the same time. Women are women: they are to be loved. Women and love: they go together. They are there: love them. Now," he angrily barked, avoiding a direct attack on Paris' questions.

"I'm not questioning women and love. All I'm—"

"No more," he cried. "I'll not listen. I refuse to run my life to your dictates," he said and he left.

Paris had really hit home. It was a bull's eye. No need to take aim; he was right in line. He heard the squeaky door to the main staircase slam. Back to his cubicle he strolled. He packed his pipe and lit it and sat on his bed pondering the situation. Paris knew he spoke the truth but something he had to realize was that people did not care for the truth about life or about themselves. Truth was merely an abstraction used to justify academic tastes. No one really lived for truth because life was so contradictory, now hot now cold, now new now old, now life now death in one ball of Now; that truth to be lived was painful and most did not care for pain whether it was false or true, it was simply there in its full reality. Truth was something you realized when you had to, when the suffering required that you slow down and begin to ask why everything is the way it is. And if you lived intensely enough, in spite of the fact that you were not required in any way to do so (since it was only for free spirits that such an aging process could be justified) you lived to find that the battlefield of truth claimed many casualties, that the quest for truth was embroidered in the seams of death, and that the quest was learning how to die. And if you died long enough you found the truth: that life was worthwhile despite the wrecks it makes of lives and more lives. But this quest was a solitary affair or, on occasion, a communion of taste, and those who did not see truth as necessary to their living, resented those who had embarked on it. Such was Fleming. Paris was slow to find out that truth yields despisers of truth. Such truth was a form of medicine that, like most medicine, had to have a patient's will to live in order to heal. Fleming did not wish anyone's medicine for he, too, was as proud and as sensitive as Paris. But Fleming, by comparison, had not suffered anything but Paris had.

CHAPTER 8

As the weeks of summer wore on, Fleming took an interest in two other girls in the manor with whom he had many good times, the usual for his sybaritic tastes and epicurean temperament. Blythe had discovered long before that Fleming played musical beds with the wanton negligence of a bacchanalian with a wine-drenched mustache and lips in love with lust. It crushed her spirits for she was sensitive; sensitivity presupposes awareness and is the first movement toward becoming poetic. She became more hardened that she had ever been. Men were bastards. They really are. They poke you and then leave. Such were her thoughts throughout these weeks. Her bitterness hardened her heart and for the failure of one love cursed them all; yet mingled with this bitterness was a secret coiled within, that she truly cared for Fleming but would not dare to admit it to her conscious thought.

As for Fleming, he was quite aware of Blythe's feelings. She would often ask him to visit her but at the last moment would find an excuse appropriate to the situation. Sometimes she would venture into room 33 looking for Fleming but would find he had gone to a local pub. Then she would follow him there and, once found, he was usually so drunk he could only sing and dance. Her presence made him a bit uneasy. They had been together for nearly a year (such is the way of fickle people) and then at the first opening, he applied himself in another direction. At other times, she would simply try simply talking to him but even that failed to work since his other girls would come in and take over the conversation, thus excluding Blythe in fine fashion. She despised catty women too. Fleming simply could not and would not commit himself to anyone.

Blythe represented commitment. Not that Blythe was hot to grab a husband while she could. It was not that at all. She believed, half naively or even defensively, that a fine body might grow into love for a fine mind. The body was her first attraction; men usually went for the body. Men are born with lust in their mouths. So she figured after the novelty of the sex thing was over, the mind thing would grow. Such was not always the case. Some men just wanted body. All body. Fleming had behind him, in the softened hindsight of personal biography, a long line of women. This explained his aversion to anything that smacked of the marital bed. He reasoned: why get married when you can get all you want outside of it? And besides, who wants legal sheets tying two people to hearth and home? And all the petty bull of a divorce? So stay free and commit yourself maybe to your career but not to anyone beside yourself. He saw marriage, then, as a legal bind, not as Blythe saw it, ideally speaking, as a marriage of minds as well as body.

What made Fleming mad was Paris. He would always bring Blythe into the conversation for he knew his friend's dislike for being reminded of the past. Paris was a stage for memory. They had several arguments, even debates, on the whole question. They would spend hours late in the evening discussing into the early hours of the morning, as the time passed as the bell tolled outside. They would have to leave their room for a peaceful place to talk since room 33 was a nightly scene of a myriad of fandangos danced by Jocko and company who left not a board unhinged when the midnight hour was ready to toll and their bellies were filled with bitter and sweet ale. Every pub in the area knew their faces. The fat lady who ran the Gregory Arms and who had the enlarged mole on her neck knew them. The Welby Arms, the Checker's Inn, the Blue Bull knew their familiar well-lit faces. And the Britons, involved as they were in dart games in the pub corner, knew they were out swilling Macheson Stout or Newcastle Brown Ale, otherwise known as "lunatic brew."

This night was not much different. Minivans and minibuses had left loaded hours ago for the pubs and as midnight was about to toll, gravel scrunched and grunted in the bullring as the singers came in full of brew. Headlights flashed, doors slammed, and an occasional scream of pleasure or pain could be heard. Jocko had drunk heavily on Worthington ale. In moment-flashes, he had already smashed two windows in the manor.

Only in between the shouting and cavorting of buzzing bodies could the shattering glass be heard at all. Half the faculty was embalmed on gin and tonics, whisky sours, and dry martinis as they certainly would not have the hearing to hear that the students had returned. Old ale bottles proved to be Jocko's ammunition. Another window flew out; its frame trembled, faltered, then totally collapsed. From the commons room, "we all live in a yellow submarine" could be heard groaning from beneath the burden of having been overplayed by the various parties concerned. Jocko and Sparky were howling at the top of their voices; Mary was high; Cassie too; Blythe was the only one really drunk since her drinks were calculated to erase memory. Another window flew out as Jocko stood in the dim light of the manor and hurled another ale bottle gleefully. He was becoming good at it. He would whirl his arm as fast as possible then let go. The bottle would soon find a nice plate glass of antique vintage and smash it. It was fun to destroy things, especially if that, too, was an escape. Some other fellows helped Blythe into the manor and on to the elevator. The sudden jerking of the elevator caused her to vomit all the way to the third floor. At the top she vanished into her bedroom where the retching intermittently continued. Her sensitive mind and sometimes frail constitution made her sicknesses even more extreme since they exerted a kind of tyrannical control over her often flighty moods: she was how she felt. Poetry, in a sense, was her name.

Jocko sang ribald songs as he climbed the stairs; Sparky skipped each stair and uttered crass remarks better left unprinted; and Cassie Pappas quickly flew into the commons room and began to dance. Just before he reached the floor of the boys' wing, Jocko found an empty Carlsberg bottle and flung it at the manor window which shattered on impact. This time somebody above heard it. A door opened in the faculty lounge and Jocko and Sparky quickly hid in the shadows. As they hid from those faces above who now peered over the balustrade, Jocko noticed a couple standing off in the shadows. It was none other than John Diamond, the Casanova of the cedar staircase. He spent his hours with hustling coeds who appeared matronly beyond their age. One of his favorites was Daphne Fox, a junior in home economics, who wore high collars and extra long skirts to conceal her legs. She seemed to be in her fifties, old before her time. Jocko and Sparky both noticed John in the shadows and even though they were drunk the corny conversation between John and Daphne about the risqué attire of others was making them both nauseous.

They heard the faculty door close and that was the signal to make it to room 33. They left John Diamond in the shadows whispering sweet nothings to Daphne Fox. Jocko was glad to be home in the safety of his cubicle; Sparky only came in to find Jean Pence, a sophomore in psychology with large buttocks that filled out her pants, lying diagonally across his bed. Jean had been waiting for awhile for Sparky. There was not much between them save a feel here and there. Zee was lifting dumbbells again as you knew some coed had not come through with the sexual goods. Paris and Fleming had gone off to debate points of interest while Peter lay quietly in bed, idly listening to the ticking of his grandfather clock.

Not much time passed before a stirring of concerned voices were heard. The broken windows were discovered. Zee finished pumping iron with his dumbbells and ventured to the Puck Show below operated by Gabby the Porter, a fat Irishman with a red nose who could drink you blind and who made a continual quacking sound with his mouth and nose. Activity buzzed. Two professors were down there as well as the Duke of Earl who ran the place with aristocratic overbearing. Everyone passed the blame around a circle; everyone was happy if it was not his or her fault but it was. Evading responsibility is the first cousin of non-commitment. And the buck passers were there passing the buck. False stories with half-truths filled the air and the destruction of windows caused a rumbling of hysteria throughout the manor. The Duke was quite angry and regarded these American students as uncouth, thoughtless and uncivilized. Erehwon Manor as his responsibility and much of the furniture and architecture was irreplaceable. Artisans like that no longer grew on trees. They were rare since mass production undercut originality before it had a chance to be. Music in the commons room stopped on "we all live in a yellow submarine." The search was on. Word traveled fast. Jocko and Sparky got wind of the search and Sparky decided to stick it out with Jean by his side. Jocko decided to flee to the top floor and pretend he was taking a bath. The upstairs bath tubs were convenient for situations like this. When the door locked, it locked tight as a drum. With over three hundred rooms in the manor and revolving walls that led into labyrinthine passages, the search was a noble gesture but almost always doomed to failure. Potential witnesses were questioned; some even sobered up for the whole affair while others, sobered by the thought of a search, began to drink again to forget. The political activists even put out a one-page pamphlet declaring the search unconstitutional and another example of capitalistic imperialism abroad. After several hours of questioning students, threats to enforce student body rules, and other maneuvers designed to extort evidence of some kind, the search was halted and would presumably be continued the following day. Word reached Jocko who had in the meantime finished reading *The Last Temptation of Christ* and he crawled out of the huge, pearl-colored tub and returned to room 33. Jean and Sparky were still awake although no light shone in their cubicle; Peter and Zee were both asleep. Paris and Fleming were still absent as Jocko quietly slipped between the covers the maid had made that morning.

Next afternoon student body president John Barff called an emergency meeting of the student council to discuss the vandalism that seemed unabated. No one was going to perpetrate such atrocities while he was in office to preserve the peace and bring the culprits to justice. In fact, after Jocko had smashed windows, he was now engaged in a smashing good time with pretty hazel-eyed Magena Flores. Barff was quite upset when he heard the news of a smashing good time someone was having smashing windows. His term of office was a series of empty promises on how efficient he was and how he recognized the seriousness of his duties and all the other ifs and buts and power lines of authority-seeking. Suddenly he was faced with rumblings from his superiors, especially the Duke, who made it plain that vandalism would not only not be tolerated but the guilt culprit or culprits would be punished to the full extent of the law in their jurisdiction. The Duke wielded influence with several members of Parliament in the area surrounding Erehwon and if substantial damage was inflicted on the manor in the future, he would not hesitate to have the manor policed.

The meeting went well so far as Robert's Rules of Order could go. No one who knew who had smashed the windows said a word about it. Frustrated because no one confessed, the president suggested making more rules to govern student conduct. The students despised law; youth has the wisdom of rebellion on its side. More rules seemed a grievance and some students wanted a redress of grievances. Jean thought more rules were an unnecessary waste; Sparky objected to more laws saying the law only encourages offenders; Zee argued hotly against them, arguing more rules were simply another form of inhibiting human growth and that the judges selected were not well-versed in an understanding of human nature to know when the law should be flexible and went not to be; Joan Bradshaw thought the proposed laws were simply going to dampen the spirits of the entire manor; Fleming thought it a crime to enact new laws simply because some windows were smashed and he thought laws were simply another repressive mechanism that killed a sense of freedom to express oneself. He argued that aggression is a fundament drive of human beings. And if this drive is thwarted, it only bottles itself up until it demands an even more outrageous form of violence. Then Paris offered a larger perspective. "Laws are traps," he said. "They smother vitality and life that wants to breathe." Paris then argued that people should practice non-violence toward all living things and that even windows were, in a sense, living things. He was a great lover of reverence for life. To him destruction was already plentiful in the cosmos; it had its own processes of decay. There was no need to contribute our destruction of it. Was there not enough evil in the world without our having to make war on man and God and environment and the whole planetary system? Certainly aggression is present in all of us, he said, but understanding is not all that is to be done. Understanding must include action otherwise nothing happens. Fleming, he said, understood the drive of aggression but stopped there. Now, Paris continued, we need to do something. And that did not mean piling law on law. What was needed was a revolution in values so that we appreciate this world and our relationship to it. People need music in their souls, not a chance to rage against anything and everything. We must cherish everyone and everything. Only a reverence for life could establish a purpose to human endeavor and possibly prevent the senseless destruction of art and science.

There was a brief applause; Paris was embarrassed at himself. Fleming patted him on the shoulder. Having found considerable opposition to governing conduct with new laws, John Barff was shrewd enough to forego pressing the issue, even though the Duke was alarmed by the willful and irresponsible destruction of property. When Jocko heard the news, he was relieved. He resolved that, within the bounds of possibility, he would not smash windows again. This came after Sparky mildly chastised him for the drunken rampage of the night before.

That night Blythe paid a visit to room 33 to see Fleming but he was not there. Maybe he had gone somewhere with Joan Bradshaw, although no one knew it or, if they knew, would not tell Blythe about it. That would only cause chaos. Peter stood at the door chatting with her. He knew Fleming well. But he also saw in Blythe's strained face a neurotic tendency that he tried to deal with in a sane manner. She liked talking to him but grew anxious about Fleming's absence. He was so hard to find these days. He was always gone, for business or pleasure. It did not make much difference. He was simply not around. Nor was it a case of playing hard to get, a game insecurity plays. To avoid her was not necessarily his aim; he simply did not like to be reminded of past deeds and obligations. The past was an embarrassment. Paris always knew the past. His was the historian's art: to dramatize the past and blend it with present realities. And he reminded Fleming of the past, especially with Blythe.

Noise was in the air, especially coming from the commons room. They could hear the sound of someone washing their hands. Paris had just come in. He had not seen Blythe in ages it seemed. His eyes lit when he saw her standing in the room with Peter. He gave her a warm smile.

"Long time no see," he said, drying his hands on a towel. "Peter keeping you company?" Delighted, Blythe smiled despite her sullen face with sunken eyes and tried looks. It was satisfying to see a friend's face and hear a friend's voice. Words can comfort despair. Especially words Paris spoke. He had a way of being somewhat detached from the ordinary worries of living yet at the same time an uncanny ability to read the faces of others. But most of the time silence was his character, that is, if you happen to enjoy Chinese calligraphy. Blythe had not felt so welcome in a long time. To be with Peter and Paris was a delight.

"Yes, it's great to see you again," she said with the sincerity sensitivity can show. Paris knew from her facial expression she wanted to talk so he asked her to his cubicle while Peter crawled into his bed to listen for the tolling of the hours on his huge clock. Quickly Paris straightened up his cubicle, hung up his shirts, pulled books off his bed, and folded a sweater so it would not wrinkle. Blythe made herself comfortable on his bed. She looked upset and Paris knew it. Her sensitivity came through her sometimes desperate attempts to hide it with the tough skin of experience. She did not feel threatened by Paris; he was a friend with an open mind, a master of the counseling art. He sat in his desk chair with his arms resting on the chair arms, feet on the floor, legs open and relaxed. Such a position said something for the judgment of Paris. Being open, he could listen. Listening, he could hear down into the depths the despair that flew out like bats out of a cave. She began lightly as though she had wings on her feet and, like Mercury, could carry a caduceus between the gods.

"Yes. Been a long time, hasn't it," she said with a flattened tone, a tone of sapped vitality.

"Certainly has. Haven't seen much of you since Windermere and Grasmere," he said with understanding. A long silence ensued in which much communication occurred though neither of them uttered a word. Worry outlined her face; anxiety made her hands twitch nervously though when she became self-conscious, she relaxed them. The silence was a graduated movement toward a greater degree of depth. Then out popped the angling line.

"Where's Fleming tonight?" she asked.

"Haven't a clue," he replied.

"Where is Fleming every night?" she echoed with almost narcissistic abandon.

"Here, there, and everywhere," he said, "everywhere but here."

"You're telling me," she said flatly. There was another long pause. Then: "I despise him when he does this. When he goes out on me," she said as her composure began to spring a leak.

"I just hate him. I really do." Another silence. The tension that had built up in her did not relax. Her fingers twitched nervously and a look of sober reflection now mapped the lines of her young, poetic, and radiant face for it was sensitive though accustomed to the trials that drew lines on the face of most people. Paris then spoke with the softer tones of sympathy.

"You don't hate him." Eyes met frozen for an instant then relaxed. "No," she replied, "but I cannot stand him treating me this way. Do you know he hasn't in the last few weeks even so much as talked with me? Do you know that? Ignores me like I'm camel dung. What am I? His personal and private whore conveniently known as 'lover?' Am I? He is a bastard to think so! Men think women are playthings. I hate that. Thinks he can have me any ole time. The bastard. The son of a bitch," she almost screamed.

Paris said nothing. Blythe continued almost hysterically:

"The rotten bastard. The whoreson hound, the lying cheat, the savage son of a bitch! Damn him, damn him! How I despise liars, those who have all the great truths! His truth is in his pants! The chicken-livered

red beedle, the fork-tailed scorpion, that python of the blue eyes, that anaconda with the loving embrace! I can't even remember swear words for the rotten son of a bitch!" Just then she took out an atomizer and quickly sprayed it to avoid triggering an asthma attack. Then she continued: "Why if I were Irish I'd have a host of swear words, but since I'm not I'll have to mimic Celtic imagination. I just think it's a damn crying shame when people take each other for granted. Does he really expect me to wait around? Why wait. Action is now. And he spends his action with that damn Joan Bradshaw. Spends all his time with her he does. All his time. Never comes to see me. I'm sure he has slept with her by now. He's prone to that position. Tell me why. Why, oh why do I really care? Is it love or despair? That I despise men in general for their damn asinine ways."

Again Paris said nothing. He just let her pour it out.

"You know what I wish? What I really wish? That I could find someone who treated me like a human being. That took me seriously enough to care. What is it like to be a human? To love, to cherish, to really care whether your love lives or dies. To take time of life to really care. Is that impossible? Is it? Nothing is impossible. Would it not be a better world if people were human and not slitting each other's throats for money, power, and prestige? The whores' trinity. The whole bag of neuroses. Why can't people learn to love one another, to try to get along? Why must we constantly wage war against ourselves? We're always at war, seldom at peace."

After several moments, Paris echoed her last sentiment almost to himself but yet audible enough to hear if you listened closely: "why do we deal treacherously every person with their brothers and sisters?" He then turned to her, a person he had known since freshman year when he met her at a fraternity rush party. Old friends have mixed currents that pass away or lean on memory for support. But this was a present with a problem.

"I suppose you want a reply, not an answer," he began softly.

"Just say something," she begged. "Anything."

"Well, how do you feel now?"

"About what?"

"About telling me all this."

"I don't care. I trust you. You are my guru," she said with a humor that laughed away too great a suffering and allowed her to view suffering in a perspective, the immortal laughter of the holy.

"I'll lay out your fortune like a fan," he remarked with a flattened humor.

"Shoot," she said, lighting a cigarette, sitting with her legs crossed and head cocked attentively. Relaxing in his chair, Paris stroked his chin pensively and thought of proverbs of comfort and counsels of wisdom.

"First of all, I don't think you hate Fleming. Only great hate can come from great love. It seems you care for him in a most loving way. Second, try not to despise every man because of the failures of one. True, he hasn't been beating a path to your door. But relations change: sometimes hot, then cold. Sometimes tensed; other times relaxed. Yes, men do abuse women but women also abuse men. That, too, is sometimes part of relation's scenario. There's abuse as well as splendor; hate as well as humaneness in all relations. And that is real."

He paused and watched her eyes focused on him, listening to every vowel through the smoke.

"As for someone treating you as a human being…well… Love here, there, and everywhere. Without putting on the masks. Love beyond yourself. That way you will return to yourself. Love all the hideous as well as the beauteous forms that surround our little life. We cannot demand someone to love us. Not Fleming. Not Joan. People resent force. They may admire or enforce it. But they resent being forced. The world does not always conform to our expectations of it. The world, my dear Blythe, is not built to suit our conception or truth or perfection. Why rage that it is not so? We can struggle, despite our being denied in some way, and endeavor for truth as far as that is humanly possible. But there is no sane reason to despise people who are not as godlike as we delude ourselves to be. People are people. Fleming is Fleming. Paris is Paris. Full of faults. We are poor vain creatures forever struggling for some light."

His voice drifted off as he watched her face in the light for there seemed to be a glow to her cheeks whereas before they were pale. Her hair, her lips, her eyes all seemed bathed in an iridescent light, a clear light like she had just been rescued from prison. She had not smoked all of her cigarette but had let it burn down and she quickly crushed it in an ashtray. Her lips were full and she licked them pensively as though absorbed in his words and, more than the words, the thoughts they conveyed. In the next few minutes, all she said was "wow."

Paris Brandon, a student of philosophy and religion, had thought about problems of ethics, aesthetics, logic, political systems but had also ventured into the realm of psychology which opened the door to the vast treasures of wisdom lodged like chunks of diamond in the pages of reflective religion. He had learned early that life was a continuous death and death a continuous life, that truth was fought for by the reputations of people, not necessarily for truth's sake alone. Blythe, though accustomed by necessity or for her own self-image to being as dispassionate as possible when such moments were appropriate, let herself relax. Even her asthma which often flared up in tense times, did not bother her this evening. She felt a serenity when the self stops neurotically warring with itself. It was a rare experience when the fires, when disciplined, begin to burn in another direction.

She finally sat up, knees pulled high, and stared at him with a warm feeling.

"Your words. Such beauty's eyes and teeth," she said bordering on a poetic radiance.

"But words are snares of old times. They cannot always help us remember the present or live the past. They are snares. And some live and die on a word. That is their sacred syllable. Beauty has power to bewitch; the devil's with him. Be careful. Not all the words you can say, read, or hear can take the place of you now. Now you are whether you like it or not. Words are brief crutches that keep people in memory. They fly out like golden eagles in imagination. But they can break their own crutches. By silence. Words are snares; they commit us to memory, imagination's fraternal twin," he said with a characteristic low tone. He knew Peter was listening to ticking time but also to their words as well, a fact Paris did not mind, but he still like to keep such affairs as private as possible. He continued: "So take the meaning and let the words go. But then we have to resurrect them now and then to relearn what meaning situations demand. Then we fit the flesh together to develop muscles of the spirit…"

She sat back and measured, as far as that was possible, all he had said. At that point the bell tolled the hours. It was ten o'clock and a slight wind whipped at the western windows that overlooked the rolling plains of Lincolnshire. The bell erased her measures for it had intruded and reminded her of her original mission: to see Fleming.

Just then boisterous singing intruded; a door slammed; shouting came from the long hall that led to room 33. Blythe sat intent, listening for Fleming's voice. Yes, it was Fleming singing ribald songs. Serenity vanished from her face; it had lasted only a few moments. Peace is a prologue to new wars. Disturbance continually finds its own victims. Wars want blood and pride. Never mind the truth. Just blood and the satisfaction of some vain idiocy in whatever name it could be given. Peace did not last long. There would always be something or someone who despised peace and made you war against yourself.

Paris watched as her face became concerned, lines drawing together then far apart. He knew suffering was everywhere and it was sad to watch it overcome her sensitivity. Fleming came in like Leif Eriksson discovering the new world of Vinland with drama and flair. It had been a merry evening and he enjoyed making merry with a hearty laugh, good friends, and a good pint of bitters at the Welby Arms. He sang: "come and sit on my face if you love me…" He weaved into Peter's cubicle and beheld him lying there with a look of sweetness on his face.

"By saints Peter, Paul, Mary and Nietzsche. Is this the face that launched a thousand ships and built the topless towers of El Vaticano? Ah, sweetness lying there with your t-time machine! Well, I'll be a devil's cousin and plant lips, eternal lips mind you, on the mouth of Paradise! St. Pete, how you doing tonight?" he said, nearly stumbling over the foot of his bed. Peter looked at him bemused; he had been dreaming for the longest time or so it seemed. Now he blinked once or twice to find who was screaming with the language of the saints. After rubbing his eyes, he recognized a drunken Fleming hovering over him.

"You saints need to get out more often, Pete. There's p-plenty 'o pints 'o bitter you can soak your guts with in the world. So get up on your hind legs and become the saint you are!" Peter sat up, still groggy.

"You and your saints, Fleming. You old Julian the Apostate you. Go out and fill your belly with cheap ale. Ain't worth more than two bob a glass and you have the nerve, Fleming, to come trampling in here and tell me I'm not on my hind legs. Look, I keep the time while you give your women the time. We're both sinners aren't we? And that ale you fill your guts with …hell I've drank better horse piss…" At that Fleming let out laughter that lasted for several minutes.

"By Jove, St. Pete, and all the other ones I recall…you've got the sickest damn humor this hour of night. Horse piss. Really now, we're just drunk with humor. Humor makes me drunk. I can laugh myself to death without a reference to St. Peter. Imagine you lying here with your clock. By God, you and me Pete, we gotta drink this civilization down. Mingle gall with our ambrosia. You know. Let's drink the place down some night. Get you hundred pints of bitter and me a hundred pints of sweet and together we'll drink the world around!"

St. Peter made that curious grin so characteristic of him; he always grinned that way when Fleming invited him to go drinking. Not long before, Peter had drank Fleming blind at the Checker's Inn; he couldn't even hold up his arm to throw darts much less stand to throw them. Fleming had to be brought home sprawling and birding every step of the way. He was sick as any could be and swore he would never touch the stuff again but he drank again the very next night. So much for good intentions.

At that point, Blythe stuck her head through the cubicle curtain and, with a slight, sarcastic grin, stared at Fleming who turned around slowly to follow the direction of Peter's eyes.

"Well, I'll be damned, if it ain't…Blythe. What the hell are you doing h-here?" She smiled a bitter smile and smirked forcefully.

"I just came by to see my beloved Fleming."

Fleming looked like he had just seen a ghost come from a closet.

"Beloved? How thoughtful of you, my dear. I mean it's been a long time. Where've you been?" he said, hovering now toward her.

"Where have *I* been? I haven't seen you for ages, mister. Where in the gates of hell have *you* been? Ha? Have you been playing kitty catcher again, Fleming? Out to get as much pussy as possible I suppose." At that, she realized they were still in Peter's cubicle.

"Let's go Fleming. This talk is probably grossing Peter out. But Peter protested: "Oh, no. You are welcome. I enjoy a lusty tale now and then."

Blythe gave him a puzzled look.

"Even saints burn with lust," she said as she took Fleming by the hand and led him stumblingly through Peter's cubicle curtain. She had much on her mind and even more on her chest. He lay across his bed, gazing with glassy eyes at the light that gleamed through his curtain. Discreetly Paris made his exit along with Peter who left reluctantly.

They had the room all to themselves. Privacy was a luxury no one could afford to miss. It was difficult to find a place or even a moment to talk since everything was so hurried and souls lost their balance on the precarious course of continually changing events. Blythe lit a cigarette with an intent face that stared holes through Fleming as she sat next to the bed, leaning back in her chair.

"It's been a while, love," she began as she blew smoke rings toward the ceiling.

"Of course, my dear. Time mellows all, isn't that true?" he said with a slight twitch of his neck as his eyes shot at her through the smoke that seemed to curl endlessly from her lips.

"Well, it hasn't mellowed me. Love does not mellow lovers in love, Fleming. It only fans the fires. At that, he gazed at her incredibly.

"You're not in love with me. That's bullshit."

"Well, let's put it this way. I grew quite fond of you and I'm growing now," she said almost as if she felt it necessary to be overly cautious. Fleming was impatient. He did not like the scene. The props were insufficient; he was defenseless and her words felt like blood staining the present with the past.

"We just had fun. That's all. Sure, I like you Blythe b-but…"

"But you just don't feel the same way. Same old story," she added under her breath. Anytime things got tight there were plenty of excuses to leave. Fleming felt cramped. This was not fair to ruin a good evening of drinking. Why should he sit and listen to her half-maudlin ramblings?

"Hell no I don't. I mean I do but I don't. Hell I don't know…" he said, drifting into space.

The road to oneself was the steepest. Fleming did not like self-analysis, especially after drinking at the Checker's Inn. The local anesthesia was wearing off and he felt the full impact of the situation, a situation in which he felt helpless to adequately influence. He had not realized the full extent of her feelings for him. Their fun was fun at the time. Why was it so important now? Couldn't she just forget him as he had tried to forget her? After all, sex was fun. Pure and simple. It was a good trip. Why make trouble over the past? Life must be lived now.

"I've missed you Fleming," she said almost as an afterthought. But her words only further imprisoned him in this situation.

"Well, time's a-wasting," he said as he got up and began to leave.

"Fleming. Please. Don't go," she said as she took another puff and let the smoke stream from the corner of her lips.

"Blythe," he said, rising, "you've ruined a good evening of drinking. I'm nearly sober thanks to you. Nothing worse than getting too sober too soon I always say."

She rose and put her hand on his arm; there was a stiff moment in which all of the past seemed to climb out of the woodwork, sum itself up, and then vanish into a thousand passing faces full of rosy color and ethereal light. Blythe was getting desperate by the moment; she had something to tell him but felt crushed by her own embarrassment since she felt it would seem she was only telling him this to possess him. But such was not the case. She had been holding this information inside her for weeks, now looking here and there for an opportunity to tell him while he was in a reasonable mood. Then, with a flash, she eased her arms around him and pressed her face into the knit of his bulky sweater. This was enough clinging to arouse Fleming's sarcasm.

"Honey, why don't you get on all fours so we can play easy rider." This only aggravated her sinking image of herself. Seeing that this had no visible effect but to tighten her arms about him, he continued to taunt her.

"Look, we had fun. A great trip. I'm a Lutheran. You know I at least get to know girls before I begin balling them," he said. This was dynamite.

"You son of a bitch. You son of a bitch. You damn son of a bitch," she screamed into his chest then even his heart might hear in an odd sort of way.

"Like I say get that ole tongue in there; you don't know how long you'll be there," he taunted, unmoved by her name-calling.

"You ought to be a politician," she snapped bitterly, "you are insensitive enough." This delighted Fleming who despised politicians anyway.

"Politicians are merely preachers of another order…" he replied.

It was only a moment or two before he began to feel the heavy sobs deep into his chest. This was no jest. Call it intuition that reveals the wordless by face or hand. For the first time Fleming sensed her seriousness and it bothered him. It was not like Blythe to be that serious since she hid herself behind a surgical shell of cynicism and apparent indifference. Shells were made to ward off hurts and after awhile the person who dwelled in a shell became so constricted that the mind suffered hardening of the arteries. Shells were a tacit refusal to dance. What was once poetry now became prose. But a daemon in crisis reopens the shell and the sacrament of person shifts into the new and the now. Such was Blythe. She was reopened. The surgery now needed was understanding and love. Fleming was hard put to give such medicines of the soul. Never before had he seen her in this light and lights changed from moment to moment and day to day. Finally he sat again on the bed.

"All right, what in the hell is wrong?" he asked. Blythe fidgeted, relit a cigarette, and paced around the cubicle. Anxiety mapped her face, her poetic and radiant face.

"I think…I am…pregnant," she said with a face that etched its lines and expressions in a stone-like glare.

Stunned, Fleming laid back and stared a long while at the ceiling reflected in the lone light. He frowned and felt the weight of care hasten his heartbeat. Why me, he kept thinking, why me? This must be a trap. Of course it's a trap. To be possessed: is that not a criminal act unless you want to be possessed. Ah, the nerve of her. To be possessed: is that not a slow murder? Why me? Why all hell on my shoulders? Pregnant of all things. His thoughts left him long enough to talk to her head as it appeared through a smoke wreath that curled like a shawl around her neck as she paced in one direction and then another.

"You're kidding. You must be kidding. It's all a joke. A mere jest," he said, acting more upset than he actually was. She puffed her cigarette.

"Folly is a jester but I am not. You may not believe a word I say but reality is alive and kicking. I did not think so at first. I was afraid to say. But it was confirmed the other day."

"By a doctor?"

"By a doctor," she said, steadying her gaze again at his glassy eyes riveted to the ceiling.

Fleming laid there like an empire he had begun and built and without warning one morning collapsed about his ears. The loss wrote its score on the frowning lines about his usually jovial and jesting mouth. What was so surprising was the he did not in all honesty know how to react because it was difficult to tell whether it was simply a ruse to lure him from his other loves or to scare him into getting married. Finally, before he could decide on the issue, she ceased pacing.

She knew Fleming well enough to sense he was calculating an escape. He was a fine calculator; his shrewdness in life kept him in business. But how could he even begin to feel as she did? Did he feel a periodic pelvic movement or even the symptoms of pregnancy? How could a man ever understand a woman or a person understand oneself, let alone another? Hard it was to wear another's skin. Even harder to wear another's persona! Not one time did she tell him of her uncertainty of paternity for she had been forcibly raped that night in the Lake District aboard the Swan Barrow. The man with the bandaged head had smacked her pleading and disobedient face, and raped her on a couch in a room far below the promenade deck. She was not sure whose baby it was. All she knew was she was pregnant. Out, out of her mind she shoved the terrible thought that a rapist had impregnated her and because this was such a painful thought, it was cleverly disguised and locked in the closet of her mind. But painful thoughts, like skeletons, reappear from every closet. It was just a matter of when. She would rather assume Fleming had done the deed and that a pagan fetus was developing within. Had he known she had been raped, Fleming would use such knowledge as a way of escape from the current situation. She knew this and possessed the cunning and perhaps wisdom of knowing when to speak and when secretiveness was required. As it was, Fleming cussed and swore for awhile for the news had thoroughly diluted his drink this evening and perhaps his very future as well. Why did fate hurl poisoned lances and aim to pierce the eyes of men, he kept lamenting half-aloud. Could a man embrace such a pregnant fate? Women bore sins and crosses as well. But could Fleming bear such news as this? He could not and would not.

"Here's a solution," he said, his finger pointed skyward. "Get an abortion."

"An abortion? How typical of you to suggest it, Fleming. I figured you'd pop that one on me. God, what are you, a devil?" Fleming looked incredulously.

"What's wrong with that," he demanded.

"Nothing is wrong with it. But it is so typical of you. You drink your guts to escape every day and then before a birth want to escape. No wonder you cannot deliver anything. You're too busy problem solving. As if everything in life is a problem ready to be solved."

Fleming laid there, his hand pressed to his forehead like he had some grief to pose for in photographs yet to be taken. About this time Fleming felt not only hot about the collar but felt his mind had fled to live in some primitive nativity. Christ almighty, he kept repeating to himself. His mind had fled; it needed solitude, it needed rest. His groans made him sound like the lamentations of Jeremiah outside the doors of a sanctuary. Zap, his mind returned.

"Look, if you have a problem, why not solve it? Doesn't that make sense? Life is problem solving. We have problems every day, right? So we solve them. Or try to. So the problem is pregnancy and we solve it. Just like that!" he said, snapping his fingers cheerfully.

"Just like that, eh?" she said with a snapping mimesis. "You bastard. Do you really just solve things with the snap of your fingers? You don't feel what I feel. How could you? You're not me. So you wind my feelings, like umbilical cords, around your fingers and expect them to snap like threads the fates cut? What bullshit! You think you can rip life out of a womb and solve a problem thereby?"

Fleming was grinning now. He could not believe his ears.

"Why make such an issue of it?" he said.

"An issue of it?" she said with exclamation, hands now on her matronly hips. "How the hell can I not make an issue of it? I'm the one who's carrying a baby around. Am I not the bearer of birth and death? I am a woman. And you tell me to simply abort. God, what a crass dude you are!"

Fleming was becoming bored with her continual ranting. His evening had been smashed.

"What can I say? What can I do? What do you suggest?"

Blythe herself was puzzled. She did not know what to do. It was not Fleming's suggestion that bothered her. It was his cavalier attitude that made her blood boil and her face fume. Easy it was for some men to escape the noose. They were so quick to make a practical, factual solution to everything. Such hard-headed practicality flowed against the poetic and womanly grain in her; it made her sick that life had become computerized problem-solving. For all her feeling of discontent, Blythe was practical as well if not realistic. She knew he was right and had suggested the only practical solution since marriage was not what they had in mind. Marriage meant very little to them. Yet she did care for Fleming. For the most part, they lived for pleasure and musical beds. Marriage was for them when they felt the need for a secure interlude but then again divorce was usually necessary for them to continue playing musical beds. Abortion seemed the only way. She thought for a moment about being a single mother. The idea appealed to her. She might just do that or at least feel out Fleming's feelings about it.

"I'll be a mother." Fleming shot a curious glance at her large round eyes.

"A mother!" he shouted but then quieted himself down so no one else could hear. "A mother?" he whispered. "You're crazy."

"Crazy am I? You're crazy for aborting life even before it is born. You and your problem-solving."

Fleming sat up with an intense look. He went to his cubicle corner where his clothes were hung and felt around in his shirt pocket until he found a cigar and lit it. Together they created a lot of smoke. With Blythe chain-smoking and Fleming's cigar-puffing, they clouded each other's thought with grey rings. Fleming was really angry at her obnoxious stubbornness. He figured it was easy to say no to everything; what was most difficult was to say yes to everything. Life and death wished a yes. No was simply an interlude for reason. The prospects of her becoming a mother really bothered him; why did maternity have to be dragged into the affair? It was simple, clean, quick and easy to have an abortion. Being stubborn only enhanced the possibly tragic in life. But she did not seem to care. The thought of his paternity crossed his mind. What if the child should show a certain resemblance to him? How embarrassing! Excruciatingly it would be to live and knew, just know, everyone knew you had refused to even nominally claim the child. But it would be hypocritical simply to give the baby a name if you didn't really love the person and you married them for pity or respectability or rationalizations. Or would it? He dismissed the explorations of this mind as idle fancy. Marriage was a wedding of minds and body music. Thus far, he was not interested in marrying anyone, including Blythe. At this point, she spoke up through the circle of smoke the almost screened their faces from each other.

"Am I really crazy?" she began rhetorically. "But is not all humankind a family? We are married to one another in oh so many ways. We breathe the same air, eat food, want shelter, feel pain, and die alone. Are not men brothers? We are married to earth, stars, and sky. How can it be crazy to be a bearer of life?"

Fleming was really puffing his cigar now; it fumed as much as he did. His mustache twitched as he stroked it through the smokescreen that had come between them.

"Well, that just sounds fine, honey. I hope you win next year's essay contest as well. Of course all humankind is one family. Ideally, yes. But hell is here on earth and you have to live here. I wish all men *were* brothers. But such is not the case. We must learn war no more to do that. It is not crazy to be a bearer of life. But the legality of…"

"Oh, so that's your bag now. The legality of it. Does only law make a thing right? Because it's legal, is it legal?"

"For God's sake hold your tongue. My God…a legal debate going on here. Hell all I'm trying to say is that it's all very beautiful. The way your imagination strums the guitar strings but reality is a little bit more complex than your childish dreams. You're too damn idealistic for this world. People don't live dreams. If they do, then end up freaky. Or in a mental hospital. Know what I mean? It all sounds so easy. So idyllic. Man is a family, etc. But believe me, Blythe, men hate. They really do. All you can do is deal with all the hate. All the hate in the hearts of men…" he said, drifting off like he had realized all too suddenly how unreal his version of reality. But Blythe liked the challenge of doing things differently. The road to punishment was doing things differently. When you did things differently, when you dared to be human, resentment, envy, jealousy, pride followed as cortege. Punishment was there for the "crime" of doing things differently. Public opinion was fickle enough to adore your successes and mock your defeats. That is how people are. And no matter how strange or wonderful you are, there is resentment and envy lurking even in the hearts of admiration and respect. Blythe knew this but still she kept toying with the challenge her condition inspired.

"Don't play with fire, Blythe. It just won't do any good," he said through the smoke. At that point, Blythe decided words no longer sufficed. She would act her own parts when her drama became increasingly dramatic. It was a bold course to take since the paternity was uncertain and if she really meant to pursue her course, the stains of public opinion would deepen as the days passed. Just then she vanished through the smoke.

CHAPTER 9

The afternoon faded and the sun began to set in a prolonged burning. Enid nestled into Paris' shoulder, almost cuddling him. When he looked up, he could see Fleming's grinning mouth, twitching mustache, and dark lusty eyes. Joan had her head in his lap and snuggled into his crotch, a position that both stimulated and cramped him. Trees swayed outside in a gentle wind; sky took on tints of pink that blended into a deep blue over the North Sea. They had not wished to take the train to Edinburgh so Fleming suggested they go by car. Meanwhile other students listened to the rhythmic clacks of the British railway trains. Paris thought how the sky far off to the right resembled Enid's eyes; they dramatically contrasted with her roseate cheeks and hay-colored strands of hair that swept across her flawless face. Paris could gaze at beauty forever. He relished the long moments when she would listen to his heartbeat and snuggled warmly into his arms. Her presence nearly had an intoxicating effect. Paris was not himself when he was with her. Her presence inspired him with beautiful thoughts, poetic insights, and words nearly unutterable. Part of her beauty was her nonattainability; this only served to intensify his longing for her. Yet she did not flaunt this in front of him. He knew from the beginning where feelings stood. She was more honest than some were inclined to be. But her honesty also served its purpose too. Her very virtues were, in a half-crazed sense, temptations of the meanest sort. Paris lost his balance in her presence, even in the presence of her virtues. Yet he concealed his sensitivities to her for that protective defense was necessary if he was to be with her at all. He had to almost pretend that he did not feel anything toward her. Loving words could not be directed at her; so they were deflected and issued as poetry. It would have been utterly embarrassing if he had ever said loving words to her; it would have stained their relation for its continuance, his denial of his own feelings, and her affirmation of her love for her fiancé now at war. Although such a practice cramped him, the return of her to him was more than ample compensation. He reasoned thus: your energies must be put to use toward a direction even if no goal is in that direction. A future together was a goal he had to renounce if they were to travel any miles at all in any direction, since he knew that that goal was an impossible dream. So he traveled with her as far as he could and knew there would be a time in the near future they would part and probably relegate their times together to fond memories and sweet records. Yet now the miles stretched youthfully before them and in their eyes played love and laughter.

Already shadows cast their long, gloomy fingers across the shoreline lined with white North Sea foam. Earlier Paris had heard a line of poetry from her lips: "It is desire that makes desire worth desiring." That line fastened itself to his brain and kept repeating itself to his memory and memory repeated everything it could. He could not get her out of his scent. Enid could bowl him over. It is so hard to describe her. She was like a portrait of infinite beauty; her eyes invited oceans to bathe her eyelids; her lips, when they smiled, sang a thousand love songs; her long white neck issued a temptation at every turn; her nose exuded a knowing presence. Beauty was her throat and her name. He was wild-eyed. Love knew no bounds: she was the summation of all that divinity has flesh for. Poetry caressed her cheeks and paid homage to her temples. Music played with every tilt of her head; her voice was a fount for the sacred muses. She was a woman, the wonder and beauty of the world. Such were his thoughts as they drove along the seashore.

It was nearly seven-thirty and it would be dark by the time they arrived in Edinburgh. From what he had noticed of the landscape of Scotland, Paris thought it was a land of exciting contrasts. The trees lit into him and inspired him with poems. Waves that painted the beaches were like mustaches that puckered to kiss the shore. It was a high, rugged land, with crosses between shadows and assaults of the imagination. Shadows impressed him for in that soul of art, light's twin, he saw deep within himself the shadows that gave art to himself. Dark descended like some wounded groin and the lights of the city cast long beams against the rugged rock that founded the city and supported it. They met the rest of the group at the St. Andrew's Hotel. They all had assigned rooms. The bathtubs were burnt black and had not been used for the last few years. Food was fine except for the tapeworm that lurked in the half-cooked pork sausage. The men slept on maroon air mattresses that leaked while foreign girls outside plodded their wares on the streets below. Paris and Fleming quickly made their beds for the night. Accommodations were not exactly what might be termed entrancing but they made the best of what presented itself.

Fleming now lay on his sleeping bag, puffing a cigar.

"That was a nice trip," he began.

"Yes, it was," answered Paris.

"You miss Blythe," he asked.

Paris looked up from unpacking his bag.

"Miss Blythe? Why? Should I?"

"Just wondering. I thought you might. You thought we made a nice couple and all that," he remarked.

"Just because you make a nice couple does not obligate you forever," replied Paris.

"Of course. Yet somehow I got the impression that you liked me and Blythe together," suggested Fleming, carrying the conversation forward.

"We get accustomed to faces. After awhile it makes a difference. Time differentiates. Soon one face means more than another," replied Paris with a philosophical air.

"Habit merely," replied Fleming. "We must crush habits. That's the only way we can adapt…and be ourselves," he said with a tone of finality. To him every end was a beginning. Nothing ended.

"True, we must crush habits that enslave us. It takes courage to destroy a habit that is destroying you. Of course. But when people are involved, habits are not easily broken. Habits become mistresses of repetition. But it is difficult…" he said with that almost characteristic drifting voice that fell on the other side of breakers roaring for the shore.

"To break people who are habits…is that what you are saying?"

"The words are yours." If words can crucify (and they can) Fleming was busy pounding nails into Paris.

That comment irked him, touched a sensitive nerve and caused him to become self-conscious like suddenly being expelled from Eden.

"Yes. But you implied it. Blythe was a habit. We saw too much of each other. Too much."

"And so you cast it off. Just like that."

"And why not? said Fleming, his brows knit in lines of anger.

Paris said nothing. For several moments Fleming blew smoke that floated, glided, and wafted with every wind that blew.

"Why not?" he continued.

"Why?"

"Why not?"

"Why," he repeated. Fleming was getting madder by the minute. It was not often anything upset him but he respected Paris' opinion and Blythe was a sore spot that would not yield.

"Because too much is too much," confessed Fleming, now biting his cigar pensively. His eyes searched those of Paris who did not squarely meet Fleming's.

"Because you might actually…feel something for her," suggested Paris with a deliberate cold stare into the center of Fleming. Fleming shot him a glance that was glassy and bold. To him the whole conversation smacked of heresy.

"Aw, bullshit. I've never heard such crap. I swear Paris Brandon you spend all your time worrying about other peoples' affairs. Sure I like Blythe but hell if you get tired you get tired. I have no obligation to her whatsoever. We have no engagements, no future together, and certainly no wedding date. Good, God."

Paris gave him a steel glance. Such talked stirred storms within.

"That is not what I meant. Not what I meant at all. I'm not talking about obligations to engage or marry. All I'm saying is that you use this freedom stuff to continue stiff arming people. That way if someone you really care for comes along, you push them away. Love is freedom toward communion. And you think freedom is only a repellant movement. Not so, my friend, not so. You've seen too much of her, eh? You are simply addicted to novelty. That is why you spend all your time with different faces. You despise the thought that you may actually love someone. And so you run away. We flee too great a love. Don't we? I remember how you've told me so many times how you really found Blythe to be the one girl that could understand you. Then along comes a new face and in the name of freedom or rebellion or creativity you abandon any relationship you might have with another human being. That's why Joan means so much to you now. She's a good surrogate. An escape to replace Blythe. Yes, you can like Joan. I'm not saying you don't like her and all the others as well. All I'm saying is that it is not a matter of seeing Blythe too much. It's a matter of fearing your own self…that you might actually love someone. Might actually have lost a fine relationship."

Paris felt exhausted and lay back on his now unfolded bag. Fleming put out his cigar and went to the bathroom to wash. A pensive mood hung over him and wrote lines of anxiety into his forehead. Paris' words were deep brands. They possessed a sincerity rarely found. They burned into the flesh and Fleming felt for the first time a need to re-examine why he and Blythe were estranged. Somehow what Paris said struck a familiar chord and such a chord undermined many of the rationalizations he had made to justify seeing other women. Blythe fascinated him for some reason. He did not know why. All he knew was that she had been the only girl in his life he had ever taken half-way seriously. The judgment of Paris was usually sound. Fleming returned, drying his face on a towel.

"You have something there," he said. "I don't know what it is but you have something on the line." Paris remained almost expressionless. He stared at the long roof that stretched down the hall.

"What makes you think I need novelty?"

"Your life is geared around it. Novelty is a way of coping with boredom. And man is boredom's fool," said softly.

"Of course. But I don't feel bored. In fact as long as I keep busy with books and papers and women, I'm never really bored. I think you exaggerate this boredom, Paris."

"Perhaps. Perhaps not," was his comment.

"There are many perhaps between here and there."

"Yes. And time and eternity."

"Let's not be frivolous. Someone might be listening and review our frivolity in a publicly frivolous manner," suggested Fleming whose frivolity was his avoidance of taking frivolity in a seriously frivolous way.

Paris laughed at all that. He was continually amazed at the repertoire of evasion Fleming employed to deflect anything that might be overly direct or on target. Paris enjoyed the art of deflection for he believed everyone deflects something sometime somewhere.

"No let's not. But to repeat…I think your need for novelty is simply a need to avoid…making lasting relationships. It is a plot in which you bury the old actresses whose closeness expresses your stresses."

"Talk about repetition!"

"It's one thing to talk about it and another to live it."

"You're being repetitious," suggested Fleming, lighting another cigar and he turned it in his lips.

"Maybe. But novelty is fine. Everyone needs novelty. A new place, new persons. A chance to get away. But we come back to some place to begin again. To begin the flight again. All I'm saying…"

"You say too much, Paris. You talk too much. That is your problem. Maybe *you* don't have enough novelty as you call it. Has Enid become your habit? Your vows make her a habit. Why don't you date Sally or Candy instead of analyzing me? You spin your globe and I'll spin mine."

Paris sat on his elbows with a disturbed face.

"Maybe you are right. I talk too much," he said softly. Fleming felt he had put a stop to the criticism which was an incentive to believing he was now blameless. Arguments and counter-argument were ways of justifying feelings and like a lawyer, they put away their briefs for the night. Soon, one by one, the other students began to straggle in from the pubs, the alleys, the women.

As he lay on his mattress, Fleming had really smarted about what Paris had said. At first, Fleming thought his counter-argument had left the issue stillborn. But as the evening wore on, Paris' words began to touch neuron traces he knew to be headed toward his brain where they would fill the night with private debate. Paris had left to go to a pub. Fleming, too tired, declined. His mind was still restless. Maybe Paris had something. What was so monstrous was that Paris had an ability to perceive quite accurately what bothered others. And the truth he spoke was empathetic enough to make his observations kin to truth-as-perceived by the bothered. Although Paris spoke the truth, Fleming resented it. There was a subtle "I told you so" air about Paris that made Fleming nauseous. It was incredible that someone could read the deepest desires of the heart, the primal yearnings of the human spirit by the stethoscope of empathy that listened accurately enough to hear even a snowflake as it lightly landed on a winter window pane.

Fleming was torn between the understanding that probed accurately and frankly knew, just knew, too much insight and the need to have someone, almost anyone, understand and articulate what he himself could not articulate. He loved Paris while resenting him. So Paris had shrewdly and wisely backed off. He himself knew the pain of the sharp scalpel and how it hurts to probe too deeply. That is what you had to do. When you probed, you had to know how far to take someone. The child has to begin at the shallow end. Only insofar as he grows can he stand the deep waters only. And no defense would be so defended against as having the sheer tactlessness or hopefulness as to take the child too deep too early. You had to ready yourself. You had to be ready. Otherwise you might drown. Paris knew it was safe at the shallow end; most preferred the safety of it; masks were difficult to rip off. Fleming was not ready to do anything of the kind. His safety meant too much. And there was safety in not having to repeat anything, eternally speaking, and to continually enjoy varieties of the flesh that religiously presented themselves to his religiously gargantuan appetite.

Paris had seen Enid fall asleep before he ventured outside where the night was filled with stars and music became the beat of time. He put on his Scottish bulky-knit sweater with his long, white collar hanging in contrast to the deep blue knit. Cars passed by. Edinburgh Castle gazed over the city from its dank, gray façade; a few pubs were open and men in heavy sweaters sat at the tables and drank and talked and enjoyed themselves while Paris sat and thought, vaguely gazing in the direction of a hot dart game in the corner next to the mahogany deep walnut paneling of the bar. The men fired jokes at one another. Wit, as it turned out, was a measure of game prowess and they excelled at making their games witty. For them, it was a fun-filled night.

Paris sat at one table. A couple on his right had an intense conversation going about a mutual party. The woman kept accusing the man of infidelity. He defended himself by saying only the devil himself could live with a shrew like her. They drank scotch on the rocks heavily. Since her nickname was "Rawhide," she seemed capable of allowing his cutting remarks to slide off her rough hide, a fact which prompted Paris to muse that the man was probably justified in taking the position of infidelity. On his left sat an older man, who as it turned out was named Fritz, dressed in a dark suit. He had a ruddy complexion and a full black mustache and a distinguished air about him as if he professed something at a university. His high forehead indicated a massive intelligence and the pipe he smoked he held in a manner suggestive of a thinker. His hair flowed over the fullest part of his scalp and his ears were barely visible. He sat quietly staring into space as if his mind was lost and dwelling somewhere else in the cosmos. Paris could not help but notice the man's hands. They were delicate, long, and ivory in contrast to his ruddy cheeks. They seemed as if they were the hands of a saint since they were so intricately attractive.

For a long time neither spoke. Paris drank two glasses of ale and felt fine. His thoughts were sore since he felt he had become a bit too heavy with Fleming. It was sad to see people only steer for the shallows. Error was always a necessary foundation for truth. But even error was necessary for truth. He knew the temptations of the shallows intimately. Security was a strong temptation. As long as one did not have to breathe the air of freedom, the shallows attracted. But the freedom Paris aimed for Fleming to realize was that once in the deeps, he would know that the shallows and the deeps were both illusions. First, he had to convince him of the reality of such illusions. Words are wombs of illusions. That he knew. Novelty was a need to continuously pass from illusion to illusion. Only the repeated illusion could reveal itself as such. Novelty was needed to prevent thought for it constricts and cannot run a good footrace with novelty. Fleming needed novelty to stay interested, to stay alive.

As these thoughts passed through his mind, Paris noticed Fritz was often looking in his direction as if to talk to him. Fritz paused to take a sip of ale. His hands searched for a match. There was none. He leaned over:

"Have you a light?" he asked.

"Yes. Here," replied Paris. In the dim light, Paris noticed Fritz's eyes were very dark indeed. They were almost black and they flashed with ferocity and tenderness. He relit his pipe and soon curls of smoke rose from beneath his mustache. A conversation soon started with Professor Nietzsche.

"What do you do?" asked Paris to get his mind momentarily off his troubles. The man grinned an almost ferocious grin, showing extra white teeth beneath his black mustache.

"What do you think I do," he returned with a question.

"I don't know. A teacher perhaps?" Fritz laughed a hearty laugh and slapped his knee in a delicate manner.

"It's a hard field to mask," he said. "Yes, I am a teacher."

His curiosity aroused, Paris asked: "What do you teach?"

"Theology. Formally, that is. What I really teach is how to cope with life. How to cope with death. Nay, how to cope with God. Theology."

"That's a mouthful," Paris replied as he ordered another Newcastle Brown Ale. Fritz called over the bartender and ordered a German beer called Hummel-Bräu.

"You're a student I presume," he continued, drying his mustache after a long draught.

"Yes. An American."

"I am too. What part of the states?"

"California."

"I've been there. Went to a place called Little Switzerland near Sonoma. They serve great German beers. Sang some great beer drinking songs like Eins, zwei, drei Gezufa... and had a great time." After a minute or two:

"Why do you teach students how to cope with life and all that?" asked Paris in an almost naïve way.

"What else is there to teach? What is education if not self-therapy? What is theology but self-therapy in another dimension? Life is the education for situation upon situation. How to relate, confront, cope," said Fritz, gesturing with those long, ivory fingers that alone were enough to attract a listener.

"So you approach it like psychotherapy?"

"Yes, there are so many different words for the same thing. I teach that if there is time, there is eternity. I let their dark be my light. I teach them love as well as rage. Hope as well as courage. Devil as well as God. Unmeaning as well as meaning. Is that not all life and death? Silence and noise. To teach, you must be a student. That is when the ears have the least grease in them. One begins to associate sound with symbol and avoids the aphasia of language disturbance. That is why I teach. To develop a soul: to light love in the world and laugh at the fight of chaos and order. Everywhere there is ignorance. Everywhere. Clear thinking, yes; the why of life, double yes! You can get high on yes, you know. No is a way out. It always will be. But music says yes and plays her own divinity. That is why I teach."

Paris listened almost in a rapture. It was difficult to take it all in but a sage was cleaning his ears, performing a private purgatory in an Edinburgh pub. Why can't all teachers be inspired like Fritz with his black mustache and ivory hands? Fleming was lost somewhere in his mind. Paris thought this was education. Here was wisdom, however transvalued.

"How did you arrive at this vision?" he asked quickly.

"From relation. All relation. Patient-therapist. Patient-doctor. Parishioner-priest. Student-teacher. Relation is the healing of alienation. A way of getting out of neurotic cycles. Vicious circles. It is like the ministry of reconciliation. Self-transcendence. The transcendence of past examples of hatred, exclusion, and other forms of stupidity. Flight to the divine. As Plotinus said: the flight of the Alone to the Alone. Education for self-reliance. Education is the medicine for the curious and a fountain for lovers of wisdom. Education is animating the divinity of flesh. Education must teach the why as well as the how of life. Otherwise it misses the point. It becomes boiled down to a listing of facts; and life is not all facts. It is living itself. We need to inspire as well as to relate. Aw, but I am boring you with a lecture…"

"Oh no. Go on! Go on!" exclaimed Paris whose eyes were lit fires. "Please. Tell me more." He shook his head slowly and then paused for another draught of ale. "No. I lecture too much already," he said with a grin showing the whiteness of his teeth. "There is one thing a man must know…" he said, shaking a raised finger.

"And what is that?" asked Paris, already seduced.

"When to talk and when not to. I have talked too much already," he said.

"No. I disagree. It is wonderful to know men have visions even when it is hard to see in the world."

The professor wiped his dripping mustache with a handkerchief.

"Visions. Ah, yes. Visions. Too many have none. And they die for want," he added. "But tell me, what is it you study?"

"Philosophy," replied Paris.

Fritz's eyes lit up.

"No wonder! No wonder!" he exclaimed.

"No wonder what?" asked Paris, puzzled.

"No wonder you enjoyed my rambling."

"Yes. They are close."

"At times. In minds."

"Indeed. Indeed. They talk of life too. Philosophers do."

"Some only talk of thought. But I like those who put life into thought since life outswims thought," confessed Paris. Fritz stared at him a moment as his eyes danced.

"It is rare to find anyone interested, isn't it?"

"Yes. It certainly is. Most are concerned with getting and taking. That is their business."

Fritz was floored by Paris' astute observations. Both began to see once again the value of dialogue for only then could life be a carnival where it was fun just to go from booth to booth and listen to the salesmanship of the world.

"Amen," replied this professor with the black mustache. At that point the bartender came to their table.

"You gents drink up. Almost time to go." The two had not noticed how the time had slipped away since they were so involved in their conversation. They finished their glasses and strolled outside. A cold wind cut through dark of the city and cut right through their clothing even when their collars were pulled up. They huddled beneath a street lamp. Fritz gave Paris his business card which read:

Fritz Nietzsche, D.D.
Professor of Theology
Phone: (888) 777-3334

Paris thanked him and Fritz said goodbye and good luck as the weather killed any desire for further conversation. Paris was sad to see him go. How conversations can make friends, he thought as he strolled toward the St. Andrews Hotel with his collar braving the bitter wind that played its bagpipes from the heart of the highlands.

CHAPTER 10

The next morning dawned somewhat bright and they all went on a bus tour of Edinburgh. Up and down the streets, across the Firth of Forth, followed by a tour of Holyrood House—these all mapped their day. Enid stayed with Paris and grew on him as days passed and the love their arms and hearts expressed grew although neither acknowledged its existence. Fleming escorted Joan through the cobbled streets that glistened now and then in the partial sunlight.

Fleming suggested a nice café lunch. He and Joan and Enid and Paris took a small table near a large window. Several others in the group did likewise. Soon Blythe and several other girls ventured into the same café. Her presence did not exactly fill Fleming with spasms of joy. All it did was to quicken his resolve to resist. And resist he did. Blythe sat facing him and he did everything human possible to avoid her eyes that continually searched his. It made him uneasy to be spied upon; it gave him a sense of paranoia to see her girlfriends quite sympathetic with her plight but Fleming was strong even though he did feel uneasy. His uneasiness was caused by yet another consideration: efforts to turn Joan against him. Women had a way of getting what they desired even if it came by an entirely novel route. So far, Joan seemed immune to any outside influence in any direction that required her to feel anything hostile toward Fleming. Blythe was in a quandary. She did not know how she felt. She could not bring herself to tell Fleming about the man on the pleasure boat at Windermere. Yet she was confused more and more about Fleming potentially being the father. It sent her into a severe depression for long days at a time. She contemplated suicide. She tried to think of ingenious ways to abort the fetus without going through the mess of an abortion. She simply did not know what to do. It was obvious Fleming did not care either way. Yet the pregnancy would ultimately show and there was nothing she could do or say. She awaited her breakfast sitting between her girlfriends whose art it was to gossip. They were friends in the sense they shared similar activities and interests but when a crisis would come they simply did not want to associate with someone who was no longer the shining star of prestige and recognition. So they backed off in the face of current opinion which was usually the affliction being inflicted. It was their solemn duty as superficial friends to bow before the opinions of others. To see Fleming drinking coffee and eating breakfast with Joan did not tempt her taste buds. It only drove the depression deeper. What made her nauseous was her so-called friends gossiping as if they were perfect with no stains on their petticoats. Suffering means nothing unless there is someone to hear, to share, to listen. And all her friends did was to frustrate her suffering by their constant insensitivity to it. They were sympathetic as far as lip service could go but they were, in reality, quite insensitive to the extent of her suffering.

She calmly ate her breakfast and felt her body become a form of nourishment for her baby. Then, Judith, a home economics sophomore who was planning to switch to political science, spoke up.

"Don't worry about a thing, Blythe. What's a home anyway? It is so good to be free from all that garbage they feed you. I mean about having a home and kids. The whole scene. It is just crazy. What we women need is political power. Hell a woman's got to stand up for what she believes or else she'll be walked on by men. Men are always that way. Aggressors. Traitors. Bastards. I can get my own damn job. My dignity requires it. I mean why be pushed around all your life? By myths, illusions and all that sort of crap. I'm a champion for liberty, women's liberty. Why, just look at Fleming over there with that feminine object, Joan Bradshaw," she said, pausing to pop one of her pimples. "Look at those big boobs. All she does is wear tight sweaters so men will notice," she said, feeling the flatness of her own chest. "And those legs. How putrid and how utterly daring she is sitting there like that," she said, pausing to scratch her bony leg. "I'll tell you," Judith went on, "being an object for those bastards is no sort of freedom at all. Men are traitors. They say they love you to get into your pants. Freedom! Freedom now and forever. Unshackle the chains of illusions, girls!" she said in quiet somewhat Marxist declaration.

"I've been furious with men ever since they tried to invade our campus at my undergraduate girls' school. All of us women together against all men. What delight! And what vibrations! Those sneaking men came around trying to get into our pants. I know it for sure. They're such bastards. No good sons of bitches. That's what they are. Down with home and family! Imagine. At my undergraduate college for women they told us not to go on, that we had to be married at least by graduation time. What a myth! You had to be married by the time of graduation. Oh, it's all so phony. Why I loved, dearly loved, some of my girlfriends more than I could ever love a man. Men are so hard, so aggressive. Isn't that right, Pauline? Pauline adjusted her bra and nodded with utter solemnity. There was something grave in their solemnity. None knew what was grave about it though each felt it. Blythe finished her eggs and drank some coffee. She did not really feel like eating but felt that healthy food aids good health. Her eyes were fixed more or less on her food and she became impatient with the conversation of those trying to comfort with slogans and other party feelings. They did not and could not understand. How could they? They were too busy jabbering like old fools, she thought. Could one understand the pain of another? Pain is best understood when it is remembered. And if memory falters, so does empathy with the sickness of another human being. Words need silence to console.

At first, Blythe had not felt anything special about Fleming. They had slept together on many occasions. It was nothing new: if you've slept with one, you could sleep with all. At least this was Blythe's situation. But she would not sleep with anybody she did not like. It was people who were special, who cared, or seemed to. But her condition caused her not a little anxiety due to basic feelings of insecurity. She could easily abort but something inside her did not want an easy way out. In effect, she chose her own pain. Not only was she attached to her own stubbornness, but with the idea of having Fleming's child. What compounded her anxiety was the thought that her child may not even be his. Wishful thinking became a potential substitute for reality. The more she thought of his getting away, the more anxious she became. Anxiety grabs for even a straw of security be it illusion or mirage. It was partially her vanity at work which made her cling to the idea of marrying Fleming. She could not for even a moment stand the thought that another woman might lure Fleming totally away from her. The thought turned her stomach and she abruptly stopped eating. Judith looked up from her coffee.

"What is it?"

"I want to go," Blythe said, slowly.

"Where?"

"Who cares? I want to go. Now," she affirmed with a solid determination. Judith finished her cup and Pauline reluctantly pushed her breakfast aside. They all paid and left. Blythe declined to look at Fleming who sat puffing a cigar and joking with Joan.

The sun was bright as they strolled down the street. Pauline was miffed because she had to give up her breakfast. Judith was there to sympathetically pick Blythe's mind.

"Fleming get to you?" said Judith.

"No. What do you care?" she said, rhetorically cross.

"Just trying to help."

"I don't want it. I have enough trouble as it is without your reforming zeal," she said caustically.

"I'm sorry, Blythe," as she gave her a tender kiss. Blythe did not respond as Judith had hoped. To get her mind off men was her challenge in life. A strong male ego was anathema to Judith. It must be deflated at all costs. Men were competitors; they had to be defeated. And one way of defeating them was to take their women away with a greater love than any. And that was to cause women to love women. Then the male threat no longer had any power. It dissolved in non-relation. Blythe was unaware of this particular tendency in Judith, but she did feel safe with her in a sense. It was not Blythe who experienced Fleming as a threat. Judith did. And Judith projected her feelings on the helpless Blythe, which was, in fact, also a desire to manipulate Blythe for her own ends.

Judith needed someone to rally around her cause. What could be more natural than men who were her enemies because they continually stole her lovers away from her? Politics was a mask she used to intellectually justify her own sexual behavior. She wanted Blythe and since Blythe had been rejected by Fleming, Judith was on the inside track for Blythe's affection.

That night everyone attended a concert at Usher Hall. All stood when the orchestra played "God Save the Queen." Afterwards they heard Tchaikovsky's *Hamlet, fantasy overture* and his *Symphony No. 5 in*

E minor. Fleming was again with Joan and Enid was again with Paris. Blythe could not keep her attention focused on the concert. She slipped into the hall where her asthma gave her fits. After she calmed herself, she was able to return to the concert with Judith at her side. For her, life was simply and utterly depressing. The source of her happiness was Fleming, an obsession recently elevated to that status in proportion to an increase in anxiety feelings. The more insecure, the more anxious. The more anxious, the more grasping and possessive. The more possessive, the more self-defeating. This was her current circle. Of course, Fleming did not want to be involved in any way. He did not particularly relish handling the problems of others, especially when it concerned him. So he continued to enjoy Joan's company if not her body. The concert was given by the Moscow Radio Orchestra but such a treat only made Blythe more nauseous. Out of empty space, she got the idea that she should just leave school and leave everyone. By this time, her self-sorrow, which is anger by another name, melted into such a large proportion of self-pity that she just had to leave. So in the middle of the concert, with guests quietly listening, Blythe, with partial attention-getting intentions in the world, rose and quietly marched out of Usher Hall. Her movement caught Paris' eye but he made no move. A minute later he felt someone pulling on his arm. Turning, he saw Pauline. She whispered something in his ear and without delay, he left. Outside, he saw Blythe resting her head against some railing, staring gloomily at the sun. He motioned for Pauline and Judith to leave. Reluctantly, Judith left her quarry but let it be known it was not for long. They both went back inside for the rest of the concert.

Slowly Paris ventured up to Blythe. He did not have a serious a look on his face. It was more curious than serious.

"Blythe," he said softly. No reply. He touched her arm.

"What," she said.

"What's bothering you?" Her face grew fierce for a split second then she softened their lines.

"What do you think is bothering me?"

"Fleming," he replied. She shot a look into his eyes then resumed staring at the sky.

"So you've got everything solved, eh Herr Doktor?"

"No. Nothing is solved. Is there anything I can do?" Glumly, she shook her head.

"Nothing in the world. Nothing in the world," she repeated, staring at cloud formations off to the west. Whenever depression hit her, she would stare at the cloud formations as if daring them to rain on her.

"Nice clouds, aren't they," as he too leaned his head on the rail.

"Yes. There's a man. See. The large part's his nose. Looks like a pipe in his mouth. There's his chin. See. Where the light filters…" she said with an almost childlike abandon.

"By God, you're right. There's a man out there. Pipe and all. Wonder how he likes it. Up in the air I mean."

"How should I know. I'm down here. An earthling."

Paris seized her focus on cloud formations and tried to sprinkle them with stardust.

"Ah, yes. We both are earthlings. I have a pipe too," he said, pulling it from his coat pocket. He showed her a dark briar pipe then slipped it back into his pocket.

"Paris, you have a way about you. You understand. I know you do. But I can't stand living any longer," she declared.

Paris almost had a grin on one side of his face. It was a curious grin, one of familiarity.

"Have you thought…of suicide?" he asked, almost gingerly.

"No!" she exclaimed quickly. Then Paris looked at her seriously.

"Why not?" he asked.

"I don't know. Why should I?"

"I don't know. I just thought I'd mention it…seeing as how you haven't thought about it," he said.

At that, he began to pack his pipe and lit it. A wreath of grey smoke curled up, shifted with the breeze, and vanished out of sight. A wry grin mapped most of the lines of his face. How many times before he too had plunged into the backwaters of depression, the first movement of despair, and somehow found something or someone worth living for.

"I'm not afraid of death," she said.

"Oh, I know," he quickly replied. "You think death is the last thing?"

"Of course. Nothing is after death. Nothing," she said with almost dogmatic insistence.

"You're sure about that?"

"Of course. Don't tell me you believe in heaven."

"Maybe. Whether it's heaven or hell, I don't think it's the last thing," he said softly. "You just die the death to learn to live."

"What do you mean," she asked, curious. So curious was she that for a brief moment, she was not wholly absorbed in her obsession. He reached into his coat pocket and pulled out a well-used piece of paper that looked like it had been folded and unfolded a hundred times.

"What's that?" she asked, curious.

"Something I'd like to read to you."

She shrugged her shoulders as if indifferent and almost nervously pulled out a cigarette and lit it. Still, her curiosity had been aroused and in her despair and depression looked to Paris for some consolation. Paris cleared his throat and read:

"When death is the greatest danger, one hopes for life; but when one becomes acquainted with an even more dreadful danger, one hopes for death. So when the danger is so great that death has become one's hope, despair is the disconsolateness of not being able to die."

His voice drifted off as was his custom. A few moments slipped by before he wished to know what she thought of it.

"Well," he said.

"It's heavy. Who is it?" she asked.

"Kierkegaard." She nodded for a few moments.

"How did he know so much wisdom?"

"I don't know," Paris replied. "Maybe he lived it. Then wrote it down for other despairing fools...like us." A faint smile briefly came to Blythe's face.

"What are you in despair about?" she asked.

"Hard to know. Nothing definite. A kind of dread…"

"I see."

"When relations abort, there is despair and loneliness. A sad affair."

Blythe shot a wondering and inquisitive look when abort was mentioned; it was a way Paris had of divining the recesses of a human soul. Like a physician, he probed the layers of tissues that lay directly upon the heart and gently, ever so gently, began to touch and define the sickness of the soul in combat with the disease of despair.

"I know. Some abortions simply are not therapeutic, are they?" she said.

"No. We are everywhere pregnant with sins and despairs. But there is joy. And it can be breathed. That is, if you can get out of the way of your symptoms like envy, lust, greed, sloth, gluttony, pride, and anger," he said with an almost light-hearted bounce to his voice.

"Sounds like the symptoms of everyday, doesn't it?"

"You could say that," he said.

He re-lit his pipe. She stepped on the butt of her half-smoked cigarette.

"Well, Herr Doktor, you medicine man, theologian, and philosopher what do you recommend?" she asked.

"Well, I'd say approximately a thousand milligrams of eternity. Take two tablets everyday," he said with an ironic grin. "Let eternity be your now. Cease choosing resistance to yourself. For health of body and serenity of soul, learn the arts of repose as well as action. Be not afraid to live. Dying is all too easy. And all too human. Work through your despair by working. Learn service to others but do not hide in it. Make your love a labor, your labor a love. Oh, and don't forget one tablet in the morning and one at night before bedtime. Meanwhile try to get rid of the symptoms you carry. That way you will not be stillborn."

Blythe smiled for the first time. All she did was nod and nod and nod. She really found Paris a gem in a desert of hard-baked clay. It was a way of watching her heart warm. After all that, she felt very close to Paris. He possessed a rare gift: to accurately articulate another's feelings. They stood there with a light breeze blowing through her hair and taking his smoke and blowing it away as soon as it curled from his lips. A decision was reached. She had to tell him about her condition. His remarks had hit home as if he already had half-baked expectations that she might be pregnant. A few more minutes passed as he slowly puffed his pipe and she stared at the sky with an almost blank stare.

"Paris," she said finally. He peered at her as a screen of smoked rose, curled, and vanished. "How did you know...I am pregnant?"

"I didn't." She gave him a doubting look. "Honest. I didn't," he repeated. "Who is the father?"

"I think it's...Fleming."

"No wonder you're depressed. How could you help being depressed?" He looked inquisitively at her. "Have you told him?"

She nodded.

"And he said no dice?"

"No dice."

"How far along?"

"Only a few weeks."

"Have you thought of an abortion?"

"I don't want one."

"Why?"

"I don't know," she replied.

Paris scratched his head and poured out some of the burnt ashes from the top of the pipe bowl and they blew away in the breeze.

"It's a sad juncture to be caught in your own acts. Especially you who are both protagonist and antagonist. Sometime we direct, produce, and act out our own tragicomedies."

"That I know," she replied. He took his finger and pulled her chin around until he could look her straight in the eyes.

"Knowledge should be your liberation. But instead it's a libation. Too much knowledge might be as bad as too little. If you know this, why don't you do what is necessary to live?"

"I don't know," she replied without an expression on her face or lips.

Paris' brows came close together as they did when he was puzzled or angered and it was easy to see he was in deep thought.

"If you know what to do and do not remedy it then…"

"Then what?"

"Then you've chosen your own fate. You love your fate. Right?" he asked with a bit of curiosity.

"No. Not necessarily. I simply want this child." Delicately Paris examined her face and all that it expressed. It was an ambivalent face. The lines sagged at the mouth but she was quick to smile and her smile possessed an irresistible charm. Her integrity was evident, so he thought and decided that if she really wanted a child, why not?

"Well and good. Then don't bother Fleming. It will be a trip to hell. But if you find the going rough, keep your mind on your goal, that is, if you need one, when all the praise and blame is hushed you can live in peace. Don't worry what others think. They don't know how to live, much less to think. There'll be the jealous ones who don't do anything but stand around and be jealous while condemning you. Envy will be there too with his green eyes that glow in the night, paying worship at the shrine of comparison. They will all be there. So it's up to you to deliver your own pain…"

"I know," she said. "It will be hard."

"But try not to blame Fleming. He may be the father but if he doesn't want to marry you or claim the child, it is not your duty to put fault or blame on his doorstep. Life is something you bear yourself. We can't expect everyone to turn on when we flick the switch."

"I know," she said. "I'm glad there's someone like you. Someone to talk to."

"That's what I have ears for. To listen and maybe learn," he said. "Well, Enid's probably wondering what happened. Let's finish the music and down it like wine."

Smiling, she strolled with him into the theater and listened to a fine concert. Fleming sat with Joan and enjoyed the entire performance. Blythe returned to her girlfriends with a much lighter burden. Or so it seemed. Anxiety is not necessarily removed with comforting words or pharmacological suggestions. Her eyes kept landing on Fleming and she continued to crave him, to want to hold him forever and pretend with all her soul that things would be like they were and would be so in the future. She could not stand living now, not with him dating Joan. The art of tragedy, however, is a refusal to live now. Too often we romanticize the past, idealize the future, and suffer through the present. That is what Blythe did. How could it be otherwise?

That evening all had dinner at a plush hotel. Blythe did everything in her power to sit next to Fleming, all to no avail. She tried to tip over the soup bowl so some would land on Joan but it did not work. She slashed Joan's purse with a razor blade but Joan said not a word. It was as though an invisible glass separated them. Jealousy ate her, bit by bit and finally consumed her. One drink followed another and soon she began to slur her words. Joan looked at Fleming out of the corners of her eyes as if to ask what to do. Fleming sat silently between the jokes and fun all were having, except one. Paris caught Fleming's eye and motioned for him to step outside. They discreetly did so.

"What's up," asked Fleming.

"I think she will make a scene."

"So what."

"Well, the drunken tongue is often tipped with slander. And you know how a scorned woman can be. They're not too nice when their hurts begins to surface. Get me?" said Paris, staring out at the street lamp beams in the night.

"Let her slander. Her words cannot hurt me."

"That's very brave of you, hero, but I'm not sure if Joan will be in love with words of hate. Especially when Blythe sharpens them into barbs. She makes her words razor sharp. And they cut," suggested Paris, standing with his arms crossed. He did not expect Fleming to do anything since he was impervious to Blythe's whining as he called it.

"It is silly to stand out here and worry about what Blythe will do."

"Have it your way. Her anger and rage are tempests that will rock your boat. Don't underestimate the rage of a woman."

"Thank you, counselor. Let your briefs be briefer next time."

He gave Paris a smug smirk and cockily returned to the supper where Blythe, already high, was just about to let her feelings have full expression. Fleming did not care at all. He simply winked at Joan and began to cut his steak.

Paris leaned over to Enid: "I think there is a scene brewing."

"I hope not. That's all we need. I feel it too though. Events are foreshadowed in the bones that intuit them. Hear her laughter," she said, making obvious reference to Blythe whose lips were lit by hilarity and jovial laughter, all of which was a mask, for as soon as the drink would deaden awareness, when all lines of reason and coherence dispersed into an angry and infantile blue, what she felt would surface as it did now. Perhaps she was not conscious of how she felt while laughing. She was numb to it. All she had to do was trust even her blurred senses long enough and what they perceived would cause her torment and anguish, not just the pain of her mind's reaction to the present and even more acutely pain remembered. It was as if the pleasant memories of all the times they had had as well as the songs they had sung together— all these memories of pain and pleasure only added gall to the ambrosia.

Judith reveled in her loud aggression. It thrilled her to see that even Blythe could be influenced and molded to her heart's desire. By contrast, Pauline felt somewhat embarrassed by her remarks which, one could sensibly sense, were not in the best of taste, at least among the well-mannered and fastidious. Like a child, Blythe wished attention especially from Fleming. When she saw the happiness Fleming and Joan experienced as two humans very much infatuated, her memories flew back to her own loving embraces with him and such pleasantries, glued as they were to the context of her mind, infuriated her and filled her with a slash-and-burn rage.

She wanted to rage at everyone to divert attention, to tell everyone to screw the world for out of an unlucky relationship, she judged all men and all relationships. No one could do that to her. No one. She would not put up with it. After all, she really felt something for him but it was now poisoned by her thoughts. Thoughts have a way of influencing the perceptions of the brain. When thoughts are sick, the perceptions will be sick as well. When they are healthy, the perceptions will be healthy. And some thoughts victimize the brain forever, much like the loss of meaning in life and the lethargy that accompanies depression. Her thoughts were arrows of hate. Her actions, gestures, facial expressions, silent speech told as much as a long-winded speech. She wanted to embarrass him, to do anything to get his attention. Pride kissed her mirror-image, self-pity, and then turned quickly into scarlet rage. She drank more and more, concentrating less on her meat and potatoes. She called men phonies and aggressors to which Judith applauded gleefully. Still everyone ate and talked and paid very little attention to what was happening at their table. It was not long thereafter that she began to remove her clothes bit by bit in the style of old time burlesque. Surely that would garner the attention she craved. Ladies gossiped and men stared wild-eyed. Her hips, though large, were shapely and as her blouse fell to the floor people gasped. They could not believe their eyes. Her stomach protruded just enough to draw attention on a canvas of stares. But it was a beautifully body, the divinity of flesh, and it drew attention like moths to light. Onto the table she hopped and began to sway to the music which played softly in the background.

Fleming said "What a grossout" and tried in vain to continue eating his dinner as Paris gave him a knowing look. The wine buzzed in his head and his embarrassment was offset by his newly-erect fascination with her swaying loveliness. Joan was angry that Blythe should have to be in the spotlight and she felt enough envy to tempt herself with competition for attention and recognition, for the ego makes demands, sometimes unreal, that can distort otherwise immaculate perception. She watched as Fleming instructed his pupils with the love of the dance and felt as though she should compete but decided it was silly and stupid to use her body in that way. To herself, she reasoned thus: why abuse the body if it is divine? By contrast, Judith was utterly absorbed into the beauty of Blythe's body. Her eyes careened smoothly down her legs, absorbing every inch. Long and longer she studied Blythe's thighs and hips. She longed to be making love to her right now. But no, she must restrain herself, must hold herself until the proper moment when she could get Fleming out of the way and naturally proclaim her love to her love. Her time would come. Patience and waiting are a way to wait for a coming. And her time would. So she stared at Blythe's slender legs and milk-white skin. How she longed to have her. Oh, how wonderful was desire yet how frustrating, for with every imagined or real pleasure came real or imagined pain. But to her, even pain was pleasure. They all watched in amazement as her hands expressed themselves in slow, graceful motions. It is a great triumph for her for she knew how frustrating it was for a man to be aroused and not be able to come. This was a way of punishing them by giving them a bit of pleasure. And she enjoyed, though not as much, the thought that Fleming might be embarrassed.

As the drink began to tell and give her brain a dulling sensation, the faces that eagerly watched her began to blur as well. They were all consumers bent by consumption, an ancient disease that encouraged observers to observe the entertainers. The faces all blended into one yet they were all present: the girls jealous and with gossip, the men bug-eyed with stares and soon for the moment at least, she felt their opinions were merely pigeons of care that alighted on her shoulders to coo and woo the days away. Opinions were like flies; they carried the fruits of comparisons to logical conclusions. Open the door and you were free, not afraid of opinions. And that is how this ring of merry consumers expressed itself. They had to consume because they were too stiff to dance. They had to be entertained because, being vacuums, they could not entertain themselves.

And so she danced even if it was to embarrass Fleming and gain his attention. She also began to gain some insight into herself. And so she danced and gyrated her hips and simulated intercourse and the men drooled with lust on their lips and eyes on her hips. Each was hot under the collar and sweaty with desire. And it was a flattering to be desired. There was something powerful about using the body to influence others. Nothing had to be said. In fact, the best language of the body was motion for motion verbalized silently. And, as their faces bore testimony, they seemed to get the massage. Judith was in ecstasy as well as the men and boys. She had not even had to seduce Blythe to see more of her body. Her future was in hope and hope was purely an imagined future but it fortified the present with its wedding veil of illusion. She was determined to hold and love, if that term is at all correct, Blythe who simply danced away the hours despite complaints from the hotel management. Her body became a bath in perspiration. Her forehead was lined with nuggets of sweat. But the dance was over for now. She had the attention she wanted as Fleming did not take his eyes off her for a moment. Even eating was replaced by gazing and being continually surprised by her loveliness. Everyone watched her as she redressed her grievances and took her place at the table. By now, her food was cold but it made no difference. Attention was what she had wanted and she had it. The party soon broke up and the night was made tender by the appearance of stars.

CHAPTER 11

C uriously, much of attention to her also came from Judith who spent the rest of the time in the weeks ahead trying to control herself. But to control oneself was made especially difficult if one had to fight against the possibility of being uncontrollable. She fought her need to be self-controlled. And the more she fought this within herself, the more conscious she became of the need to control her uncontrollable urges. Hence, her desire for Blythe began to obsess her. She grew jealous of her whereabouts, kept tabs on her as often as she could, and discouraged men from seeing Blythe whenever possible. She continually gave Blythe the pitch about being totally independent of men, that she was a big girl now, that men were simply after women to exploit them, and that she, Judith, would act as Blythe's companion in the months ahead. Blythe listened to her propaganda and soon began to view all relations in terms of power struggles, dominance-submission games, sado-masochism, and eclipsed any sense of agapic love, love that frees and is free of the desire to possess and exploit, there might be in any authentic relationship. What was embarrassing was her pregnancy. Here she was an independent woman in need of no one since to need someone was regarded as somehow 'feminine' and this was taboo. After all, she was independent, was she not? She had confused solitude with isolation and chosen the latter course. To be independent, she soon came to believe, was to be in non-relation or only relationship with Judith who seemed to be her only friend. Men were out. Who needs them with all their stuffy self-importance, always trying to make women submit to them. The thought of them made her nauseous. Thanks to Judith's kind counsel, she had become a true believer and confused independence with non-relation.

As the days and weeks rolled by and wind gusts swirled autumn leaves around, she came to rely more and more on the propagandistic source of her independence as a released woman. She would not conform to most anything since this might suggest she was not a nonconformist. And, as she began to think for herself in all matters, she was deceived into thinking only her opinions were significant with respect to the cosmos as a whole. Only Judith's opinion remained on a semi-equal par with hers. But Judith stood to profit from all this for she was gradually, ever so gradually, maneuvering her lovely paramour into a position which would be exploitable. Her truth was used as a lie. And Blythe became stiff with her opinions and began to fancy herself as an intellectual with all the answers, a slightly different self-perception than before. The intellect was another source of games and lust. It could be used, as with anything else, to any purpose. In class she would have the answer for Professor Arsse before anyone else. It buoyed her ego to feel such a thrill and satisfaction to beat others for the sake of self-importance and tinseled sophistication. And it was a pleasure to outwit men too. It only reinforced her own self-perception or self-delusion that she was fast becoming quite powerful. Even Judith was awed and amazed at Blythe's beautiful brain. At the same time, she was beginning to feel apprehensive lest her plan not come to fruition. She had to somehow soften Blythe and make her a less viable source of intellectual achievement. Gradually she began to open up her bag of tricks and touched Blythe here and there. Maybe a tap on the buttocks, a gentle play with her hair, a touch where a touch might do the most good.

Blythe responded. Pregnant as she was, she found Judith to be her only true friend in the whole nasty world, a world she felt she had to compete with since it was full of men and the high-blown needs and self-important assertions. The world was not receptive to her striving to be a nonconformist since she went out of her way to deliberately cultivate a nonconformist reputation. There was one problem: her competition with others only made her nonconformity into another conformity since she excluded cooperation with others from the arena of life. This made her rebel even when it was ludicrous like the time she announced at lunch that the British were tyrants if they only offered tea to coffee-drinking Americans. And that she, for one, would defend anyone who, along with her, challenged the British government in its so-called oppression of natural drinking habits. The Britons answered that all along coffee was served three meals a day. It was embarrassing for her to face her folly but this only drove her to strive for perfection even more.

When it became apparent that only her opinions mattered, others did not respond. It was admirable to be a nonconformist but this was ridiculous. Obvious it was to everyone that Blythe was losing the art of being gentle for to be gentle is to be flexible, without rigidity, and able to flow with the flow of life. Even Judith could not control as much of her as she thought as she learned one day while giving Blythe a massage.

"You ready for exams next week?"

"So. So," replied Blythe with a shrug. Judith moved her hands leisurely around her back, moving them from shoulders and neck down to her curvaceous buttocks.

"You don't care?" she said, staring at her buttocks longingly.

"I don't care that much. Besides, I think exams are stupid. They are a waste of money and time. An exam cannot test everything you know. It can test only what can be tested. That's all," said Blythe with a satisfied tone.

"I agree," said Judith as she ran her fingers up the inside of her legs.

"You seen Fleming lately?"

"Don't mention his name. The bastard," she said bitterly as Judith held her leg for long moments as if to eat her flesh so tempted was she to caress it. For the time being she was content to play with her with her hands. Coolly she studied Blythe's figure with its supple lines, the way her buttocks seemed almost bell-shaped even as she lay there quietly in a pose of repose. How she longed to be in her arms, to taste the wealth of her body, to hold and possess her as a rich man sometimes clutches his money bags. Seeing her there almost drove her out of her mind. The pangs of pleasure were sweet as a light delicacy tantalizes the palette. Up and down her fingers massaged. Tight muscles softened. Nerves calmed. The flesh became relaxed and a halo of beauty surrounded her naked body. She was an angel, a divine body. And Judith could hardly contain her inward joy at the sight of those hips and thighs and long legs that had been so abused, she thought, by those insensitive men. But her self-imposed silence and restraint would have to continue a bit longer. Judith did not want to compete with men. That way she thought she could own her.

"Haven't seen Fleming lately, eh?"

"No. Not lately. Don't plan to either," she said as Judith's face was aglow with sheer delight. Blythe's flesh felt warm and soft to her fingertips although she was slender and her body was hard as well.

"You dating anyone else now?" she asked as her fingers gently rubbed the sides of her breasts in one continuous stroke.

"No, I'm not in any position. A pregnant woman is in a position to labor."

Again a warm smile of delight rose on Judith's face. Such news was utterly a pleasure. Sheer delight. An impossible dream. Her pregnancy had become a temporary advantage.

"I guess you're right. It's good to be here…with you. I've grown accustomed to you. I enjoy your company. We get along. And that's important in life. Social relations. Especially with somebody you trust."

Again she gingerly stroked Blythe's buttocks and then held them in her hand the same time she pronounced "trust." Blythe did not mind. It was pleasurable to know somebody was not offended by her recent bookish excellence. And the massages were stimulating to say the least. When Judith would tickle her, a light almost childlike laugh would bubble from her otherwise quiet stimulation. "Yes. I think a lot of you. You understand. And you're not jealous or anything like the others," she said with a naïve sensibility.

"That's right. I understand you. And whenever you need someone, I'll be here. That's what love's all about, don't you agree?"

"Oh, yes. Love is friendship with passion in the game."

"That's a good way to put it. Tell me…what do you think of passion?"

"How do you mean?"

"How expressed."

"Oh. Kissing…" she began.

"How do you kiss…passionately. Pretend I am your date. Show me a passionate kiss," suggested Judith.

Blythe was almost startled at the suggestion. But without hesitation Blythe put her arms around her neck and kissed her and their warm tongues met. The warmth of their mouths only served to raise their temperatures. And with that Blythe hugged her with an almost violent reaction, a double-edged sword, that made her want to know and belong even if it might be a different way to be. Feelings of sheer loneliness welled up in these violent grasps at Judith who was almost offended had it not been balanced by the pleasure of seduction.

How long she had waited for a kiss, human lips, anyone who cared, anyone who showed concern, anyone who would rescue her from the hell of her self-chosen pain and solitude. Care and concern and compassion are the trinity of love. She had not allowed herself to admit these needs, at least to her social self, that she had starved so long she did not realize the range and depth of her hunger for the utter joy of a concerned friend. So what if she made love to a woman. There was pure joy in it. There was touch, the poetic lines of skin. And touch made her skin dance and dance with joy and celebrate the mystical communion of touch. Ah! Alas! The joy of body on body and the touch of touch and the hunger of need expressed. Passion was worth the whole of life. For without passion, its music was turned off, the inner spirit dried and blew away. Passion had a friend in its supposed enemy reason. So she relaxed and spread her legs as their hair rolled from side to side in their ecstatic embraces. Nothing could have made Judith's day happier than to be with Blythe whom she had wanted to love and desire and possess. Blythe kissed Judith all over her body and Blythe, too, was in a state of ecstasy. This was as wonderful as she had experienced with Fleming and the mere thought of him brought unpleasant associations which made her feel anxious. Anxiety cut into her joy and rendered it pain. And the more she thought of her stress, the more she forgot the present as it was clouded by the past. And then it happened. The wheezing began all over again. The gasping for breath was usual and Judith had seen these attacks in her before.

"I'm sorry," she said after a few minutes.

"Don't worry," Judith replied. You'll be alright. Just give yourself time. Time to live. Time to relax. There. There. The wheezing's over. Here's a kiss." She bent over and kissed Blythe deeply. Blythe was starved. She wrapped her arms around her as if to never let her go. But never is unreal. And Judith would take her unreal and make it a form of something real. For the meantime, they lay in seemingly unbounded splendor as the afternoon eased into early evening to take over as the dark extension of day.

CHAPTER 12

The midmorning sun warmed their faces and made them glow as they laid there in tall grass and stared at the ever-changing transformations of sky.

"The sky. See how it moves," said Enid.

"Yes, it just keeps moving or maybe we do. Which do you think?" asked Paris, pausing to chew a long piece of grass.

"Maybe the eyes do. They keep floating like wisps of cloud," Enid replied as she rested her head comfortably on his shoulder.

"The eyes are keys to mind or brain. They might be clouds. And all the beauty they see is optical angles and coincident lines. Life is converging lines."

"And they converge on love."

"And the love is love without an object," mused Paris. He stretched his legs.

"That was beauty the tongue writes poetry for. Yes, you do have a eternal poem inside you that wants to come out and cry with joy. But I guess sometimes we're afraid that if the poem comes out, we can't concentrate on business. But that's an excuse for evasion."

"I totally agree," he replied, "it somehow gets suffocated. Somehow it gets strangled by all the fret and bother. I guess that is why the poem, that is, the eternal, does not materialize often. It just stays inside and we drown it with beer and pretzels."

"Why do we lose our poems?" she asked as she turned on her stomach so she could see his face.

"I don't know. They just lose it. Sell out. And kill off their inner fire which alone makes life worth living. It takes a labor of love to make a poem."

As he chewed on the grass, her big blue eyes searched his face. It was pleasant to find someone who understood, someone with whom she felt she could talk.

"You think love a labor?" she asked.

"Yes, it is," he replied. "It takes time and infinite patience. And suffering too."

"I guess there's poetry even in that."

"Yes, the spiritual is in the eyes. There's a universe there colored by rhythm and change. The night, the day are all one aspect of eternity."

Her inquiring blue eyes contrasted with her smooth, fair complexion.

"When is eternity?" she asked.

"We are it," he replied.

"We are?"

"We are," he replied as he tossed the grass away and began to munch on a new one.

"Right now?"

"Right now." She rolled over on her back again and breathed deeply as she snuggled into him.

"It's just great to be alive," she said.

"Yes. We don't know how fortunate we are. We seldom do."

"Why is that," she asked.

"We are too busy losing our poems. We elude them for something else. We put on blinders because we're in a race for our lives somewhere else over a mountain or across the sea. Poems allow us to live here and now. But they lose their poems so they don't have to admit they are them. And pretty soon blip, a life goes by and then we wonder if we have ever lived to hear a poem, our poem, or any poem from within. That is why I reckon poems are dismissed as irrelevant or sentimental. We would rather live ignorant than live poetically. We want to turn off the music and pursue illusions for illusory happiness as if happiness could be caught with a butterfly net. I must be boring you by now."

"No. No, you aren't. You aren't at all. I agree. Beauty is sometimes worth the living and the dying."

"That's possible. You know, all this while I have watched the sky change. It changes all the time yet it seems the same because it changes all the time whenever we look. The sky is a canvas of wisdom. Its colors, its changes all seem somehow the way the sky should be—the way it is."

"Isn't it something? How it changes. Just changes and changes as if it was trying to tell us something. Trying to say 'accept life' in our ear," she added.

"Yes. But even the change changes. We don't think it will but it will. It's like an old passion that hovers over us like a shadow and it becomes so big we cannot see around it. Then one day—poosh—it is gone. Just like that. And you never think you will change but you do. All the time. Every blink. Every moment we are different, like the sky. Assuming a shape we had not before. A pose, a play, a mask we had not acted out before. We become the sky inside. Lightning and tempest and calm and sunny are the skies inside. But we forget that, too."

"Yes," she said "we forget the obvious in pursing the not-so-obvious. The little things. The trivial. Or seemingly so. They make up a life whether we like it or not." A big smile came on her face and she playfully stroked his chin.

"Your eyes are like the sky. A man's character is in lines. Moving lines. Like you could use an ophthalmoscope and see forever in the obvious. An image forever moving is the time you see with."

"Your eyes are pensive and poetic but I kinda like you anyway."

At that he tortured her with tickles and she rolled over and over in the grass and they played and frolicked and laughed to their hearts' content, a sacrament to hay and sun. A car passed by packed with pub lovers. They waved and laughed and she tickled him until tears streamed down his face.

"Oh, please. No more. No more. Oh my God. I laughed so hard I hurt," he panted. "Whew!"

"See what you get for tickling me? A tickle back. In the old rib," she said as she set about straightening her hair and pulling grass out of it.

"Ah, poetry in the grass."

"Poetry in every roll," she replied, leaning back on her propped arms.

A big grin lit his face.

"You roll your own poetry, eh?"

"Every once in a heap big while," she replied.

"Ah but the sky," he said looking over the heavens. She looked at them too.

Wispy patches and thick billows curled over one another as if winding around the sunlight like a snake, alternately lightening and darkening their faces. At one moment Paris' face would be bright like an angel; Enid's would be dark like a demon. Then the reverse would happen. It was life. The ball of mood was passed around between the players.

In a nearby field, they could hear sheep tinkling their bells as they grazed on the luscious, deep green grass beneath the curled limbs of oaks. Paris turned on his side.

"The grass is sweet. Look at it. The green earth so beautiful, so warm, so new. Just to appreciate the earth. To hold it dear and clasp its lush grasses to our breast. And to lie in deep grasses with poetry on our lips and write sonnets. A hot sound, a kiss, a touch—some can never love too much. Ah, but the grass is sweet deep down. Just to see it and touch it. Is that not a miracle? And is it not a miracle to have time to behold a miracle? Yes! Time enough for those goings on we do not notice, that expanded peripheral vision so that we might see a thousand times farther in the closeness of a man and a woman. I hear a harmonica."

They rose above grass level and saw an old man dressed in a Swiss Alps-like outfit.

"Hello," they said as he passed. He stopped, smiled, and made his way to them.

"How be ye these days?" he asked as if hard of hearing.

"Fine, sir. Just fine," Paris replied. "That's a fine harmonica you play."

"Oh, this," he said, blowing it briefly. "Just love a merry tune. Makes the grass grow, you know."

Paris grinned at Enid.

"I see. The grass is sure high here. You been playing around here long?"

"Naw. Just once in a blue moon. But I like to play and dance. That's the only way I go sometimes," he said. "Must go. The afternoon's a-goin' and so am I. See you kids later," he said as he waved goodbye.

"That's a nice man," Paris commented as he watched him return to the road and wave goodbye.

"I'll play to that," she said.

"Ah but tell me what is it that we want to say on this fine later summer day? What are we looking for? What words out of the deep? What springs where fountains play? Is it beauty that inspires eternity or eternity that inspires beauty?"

"Who knows? I certainly have no idea," she said with her blue eyes wide with wonder.

"What do you think beauty is?"

"The sun and moon and stars," she said "and the love worded by silent eyes."

"I see you've kept your poems. Lay 'em on me."

"Beauty's the skies of your mind and the divinity of a flower," she replied.

"'Too late have I loved thee, o beauty so ancient and so new. Too late have I loved thee,'" replied Paris, quoting the *Confessions* of St. Augustine. Her big blue eyes rolled over to him. His teeth shone brightly in the temporary sun.

"And what was that all about?"

"Loving beauty too late. Divine beauty so ancient and so new. Lament and amazed affirmation. What you were saying before. The aim at higher levels of beauty for beauty is the eye God sees me with. We see eye to eye."

"I see," she said. "Beauty loved too late is loved anyway. It is the way of perception after one has lost the veil of illusion and is wed, instead, to the quest for truth."

"You took the words right out of my mouth," he said as he rolled over and gently touched her soft cheek.

The blue of her eyes and the gold of her hair set against the late summer's day was a contrast that made him feel an almost irresistible desire to kiss her. To kiss her would be a delight even though she often warned him that she was promised to another. It seemed somewhat futile to love someone whose previous commitments could not include you. But he dared anything even though it was awhile before he acted. So he decided it was time. As if a kiss could shake the planets out of their orbits, he mused. So he leaned over and caught her unaware and pressed his lips into hers. Although she hesitated, she returned the kiss. And they kissed long as if stars were happening and satellites were orbiting and their kiss made their hearts beat faster as their arms sought one another. No words interrupted the kiss. It was the way it was. Long. Close. Warm. Tender. It was poetry. Their lips kissed warm and tender. Paris had some learning to do. But that would come later. For all his philosophic learning, he had yet to ripen into a wisdom which is beyond the fruits of mere understanding. But tomorrow he would learn. All his knowledge had not made him stuffy with a snobbish understanding. He was ready.

CHAPTER 13

"The nakedness of woman is the work of God"
—William Blake

Fleming turned over. Joan lay next to him at the hour of five o'clock and the cock crowed not far away. A portion of her back shimmered in the faint light. Strong, proud, intelligent, her lips were full and her hair, though pulled to one side, fell over with that beauty only naturalness knows. Below, he could almost touch whiter breasts pressed into the sheets almost hidden. He lay there thinking of nothing in general. All he knew was he liked her body heat that radiated from her rich yet soft skin that filled his nostrils with a heavenly scent, a scent much different from the usual smell of beer farts that were Fleming's early morning trademark. He had to unlearn such spontaneous sphincteral exercises that even offended one of the maid's dogs who, upon smelling Fleming's doings one morning, put both paws over his ears and wept.

But now (or so far) the scent was divine. He turned on one elbow and just gazed at her. He could not for the moment go to sleep so he just gazed. And there was beauty in gazing itself; it was a palace named "abiding." And he gazed at the long, sleek body and skin and wondered how it was sometimes between the parts of pain and the speeches of hurt there could be revealed a sign of beauty such as this flesh, this woman. There was nothing particularly special about her; she was just another student. Yet in her nothing special, there was something special. It was that she was there. In bed. Next to him. Warm and loving. And that was somehow beautiful in his gaze. It was because he could not go to sleep that he was even awakened to such a fact. After all, there was really nothing else to do but gaze and his gazing was his own meditation. The eyes see no gems if there is no dirt to hide them. It suddenly hit him. The fact hit him. Why did he not notice all this before? He did not know the answer. All he knew was that he noticed. What he noticed was the beautiful. And he was happy.

Distantly, he heard the cock crow. Such a trumpet heralding the dawn, he thought. The few minutes he spent gazing had been a dawning. And the sun would be brighter as the day rolled on. The time was as if gazing into the heart of a rose with new-fallen dew perched lightly on its petals. There was something fresh about beauty, her beauty. And it dawned on him in a far-out sense beauty is everywhere not only next to him beneath the covers. Beauty is everywhere. But everyone is too busy shopping to see it. Naked, a man had immaculate perception.

But then he turned over again and went back to sleep. It was not long before it would be time for class. He heard voices. Jocko and Sparky were talking low. He opened one eyelid. Imperceptibly, with the quiet of a cat, she had gone to the girls' wing. A cold flush of air filled his cubicle curtain since Zee had opened the windows. It was a cold air and it made him curl up snugly in his blankets. Half-asleep, he rummaged about in the closet of his mind. How delightful had been the early awakening when all was still and quiet was itself a song for no one's ears. She had been there and had vanished. They had talked late and his fatigue made him want to do anything but attend class. He felt dead, a dead weight. Yet earlier in the morning he had felt light. The droplets of consciousness change drop by drop and everywhere change shifts and shows permanence the illusion of now.

"Rise and shine," said Zee whose wiry body was bound for a life in the army.

"Go back to bed," murmured Fleming from beneath the blankets.

"Rise and shine," insisted Zee.

"Look, Zee, I feel like some more sleep. So flip down the curtain, all right?"

"Rise and shine," repeated Zee, now grinning.

"You copious cockbite," snarled Fleming who picked up a shoe and threw it at him.

Zee dodged it.

"Son of a bitch," muttered Fleming, becoming more exasperated. Zee reappeared and flipped the curtain down. But before it reached its normal position, it filled with a rush of cold air that left him freezing. He was pissed.

"Copious cockbite," Fleming shouted. The early morning wind froze his bones. Machete-like, it cut through several blankets and turned everything cold. It was Zee's custom to pump iron with the wind blowing on his back. That was he felt he could breathe the air of the heights and feel brisk and tough as if he had been climbing the Alps. Fleming darted from his bed and made his way to the window and forcibly shut it, freezing all the while. Zee grinned as he combed his hair cut in a military style in the mirror. With contempt in his voice, Fleming said thanks. Zee just grinned. That was one way to wake Fleming. But force sometimes engenders resistance; so Fleming resolved to go back to sleep. Zee left. Everyone had left and gone down to breakfast.

He climbed in bed and thought: Ah, the beauty of solitude and moments of quiet! How few and far between!

And soon Fleming was sound asleep. It was cherished for its brevity. And it would be all too brief once breakfast and classes finished.

Time dropped more light. And before he could understand what was happening, Fleming opened his eyes again. It was Paris who stood there examining some of the books on his desk. He looked at Fleming when he saw him stir.

"What's up?" asked Fleming.

"Nothing much. Just decided to cut class. Thought I'd get some sleep. Couldn't get to sleep. We supposed to read about Elizabethan England?" he asked, holding a volume of history.

"Yep. Have an exam on it pretty soon."

"Sounds delightful."

"You know, I realized something today."

"What?"

"How beautiful it is to gaze."

"What about it?"

"It's beautiful. To gaze at beauty is a wondrous sport."

"I agree. But what occasioned this great realization?"

"This morning. In bed."

Paris looked puzzled.

"Joan?"

"Of course. I could not sleep."

"Great realizations sometimes come in bed."

Fleming grinned broadly. Paris lit his pipe and soon a wreath of sweet-smelling smoke curled about his pillow-propped head and rose to the top of the cubicle and then as gently wafted away.

"It was something I would never have realized if I had not been inconvenienced by not being sleepy."

"What was it?" Paris asked as his curiosity uncoiled.

"Joan's body. The way it shimmered in the light."

"And just gazing at her body taught you most of the learning you need for an education?"

"Just gazing."

"There is something rather than nothing. Just ponder that, Fleming. You opened a different book. The book of seeing. And it has so many shapes and colors and popcorn. Just seeing. This is an education few receive and fewer learn or even bother to learn," suggested Paris as he puffed.

"I know what you mean," reflected Fleming. "It is really amazing how many educations there are."

A smile crawled onto Paris' face. This was old stuff to him lodged in the yellowing pages of his memory. How gratifying it was to think that not everybody was thoughtless. It was also something that made him feel old but inspired. A problem, once abandoned or once solved, was only remembered if communicated by eye or by dance or by rhythm or by word or by silence. What was so novel was to hear someone else going through a similar process of learning. A problem solved became old and mellowed but it became new in newer eyes and newer dawns. In truth, he was not chronologically older than Fleming. He was older only in the sense that he had faced similar situations and occasions before and for him they were old. Repetition was a renewal even if you yourself did not do the repeating. That was how it went. If you asked questions of life, you may not even get an answer. But at least there was the curiosity and courage to address life at all. And when unexpected situations arose, there was a confidence and self-dignity that did not allow you to be devastated by grief. Paris had asked and would always ask questions of life. And a man became old in the asking.

"You sold on Joan?" asked Paris as he emptied his pipe.

"Of course," replied Fleming, looking askance at him. Paris got himself into a thinking pose and rubbed his chin.

Fleming began to get nervous, so much so that anticipated Paris' thoughts and said:

"You're wondering about Blythe."

"Who? Me?" he said with a half-hidden grin. He sat with his arms folded with a curious look on his face. There was a long pause. Paris would not say anything and his silence was more devastating than his talk.

"Go ahead and talk!" exclaimed Fleming.

"About what?" demanded Paris with a dark frown.

"Blythe," replied Fleming.

"There's nothing to say. You know my thoughts. I don't have to put them on paper for you."

Fleming rose and walked out. Paris made no attempt to urge his return. He just sat there and puffed on another pipeful. Fleming did not like what Paris could imply by silence. And he did not like it because he knew Paris did not agree with his views on that point. Blythe simply was a sore spot between them.

Blythe meanwhile was becoming more and more active in politics and social issues. Her pregnancy was known and accepted. There would be no need for a marriage since her affections had turned awry and taken the name of action. Judith was her game, her only confidante who could handle her in a sexual way but could also intellectually discuss everything from zoology to political action committees. She became actively engaged in programs that opposed the accepted value systems and political hierarchies. And, as she did so, something happened to her of which she had only been faintly aware. In her zeal for a cause, she became alienated from those who did not share the same views. When she spoke before groups in Grantham or Nottingham, she felt deeply the need to have much feedback, positive feedback so she would know where she stood in everyone's opinion. And to those who did not participate, she exhibited a haughty contempt, described by one caustic Darby reporter as "the vicious bulging eyes of a rat in an experiment with her own self-conditioned bias." Those who were apathetic were increasingly irrelevant. They became storybook fables in her pre-enlightened past. Everything was now for the cause or as she termed it "revolution." Family and friends drifted away. They simply did not measure up to revolutionary aspiraions. But Judith satisfied another side that still held sway in her life. And Judith increasingly became a true opportunist in that she experimented with Blythe. It was as if Judith was Blythe's blind spot. She could analyze and argue both rationally and coherently until it came to Judith. It was there the weakness of Blythe's persona revealed itself. Even reason expresses emotional roots; philosophy is the flower that blossoms on the stem of psychology. The illusion of reason and passion is mutual exclusiveness. One does not exist forever in isolation from the other. And so it was that Blythe could argue an airtight case against any given, any value, any accepted current fashion only to find a gaping hole left unpatched in the web of her arguments. Judith was a catalyst that could stimulate or depress since her presence was enough to put Blythe off balance. It is rather difficult to philosophize on the virtues of rational discourse in the midst of passion.

CHAPTER 14

T he sky spelled late afternoon. Already everyone was on board and with a heave, a shrug, and a groan the heavy ferry pulled out from Dover and churned the channel waters into a foamy brine. The wake bubbled and popped as the white cliffs of Dover disappeared.

Luwanna drank one gin after another; John Diamond courted with a mug of ale; Enid and Paris quietly sipped a Macheson Stout; Jocko smoked a small Navy cut cigarette; Sparky and Jean talked out on the promenade deck as did Fleming and Joan, watching the drops of life ooze away like wine that blended into the Dover cliffs in a memorable contrast to the nearby houses with tall chimneys. Ev sat and drank and ate in a gourmet pose. Peter strolled about the upper deck and searched seemingly in vain for a sign of France. All he wanted to do was shout "Vive la France!" when its coastline finally came in sight. He loved the French language which he had studied in high school with Dr. Geza Kadar, Monsieur Baldemar Barson, Madame Fontaine and Mademoiselle Mary Anne Florea who had studied at the University of Grenoble. Duci enjoyed a drink at the bar and Zee Ferguson watched the waves split by the ship's bow.

Blythe sat by herself near the front of the ferry. Judith had ostensibly gone to get a pack of cigarettes and a bottle of Pinot Meunier, although she usually preferred French and German wines. She had been gone nearly half an hour. At the bar Judith had met a black woman who intrigued her and with whom she struck up a conversation. Soft, luxuriant skin almost copper-colored, she had a bright smile and curvaceous figure. Judith's charm was nearly irresistible especially when she spoke concerning inalienable rights of womanhood. The woman listened intently, her dark eyes cheerfully somber, and did not say much. Judith watched the way she lit her cigarette. She had a continental aura. The woman spoke clear English yet was from Paris. She too was attracted to the fair-skinned Judith with the eyes that sparkled and lips that charmed. Judith stared at her lips as she spoke; they were dark and not especially thick and a red tint made them alternately smooth and pleated. Judith was attracted to her eyes, those dark, bold eyes that promised a fire inside. They drank and talked for another half hour and then agreed to meet later after sundown. Judith then remembered Blythe who was sulking as she wrote a speech on the right of an abortion for anyone who wished to have one. Although she did not want an abortion in her case, she favored abortions for others. Judith came softly and slipped her hands on her neck and then kissed her neck playfully.

The sun was rapidly setting so the moon of one's life could begin to rise.

"Where've you been?" asked Blythe as she completed one of her sentences with a strong plea.

"Talking."

"Anyone in particular?"

"No, nothing in general. Lots of music. *Diamond Divas Band.* You like a cigarette?"

"No. Just finishing my speech. I wanted to read it to you as I went along but..."

"All right. Lay off. I've a right to talk anytime I want. I just felt like talking in there. Besides, you finished your speech out here. So, it helped us both right? Sure it did. One must finish alone. It does no good to chatter with idle speech."

Blythe sulked but wanted to exact as much apology out of Judith as possible. That was her attempted play at guilt. But Judith felt no guilt. It was simple as that. And Blythe found her sulking did no good. It only frustrated her further. Judith lit a cigarette and stood gazing at the waves as her politically-conscious companion exhorted and extolled the freedom to abort. But as Judith watched smoke curl into the wind, her thoughts were on the woman inside. She wanted her and wanted her without delay. Trying to get away from Blythe had become a problem. Before, it was a delight to be with her. But now Blythe was excess baggage that lost its importance as the capricious currents of desire flitted about with fickle fashions. Erotic love flew from fashion to fashion. Unless it was in fashion, it could not be. The fashion of the day reflected erotic play. But Blythe posed a problem. What to do? Finally, she suggested they go in and mingle with the groups that talked inside where it was warmer. Blythe agreed. Once inside, Judith scanned the entire ship for her friend. Nowhere in sight. Apparently this satin-lovely lover had already slipped outside where they had agreed to meet. Soon Blythe struck up a conversation with Paris and Enid who were singing a medley of songs to themselves. Paris had not talked with her for awhile so they began with Enid leaning her head on his shoulder as he talked.

Seeing her opportunity, Judith excused herself. Outside by the emergency lifeboats, stood her new friend, Yolanda, who was barely visible in the dying light until Judith came closer. Her fresh lipstick made her lips seem even lovelier than before.

"I see you already have a friend," remarked Yolanda with her arms folded next to her black purse.

"Oh. Yes. A love that has faded." Yolanda smiled.

"For a day?"

"No. Forever." Yolanda looked skeptical at the lying lines of Judith.

"Love can always be resurrected for a future date," she countered. Judith did not like the reception; her knitted brows soon passed and her forehead lines vanished.

"I'm sure that's true. In this case, she is fading." Again, a softer smile from Yolanda. Judith noticed her long and slender fingers and her imagination created scenes that were so passionate they were almost utopian. Judith offered her a cigarette.

"Sure." She lit it.

"Nice night out." Yolanda agreed.

"Where are you going?"

"Paris."

"Can I see you there?" Yolanda smiled.

"Of course. I was hoping you would ask. Paris is for love." replied Yolanda who raised Judith's expectations as well as her temperature.

"Days and nights for love. That is what Paris offers," suggested Judith who looked about her suspiciously to see if anyone else was within the range of eye and ear. She moved a bit closer and tucked her arm in Yolanda's and together they strolled aft. Only a faint light from a cloudy moon even intruded over the darkened channel waters. In awhile they would sight the coastline of France. Yolanda kept pressing her exquisite lips together as her heart beat faster as the adrenalin poured into her bloodstream. Judith put her arms around her and gently brushed Yolanda's breasts. Finally Judith kissed her deeply and Yolanda threw her arms around Judith's neck and rained kisses on her soft, warm lips. The scene was deeply moving as Yolanda let forth a flood of furious passion as she had never kissed a white girl before.

Just then a door slammed. Judith pricked her ears. The night was sufficiently dark so as to conceal them. Even so, Judith stopped kissing her new-found love. Together they crouched near the railing and listened. Moments passed with no sound but the throbbing hum of the engine. Then they heard another slam. This time through the darkness, almost imperceptibly, Judith could see someone move but could not distinguish gender for gender was only possible in some kind of light. More time passed like the wake that follows ships. Then the person climbed the ladder that led to the observation deck. By her bare outline and gait, Judith could tell who it was. There was no way to escape. They were cornered. Even in darkness Blythe stared right at them. In a moment, she scurried down the ladder. Judith did not move. Like two statues, Judith and Yolanda crouched, frozen.

Blythe wasted no time.

"Judith," she said. Judith rose and smirked. "What is the meaning of this?" Blythe said, indicating Yolanda who was now rising.

"None of your business," Judith curtly replied.

Blythe slapped her; Judith slapped her in return. A fight began. Yolanda stood there, flattered by the scene. Judith knew judo but did not want to flip Blythe out of a certain mocking deference to her condition. It was less than polite to use judo on pregnant women, especially when it might cause a miscarriage. So they pulled hair, a good ole form of combat between some women. The screams were not loud enough to provoke anyone else's attention but Yolanda thought they would kill each other for sure. Judith did get Blythe on the deck and pulled her several feet which infuriated Blythe. Only minutes before had been a tender tête-à-tête between Judith and her dark woman where words of love were inspirations for sublime poetic heights. But now the swearing would make a drunken sailor blush. Blythe popped Judith a solid punch to the jaw and Judith was out. Blythe kept repeating "you damn bitch."

Yolanda did not step in and her hesitation drew Blythe's attention. Blythe swung and hit Yolanda in the mouth as Yolanda dug her nails into her face and wished to gouge her eyes out of their sockets. Around and round they went, clawing, screaming, and swearing. Then Yolanda punched Blythe in the face. Shocked, Blythe began to step backward, her eyes grown huge as she stared for a nano-second at the darkness. Shock turned to rage and with a war whoop Blythe charged at Yolanda who dug her nails into Blythe. Her teeth gritted, her cheeks rose to fury and she grabbed Yolanda's windpipe and squeezed with superhuman strength. Yolanda's mouth opened and gasped for air. Still Blythe squeezed with revenge in this private uncivil suit. The scene could be called action for damages for which, in the fury of the instant, there was no remedy at law. Blythe pressed harder and harder and, as she tired, her strength increased almost like an anaconda wrapping itself around explorers in the furthest reaches of a jungle. Yolanda's will to live was ebbing; her air certainly influenced her will but her will, propelled as it was by the most primitive of instincts, fought back. No, not now, death is not now. So she fought back furiously and in one last-ditch effort, dug her fingernails into Blythe's wrists and gouged them with every last bit of strength and determination for she was not ready for death, at least not in this way. Just then, Blythe's pressure began to break until a trickle of life-giving air filled her lungs. Again and again she summoned every bit of strength from an African heritage that had withstood the severest heat of tropical suns and finally, in a few moments, broke the lock of fingers from her windpipe. Blythe began to pummel her in the face and somehow Yolanda pushed her off. Then Blythe backed off, gasping for air.

"Get out. Get out," Yolanda snarled as blood dripped from her chin.

"I want my lover," screamed Blythe.

"Your lover. Your lover indeed. You don't try to kill someone you love, you stupid bitch. Now get out. Go on."

Blythe paused and stared long at Judith sprawled on her back. Blythe knelt beside her and began to touch her face. At that point, Yolanda came at her and threw her a right cross punch to the jaw. Blythe fell back and lay there a moment, stunned. Yolanda began slapping Judith's face and put smelling salts to her nose that she kept in her purse. Blythe watched with dazed eyes as Judith began to recover. Blythe made a move toward Judith; Yolanda doubled her fist and shook it at her.

"You want some more?" Yolanda asked with a threat to continue the fight.

"No. No more," murmured Blythe who got up and leaned against the railing. She watched as Judith woke up in Yolanda's arms. A sudden pang of alienation struck within her, a parting that gives a foretaste of death itself, a reminder that even the togetherness shared today, even the seeming permanence experienced today, will have been transformed tomorrow.

Blythe had felt such sorrow before no matter what she did or said or thought. In fact, no amount of achievement, accumulation, or gain could erase the opposing twins of joy and sorrow. She had felt the same when Fleming had to be renounced though her heart burst with its aching of passion and longing for reunion with him even at the cost of her soul.

She moved away from Judith and Yolanda to the deck that overlooked the bow that split the waves. Sitting for a long while there, she watched as the waves beat against the bow and casually rolled along the sides of the ship and mingled with the wake that followed. It seemed as if she were bound for another shore. And all of this was transition from the ultraviolet to the infra-red and all the frequencies in between and even those whose frequencies went beyond the normal range of perception; all of these were simply mere symbols of transition.

The English Channel became a channel through which one passed between the continents of self-perception. It was only through departure, a loving hint of death's fragrance, that she even died enough to consider what in her was worth a life. When sharpened by sufferings, lusts, self-compromises, artificial parties, and facial make-ups for all the faces in her mirror that would appear, that a life could become sharp, and, like a bow, split waves so that one's death honed the ability to live one's life sanely and in perspective. Then and only then in retrospect (the aft called memory) could one see the sharpened character (with rusts burned away), the values of departure as well as its twin, arrival. Only then could she be done with the matter.

It seemed that no one was secure since everything was changing, advertised, and sold so fast there was no time to be secure anytime or anywhere. Becoming was a channel that flooded any thought of security. Everyone had to continue becoming so no one would lose out and when you reached your destination, you found it was one of many destinations. And you laughed at yourself for giving it a sense of finality. And then you wept for knowing there was another destination. And still another, all destinations unknown. And you knew that as the bow split the waves of becoming and washed and beat against Acheron's bark, there had to be an alternative in her life. Despair was her lot. Her loves, both male and female, had departed. It was fruitless to bother with Judith now even though she loved her as much as she had loved Fleming. It seemed to her in this disappointment that all she could reap from this was a row of tears. And then something strange happened as she gazed at the bow that split the waves of becoming. It did not offer itself with any overwhelming power. But this would not have occurred if it had not been for her despair which lacked a sense of the infinite. She wondered why in each case there was such pain and sorrow at each departure of her loves. And then she discovered to her gradual amazement love in the agape-like sense in that you had to become a bow in order that you, too, could split the waves of becoming, for only by splitting the waves could they be united in the wake of understanding. She decided that, as far as it was possible, she would be a bow to herself.

As she stood there, she felt within herself a new birth. Freedom was freedom from oneself in order to also serve others since your self-obsession got in the way of serving others. She was bound for another shore and all this, in her despair, was a form of passing. And a secret calm was hers for the feeling, and she felt, even in the cool wind, a warmth inside that somehow had surpassed the hair splitting of her earlier days.

CHAPTER 15

Fleming and Paris spent the night in Calais at four francs a piece. The rest of the group had gone on to Paris but they had played around all day and missed the seven o'clock train. Fleming was mad that he had to be parted from Joan and complained bitterly that another student was in hot pursuit.

They sat on the dilapidated mattress with a dim light burning over their heads in all its futility. It did not seem to light anything at all and, moreover, it made the room seem more surreal than it was. The couch was full of holes as was their mattress but the wine tasted exquisite.

"I know that son of a bitch is after her now. The bastard," said Fleming as he took a swig of wine.

"How do you know?" asked Paris, spreading butter evenly on his bread.

"I don't. But you know Joan…"

"No. What's she like?"

"Like every woman I've ever met."

"Oh? How's that?" asked Paris.

"Out of sight, out of mind," replied Fleming, breaking bread.

"That quickly?"

"That quickly," affirmed Fleming. He broke some more bread and stuffed it in his mouth.

"That's outa sight," Paris replied, feeling high. "You know it's a pity that half a life is spend in playing games with people who insist on making up the rules and then bending their egos to fit them..I mean it's really tragic when your security is threatened the moment Joan is out of sight. Why must love be a game of cat and mouse?"

"Maybe because the cat and the mouse are the players…" replied Fleming, who took a long swig of wine. Paris chewed bread awhile and kept silent.

Then Paris spoke.

"Maybe it's a game of cat and mouse because the players perceive themselves as cat and mouse and can therefore justify playing the game of cat and mouse."

Fleming looked perplexed and countered:

"Your intellect is a game for fools."

"Is it always?"

"I don't know. But I wonder if your intellect does not create more problems than is necessary," he said taking another swig of wine. Paris was thoughtful for a moment.

"The intellect is beautiful. I believe it can help us. And you are right when you say it can be a façade for an evasion of psychological problems. But I do think it is trustworthy and can be beautiful in itself. Not all intellectualizing is evasion or fantasy. If it weren't for the intellect, how could we appreciate anything? So I wonder if the game of cat and mouse is not simply a fixed form of self-perception. I am asking this for real. I want to know what you think. Remember it is possible to use psychology as well as anything else for the purposes of evasion as well."

Fleming's thwarted sour face included a not-so-faint frown. Paris had a way of making him think without referring constantly to why thought could be psychologically unsound.

"All right. If you insist on creating an intellectual problem, I'll go along for the ride. Yes, it is possible that how you perceive yourself can be a fixed role and that you feel obligated to always play that role."

Paris washed his bread down with wine.

"But the role as you perceive yourselves is simply a convention. That you must be a mouse or a cat because it is expected of you. And if you don't then…"

"Then what?" asked Fleming, becoming interested.

"Then people get sore because their egos cannot fit into another context. Even games can become unknown, unfamiliar."

Fleming thought for a moment then spoke:

"But unless you play the game, how will anyone even know you?"

"That is a good point. But I am concerned about even that. For if you play the game as you say, does anyone ever take the effort to know you other than in the roles of cat and mouse?"

"No. It takes a while to get to know someone. Sometimes the masks are on tight. And it takes tragedy or tenderness to get at least one of them off," said Fleming, pensively chewing.

"And you know, my dear Fleming, what makes it so hard for anyone to get to know someone? The incapacity to know oneself. Self-examination is acknowledgment to the bowels of chaos and desire woven into the fabric of existence itself. Cat and mouse is a game we play with ourselves. We hate and love the several parts we play simultaneously. Cat and mouse is a reflection from within. A game. A mere game. Yet how sublime."

Paris took a long drink. Fleming sat and played with his mustache.

"I don't follow your train…" he said.

"Don't worry about it. It is this that cat and mouse is a reflection of what goes on inside ourselves. Cat and mouse is there because it was first played within. And within is a prologue for without."

Paris lit his pipe after a search for it in his duffelbag.

"You mean within becomes public property?"

"Of course. The game only reflects what was once a private affair in the fiction called the mind."

"I see," said Fleming.

And the two sat there in silence for awhile as the night crept upon them on padded feet. Outside, much of Calais was quiet except for piano music that played on the air from some undetected source and the moon shone briefly through the partly cloudy night. Humidity was somewhat strong but a gentle breeze cut the otherwise thick and sleepy air.

"Now to you," Paris began again. "Because Joan is gone, why must you feel anxious?"

"I don't know. I just do. That's all," he replied with a sense of an almost pessimistic doom.

"What? Has the great lover Don Juan gone stale? And for a stud to do such a thing! Why 'taint legal," mimicked Paris.

Fleming did not care to be ribbed in this fashion. Paris had a way of holding a mirror up to world after world.

"All right. All right. You've had your fun. So cut it now," protested Fleming.

Paris now only occasionally took a few sips of wine. Long puffs floated from his pipe and curled to the ceiling with warped wallpaper.

"But why does it matter so much to be parted?" Paris asked with a philosophical flavor.

Fleming looked at him seriously.

"I don't know. Maybe because parting is a premonition of death itself. A dress rehearsal."

Paris' eyes twinkled.

"You mean parting aches for the freedom it delivers?"

"Maybe. But freedom or no freedom it hurts."

"Of course," said Paris, puffing on his pipe. "Freedom or liberation depends on dying a little in order that life may mean something."

"Maybe so. All I know is what I feel. Your intellectual arguments do not satisfy my stomach. I know what I feel. And I know, just know, that bastard is going after her."

Paris held up his hand as if to stop traffic.

"Don't let the thought feed on your mind. Relax. If she's any kind of woman, she has her head together. Your jealousy is your insecurity, your feeling of deprivation. So you're anxious for your standings. Your demands for complete security from Joan are at best ephemeral. Why should you be jealous? If you have something to lose, you're jealous. But that implies there's someone you own or want to. You don't own anyone. You are foolish for trying and they are foolish or perverted for letting you own them. Pain and a sea of sorrows result. You cannot depend totally on another for your happiness. If you do, you are sunk. Don't worry, Fleming. Your possessiveness feeds your jealousy. No wonder you talk like you do. We create hell to live in. The mousetrap is our own. We are our own traps. And we bait one another with lines drawn from an everyday word association. So go on. Be anxious. Worry if you must. We are all-too-human but loveable even in our stupidity...that is when someone realizes the utter damnation and beauty of the situation...shall we say... wearing skin and breathing. Being human on the cross of life and death. Maybe with a vengeance..."

A long silence unfolded for each of them in its melodious arms.

"It is hard to live truth, no?" asked Fleming after awhile.

"The most difficult road is to live your truth. Yet it is a way of self-healing," Paris replied.

"Aye. And self-destruction," replied Fleming, stroking his mustache. Throughout the conversation, he had continually drank his part of the wine which was nearly gone and his lips were a dark red beneath his mustache.

"Perhaps. But to live truth is a way of building a foundation for however many castles you have built in the air," said Paris.

Fleming began to look tired; his mind was already fatigued. All he knew was somebody was after Joan and Paris had issued his message from Parnassus while being entertained by the muses among the sacred fountains of his mind. Paris sat on the bed and removed his clothes and knotted his socks. He knew he had not phased Fleming out of his worry about Joan but it had been worth a try. It was easy to remember a quantitative truth because of its tangibility, but a qualitative truth, that is, a truth discovered by life and living as apt to be forgotten and lost. That is why such a truth had to be taught over and over again. So much wax filled the ears in the meantime that a person grew hard of hearing, hard of hearing the silence in every word and hard of seeing the unseen in every seen. But that was how it went. Some never dream that life flits by like a freight train in the night. The best always seems reserved for last. Life is seldom enjoyed not simply because of the inherently tragic elements in life but because much of the tragic is self-chosen through a thousand projected follies of the race. Seldom is it realized that one breathes and they are there. In that which abides.

"You know," Fleming said after awhile, "I am too tired for the debate tonight. Just too tired."

Paris sat up in bed.

"You tire yourself with constant worry about this and that. And Joan is the least of your worries whether you know it or not. And your worry is the least of your worries. Whether you know that or not too. Thus endeth our intellectual chronicle. Close your eyes like the Buddha of Kamakura. Tomorrow is a new birth just like today. We'll hit Paris tomorrow after a good night's sleep," said the otherwise silent Paris Brandon. Fleming could be heard moments later brushing his teeth.

"The water is foul," he mumbled through the paste.

"The weather is not so cold out," Paris replied. "Not bad for four francs a piece," he continued.

"Not bad? It's on the rats' reject list. This is what you might call a hole. I've seen better dungeons," said Fleming, combing his hair.

"What are you doing?"

"Combing my hair."

"What the hell for?"

"I want to look nice."

"For whom?"

"Joan."

Paris heaved a heavy sigh and shook his head.

"No one can put down desires but he that has overcome them. Well, I hope she likes your style."

"Naw, I'm doing it for you, Paris."

"No guys in my bed, baby. No thanks," Paris said.

Fleming laughed and began the water in the sink.

"What now? A shampoo?"

"No. Just want to wash my face."

"Oh. I see," Paris replied with a smirk. He shook his head. It was hard to understand how many faces had to be put on in order to survive the play. But, on second thought, it was not hard to understand once you knew the makeup of things. After nearly an hour of pre-bedtime fixings, Fleming jumped on the mattress. Stuffing flew out and caused them both to sneeze.

"Can't you get into bed quietly?" asked Paris.

"Goose feathers are good for the old lungs. Helps open up nasal congestion."

"Hit the hay," commanded Paris.

Fleming opened the large-framed window so that the night air would clean out all the mattress stuffing and clear the air from its pollution. For minutes he laid there, reading and drinking from a new bottle of wine he had hid from Paris. Paris turned over and gave him a wondering look.

"What're you doing now?"

"Reading poetry and drinking wine. Can you think of anything better to do in this world? As that wonderful poet Omar Khayyam put it:

"A Book of Verse underneath the Bough,
A Jug of Wine, a Loaf of Bread—and Thou
Beside me singing in the Wilderness—
Ah, Wilderness were Paradise enow!"

"Why don't you shut off the light and let's get some sleep."

"I must finish the wine before our flesh goes down and let poetry flow until time herself flows down, down, down," chanted Fleming.

Paris raised himself up and applauded:

"Bravo! Bravo! In concert with the cosmos no less!"

Fleming smiled sarcastically.

"Ah, in concert. Why you are worse than me Paris," Fleming said with utter disgust.

"You know me, Fleming. I am just the reverse side of you. And that's a secret even sides don't know."

Fleming was pissed. He did not particularly like seeing himself in another's face. And Paris was one who could show him to himself.

"Well if we've got to spend half the night in your poetry and wine, then let's have some."

Reluctantly Fleming poured him a cup of red wine from his suitcase and Paris made a toast:

"Tomorrow Paris. We'll enter the city of Paris like Henri de Navarre: 'Paris is worth a mass' But a toast to the French. Sophisticated and fashionable, connoisseurs of cooking and the arts, the people with wine flowing in their veins. From Caesar's conquest of Gaul to Fleming and Paris toasting her in Calais. My God, it is the soul which is the essence of life and love."

At that point they drank more wine.

"You know I am supposedly descended from the House of Bourbon," boasted Fleming.

"It's burgundy on the house today. 'Arise you children of the father-land, the day of glory has arrived...'" as Paris sang a few lines from the French national anthem.

Fleming waved his singing away.

"Yankee go home!" exclaimed Fleming. "Yankee go home!"

They both laughed and the wine helped them feel happy. By now Paris was slap happy and dead tired. It had been a long day. The wine all night made his head feel like it could touch the sky. He grabbed for Fleming's bottle.

"Not this time."

"You socialists think you own everything."

"Who is the socialist," gulped Fleming.

"A toast to some theologians everywhere for at long last opening their minds!"

"I'll drink to that," said Fleming, trembling as he poured wine into Paris' cup.

"Read some verses of the bourgeois mind," said Paris lying back to listen to Fleming's silver-tongued horseradish. Fleming read:

No one in bamboo but the wind
And words now lit with rush.
No one in wind but bamboo rushes
And rushed darkened with wordy brushes.
Be neither term
And fly the coop that dissolves in flown
The way is to be down grown.

"Windy poetry for a calm night," sang Paris. "Another. Quickly."

"Oh, yes," snorted Fleming, "here's one called 'To the Old Professor: a program for future fools'"

"Sounds good," said Paris enthusiastically.

Entangled in labyrinthine ways
No one passes.
You cannot see even with your glasses.
After all, the world's a footnote
To where your realm begins.
You've been out so long
How can you be in?

Paris rolled over with laughter. Fleming laughed and fell out of bed.

"This is the funniest four francs I've ever spent," giggled Fleming.

Paris was red with laughter and in laughter he was creating beyond himself.

"The francs don't make it funny. The poetry is fun," countered Paris in mock seriousness before he again spilled his laughter.

"Hell, it's not *that* funny. Those bourgeois poems really capitalize on humor, no?" said Fleming. Paris wiped the tears from laughter about the eyes.

"Nothing like a good laugh. Laughter is a temple of the holy for it is spirit who animates."

"Yes, laughter is fun. Relieves the race for a moment or two," replied Fleming who yawned and fell back in bed.

"Aren't generalizations the fun of half-truths?" laughed Paris.

"Certainly. Most certainly. From such lies arise. That's youth for you."

"Are you sacking it now?" asked Paris.

"Yes. I am tired. Had a long day. But tell me something."

"You think we'll remember these times?"

Paris gazed at him with an understanding face.

"Yeah. As long as we breathe in the time of memory. Later, we'll romanticize them. Sometimes we romanticize the past when the present is not so alluring. That is one escape."

Fleming seemed almost sad, a sadness about the mouth, a sadness that made it droop during the transition from one state to another.

"I am glad we remember," said Fleming.

"Why?"

"It is good to be able to escape even if only for a short time."

"The present is hard to live with. Maybe it just seems that way. It is hard to live now. Maybe because we don't want to for some reason or another," whispered Paris with a yawn. "Don't you think it is time to hit the sack, time to rack?"

Fleming smiled even though it was a sad smile. With that he turned off the light and the only light was from the wide window that opened onto a dusky blue light, half moonless, though not especially cold. It was humid enough to warrant a surprise for them as they slept off their drink.

Outside their window was a stagnant pond which was the breeding pond for hundreds of mosquitoes. Like airplane squadrons, they flew from the moss-grown water and circled and zoomed through the humid evening sky until they spotted Paris and Fleming having fun on four francs a night. In double formation they soared. As they approached the snoring forms, one of the squadron leaders noticed Fleming was not covered on the buttocks. "Let's get him," he said and led the way. One by one the mosquitoes attacked Fleming and Paris. Soon whelps appeared all over their bodies. Hands, face, feet, arms, back, rump were all targets of the nocturnal raid.

Next morning, Fleming peeked at Paris curled on his mattress. He noticed that there was an odd shape to his view of the world. There was a problem in perception. He did not see the world aright. It was somehow a slanted affair. As he emerged from the depths sleep allows to play, he realized that the world was as he usually perceived it but that it was his perception of the world that caused him concern. And then, as he awoke, it dawned on him that his perception was not really a problem at all for he could still perceive the world as soundly as possible. The trouble was his eyelid was swollen out of proportion. He reached up and touched his eye. It felt like a large lumpy mass.

"Good God, what in heaven's name has passed for hell? Incredible. My eye. No my eyes," he said as he opened both and felt a lumpy mass on both lids. "What in the hell…" as he staggered to the mirror. His eyes were puffy like puff balls and his entire face seemed metamorphozed during the night. Then he noticed the red whelps on his arms and buttocks. He scratched and scratched until the skin was red. His eyes burned and he swore swear words that could have awakened the dead. In fact, his swearing soon caused Paris to stir and find himself in a similar predicament.

"What has happened?"

"They must have come in the night. All seven thousand of them."

"Yes. Aren't we pretty? We look like two freaks. Two gigantic insects without love, country, or songs to sing."

"You're telling me. We have been attacked," complained Fleming.

"There is always some fool ready to sin against philosophy. What fools we were to lay there and be attacked by mosquitoes. Or whatever they were. Now we look like some kind of bug," complained Paris as he, too, gazed in the mirror.

"What are we going to do? We've been changed. And that upsets expectations."

"Just go on to Paris. And wait," said Paris in a philosophical tone.

"Wait? Looking like this? You must be kidding. I can't wait."

"Then what will you do?"

"What can I do? See a doctor?"

"Can she make the swelling go down faster?"

"Maybe she can."

"It should be gone in a few hours. Surely by the time we get to Paris," replied Paris. Fleming paced up and down the room boiling mad. It was so frustrating to look like an insect especially when he had been used to looking like a man. Paris sat back on his mattress steadfastly refusing to itch and watched him pace to and fro like a rooster. Finally, he said:

"Relax. Just relax. Let's get some calamine lotion. I don't look like Adonis myself."

"How can you just sit there?" asked Fleming who was mad at not only the mosquito bites but at his reaction to them.

"Do I bug you?" said Paris with a smile.

"Go to hell, Brandon," he said as he paced back and forth, back and forth, swearing. He stopped in his tracks.

"How can you just sit there?"

"Quite easily. Just by sitting here."

"I mean how can you do it?" Just then Paris found some calamine lotion in his knapsack and put it on and gave some to Fleming.

"The only way to do it is to do it," replied Paris with a teasing air.

"Since when did you become the oracle at Delphi?"

"Ever since it told me I was the wisest man in all of Athens, my dear Plato," Paris retorted which only made Fleming angrier.

"I can get my riddles right here in Calais. I don't have to go to the Black Forest for them," said Fleming, making a gesture due east and presumably toward Germany.

"Relax I tell you. The calamine lotion will help. The swelling will go away in a few hours. Mosquito bites go away. It's the crucifixions that linger," Paris said. Convinced, Fleming sat on the bed and began to think about other things. He decided to pack; he had had enough of Calais.

"I guess you're right," he said.

"Sometimes you have to keep the faith."

Paris packed and both of them no longer complained, although Fleming itched and bitched now and then as the itching flesh itched and flaked.

That afternoon they caught the train to Paris, a train that chugged and sent voluminous funnels of light and dark gray smoke out to the sides where it floated and drifted above the small farms each with a pond and some geese, and then soon rose and vanished into the air. In the cabin Paris and Fleming sat across from a young girl with long, slender legs. Next to her was a matronly woman who stared at their every move. Fleming moved next to the girl and Paris moved on the other side next to the woman. Paris struck up a conversation about the weather in half-French. This took attention off of Fleming who was sizing up the girl. He leaned over and began to whisper in her ear. She did not care for his words and at first ignored him. Then he did a silly thing. He touched her legs and her reflex action was so quick that before he knew what happened she had belted him across the face and left the cabin. Upset, the woman also hauled off and slapped him and left the cabin.

Fleming sat dumbfounded. Paris shook his head.

"What did you say to her?"

"I told her I wanted to warm her up for Paris. She didn't like the idea. So she belted me and took off."

"Just because you wanted to warm her up?"

"By getting laid here and now. I called her a young lay-dee."

Paris just stared at him with a puzzled nod on his face and a wonderment that could be described as an itch.

CHAPTER 16

The underground metro closed its heavy doors with a gust of wind. Paris looked up the cobblestone streets of the Latin Quarter at Fleming who waved him on. They came to Hotel Diana and put their suitcases on the floor while Paris got a room from the attractive Jewish woman who laughed as she talked. A pet poodle sat on the counter and watched the transaction with a professional air. The poodle had seen a "professional clipper" in the not-too-distant past. The woman had curvaceous hips and a long strand of pearly beads. She gave them a key and pointed the way up a long flight of stairs through a narrow corridor to their room that overlooked the busy boulevard below. The rest of the group was lodged nearby. But Blythe was lodged next to them in the hotel.

As they changed clothes after their long trip, a knock came at the door. Paris opened it.

"Blythe, how *are* you?" he asked as he invited her in.

"Fine. Just thought I'd drop by."

She came in and sat on the sofa and did not appear to notice Fleming who had certainly noticed her.

"What happened? Did you miss the train?"

"Yes. Spend a horrendous night in Calais. Mosquitoes. They ate our flesh in the name of preventive medicine."

"Mosquitoes?"

"That's right. Welts all over. You can still see them on my arms." He showed her his arms and face.

"Really screwed up our view of the world. There was a mistake in perception, right Fleming?" Fleming nodded but for a moment seemed embarrassingly reluctant to answer.

"Yes, there's nothing worse than mistaken perception. And we had it," he said almost matter-of-factly. It was obvious Fleming did not feel at ease with Blythe around. Difficult it was the pass from intimacy to mere friendship again; the past became an all-too-human reminder to the present. Paris busied himself with putting clothes in a closet and humming to himself. He took a kind of pleasure in putting Fleming with Blythe for he felt Fleming had left her out in the cold.

"Your eyes. They're swollen."

"Yes. I know," replied Fleming who snarled under his breath at Paris still humming a tune. It only made Fleming mad again; he could just see a broad grin on Paris' face as he sweetly hummed his tune with all the nonchalance of a Swiss mountain climber.

"Those mosquitoes really got to you, didn't they?"

"Yes, they were successful all over," he said, itching his buttocks at the mention of 'over.'

Blythe laughed an almost nervous laugh. She too was feeling the absence of Paris in the conversation.

Just then Paris stopped humming and turned to them.

"Paris is just gorgeous, isn't she? A lovely city. Don't you agree?"

Fleming pantomimed a hearty 'screw you' in his direction.

Blythe said: "Yes. Why yes it is. A lovely city indeed."

Paris had a broad grin on his mug again.

Fleming gave him a 'thanks fella' then smiled sweetly as Blythe turned to him again.

"Certainly is a lovely city. Paris is just lovely," he said with an attempt at seriousness. There was a long pause.

"Well, I'd better go," she began. Then Paris stopped humming "I'm in the Nude for Love" and "A Hundred Years from Today."

"Oh, no. Don't go, Blythe. It's time for tea," he said as he dashed out the door. Fleming's face drained and put on a velvety wan coloring. Blythe sat there, holding her arms by her barely visible fetus as they idly chatted the way ex-lovers chat for fear of talking seriously, another reminder of the past relationship that, like a hungry wolf, prowls about the doors and causes a shiver on otherwise complacency-lined skin. In the time that it takes a male peacock to preen, Paris returned with a tray of teacups, a pot of tea, and tiny rolls.

"Here you go. A way to spend a French afternoon," he said with the suddenly-plumed décor of a steward. They sat and dinned with an occasional toast. Paris followed the tea party with two bottles of wine, a Johannesburg Reisling and a Moscoto de Canelli, he had purchased en route to the hotel. Fleming could not help staring at the fetus as if it were a mask of guilt that somehow returned to haunt him as more wine flowed in his veins and he felt a sense of pity for the way she carried his guilt around inside her.

Soon Fleming was on the bed half-dazed; the wine had enveloped him in its luxuriant charms. Repeatedly he felt a desire to kick Blythe out the room for her presence reminded him their hot scenes in the Lake District that both stimulated desire and forgetfulness as his thoughts paraded across his brain like shooting stars across a summer sky. For his part, Paris kept entertaining Blythe with songs and anecdotes, a mini-lecture on wine bouquet, and a discourse on eternity. Blythe was amused but kept wondering if she had intruded on them but now that wine was readily flowing she did not especially care. Fleming was soon snoring even though a resounding series of snorts indicated he was not finally asleep and continued for several minutes. Paris had not talked to Blythe in such a long while. It was like having to get re-acquainted.

"Looks like our friend has gone to another world," Blythe said.

"It's been a long trip. All the way. Sleep is his home: a wine and rest. His is the quotable snore."

"Have you noticed a change in him?" she asked.

"Yes. I don't know the source of the change but he reveals a certain kind of poise now, less likely to vent his sarcasm on people around him," replied Paris who regarded her with a curious air.

"Tell me," he continued, "what's been happening to you these past weeks?"

Blythe smiled but her mouth corners drooped as a kind of sorrow.

"I've ventured a few things and that is not a source of sorrow and found out a few things about myself...and others."

Paris sat calmly with his ears perked like an alert Dalmatian. He lit his pipe, crossed his legs, and listened.

"Go on."

"And I've changed and am changing all the time. Yet something, I don't know what, remains the same."

"That sounds like a preface to self-knowledge."

"It is."

Paris nodded as a cloud of unknowing wounds its way out of his pipe bowl now orange with fire.

"I've found no finality to relations yet all is real only in relation. That I've nothing to do with the empty spaces yet life is only livable in that perspective. My knowing is my unknowing. My desire to possess is my personal hell. I love sex yet it, too, is a possession. And that my life, in the turmoil of remembering and imagining, is never content with where I am at. Never content. My body is tramped on it by the ingratitude of others and myself. Life without love is death. Love is the very meaning of life. It's amazing, Paris, but true. And I don't mean screwing all the time. I mean the way a sparrow sits on a rose stem. Or a star twinkles in the sky. The endless parade of perishings. My heart has been broken many times. Crushed. And yet my heart keeps mending even in the arms of despair, loneliness, self-hate. I've found out, maybe the hard way, to bend with the matter is to unfold the spirit. All my political campaigns were forms of self-aggrandizement. How I would pride myself on despising everyone, the mediocre fools in this mediocre world. Remember all those speeches I made? All those sisterhood type speeches and they were ways of fooling people and even fooling myself. I've lost in this world, a born loser but I keep telling myself the sun will rise again tomorrow. The sun has spirit and if we could be like the sun and love then maybe we would have the vision of within..." she said in a whisper as her voice drifted off.

168

Paris re-crossed his legs. He was barely perceptible through the cloud of unknowing that wound its way around his shoulders, neck, and head. Then he grined.

"What can I say," he said with the aura of an old, gentle, and wise Chinese sage.

There was a silence between them that said all they wanted to know. Paris puffed on his pipe; he was surprised by the extent she had changed.

"We are as we perceive ourselves even if it is error. You have changed your perception of yourself and are as different. If you are at home with that, that is a change for the better," he said, now sitting cross-legged like a happy Buddha.

"Seems you have grown from your pain, from confronting death several times. That makes life the sweeter," he continued as his pipe went out. He relit it and smoke curled out again.

"I'll tell you, he did not know what he was in for when he left you," he said with a nod toward Fleming.

"No, Paris, I understand him. He is a lover but in a different way. It is struggle either way. But he has his and I have mine. Sad but true."

"Aye, the truth can be sad lot," he said.

A faint smile came on her face and she nodded to which Paris responded with a grin.

"It is so good to talk to someone…who listens…and understands."

"Such is the secret of confession. Some things are best shared," continued Paris.

Before she could reply, there came a snort as Fleming growled, coughed and grumbled his way toward daylight. Strangely enough, he did not recognize where he was. His face was sweaty and he lay there almost frozen without recognizing where he was.

"Have a nice sleep?" Paris asked as he removed ashes from his pipe. There was no answer and as Fleming just stared at him with a somewhat frightened look on his face.

"I said did you have a nice sleep?" Again Fleming just stared with an almost frightened look. Paris went to his bedside and looked at Fleming with a puzzled frown. Fleming just froze.

"What's wrong? Fleming it's me. Paris."

Fleming just laid there with a frozen, frightened look.

"Hey. What's going on? You have a nightmare? Tell us about it. It's me. Paris."

He reached and touched Fleming who froze a moment then relaxed. A foreign gaze was directed at him and Paris felt a cold chill as when one sees a cadaver for the first time.

Blythe gave Paris an inquisitive glance.

"Probably a bad dream. A nightmare perhaps," he said as he sat beside her and thought.

Because she did not always think, she asked questions.

"What's wrong with him?"

"I don't know. Like I said, it's probably a bad dream."

"Are we just gonna let him lie there?"

"What can we do?"

"Shake him," she said.

"Shake him? My God, the guy's frightened as it is," replied Paris, "just let him alone. He'll come around."

Paris was right on target for no sooner had he said that but Fleming sat up in his bed stared around the room and solemnly at Paris.

"Am I here?"

"Yes, you are," smiled Paris.

Blythe's eyes were dilated. Intently she watched as did Paris.

"Am I really here? Now?"

"Yes, you are," Paris replied as Blythe gave him a puzzled and contemptuous gaze at the same time.

"Where am I?"

"In a hotel room."

"Where's the room?"

"In Paris."

"In you?"

"No, France," suggested Paris with a wry, almost comical humor.

"Where's France?"

"Up yours, Fleming," he said with a Buster Keaton deadpan expression.

"Where's France," he repeated without inflection.

"In the world," he replied, having decided to go along with the game.

"Where's the world?"

"In the universe."

"Where's the universe?"

"In our galaxy."

"Where's our galaxy?"

"In the cosmos."

"Where's the cosmos?"

"In the mind of God."

"Where's the mind of God?"

"Within."

"Where's within?"

"Open your third eye and see."

At that moment Fleming snapped into a different state, having successfully completed Paris' catechism.

"What's up?"

"Down," replied Fleming.

"What's with you?"

"All is with me."

Paris was puzzled; Blythe's eyebrows arched.

Fleming's face was no longer sweaty. It was dry as dry can be. There was a calmness about the usually troubled forehead; a serenity about the eyes and if one inspected close enough, there was a certain radiance that encircled his torso. His sleep had been his wakening and he seemed fully awake and full of energy and desire though these were not immediately visible.

"Fleming, what is it?"

"Everything is it. Everything," he stated slowly and solemnly.

Paris was amused but Blythe was both curious and frightened.

"Tell me. Where are you?"

"Everywhere. In a palace."

"In a palace, eh? No, you're in a hotel room. With me and Blythe."

"That is true. But my palace is not here. You cannot see it."

"Is it in the sky?"

"No."

"Is it in Paris?"

"No."

"Where is it?"

"Within. Over and over, it is within," he said with an indefinable chant about his tone.

"What is your palace called?"

"It is called no-time."

"No-time? You mean no time at all?"

"It is out of time when time has a stop; only light can show the way," he said with a grin on his face that was really not a grin at all.

"Is there anything in the palace like gold and jewels?"

"No, nothing is in no-time. But it is full. Time is just another thing. Do not be deceived. It can only be pointed to when you have given up words. There are two windows that will show it to you. But we miss it in clouds of the confounded sun. This palace is the speed of light and yet does not move until you do. Look within and you will see the face of the divine. She is your own."

Paris relit his pipe and looked with a surprised and wondering gaze at Blythe who was giving him the same look.

"Tell me, did you see any lions and tigers on the way to this palace?"

"Of course. There are roars that do not sound and scratches that do not tear. Many lions and tigers," said Fleming with unusual phrasing.

Paris did not know what to make of the whole scene.

"Tell me, did you learn anything at the palace?" asked Paris whose curiosity, mingled with a fascination such occasions aroused, was awakened and his concern subsided for he seemed more relaxed toward Fleming's self-expression.

"I learned three things about us. About despair. We always want to have what we do not have. We always want to be where we are not. We always want to be who we are not."

Paris smiled at Blythe.

"You see, even madness has some light," he said.

Blythe was still awed by all of this and was nearly speechless the whole time as Paris in one medium carried on a conversation with Fleming in another medium.

"What would you say to a lover?" he asked with a curious glance at Blythe.

"Here are a thousand kisses tossed as bouquets. Wear them as garlands of remembrance," he replied as if he was recording time with words, which is what words do, where they are the time.

"Why remembrance?"

"Because remembrance is half of love and poetry is its name," Fleming replied who now seemed utterly mesmerized and out of contact. "My love is a remembrance put into act."

Blythe began to twitch. She leaned over to Paris: "I don't understand."

"You don't need to. This is a revelation. And revelations are always scary. But don't worry. He'll come out of it."

Still, the corners of her mouth drooped and fell for the pain could still be remembered even long after she had pretended to forget it. She did not realize how far out Fleming was. It was like a non-drug induced quasi-meditative trance; his eyes were clear; his bearing sharp; his face a portrait of repose.

"Did you learn of divine things?" After a pause, Fleming spoke:

"Yes. I learned when one sees beyond sight, hears beyond hearing, he has entered the temple for God is closer to you than you are to yourself. Look within and you will find the temple. Love is the divine dancing."

By now Paris was wondering and Blythe was entranced by Fleming's firm yet utterly calm voice.

"Some laugh and in their intense cerebral demands, miss the point. Some pray and in their sincere intense piety, miss the point. For words are a thousand ways to the divine, but in the presence of the divine, they evaporate as illusions."

And before they knew it, *they* were out of time. Their eyes fixed on his every word as if in a session of self-hypnosis.

"And you ask 'what is life?' Life is all the faces you are birth after birth."

As the two of them sat there entranced, there was a relaxed breathing, an indescribable calm, a quiet ecstasy, a reminder that through the plethora of the follies, there could be seen, if one was sharp enough, the all that was there blurred by the agitated and tangled snares of the mind.

"Life is full of hurry and waste. The best we see is but a minute drop in an ocean of sorrows. And you are what you seek for that is where your desire rests. You are what you seek. Communion is relation lit by the touch of love. It is best for love in the light. But your night may have a light of its own."

Paris could not restrain himself from asking about beauty, since he was partial to aesthetics.

"Beauty is all that you adore with your heart and blood and soul. Beauty is best in the skin. It is charming as a queen bee and treacherous as a siren. All that beauty is, is a brief coloring of dreams that history records and helps erase."

At that moment, his words ceased and there was another snapping sound like the cracking of vertebrae. They waited and his eyes opened again and he sat back, fully exhausted. Paris spoke venturously:

"Fleming?"

"Yes?"

"Was that a flashback?"

"I think so. Almost hypnotic."

"Almost?" said Blythe. "Do you recall what you've been saying to us all this time?"

"Yes. I know it full well."

"You were conscious of it?"

"Yes. But not in the way you think."

"In what way then?" asked Paris, pulling his chair closer.

"It was like an opening where I realized all that was infinite; the roses, the clouds, the sun, you and Blythe and this bed, this city: everything shone in silver and blue. Everything was there and not there. It is hard to describe…"

"No, please go on," urged Blythe, her face absorbed.

"You come upon a plain or a field of wheat that is waving in the wind and you behold all that is, in a breath of divinity. It is a panorama of openings, of somehow awakening and to realize you are no longer there and that opens everything. We always return to poetry, every one of us. When the dust lights, we become poets inspite of. That is when you see all this, all this infinity. When all our speeches are over, poetry remains with awe, wonder, gratitude. We are poets until the end. That is the music that lasts, for that is the music that opens. Poetry animates the world with soul."

Blythe and Paris were shocked to hear all they had heard. Was this Fleming? Old beer-fart Fleming? Was he that far out that he was a satellite of another country? Their ears refused the testimony as it was based on hearsay. Yet they could not deny what had been said; they both heard it. And neither was drunk or drugged with the usual perfumes of seduction or the plumes of science fiction. Here was a satirist off on a trip; clever, cunning, slap-happily ribald, ingeniously sarcastic with the aplomb of seasoned assurance. Here he was on a drugless trip. Paris frowned. His lips dropped and his brows knitted. Paris and Blythe knew something drastic had caused Fleming to stop being Fleming.

"Is this the Fleming who enchanted the maids of Erehwon?" waxed Paris with conceited rhetoric.

"Not quite," replied Fleming, almost shyly.

"What goes? I don't understand."

"Understand what?"

"You. The changes."

"The changes? Everyone changes. They just can't imagine themselves changed. That is a law of life, a book of changes."

Paris gave him a skeptical glower.

"Honest," pleaded Fleming.

"Is this the same man we know?" Paris asked Blythe.

"It is hard to recognize metamorphosis. Absence, divergence, disguise carves into the tree of life. We expect things to be like they were. But life flows and goes. Bridges are always farewells as the waters flow beneath. Maybe he *has* changed."

Paris gave her a skeptical glower.

"Maybe he *has*," she said with a shrug.

"What's come over you," Paris said.

"Nothing. Nothing at all."

Paris shook his head at Fleming's words; it was all too unconvincing.

"Tell me, how can I experience what you have experienced?" he asked.

"By struggling to realize the divine."

"How?" asked Blythe.

"By closing your eyes and watching your feet. They are pointers that keep you informed of what directions meaning may take. If you watch long enough, you will see where you are going and what you mean."

"Be clear, Fleming. I don't understand. That is too vague," insisted Paris who held his unlit pipe in his teeth.

"Just watch yourself. How everything affects you and you will know where you are. You will notice the tugs here, the tiny pains there, and you will begin to know yourself."

Paris was puzzled; he did not know exactly what he meant.

"What exactly is meant by all that?"

"Just what I said. And then every sleep becomes awakening. And once you know yourself, you can begin to deal with yourself after you have accepted yourself."

Paris was still puzzled. He gave Blythe an inquisitive glance.

"He means…self-knowledge is a gift. Only in that way can you become aware of who you are."

Paris took a puff on his pipe, thinking.

"All right. That sounds good. But the experience is what I am after. You were not speaking an ordinary language awhile back. Why is that?"

"A shift in consciousness level, merely. I was unfolding myself. Like when you said Fleming had stopped being Fleming. Same difference."

"You speak with the words of silence."

Paris was skeptical although he thought it was possible that such phenomena can and do exist. He thought it was a joke, all this nonsense about different selves perhaps because he was not a believer in that radical of a change, that a person can change his perception and see the world and his relation to that world differently. Everything began and ended with perception; the brain has that power. There was a heavy hesitation concerning all that since experiments with brain impulses and waves became irrelevant at least if one was to keep 'himself' despite the flux that constituted the eternal flow of the river of life. And with this hesitation, Paris' skepticism became an intellectually-rationalized mask.

"Well, I'm going out for awhile. You wanna come along?"

"Not right now." Blythe decided to stay and talk to Fleming who had reclined himself on the bed and wiggled his toes in a mild Parisian breeze. Paris left, saying he would be back soon and the two sat there, viewing one another in a different light, one that at once united them in such a way as to allow their past differences to assume a secondary importance. They sat there awhile very much in tune with one another. It was talking with an old love one that had yellowed within the sheets of memory.

"I see you've changed," she said sardonically.

His smile was wide.

"We are subject to change without notice," he replied. There was something about her that yet fascinated him. And her face was a mirror of memories of scenes, of times, sunny afternoons, snow-bound fireside evenings, fishing, swimming, and singing old songs. The past was a desert of bones that dried in the sun, were picked, transplanted, and blown away in the finely-spun dust of newly-concentrated memory. And he thought of the past and felt an impulse to weep, for it was easy to weep for the passing of loves in the world. He thought of what Heraclitus of Ephesus had said centuries before that no one steps twice in the same river. The jaws that time moved did not care who was eaten; the dead made a rich soil for future generations. And a feeling came over him as he laid there that everything lovely perishes. But to say that was not true, was to misunderstand life itself. And he felt a sacred sympathy, a rare moment, with everything, everything in the world. He had never felt that way before. It was true that everything lived to perish but it was also true that it was possible, in a sense, to perish to live and realize that things have a way of returning though seldom in the same way, to emerge as a diamond in a sandy beach full of pebbles whereas it had been reckoned as fools' gold before. It had something to do with the angles of incidence and refraction, how the light struck a face or a destiny.

Blythe appeared in a new light for he had changed his perception of her. She was not somebody to bed with but a person to talk with, albeit a growing fetus did not alter his reaction in spite of his renewed perception of her. He simply pretended the child was not his; the only way to do this was by massive denial, although it became, as the conversation proceded, less crucial to do so.

"Sometimes that is true. We change without notice. But sometimes we notice it. And we can watch ourselves and still be ourselves watching. Sometimes. I watched the ugliness enough, I got sick of it. And puked at myself. And wondered what was the matter."

"What was the matter?"

"Too many things to describe."

"Like what?"

"The need to be a political storm trooper. I'm still active, mind you. But not in the way I was. Speeches are fine but it became a game. And I would be in demand to perform. All the slogans and causes. And pretty soon I felt my blood grow cold. It was like a stage and I would parrot slogans and things. And then I asked myself one night if it was really what I thought or how I felt. It is difficult to step out of the limelight.

Fame is an enchantress who sings a most beautiful music. And so I sang and sang. And there was nothing wrong with doing what I was doing. But somehow we get swept up with things. We think we are exceptional and won't be. But we do. Like crabs we go out when the tide goes out, and come in when the tide comes in. There are always some crabs that don't. We try to be rugged individuals. We do. It's an honest job. But even when you do, you get swept along. You realize you're not hot stuff. Not as hot as you thought or imagined. And you entertain a hundred possibilities for your life. You can be all and everything to everybody. The world is your oyster. But wisdom knows better. But then you realize that, too, was all fantasy, maybe to relieve tension, maybe to whittle away the sticks of time. And then possibility, who is another charming seducer, becomes a cracked mirror. You realize time's wine oozes, drop by drop. And all the fussing, bitching, weeping, and complaining doesn't get you anywhere. You have to fight and muscle your way to gain a glimpse of passing beauty in this world. And have a moment's peace for a fine Napa Valley wine. Then you know what it means to take a stand, to stick where you are and feel the soil wet down deep. You realize your limits and what is more, you understand yourself enough to accept them gradually. And you find, like Göethe, that all is not a parade of sorrows which is a bed for self-pity but that strength is derived from energy concentrated with an abiding awareness and an appreciation of all that lies outside that concentration. Oh, I suppose I could have been in the limelight for a longer time but it is a most interesting thing, Fleming, is that we are always searching, we restless spirits, nature's kin, for something somewhere. And it is a wise day when you realize that your search begins in you and arrives in an affirmation of our common humanity. We are searching for a peace within as well. This takes place in fight, in action, in surmounting obstacles, of boxing our way to a knockout decision. And we find that often the one we envy, envies us. It's all a matter of perspective. Everybody's field just *looks* greener and so we want to make it ours. But there is an end to that rainbow and few pots of gold at the end of it. If we are lucky, we survive our pessimism and fatalism as do the sun and moon."

Her voice ceased like an oracle ending. And there was a moment of quiet between them, a bond, however invisible, still strong in its closeness, in its soothing, solitudinous ways. The words pointed to no-need-for-words. And he became aware that he felt very close to her and he wondered what turned love sour. He had simply been interested in his own pleasures before. And it dawned on him what it was to love the soul of another. In fact, it was a staggeringly simple fact to realize that here was another living, breathing human being for whom he began to care. He used to belittle her and outrage her with his drunkenness and cut beer farts with abandon. Now everything seemed different and he felt a sympathy akin to compassion. Here was this pregnant woman who elicited contempt when she had told him he was the father of her unborn child.

He reached out and touched her face. Her cheeks were soft and warm and lovely. And there was a radiant warmth that touched him deeply in his heart. He had momentarily forgotten all about himself and his arms encircled her spontaneously. And he witnessed in himself something that might be termed the miraculous and that was to feel the warmth and the steady beating of heart on heart. Three hearts were there and it was like an orchestra, each instrument playing out of discords, straining for the harmony beyond the need of words. Blood surging and hearts pumping converged in a steady refrain that was human life itself and in their blending together, there was a form of compassion for you never truly know anyone until you've reached beyond your own skin and touched them. Touch is the poetry of act and there was a bond of sympathy between them; it seemed they had grown old together beneath the stress of growth itself. And he felt a forgetfulness toward Joan. In fact, for the moment Joan did not even exist and he saw a tear make its way down her cheek even though a smile was on her lips. His eyes began to water, too. Soon her lips were pressed to his and he did not understand what he was doing. He simply could not understand his own actions. They made no sense. Movement was now his game.

Contrary to his resolutions and expectations, he was still very much attracted to her. He had given up on her for lack of novelty but time seemed to have a way of making even repetition novel. Kiss after kiss found Fleming was out of time and mind. And suddenly it was summer again in the Lake District. They had thought each had forgotten the other but it was not so. Even though other loves had intervened, their bodies responded to the rhythms of their past. The past had a way of returning, however different. Neither expected anything, especially from one another as familiarity had marred things before. But the familiar is made appealing by absence just as home is treasured by returning. Their travel had taught them much but now it was such a warm feeling to be in one another's arms. It was not especially favorable that time and distance, the enemies of love, should lose but every once in a while, two minds of the same current defeat time and distance and meet one another over again and reopen a past relation that at the time appeared at best abortive. But relations change. And Fleming and Blythe had to get to know one another all over again for they, too, were different although quite obviously the same in many respects. That would come in time and time takes and gives with a sublime indifference. Now all was at the feeling stage, a beginning rebirth that gave them a novel glow.

CHAPTER 17

T he evening was heavy with Parisian breezes and the air was saturated heavily with the pre-autumn humidity. Jocko and Peter sat at an outdoor café table, drinking. Along came several girls from America.

"Hi, may we join you?"

"Sure can, honey," replied Jocko, sizing her up. Seven girls and a mother-counselor sat at the tables while Jocko made an ass of himself by treating them all to drinks, far beyond his monetary means.

"Garçon, come here you French frog," he said under his breath. The waiter at Roul's on the Boulevard St. Michel came over.

"Dix bières," said Jocko, holding up the fingers of both hands. The waiter nodded and went into the bar for the beers.

"Where you from?" he asked.

"Rhode Island," replied a tall blond who gave him a pretty smile.

"Is that where Rhode Island Reds come from," cackled Peter. One of the girls frowned for she thought he had accused them of being communists from Rhode Island.

"Yes," said a chicken farmer, cocksure of her knowledge about different varieties of chicken.

Satisfied with his answer, Jocko just nodded.

"What are you studying," he asked.

There was a titillating laughter that passed over them as the question was asked. Peter and Jocko simply stared at one another in a bewildered sort of way.

"We're studying men," a brunette replied.

"Men?" asked St. Peter incredulously.

"Yes. Men. We want to get pregnant," they said almost in unison.

Jocko's eyes enlarged ten-fold as he glanced at Peter's brows now lifted to the occasion. Jocko could hardly believe his ears.

"You want to get pregnant? What the hell for?"

"I, for one, think it is a wonder that babies even are at all," said Miriam, a lovely lass from Brooklyn who wanted to be a Jewish mom.

"And I, for one, just love the process of making babies," smiled Suzanne, a student at Bradley University in Peoria, Illinois.

"I just think having a man around is the greatest thing in the world," declared Lakesha, a sophomore at the University of Miami.

At first, Jocko practiced massive denial; he could not *really* be hearing what he was hearing. But St. Peter was his witness. Everything he had heard was true. It was not merely his fantasies, not even a projection of his fantasies as he first thought. Their words captivated him. He could not believe their attitudes.

"You actually like men?" queried Peter.

"Boy, do I," replied Suzanne. Peter looked at Jocko and Jocko looked at Peter.

"This is truly unbelievable," said Peter as he snapped his fingers in the direction of the waiter. The waiter nodded and soon brought them a tray of ice-cold beers. They sat and drank and talked as the evening cast a faint pink glow from the western sky. Jocko and Peter were ready. It was going to be easy to meet one of these bonnie lassies and live to tell a hair-raising tale. They drank and drank. Peter got to know Miriam quite well and began to get a bit fresh when she slapped his hand in a friendly but warningly way. Miriam's legs were well-proportioned although somewhat stocky; her breasts were full; her eyes were lively and alert. Jocko got to know Suzanne well in the course of the evening and wished to spend the evening in a course of his own making. Lakesha was on the slender side;

she wanted to be an architect and she was quite concerned with space. In fact, she was pretty well spaced out during the chat. Lakesha had designs on Jocko, though he had not realized it as yet.

"How many kids would you want?" asked Peter. Miriam smiled a warm smile and almost spread her legs wide as she replied, "As many as…I can have."

Peter was aroused by all this and suddenly he found himself desiring to fulfill her wishes. The public was not private enough.

Jocko felt the same as he got to know both Suzanne and Lakesha. Suzanne gave him their address and before the two knew what was happening, all of them had left. Jocko and Peter again looked at one another in consternation and amazement. Had they been taken these past two or three hours? It seemed so. In four tables stood nearly forty empty beer glasses and the water came out of the bar and plopped a carefully calculated tab on the table. Again Jocko and Peter gave one another long gazes. The tab amounted to over one hundred and twenty francs. Jocko gulped as he read the bill.

"I have only ten francs and that's to last for the next two nights."

"I have only five francs. I spent the others on those paltry Continental breakfasts. Not enough food for a pigeon on a diet! Really, coffee and rolls. This place has already given me dysentery besides."

"And I wanted to go to Pig Alley," mused St. Peter who wanted to try the French women on for size.

"On fifteen francs? Boy, are you a dreamer!" Jocko exclaimed with an amused smile. Still Peter was undaunted.

"There might be some cheap ones."

"Not likely. You'd die of the rot."

Peter did not reply. They merely eyed one another with problematic glances, pausing to stare now and then at the empty glasses and remember the now disgusting transient talk.

"Where's the waiter?"

Peter turned around. The waiter was talking to the bartender at the far end of the bar. Occasionally he glanced to see where Jocko and Peter were.

"He's talking right now. To the bartender."

"You ready?" asked Jocko.

"For what?" replied Peter as if taken by surprise.

"To make a run for it."

"You mean…leave without paying? That's stealing," said Peter in a gruff voice almost enticed by the seductive plot.

"Do you want to wash dishes for the frogs?"

"No."

"Then we run. We can outrun him. Okay, what's he doing?"

Again Peter turned. The waiter was staring at them.

"But it's stealing. We were just foolish. It is not ethical."

Jocko gave him a contemptuous stare that seemed to burn a hole in Peter's face.

"That is not the point. Ethics is a moot question. Now, listen I want you to run with me. Neither of us is going to be doing dishes. The girls confused us with their lies. It's a human error. Everyone makes mistakes. That is a part of being human, right? So you undo them, okay?"

"No."

"Let's run then," he replied. Peter frowned. It was not in him to be a thief; he was surprised by his own inclination toward Jocko's exciting lure. But just then the waiter appeared and smiled.

"He wants to know if we want more drinks."

"No," replied Jocko. The waiter bowed briefly and left.

"Wait until he gets to the far end and then get up and run. Once around the corner we'll split. You go down one side of the street and I'll go down the other."

Their bodies tensed as they waited for the waiter to resume his routine.

At a signal, they sprang from the café chairs and dashed around the corner of Raoul's. The waiter dashed after them. Around they went. By looking back, Peter ran into a cart of cocoanuts; the irate seller ran after him screaming obscenities. The waiter was a fine runner on short sprints but he was no match for them. The cocoanut seller swore and, shaking his head and fist, returned to his overturned cocoanut cart. The waiter too left them to wander the darkened back streets of the Latin Quarter. Peter crossed to Jocko's side of the street and they laughed and caught their breath.

"That's cocoanuts for you," said Jocko. Peter was embarrassed but proud of himself. They wandered back toward the Boulevard St. Michel and watched the tourists and native French parade by. Jocko was itching for excitement just as Peter longed for rest. Just then two students walked by with STANFORD in block letters on their T-shirts. They were both on the lean and skinny side and Jocko felt contempt for weaklings perhaps because he had once been overly skinny himself. In any case, Peter was stimulated to action as well. They followed the Stanford students for several blocks until they found them in a dark alley lit only by the hallucinogenic colors of mysterious lions, shaved eagles and humans who ate one another for planetary peace as part of the sideshows of reality outside the main tent. Jocko invoked the spirit of his own school just as kamikaze pilots invoked the Emperor of Japan before bombing Pearl Harbor. In the half-dim alley Jocko shoved the dark-haired Stanford student.

"What is this?" the student asked.

"I think Stanford sucks," said Jocko in adolescent fashion.

"You do, eh?" remarked the taller one.

"That's right. Your admission procedures smell like dead halibut."

"What is this? A vaudeville act?"

"It's called our night out, you bastards."

The two Stanford students looked at one another bewildered. Nothing as strange as this had happened since Princeton went coed.

"College night out?"

"Hell yes. He's a minister and I'm a teamster. You wanna see my union card?"

The Stanford men appeared disgusted. The situation was leaving a sour taste in the mouth like the laxative called Milk of Magnesia.

"Not particularly. What is your damn beef?"

"I always like to beat dead horses."

"Yeah, and I have axes to grind." The Stanford men were utterly astonished.

"What's wrong with Stanford's admissions procedures?"

"Well, your admission standards are too high," admitted Peter.

"That's just the university. Nothing we can do about it."

"I guess not."

"Sorry we bothered you. Good luck in your studies."

Then Peter and Jocko walked away in the opposite direction to luxuriate in the warmth of a hot bath in their hotel room.

CHAPTER 18

"Change is the nursery of musicke, joy, life, and eternity."
—John Donne, D.D.

I t had been well over a month since they had been together. Much change had happened to them as the quiet stream of life passed on, even though they had seemingly gone their separate ways. Warm were their bodies beneath the covers and memories of their past times flitted through the ether of nostalgia that floated above them in a fantastic iridescent blue. They noticed how each had changed. Life and time had a way of altering landscapes, especially those of the mind. It was as if it was a whole new play, each playing different parts and becoming somehow plastic with respect to their real selves.

Amazing how things changed. And it made a body wonder what it was all about. You fell asleep awhile or went away from yourself on a new adventure and before you knew it, there was no familiar rug to lie on. And you only noticed how long you had been asleep by awakening yourself from the slumber of absence. For absence, very often, snuffs out love. But here, for once, paths crossed a second time. They had come together as if by a divining rod which showed them the deep wells that were often missed the first time around. They had aged in the yellowing pages of personal biography. The group experience had shown them the suffering of others and had made them feel lucky and fortunate to have been so well off. They had grown by passing through hell and found out that hell is mostly self-created.

"You like the night?" he asked. She turned to him and it caught a glimmer from the city streets below.

"The night? Yes, I like the night too. Night and day mean something when you are with your love. They do. It's as if...love makes night and day...one."

She kissed him tenderly. Nothing in this world is so lovely as to be in the arms of your love, he thought. His hands rolled over her smooth flesh and such flesh made its frailty all the more lovely, all the more divine. The human body was a divine image even if only in intention, if not in fact. The sound of her breathing made him grow to love her all the more. Yet this urgency, this majestic thought, was tempered by a knowledge that this passing poetry that stretched across the sands was, at moments, one of the most precarious and ecstatic feelings a person could exprience. And it was a realization that the ugly as well as the beautiful were poems on which time wrote the lines. And he felt tears come into his eyes. It was all too fast, too fleeting, too lovely. Then he truly understood why people wrote sonnets and symphonies, cantatas and odes. This way they could carve on brass, fading memories, and genetics a testimony to their folly, to their half-crazy and absurd notion that something was beautiful and redeeming about life that could be meaningful despite the omnipresence of despair itself.

She noticed the sniffles.

"What is it, Fleming?"

"What is what?"

"You have a cold? Here let me get close and warm you," she said as she snuggled closer in his arms.

"No. Not a cold. Just thoughts."

"About what?"

"Things words have no words for."

This caused her to lean on her elbow and ponder him in the darkness, his naked self.

"Tell me about them."

"They are just thoughts."

"I don't care. Thoughts can be villains. But yours are beautiful. Now tell me what you're thinking."

He breathed a heavy sigh. He was not prepared to go into it but decided to go ahead.

"I was just thinking how lovely it is to be with you, to hear you breathing, your heartbeat, this all sounds so childish I know, but we are lucky even for a moment, even for the fleeting dream reality plays for us, and how thankful I know you. That is what I am trying to say."

He could now see a smile on her face.

"You thoughts *are* beautiful," she said and she kissed him with all the urgency her passion allowed.

"Fleming, thank you. You have opened my eyes. Through layers we must penetrate sometimes to arrive at where the self is truest, where the heart is warmest," she whispered.

Time passed and they listened to the grinding gears of trucks below. Far off, the faint chant of trains could be heard. Next door, a couple were arguing. A vase crashed against the wall and shattered. Blythe leaned on her elbow again.

"Wonder why they argue."

"I don't know. Maybe they're under cross-examination."

"Maybe," she chuckled. "Come back and lie next to me, Fleming. There. That's more like it."

Suddenly they heard a banging on their door. Fleming got out of bed and put on his pants. He listened closely.

"Where is the Emperor Fleming keeper of the Roman peace?" shouted one.

"And where's his wench? We want to drench a wench!" shouted another. They banged even louder. Fleming quickly grabbed an ironing board from the wall and poised it for a swing. Unlocking the door, he stood back, his muscles flexed, taut, and poised to blast whoever it was in the hall. The door swung open and the two visitors charged in like bulls. Sparky and Ev were drunk and before they knew what happened, Fleming swung the ironing board into their faces. They staggered backward and fell into blobs on the floor outside.

"You bastards, what are you doing? Well, if it isn't Sparky. Members of the press corps, eh? We'll iron things out now!" he cried as he swung again, hitting Sparky on the head. Ev was too heavy to get up readily, but when he did Fleming hit him again. Fleming was really mad.

"Stop! Stop!" cried Sparky. "It's me, Fleming."

"What right have you to invade my privacy?" he demanded, his brows knit in anger.

"We were just playing a joke. Just kidding. Honest."

"Yeah. We heard you were here."

"You did, eh? Tell me quick before I swing again," he said, raising the board over his head.

"No one told us."

"You lie!" Fleming yelled as he raised the board higher with ever more determination to swing it on their heads.

"No one. We found your name on the register. Honest. Down in the office."

Then Fleming remembered he had signed the hotel register. Down came the board and he leaned on it.

"Now beat it. This is my affair," he said.

"We just wanted some fun," bellowed Ev.

"Well, you've had your fun. Paris is full of fun. Now go out and enjoy it."

"We want to say hello to Blythe," said Sparky, tipping his hat.

"Say hello some other time. Now beat it," ordered Fleming.

"Hello Blythe," Sparky shouted in spite of Fleming's orders.

Blythe came to the door in her nightgown. To her, it was a party.

Exasperated, Fleming stood there like a man on his honeymoon who has just discovered his wife is locked in a seventeenth century chastity belt. Blythe invited them in and put on water for tea.

"What're you boys out doing? Catting around?" she said with a sensuous smile afforded by women in front of horny men.

"Why yes. Looking for some action," said Sparky.

Ev plopped himself on the sofa that lurched and creaked under his immense weight.

"Yeah. Lookin' for some action," echoed Everette Lardace. That prompted Fleming's saracasm

"Well, I'll tell 'ya something, Ev. The woman that gets you in action is gonna have a helluva man on her hands," he said.

Ev thought it was a compliment and thanked him with a smile. Sparky grinned and Blythe gave Fleming a cross look.

"Found any women yet?" Fleming asked as he sat on the bed with a sigh. Sparky privately thought Fleming some kind of Casanova and kept winking at him.

"No. Not yet. But I see you have, eh Fleming?" he said, poking Ev and winking at Fleming across the room. Fleming shot him a contemptuous glance.

"What's wrong? You got a fly in your eye?" Sparky tried to feign seriousness even though he was embarrassed.

"No. No. Just a nervous twitch."

"I thought something was wrong. Either that or you're going queer on me, Sparky."

Sparky was red with embarrassment. Ev could not help laughing. Blythe made the tea and served it.

"Is this a Japanese tea ceremony?"

"No. No. It's not that spiritual. Just a tea party French style," Blythe assured them.

They sat and drank tea until Ev's kidneys were ready to release the tea in another form. They drank until it was time to go and they left, leaving Fleming and Blythe alone.

"I'm glad that's over. Maybe they can go pester someone else. Men without women is really a search for heaven," he remarked casually as he stared at her looking out the window over the streets below. Dusk was fading into night. She had high heels on and her slender legs stimulated him. It was a way she turned her ankle that utterly fascinated him.

"Women without men. Now that is hell. Oh yes, you like even love your own but then you want something else, the meaning of earth, and zap, you're on with the poetry of earth. Men and women in war and peace."

He moved to her side and gazed at the lights of Paris.

"The lights are beautiful, aren't they?" he said.

"Yes," she replied, "They come out and then go back like day and night. Then lights out. The party's over. The music ceases and words blow away with the wind. That is what it is like sometimes. Just by turning on."

"You become more beautiful the more I hear the message between the words. But we are young. Just students. Feeling the blood flow vigorously through our youth. Dreamers destined to dream on. Foolish like old men who dream."

"You know, you turn me on. Every sound is an immortal leaf that falls. We've learned a lot just sounding the sounds not heard. That is education. Time to live, not kill," she said as they kissed with a silent strength beneath each taut muscle. The night was spent in loving surrender to arms.

CHAPTER 19

All afternoon her cheeks were suns and roses. Her gait was the poetry of motion; her hips, signatures on the wind; her deeds, a will of trust. Gradually, they came to share many beautiful moments and proximity kept them prone together for long times beneath the dances of sun and moon. And their togetherness flowed along like a current that took them to the high tide and with one gigantic swoosh they were in, or rather Paris was sucked into a current that meandered with all the unreliability of a game-playing river. The altar of sacrifice was his expectations for they were like volleyball, easy prey for a spike with the fist. And he knew a time would be reached when the river of togetherness would no longer meander but shift to a series of crag-filled rapids that would endeavor to shatter any bark they may have been on.

From the first, Paris knew of Enid's inclinations as they shopped this fine spring-like afternoon beneath the skies of Paris. He knew of Ted in the armed forces overseas and that he would come to see his love before long. In the interim, the unreality of Ted's presence was more and more a substitute for a delusion as to her needs concerning him. Much had happened in the long and gradual association of being together that had helped Paris grow more and more toward Enid. Likewise, she grew toward him but in words only and words unsupported by two feet are as fleeting and unresponsive as air that flows down valleys to the sea. She had not intended anything to grow between them but human touch sometimes attaches and bingo, a new game is born.

Only weeks before, they had been traveling together through Wales and had assumed a pose of husband and wife to secure a bed and breakfast place in Cardiff. And as night is a form of silence, much was spoken in the night. From cover to cover, the night gave way to explorations of the body. It was convenience, association, and habit that allowed their mattress party to assume bed and breakfast proportions, for it was easy for one relationship to feed on another. A quick bounce of the eye from object to object does not produce concentration and eyelid penetration. Instead, the night has a way of making long pain pleasurable and Enid, after many months of soul-searching finally allowed her legs to spread from ear to ear and take on the ghost of her lover who was now none other than Paris Brandon. All had been agreed upon previously. He felt like an animal cookie about to be devoured; he could not feel the lion in his loins for he knew it was all a hoax and that when the light of day arrived again, it would be a night-time for him. There could be no future between them for Ted was the love of her life. To her life, she added the delusion that Ted and Ted only was the source of her happiness which made her love an offense to Paris for Paris saw quickly through the shifting clouds of pretense that made a mockery of the swift changes of color and mood that checkered her golden cheeks. However strong his grasp of her pretence, Paris had become more attracted to her than he actually thought and realized it only as the pain began. For her part, Enid was quick to bounce off people and events due to her contracted focus of attention, much like a hyperactive child. In that respect, her feelings for Ted were more vow than wow. Such a contracted focus of attention allowed her the dual advantages of not having to think or muse too heavily on any one person or event and also as a defense against becoming emotionally involved. The latter was self-defeating since her emotion far outran her hyperactive, contracted attention. Whereas Paris tended to be philosophical or meditative about life, Enid was far too easily distracted to concentrate on most things with a similar depth or intensity. Paris' very virtues became vices; her very vices became virtues for defenses, by way of hyperactivity, were already built in.

So they shopped for clothes to wear throughout winter though autumn was only beginning. The hurt lurked just beneath the skin even though on the surface all was gay and joyous. After the purchase of sweaters and skirts, they returned to her place for her to try on her newest fashions. She stood before the mirror in her slip as she held a skirt to her waist.

"You like it?"

"Of course. Anything looks good on you," he replied gently. Paris had become too gentle to the point of self-effacement and ransacked the tomes of philosophy for a philosophy to rationalize his behavior in previous weeks. Sexual life had made her more relaxed as well as audacious; gone were the days of her excessive naiveté; gone were the inhibitions justified by a private code of Manu; gone were the guilt feelings of a private bedside theology. She could open herself to Ted as never before, having lost her virginity to the philosophy student Paris who stoically sat on the bed and admired her with an abandon unbecoming a philosopher.

"This sweater looks nice. Red is my favorite color, Paris. Do you like it?"

"Because it is a part of you, how can I not like it?"

She smiled at him in the mirror.

"You have the kindest words to say." Kindness can be cruel, he thought to himself, especially to those who feel they must always act kind no matter what. Life was often cruel and kindness was an exception. So it was with the best intentions, however noble. There was also such a thing as being kind to oneself, especially if always being kind to others had become a form of cruelty to oneself. Loss of self-respect was not justified by philosophy. It was necessary to remain a self and to affirm the courage to be a self. And that was precisely the problem. Paris had been absorbed to the point that Paris was gone, had dried up and blown away. And that, whether he knew it or not, was a despairing crisis in his life. Abuse, twice permitted, knows no bounds. It repeats hell and erases heaven. Weeds grow where gardens once flourished and the earth rots with famine and death in the tiny worlds that surround the everyday self.

And so it was with Paris. He was no longer able to travel in his own sphere; instead, the gravity of the situation was that he no longer did his thing. Paris was no longer his own man. A puppet on a string and Enid could play with his mind with sweet bonbons here and clandestine requests there. If Enid was deluded about Ted, Paris was deluded about Enid. Illusion fosters illusion and there is no end to the sorrows of a changing face. And so he began to sink into the quicksand of himself; the more he tried to wiggle his way out, the more he sank. The self and its excessive needs and demands is redeemable only by a loosening of self-demands on the self. By letting go, it redeems itself and sees that quicksands are self-created hells.

Paris had not yet arrived at that station in life where a man learns to live his own life through himself and not through another exclusively. He possessed much knowledge but had yet to mature into wisdom. And being a plaything of someone else was not wise. It only consumed him until there was nothing there. There are some who are afforded pleasure by prolonged pain. Paris was not a masochist; he was an idealist enclosed by his own ideals, the result of which appeared to the undiscerning eye to be masochistic behavior merely. It was, in truth, a struggle to be a self in the face of all that would eventually undermine him. And the impulses toward self-affirmation and self-denial operated in him most strongly. He despised the excesses of both polar opposites but still felt strongly in both directions. If justice were done, the justice would not balance for self-denial was the side to which the scales tipped. It was to this side the gentle philosophy student leaned. What he had to learn was that fickle women, those who continually play junior miss games, are not persuaded by philosophy. Their minds do not care to study epistemology or ontology in the throes of passion. It was difficult to be a Chinese sage or an Aristotle with the fleshly odors of a mistress-paramour like Madame du Pompadour perfuming the air. Enid did all she could to attract and hold onto him while at the same time denying much to him. She was a psychological tease. Instead of bringing him to the point of orgasm and cutting him off, she would bring his mind to near completion then bind it with contradictions and behavioral paradoxes. It was an art that required an ability to play games out of two sides of her mouth; she was Janus-faced with divided attention that was manipulated by the capacious and passing whims of physical desires. How could a capricious soul in an even more capricious cosmos ever satisfy anyone? This was a question he often asked himself and could find no answer. He was a convenience, a victim of time and proximity and, as his mind was so distracted, he could think of and hope for nothing else. He ceased to live fully in the present and its fulfillments. Instead, he could only hope that she might change. But that was a dead-end street. To hope or expect another to change for or against, reveals the extent to which he had become addicted to that change. It is only a trap, a self-delusion that holds out no future and no promises for anything real, a sham that uses words unsupported by actions. Self-delusion is the folly of making oneself the sole source of personal happiness. It is not only a burden on others but a blind alley of the self. This was the quandary in which Paris Brandon had trapped himself. His knowledge of philosophy would have to shift from analyzing propositions to ethics. One of these days he would come upon the volumes of Spinoza. What he needed was a more self-affirming ethic added to the tendency of a self-effacing ethic of Jesus unless one was a money-changer. But for the moment at least he walked as if in a daze, a cloud of unknowing, a child of the darkness. He read about self-reliance in Emerson's *Essay* and especially these lines from Spinoza's *Ethics*:

> *Once a man is governed by his emotions, he is*
> *no longer master of his own house, but is,*
> *instead, mastered by fortune in whose power he is.*

Still, the road to his self was steep and most difficult and it was blinding to see the truth of oneself mapped on the horizons of one's life and mind.

She tried on more clothes and admired them in the mirror.

"This skirt is nice."

He nodded vaguely.

"All your clothes are nice," he added.

She took off all her clothes and stood naked in the light. Her body was shapely, her lips rich and full, her bosom somewhat small but inviting. She asked for some wine and the steward brought it and left. Paris was on fire. His life was a doctrine of desires. They drank the wine as he strummed softly on the guitar and gazed at the far-reaching lights of Paris below. It had been a good day full of sunshine yet there was agony written on his heart. Ted would be coming in a few weeks and Paris felt anxiety about a relation he had tried so long to foster. He could only feel futility and nothingness that secreted itself from the marrow of his bones. He was unhappy when most happy. He had lost the art of relating and saw himself as an appendage to her. And that was a source of psychic pain.

"Toast to Paris and the joys of life," she said with her glass wine. Paris smiled and toasted.

"To impermanence, the law of life," he replied with an almost cynical turn of the mouth. She looked puzzled.

"Paris, is anything wrong?"

"Oh, no, my dear. Nothing is wrong. Only thinking tells us so."

Perplexed, she toasted but only half-heartedly.

"Is something wrong," she asked again. Paris held the wine in hand and stared at the floor for a moment or two with a deep sadness on his face.

"Nothing is wrong, just sad."

"About what?" she asked with an intimate innocence with guilt.

"About us."

"You know all about us. From the first you knew…"

"Yes, I did. A man can dream, can't he?" he protested.

"Yes, he can."

"I mean…sometimes a dream is all we are…or can have."

Enid gave him a puzzled stare.

"You know, I agree about dreams. The problem is they're awfully hard to live in. They keep blowing up in your face. Dreams do. They blow up. And that is why they aren't reliable. You can't bank on them. They just are not worth it. They lead to lamentations."

Paris rolled his thumb over the guitar strings. Such conversations hurt.

"You know how I feel about you. This whole time is not just a jest. A jest may not be just. Believe me. And the times we have shared, they mean nothing to you?"

"Of course they do. They always will…"

"Don't say 'always'…it's phony. We don't know what 'always' means. It is one of the tricks words play on us and make us dream paradises of words that exist only when formed. I mean 'always' doesn't mean much when you hurt someone with it."

Enid had tears in her eyes. It was upsetting to talk about anything painful. There was enough pain without cementing it with words. She came and curled into his arms.

"There are others. I hate to admit it. But there are, Paris. And as much as it hurts, you must realize that too. But remember outside of Ted, you're the one I love."

Paris heaved a heavy sigh.

"Is that all we do? Just keep changing partners? And pass like butterflies from one dream to another? One love to another? One body to another? Is that all? If that is all, then we must change…must metamorphosize like insects that crawl on one another! Is that all we do is to pass from one god to another and pledge our capricious allegiances to another god that makes signatures with blood only?"

"I don't know. It seems that we do. That is why it is hard sometimes to tell the dream from the reality. They are parts of the same bones…and disease and death make joy worth the living…"

At that she curled into him and muffled her sobs. Paris hugged her close and gazed at her sleek legs and shapely thighs and at the night light that blinked on and off next door. He would soon snuggle next to her in bed and together they would sleep and make it through the night. It had been a long day and night was a tender caress and a tear that wound its way down over a smile.

CHAPTER 20

Notre Dame Cathedral cut a sharp figure in the early morning mists that enshrouded her flying buttresses and noble gothic spires that soared heavenward only to disappear in the clouds. They opened the door and the spacious aisles and opulent stained glasses greeted them with a spectrum of shadows and colors that words felt inadequate to describe. Far ahead lay the altar and, as they spoke low, each was amazed at the echo of his own voice. They sat for awhile and talked, each awed by the enormous and overwhelming silence of the cathedral. It was almost silent enough to hear the silence and all that a presence could suggest. The walls were witnesses to centuries. Somehow everything was bigger than they were and the long corridors of history assured them of previous wars and truces that the healer, time, had passed on for the changing present. They had come a long way, all of them, since change is a continuing death-womb that gives life to all. The games life plays are learning experiences merely; if wisdom matches learning, perhaps a man might outgrow his folly. Paris remarked on the ribbed vaulting he found most appealing; Fleming did not appreciate old buildings as such but did admit there was a certain awe and wonder about the place that appealed to his developing aesthetic sensibilities. They soon wound their way out of the cathedral and strolled along the slow-moving Seine River.

They passed a couple of young boys fishing, their poles arched over the river, as the sun struggled through the window of morning. And old man sat near the place they sat and began to talk to himself. A small boat floated by and across the way several hippies sang to a guitar one played but they could not be heard due to the heavy traffic of cars, trucks, trains, planes, and undergrounds.

Paris lit his pipe and smoked it with a contemplative concern. For his part, Fleming leaned against the concrete and searched the morning skies for a longer visit from the sun.

"It was quieter in the cathedral," Paris remarked.

"Yes, it sure was. It's good to know there's some quiet in the world," replied Fleming.

"You like Paris?"

"Of course. The French know how to live." Fleming smiled.

"Do we?"

"What do you mean?"

"Do we know how to live?"

"No, just death and profits for us."

"No, it's the same for everyone. Living or dead."

"Some just live more vitally. It is boring to live for routine only."

"I agree. It is good when life can be exciting."

There was a long moment of silence when the competing sounds inundated their ears.

"How's Blythe?"

Fleming grinned at him.

"She is fine. So fine. Amazing…"

"Amazing what?"

"How people change. They want their cake and eat it too. Never satisfied with anything. We get spoiled that way. Today the moon, tomorrow the sun and we try to buy all of life. There are things you can't buy even if you tried. But still we demand them. Still we try to buy everything…even in the face of death. To watch them change is to watch the seasons in their turn. And Blythe has returned. It is far out but true."

"You mean she has just like that…returned to her old self?" asked Paris.

"Old selves are only conditioned responses. But the old self is gone. She has changed. Nothing major. But you can see a difference. Just talking to her. You can."

"She has matured?"

"Changed. That's a more mature way of putting it," replied Fleming with a smile.

"Does all look great?"

"In what way?"

"Are you getting back together?"

"Time knows. I do not. It seems one way today, another tomorrow. Women can be like the wind; they change direction often without warning."

"Let's say that confused people change direction because they're all opposing directions that help them go nowhere," commented Paris.

"That's what I mean," declared Fleming with a tone of affirmation, having been understood.

"And what about Enid? Has she stars in her eyes?"

"Enid is fine and…well she's not so fine. Not now anyway."

"What's wrong," asked Fleming with revitalized interest.

"Her boyfriend or fiancé she never made the distinction clear is paying her a visit. Now I go back on the shelf."

Fleming was incredulous as he lit his cigar.

"Back on the shelf?"

"Of course. When a woman is playing games, men are either on or off the shelf. One day you're on, the next day you're off. Now it's my turn to be off since he is first priority."

Fleming sat and stared at the flowing river and how the sun tried to penetrate the clouds and dance a dance of Shiva on the waters of the Seine. Despite differences he felt close to Paris and it grieved him to hear another tale of woe.

"Dogs are kinder sometimes than humans are. Even so-called love can be cruel, especially when it manipulates for power and ego-trips. Our very intelligence sometimes condemns us to mutilate our most cherished ideas, principles, properties and persons. Our best intentions are not always the best. Life has a way of smashing best intentions and carries us over the rocks and rapids anyway. But there is a way of untangling all that," suggested Fleming.

"And what is that?"

"To fight it or to flow with it," he said with a tone of finality.

"You can fight it and cut against the grain and try to flow upstream and still make it. It will be difficult but the struggle is what life is all about. There is much love in conflict and peace is only a lull between conflicts. There is a peace in struggle that makes life worthwhile; without some struggle we could not live. You fight for what you want even if it is painful. A man does not shrink from pain. Life is beautiful even if only because it is damned. And that is why such cruelty is kind for you must be ready to struggle against all odds, including her boyfriend."

There was a long pause as they continued watching the river flow. Paris repacked his pipe and listened thoughtfully.

"You mentioned an alternative to struggling upstream," remarked Paris with an interest that made everything in view quite secondary and out of focus.

"Yes, there is. That way is to flow with the river to wherever it might lead. That means you are not particular about your destination. You just flow. It is not irresponsibility although that might seem to be a motive. That way is to accept the situation without fighting it. So you can accept the change and go on about your business or you can fight it. But if you decide to flow with life do not pretend you do not resent being put back on the shelf for you must get it out even if you must shout or scream or put your fist through your own resentment. After that you can accept the shelves and all the other selves that you are put on or taken off with a personal serenity beyond the power of words to describe. Love unlocks all locks and even if you must hate to love, love still unlocks all locks. Should you be healed, you have to be honest with yourself and with true others. There is no one simple way to do everything. That is an illusion that locks you in. You must be tough as well as tender. There are times to struggle upstream and times to let it carry you where it will. Best to be flexible. Only if you have a certain degree of play will you absorb the natural shocks of life. And the flesh needs play if it is to possess spirit and vitality."

Paris thought long and longer as Fleming stared at the way the river flowed and pondered the way rivers flow and what each does to each river. Barges, he noticed, went upstream while birds floated carefree with the currents. It took all kinds to play with the currents. After a few moments, Fleming asked:

"Do you love her?"

"I don't know. I really don't. For the longest time I was sure I loved her. But being put on and off the shelf can kill the most cherished love. You can only take so much then you can decide to go your own way. But I do love her. She is my dream," Paris said thoughtfully.

"Let me tell you something, my friend. Love makes people unique but at the same time quite common. No one is indispensable. No one. We are all here to serve. And if you become obsessed with someone like Enid, then that uniqueness is only something that enslaves the mind and body. There are too many discoveries in the world for it is filled with infinite variety like grains of sand on the beach…life is restless and like the clouds on a windy day shift and assume a variety of shapes and sizes and life does not wait and neither does the river for it all moves on every second scraping with worn fingers its marks on the tablet time continues to erase…"

Paris relit his pipe that kept going out. Birds floated in front of them, eating effortlessly and the fisherman, although appearing deaf, reacted as if he had heard every word. In a moment, he had moved closer to them and cast in his line. Paris and Fleming regarded him curiously.

"Nice day out, isn't it," he said with a French accent.

"Sure is," replied Fleming, somewhat frustrated at an old man moving in on their conversation.

"Good day for fishing."

"I wouldn't know…"

"Eh?" he said, holding his ear. Fleming spoke louder.

"I wouldn't know. Never fished in Paris before."

Paris cocked his head at the mention of his name.

"Never fished here before, eh? You boys don't know what you're missing. Many nice fish in this river."

"Oh sure. If you fish long enough, your fish might have ears, too," replied the old man whose face was curiously young. Fleming was momentarily puzzled and dismissed it only to have the old man come back at him with an even younger face.

"What is wrong? You don't understand?"

"Understand what?"

"What I am saying."

"No I don't," said Fleming.

"One must fish for those you love. And if you fish long enough, you will catch them. Love's a fish hook, too, you know."

Fleming stared at him with bewilderment and a bit of contempt.

"Look, why don't you go fish somewhere else," he said.

"I will but I haven't yet used all my lines."

"What other lines do you have?"

"The lines that do not die with hate or love, joy or sorrow."

"Which lines are those?" Fleming asked almost timidly now as his curiosity was aroused.

"Not the lines of your changing face," he replied and his voice was no longer that of an old man but of someone young and strong and brave. "But the lines of the poet in you."

Fleming gave a cynical smirk. Here was another quack doctor, he thought.

"Do you always bullshit people?" Fleming asked.

Suddenly the man grabbed his arm and held it firmly and bent down into his face. Through the light whiskers there was a mouth nearly expressionless and eyes that were serene clear pools. Fleming almost froze. The eyes were penetrating, but without a trace of malice or hate.

"This is no bullshit, my friend," said the man in an incredible calm. It was like peering into the calm eye of a hurricane.

"You have lines of the poet in you but you keep erasing them with your dusty passions and lusty self-delusions. Those are the lines I speak of," he said as his hand as quickly left Fleming's arm. The man held his pole and fished. Fleming was hypnotized. He was under a spell. He could not believe he was sitting next to Paris for he felt as if he was all alone and a shudder passed through him.

"How do you know all this?"

"There are ways of knowing that have yet to be discovered."

Still Fleming dismissed him as an irrational old man unworthy of his attention. And yet his attention was fixed on him.

"If you're so smart, what does it mean to be a poet?" asked Fleming.

"There's nothing to it. There are lines you never thought were there." He then turned to him and continued: "You can become the poem in yourself and all your soul to dance for that is what is essential. And that is what your soul shall be…a flower full of love and an expression of your many changing faces."

Fleming was spellbound. He did not know what to say for he noticed as the man talked his face alternated between youth and old age until his face became very young indeed. He had never seen time play such tricks on a human face. Time could play the humorist and get the last laugh on almost anyone. But this was something that anybody that served time long enough would know. At that point the old man who was really a young boy, or so it seemed, reeled in his line.

"Time to go. There are other fishing shallows and fishing deeps. It must go fish there. Your lines are talents. Why bury them in searching here and striving there to accumulate a pack of lies fit for only those whose wonder is self-delusion? Find the poetry in you despite the fact that half of poetry is a ream of nonsense that retains the wisdom of folly. Those are lines worth fishing with. Adieu."

And with that he vanished down the bank just as the sun began to linger through the clouds.

He looked at Paris who, almost magically, emerged from the smoke of his own making.

"Where have you been?"

"Right here."

"Did you see him?"

"See whom?"

"That fisherman."

"Yes. I saw him. Then I didn't."

"What do you mean?"

"It was like a soundproof room. I remember him talking to you then the sound was cut off. It was like Odysseus sealing his ears to the sirens. I saw him but did not hear him."

Fleming shuddered a certain mysteriousness that grasped him.

"You must be kidding."

"No," replied Paris who was now visible and relighting his pipe.

Fleming was perplexed and unsettled; nothing he had experienced before was like this.

"You're kidding."

"No. That's how it happened."

"Did you see his face?"

"Yes. An old, old face."

Fleming looked at Paris.

"You didn't see a young face as well?"

"A young face?" asked Paris, incredulously.

"Yes. Like he was really young, a tightrope suspended between ages."

Paris frowned an incredulous frown and shook his head.

"When I saw him he was an old, old man. How could he be young when he was old?"

Fleming shook his head.

"I don't know. I don't know. And you didn't hear a word he said?"

"No. What did he say?"

"Something about the poem in each person."

Paris was even more incredulous.

"You must have been daydreaming, Fleming. His face was the mirror of age and your dream was to unlock the why of life in those terms."

Now Fleming looked incredulous.

"Paris, I always knew you have an active imagination but this is mad. Much learning has made you mad," he said, giving it second thoughts.

"Yes, you have always wanted to see man as an eternal poem. You fulfilled your own wish through the face of another."

"You're bullshitting," replied Fleming, hurt.

"No. Then explain how I did not see his youthful side when it was most obvious to you. Either that or perception is not a good basis for a philosophy unless it is through neurology. Our perceptions are conditioned distortions. The original lie is that we cannot see our wishes. Yet our wishes are conditioned bones. Life is not limited to our conscious perceptions of it. Our perceptions and conceptions miss the point. They are surface assurances."

"Maybe you are right. I don't know what is right anymore. Life is all a big mystery even if it has been explained. For even amid the explanations there are pauses where words do not go and remain unworded," said Fleming, mulling over the experience.

"Maybe so. But what did his words mean to you?" asked Paris, tired by the analysis.

"Fire. Poetry as fire on bone. Master fire and you master yourself. Poetry's the end of all philosophy."

Paris studied his friend long and hard, incredulously.

"The sun is hotter than I thought," he said, peering askance at his friend as if to suspect his faculties.

"Do not mock me. The sun *is* hotter than thought. Thoughts aren't *that* hot. If you are burning, poetry is you," he said as if in a trance.

"Man's a poem on fire, eh?"

"Right on. A poem aflame. A poem subject to the shifting sands of capital gains and the other games he loses and wins by."

"You're sounding cynical, Fleming."

"It is difficult to watch the crucifixions of vision and idea going on all around you."

Paris was astonished. His friend was from another realm.

"What can I say?" he rhetorically asked the wind. The wind just blew, now north, then south and did not reply with words.

"What I lost in smoke you made up in idea."

"When you've lost the poem in smoke, you have lost the man. He who will kill God will kill man, mystically speaking."

"I wish I had heard him too. Just thought he was an old man. Some old guy out fishing. His hook has a long reach."

"To say the least. To say the least," Fleming repeated.

They watched how the barges plodded up the Seine and how the birds drifted with the changing currents. There was a prolonged pause as if to renew the previous conversation about going against or flowing with the currents of life. Paris was concerned to re-track the conversation.

"You were saying about going against the current…"

Fleming looked at him with a far-out gaze.

"Do you realize…how absurd these problems are? They deserve unerring contempt. They are ridiculous. To weep over something absurd. One must transcend some problems for they are not really problems at all."

"Aren't you being a bit unrealistic?" Paris replied.

"No. Not really," he said in deliberate syllables as if in a trance. "Our plots are the foolishness of dust. Our petty schemes for this gem and that. We are such fools. We get ensnared by the teeth of time and the barbed wires of care."

A broad grin outlined his face. It sounded like breaking bread.

Paris just stared.

"So I simply forget Enid and let the whole thing go to hell? Is that it?"

"No. Choose the way you wish to go and go that way. Upstream or downstream. The courageous is upstream. The wisest is downstream. East and west. Be a bird or a barge and barge right in. No one can decide for you unless you let them decide for you. It will be painful either way. But pain is life: beautiful and damned. It is up to you what you want to do. She can get you down or you can get yourself up."

Fleming's philosophizing only pointed the way. Paris was hurt by Enid and Fleming's deadly nonchalance. But he persisted for the sufferer persists until some relief comes.

"You know," Paris began, "it is pleasant to give advice even when sought but it only comforts like a cough drop. The soreness returns."

Fleming stared at him pensively as if to become almost self-conscious.

"I am sorry. It was quite insensitive of me. I get swept up on a carpet of abstractions. And they carry me away."

Paris nodded in a mode of acceptance.

"In any case, I would say date someone else. It is no good to be walked on time and time again. How about Janice or Martha? And there's Mary with that long blond hair. And what a figure. Have you seen her play tennis with Reverend Wordsworth, the outstanding music critic? She cuts a fine fancy. You could date her."

"But it would be no fun…"

"Bullshit. You can have fun with most anyone. You just have to believe you can. Believe in yourself. Project your confidence."

Paris peered at him skeptically and a sour mouth with a disbelieving twitch of the nose.

"Hrrrrmph."

"Don't give me that. Let all her boyfriends come. And believe me they will come, one by one. Let time and the river and the woods take your cares and throw them to the winds as so many leaves into the air to scatter where they will," Fleming said with an impassioned tone that indicated he wished a decrescendo from the peak of the entire conversation.

At that point, the sun broke through the clouds and they warmed up in its mid-morning rays. It was great to talk to someone who at least tried to understand. But Fleming had the old fisherman on his mind. The more he tried to remove the image and memory, the more it remained. The fisherman had become a vision, a poem on the fires of bone.

CHAPTER 21

The bed is the altar of now and neither Paris nor Fleming raised objection to that premise. Enid smiled a smile angelic with her hair leaning into his chest and she fit snugly into his arms. The afternoon sun sent softer rays now through the window shade as the day awaited night with patience. She enjoyed his presence but felt already the anxiety of meeting an old love who caused her to wonder if there was any affection left after the dual ravages of time and distance. It was difficult to leap back into a past reality, that is, unless one had a vivid memory, a prompting imagination, and a need to do so. Months had passed since their lips had met, arms encircled one another, and eyes had sought happiness in mutual love.

Yet absence can make strangers. Even old testaments of love need contact to make them new. And Ted would be a virtual idea, a sublimation of entwined bodies. But the idea would again take on the flesh and become a member of the armed forces overseas. Ted would be coming home, at least for awhile. Would he understand about Paris? Would he even need to know about Paris? Yet Paris knew all about Ted. Would it be the same? Had Ted found someone else? These questions passed through her mind like the shadows of reality they were. Although passionate, her kisses enslaved their energy to thought and that was what the war was all about. Her mind was under siege and thoughts of self-doubt plagued her even though her lips kissed someone else entirely. She was a child of her generation: no one knew what they *really* wanted. It was all guesswork, a series of puzzles, of unlearning much of the garbage from too much rearing. Shelves were spotlights of indecision and her indecision was prompted, despite her best intentions, from a lack of willingness to commit herself in any way. That way she could hold out and demand the highest price from anyone who was willing to pay. Such an angel was in demand. It was entirely difficult to commit oneself to anyone or thing; the world is a complex of pluralistic loyalties and divided people into its divisions and petty companies. Whispers of love coincided with fevers of flesh, imaginations, and remembered lusts. Ted was no exception. Yet even in that relationship, now cold with warm memories, was difficult to commit oneself to. We are often committed to arbitrary fictions. Our measures, standards, weights, balances—are all the comets in the starry skies are often fictions needed to carry on the commerce, communication, and meaningful intercourse of the world. And Ted was an arbitrary fiction. He was gone. Only Paris was here and now. Hard it was to love a ghost. Yet ghosts return to haunt the living. And here the warmth of Paris kept her warm, his lips kept her affectionate, his eyes set her poems on fire. It was impractical not to love even in the face of time and distance.

Paris had been thinking all afternoon about what Fleming had said.

"Enid. You love me, don't you?" She turned and gazed into his eyes.

"Of course. Of course," she said.

Paris wanted to know more about Ted and when he would invade his plans and toss them to the four winds.

"What is he like?"

"Who?"

"Ted."

"Oh, a very beautiful person. We grew up together. Went to the same high school, same church. Parents knew each other. We just fit together. So many years. I mean good times we had."

"How many years would you say?"

"Ten or fifteen."

"I've a bit of catching the wind to do. Like about ten years."

"It's hard sometimes how destiny plays games with you...where you grow up, go to school, who you meet in life...it's something that just happens and grow with it. Destiny has many games up her sleeve. I had no choice but to grow up with Ted and his family. Our parents were friends long before I was even born. And you learn to like almost anything. You can learn to love, strange as that may seem. Everything is there. Everything. You just have yet to focus on it. Some people don't notice the stars at night until they have camped outdoors. Then the stars are a night's entertainment. Stars are poems in the face of night. I have learned to love you as well, Paris. And I am confused. Everyone wants their cake and eat it too."

Paris had been leaning on his propped elbow, listening intently. Difficult it was to be understanding in the face of abuse. He felt there was no excuse to be number two man on the totem pole, even if the excuse was fate. Certainly he realized the impact of long-term relationships but it did not assuage his feelings for her now.

"Amen," he said. "But is it necessary to have your cake and eat it too?"

"I think so. If it's possible I think people would. It is only necessity that denies them both."

"But why?"

"I don't concern myself with why I love two men. I simply do. We are links in a chain of events that hold us in place."

Paris was getting angry at her hard determinism, namely fate.

"Fate or whatever you call it may be true but it is also an excuse. It is a lie, an evasion of any responsibility. Excuses beat dead armadillos. You sound weak and confused and undecided about anything. Fate may be truth but it is often an excuse for ourselves. And that's what you're doing, Enid. You hope it will all go away if you just close your eyes but it won't work."

Enid began to sulk; she did not like pressure for any decision for it meant a yes or no and that was intolerable. She wanted them both; self-flattery was to be needed passionately by two men. Each one had particular charms she cherished. What one lacked, the other made up in a different way. She must have them both; it became a matter of pride, a sore spot, and any method to postpone decision was used to the fullest.

"Paris, you know I love you. Please be patient with me. I don't even know how I really feel about Ted. Maybe the old spark is gone. Maybe he has found someone new. Let's wait and see," she said with an imploring tone.

Paris heaved a heavy sigh. She was putting off of any decision.

"How long can anybody wait?"

"As long as what you wait for is loved," she replied, batting her eyes at him with a deft shrewdness that clearly closed the talk.

Paris was impressed though such a postponement tactic was depressing as well as disappointing. There was nothing to do but wait or toss all to the winds. Without a word, he rose and put on his clothes. He had to get away to think things over. Her puzzled, almost frightened look, made him speak.

"I'm just leaving for awhile. Think things over. You understand," he said as the day spent time merging into twilight.

"Please stay. Don't go. Please. Don't go," she said in her nearly innocent yet shrewd use of innocence.

"Not now. I'm sorry," he said, and left. He wanted to talk to someone, anyone who would talk and yet it could not be just anyone. Outside the day was gone yet the bustle of Paris had not diminished. Cars passed him, people pushed past him, and he felt so alone, alone in all the world. Though he was upset, he had learned in the face of catastrophe the wisdom of philosophy for it taught him the wisdom of folly. It conferred a serenity of mind as when the fetters momentarily fall away and the anxious lines disappear even though the lines of age remained on his forehead. The whole affair taxed his mind as only passionate frustration can for desires are the beauty and curse of a man. What would Plato do in such a state? Think well of Sparta! Or Spinoza? He would return to his lens grinding! Or Nietzsche? He would head for Sils-Maria! Or Schopenhauer? He would return to his room and write anti-feminine sentiments! Or what of Dean Swift? He would put the whole tail in a tub and lather it with satire and spice! Zen monks would reply: "No teaching, no discipline, no Buddha." What about Ortega y Gasset? He would reaffirm his credo "I am myself plus my circumstances" and Paris would readily endorse such a sentiment. Paris had to do what he chose to do.

He went to Fleming's place and knocked. Fleming answered the door and bade him come in. Blythe was there fixing dinner.

"I'd like to talk to you…privately."

"All right." Fleming told Blythe he'd be back in a few and kissed her.

Both of them went outside and sat on a bench.

"What is it?"

"Enid."

"What about her?"

"She has the sweetest way of keeping two fish on separate lines…"

Fleming smiled a knowing smile and shook his head.

"He's coming soon from overseas…yet she protests she doesn't even know if she will feel the same toward him."

"Ah, she wants to wait till she finds out whether or not he screws like he used to, eh?" Fleming said with a characteristic sarcasm.

"Come on, Fleming, be serious," replied Paris with an admonishing tone.

"Do you think I'm kidding? Come, come, Paris. What does that sound like to you…that her love must wait till she finds out whether or not she still feels the same about him? Doesn't that sound like a lot of garbage smothered in sweet talk? I mean, really. It sounds like bullshit to me. Does she have to have a jury verdict on the matter?"

There was a prolonged pause. Paris wanted some kind of support for his actions and Fleming was not about to give it to him. It was like two dogs growling at each other.

"You are being unkind…I could have given you a hard time about Joan Bradshaw…"

"It's not the same. You asked for my advice, did you not? I say you're being walked on. It is a postponement of any decision between two men so she can have her cake and eat it too. Postponement is the axe that will cut you in twain. As long as she can keep you on the string, she's got you. All she'll do is play with your mind. Mark my words. She will. What does she need? A psychological enema whenever she had doubts about who to walk on next? Despite their appearances, women are not goddesses. They are frequently as cruel as any man could ever dream of being. And you have put her on a pedestal. Don't be a fool, Paris. If she becomes an obsession, which she is, look out for she will rip out your guts."

"But Fleming it's easy for you to talk like that…you're not involved."

"What do I have to be? Your bed partner? I can see the whole scene quite clearly and you are being screwed. You must want it or else you wouldn't let it happen. The world is not populated with saints and philosophers. It is full of imperfect people and imperfect situations. The only reason you are so addicted is the thought that you would be nothing without her. And that is a lie, a delusion. You've built her into a goddess all out of proportion—that is a disease. No one is that perfect. No one."

There was another long pause. As the talk resumed, the noise of traffic became unbearable.

"It is so hard to say anything with all the noise. It is a wonder a man can think anymore. We are baptized into noise. Good God," yelled Fleming as a bus ground its gears into his ears. They moved inside, away from the busy street.

"But that is what I think, Paris."

Paris looked strangely for a moment with a bewildered face and said an incredible thing.

"You have designs on Enid?"

"Do I have designs on Enid? Sure, I'm hot for such a hottie, cantcha see? Jesus Christ. What's got into you, Paris? This chick is nailing on your coffin lid, eh? To the point you get paranoid about the whole thing. Well, let me tell you something, you're a damn good man, a damn good one, but listen sharp now: nothing and nobody is worth losing your head over. I don't care if she's the most intelligent, most beautiful figure in town. It's all bullshit. You lose your head, your sanity and what good are you to anybody? You follow me?"

Paris nodded.

"It's all a game. As long as you are attached, you must play games and you will be made a fool every time. But if you have courage and patience, as I know you have, you will outlive your folly. This will pass. You know it as well as I. So cut the bull about Enid. That only shows how much she's got you. We become possessed by the very things we would possess. Where your heart is, that is where you'll be possessed. And what a lovely damnation it is. A lovely damnation."

There was another long pause. Fleming felt sorry for his friend since he had gone through a similar experience with Blythe.

"Some people just don't stop playing their games. In fact, they invent new ones. Life to them is just a series of games. They take all they can and give very little if at all. They beg with excuses. They live on a diet of excuses. In fact, their entire life is often an epitaph carved with excuses. And they will take if they can. What is most bewitching about their charms is their irresistibility. It may be cleverness, wit, shrewdness, appearance but with those they beg off. Are you listening? Do you hear me?"

Paris nodded.

"And the more you pride yourself on your elasticity, the more bend they will get out of you. The more you pride yourself on your rigidity, the more they will try to break you. One way or another you must learn when to be elastic and when to be rigid. Both are appropriate at appropriate times. Life has strange ways and makes fools kin to the wise. Right now we may think ourselves wise but before this pageant is over, we will be even more foolish. Don't ask me why but that is the way life revolves. All this counseling of adolescents is making me older by the minute."

There was a dead seriousness in Fleming's last remarks. A certain futility followed counseling exercises for it was not possible to counsel anybody with the best intentions. One did not always need a doctor to be cured. Sometimes the best doctor was oneself in stillness and reflection.

"I don't mean to be aging you," replied Paris almost demurely.

"You are. You're making me older by the minute. You are old father time, Paris. The chimes you ring are my own. If Saint Patrick could get the snakes out of Ireland, I think you should get Enid out of your thoughts. Life's a brief act at best. Enjoy it. Enjoy it. Enjoy it."

A smirk mapped Paris' mug.

"Thank you," he said and abruptly did an about-face and headed into the sunset.

CHAPTER 22

Almost a month passed before Ted was to make his appearance and become Enid's personal avatar. In the weeks that followed, Paris continued to see her, much to his frustration, for Ted's shadow lurked behind every smile and curtsey. The games became more intense and whatever innocent naiveté Enid once possessed had vanished with experience and a realization of her power to control and influence the lives of others.

On the day Enid went to the airport to meet Ted, Paris made himself scarce. He tried to find Fleming but soon found Fleming's time absorbed by Enid. There was nothing to do. He had dated others and enjoyed their company, but any relationship had failed to materialize. A yearning seized him and held him in its grip. He longed to be with her on days and times when life had been fun; he longed to be married to her soul and express a union of souls in one flesh. But Enid was too hot and too willing to service two at the same time. And there was a victory in that. The victory was self-flattery. As much as he loved her, he found he also, in a way, hated her. He was torn apart for as soon as he loved her, he felt contempt for such a love on the basis of playing a mere second trombone. Yet that contempt was soon opposed by a guilty feeling of being arrogant and making too many demands on her. Enid knew all this and used each phase to strategically outwit her 'companions' as she sometimes called Ted and Paris. It especially worked well on Paris because he was so gentle; he was putty in her hands and she knew it. But one thing she did not know was that putty was just beginning to harden. Sometimes momentarily guilt is overcome by intense aggression and contempt. The more contempt he felt for himself, the more he began to despise her while at the same time professing to love her. It was a relationship riddled with contradictions and psychological games which were as useful as they were puerile.

That evening in the hotel dining room Ted and Blythe sat together. Despite the noise of scraping plates and chairs being moved, everyone who knew anything knew that Paris had been dumped on even if only temporarily. He was kidded and teased by other guys and girls who saw him in recent weeks nudged each other in an affirmation of his current bout with such a sad split in his life. This evening he sat across from Blythe and next to Fleming who kept eyeing him for his reaction. There was much being said though without words. Fleming gave him a "are you going to endure this?" look. Paris replied with a shrug. Fleming gave him a serious look as if to say "You will. You'd better," all the while carrying on a conversation about asthma and its causes of onset. Blythe boasted about the lack of recent attacks, a conversation that nearly drove Fleming and Paris up the walls.

He drank more and more wine until none was left at the table. Now and again his eyes would light on Enid and Ted and the hurt would go deeper until he yearned to be anywhere but here. It was as if his eyes were co-conspirators against his mental well-being. For they inevitably landed on those two and seeing them together burnt two holes into his heart and the consequent suffering was of his own making. He thought of not going where they went but by trying to escape, he ran right into them and he would nod and Enid would grin broadly and tuck her arm ever tighter into Ted's handsome uniform. Paris was being driven by the furies of his own jealousy until they would eat his heart out.

As the days passed, Paris became rootless and in utter despair. The more he thought of her, the more he desired her and the more frustrated he became. Down and down he went until there was no longer any feeling; he became a body of numbed limbs. When he saw her there was only a faint flicker of excitement and a sense of detachment born of necessity. Behavior could become a rationalization of situations and persist as long as necessity willed. Paris became the impetus to escape or to masochistically revel in suffering. Either way had its drawbacks for humans are humans in spite of pretensions to the contrary. He plummeted in dark despair from a refusal to realize his intrinsic worth, of the despair that wishes metaphysical rebellion to be the rationalization of one's suicide.

Despair revealed the anguish, torment, and ecstasy of this moment of dust, this fragmented body that mingled the psychology of man and the psychology of God. That is how far down he could go and die until death is one's gravest hope. He wanted to rage, kill, dance, and destroy. The afternoon saw them inspect the works of Monet, Renoir, Manet, Gaugin, Van Gogh in the Louvre as he became nauseous though he smiled. At night, he saw them at an outdoor café. He pulled up his collar to hide his face. At a book stall on the Left Bank, he saw them canvassing classics and sizing prints. Enid decided the time was ripe for introduction. She called Paris over and introduced him as a "dear, dear friend" to Ted who smiled but suspected that friendship can have love at the center.

"Enid has mentioned you a lot. You must be her dear, dear friend," he said mimicking her.

Paris frowned.

"We *are* dear friends. And what of it?"

"I'll have you know she's mine," snapped a threatened Ted.

"No one owns anyone unless they wish to be," replied Paris.

Ted was becoming impatient with such nonsense.

"We have gone together for years."

"The force of custom. Tradition."

"Are you saying there's nothing between us?"

"Not at all. You just don't own her."

At that, Enid intervened.

"Ted, let's go. Time's wasting away. Let's get out of here. Nice seeing you again, Paris."

Paris turned furiously.

"I'm not a tour guide. Don't treat me with such an impersonal tone," he said with gritted teeth.

"Don't get too big for your britches, young man," Ted said with a military tone.

"Go to hell," Paris replied as he punched him in the mouth. In a flash, the two were at each other's throats, grappling, slugging and throwing their weight at one another. Paris hit him again in the mouth. Ted was beginning to bleed; Paris knocked him over a print stand. The owner began to scream for the gendarmes but none came. Over and over they rolled. Ted hit him in the stomach, then an upper cut to the jaw sent Paris sprawling on the river edge. Enid screamed and pulled his fists away. Ted began to fight with her. A right cross to the jaw sent her sprawling into a cart of cocoanuts that fell on the sidewalk. By now, a small crowd began to gather and a Frenchman by the name of Jean-Louis Kegger, with burly muscles tapped Ted on the shoulder. When Ted turned around, a fist flattened his nose and sent him to the concrete. All three lay there. The gendarmes had not come. The crowd murmured amongst themselves and Paris was the first to rise. He head felt like someone had shot it off. The world was upside down, inside out. His head felt like a ball that had been rolled for a millennium and the trees all seemed to float and embroider their branches into the thread work of a Parisian sky. Enid's shapely legs showed their beautiful curves beneath her torn dress and Ted, uniform and all, was the worse for taking leave from a military habit of command. No gendarmes came.

Each arose. Enid took Ted's arm and they left. Paris brushed himself off and beat it in the other direction. He would get even for the spirit of revenge would not let his muscles relax until he had returned the favor. For the moment, Paris had left philosophy behind.

That night Paris strolled alone beneath the moonlight as he watched moonbeams shimmer on the Seine. His thoughts were a plague that devoured him. Spurred on by remembered lust, his thoughts became all the more melancholy. His heart ached and seemed to die a thousand deaths. Off he went to her apartment. How many times had he climbed those very stairs to enjoy a warm body in loving embrace? He tried to forget but the physical presence of the room unleashed thousands of even more agonizing thoughts. He knocked. Silence. He knocked again. Silence. He knocked again. There was the sound of movement within. He listened then knocked again. From within came a tiny voice.

"Who is it?"

"Jean La Pierre à vôtre service."

"Who?" Enid called in her heavier voice.

"I don't know you," she replied.

"Ah, but I know you. We met at the Boulevard Montmartre last Tuesday. Please open and you will recognize me."

Enid left the door for several moments and put on her robe as she bid Ted a heavy silence. Paris sneaked away at the last moment, having devised another plan. He remembered around the wall was a railing next to the bedroom. It rose to another tier of roof, thus allowing a bird's eye view. Enid had opened the door, found no one there, shrugged her shoulders, and disrobed. Ted studied those hips and buttocks he had not seen before and marveled at how much she knew but suspected her of having been unfaithful to him. It was rather obvious. Paris settled himself on the roof so that just a portion of his face exposed so he could see the goings on. Sure enough, just as he had suspected, Ted was there on the bed and Enid was brushing her hair. In a moment, she came to the bed and lay next to him. They were ready to make love.

All this caused Paris a sigh and a rage. Before he could rationalize all of this he exploded and swung himself down and kicked open the window and it shattered on the frightened couple. Enid ran and got her nightgown which she could only hold up in front of her with affected modesty. Ted stood naked, his fists doubled, wiping blood streaks from off his ribs. Paris plunged into him, raining short punches to his stomach and here and there an upper cut. Ted grabbed him and flipped him and with a terrific rabbit punch floored Paris for several minutes.

"Let's get him outa here," he commanded. Enid finally slipped on her nightgown.

"Where to?"

"I don't know. But let's get him outa here. What a son of a bitch to kick in the window like that. Who'd he think he was? Superman?" urged Ted whose anger was not abated. Together they dragged Paris into the hallway and down the stairs and left him near the door, presumably to have him appear the drunk who had just passed out for the night.

After that detail had been taken care of, they returned and she began to sweep the shattered glass.

"What is his problem," asked Ted as he lit a cigarette. "He in love with you?"

"I'm afraid so," she confessed. Ted's anger had not abated; he was not only suspicious but quite upset with her.

"He must be...to know where you are...what you do...to fight for you...to eat himself with jealousy. Sounds like he's got a lot invested in you."

"What do you mean by that?" she asked with a pause.

"Have you something going with him? A relationship?"

"Maybe," she said coyly, as she continued sweeping.

"I demand an answer," he said, sharply.

She paused again and leaned on the broom handle.

"Yes, we're friends."

Suddenly he grabbed her by the arm.

"I hate liars. Of all the truth-mongers in this world, I hate liars. Do not lie to me. That was a lie. It is obvious that he is more than 'just friends.' Friends are just not that passionate."

"All right. If you want the truth, I'll tell you. That is what you want for your truth collection. We had a relationship..."

"Bull. You *have* a relationship," he said.

"All right. We have one."

"I thought so. You are so different from the last time I saw you. I was wondering what it was. I could not pin it down. Absence changes people whether we like it or not. The way you took off your clothes, how familiar you are with the male body, how you smell of the scent of roses all the time. Everything is different. You are just so different. We take little photos and we expect people remain that way. But they don't. That's why photos are a bit unreal. You are not the same person. That is the illusion absence plays. I knew it. I suspected him from the way he fought me this afternoon. The way people react gives them away sometimes. And he fought me with fists of hurt. He was hurt. I could tell. It wasn't just anybody I was fighting. I've fought too many others. I know the difference."

"Yes. He says he loves me."

Ted leaned against the drainboard, his arms folded, with an inquisitive air.

"You love him?"

"I don't know. I really don't. I don't know what I want."

"You know there's something about when a woman goes to college… I don't know whether it's the atmosphere, the courses, the values, the society whatever…but they get screwed up. They really do. Somewhere along the line they get screwed up."

"Not everyone."

"I'll grant you that. But if you sleep with someone, don't you even care a little about them? Granted you don't love them, is there no feeling at all? Or is it simply the feeling of transiency? Or the feeling of novelty? The anticipation of greener pastures on the other side of your mind?"

"Oh, certainly I care for him," she protested. "But it was you I wanted to see and be with. It is hard to be absent."

"So in the meantime you shacked up with someone else?"

"That I did. You weren't here. There was no one to talk to. And I get lonely. I need someone to talk to," she said as the slight trace of tears welled about her eyes.

"Why do you get lonely?"

"I don't know."

"Everybody needs somebody I guess," he said with an understanding sigh. "It just seems rotten that love can't transcend space and time anymore. It just gives in to the trivial moments for even more trivial reasons. That is not love. And you know it."

He lit a cigarette.

"Why is it oaths and vows no longer mean much?"

"I don't know."

"Maybe our parts are too interchangeable. We figure we just transplant our love and it grows in another body. And that's all there is to it. It no longer means anything," he said as his voice cut short abruptly.

"I don't know what it is. All I know is that I wanted you here with me. A homecoming."

"Most homecomings are funerals. We bury the dead selves we could never be. Forever."

Enid grew resentful.

"I'm sorry you feel that way. I thought you were a soldier. You could take anything. Thick-skinned and all."

"You think every soldier an armadillo? We too have tender parts. Just like everyone else," he replied. "It just kills me to think that I'm off getting my ass shot at with bullets and you're back her getting your bedroom pleasure with some son of a bitch you don't even care about."

Enid just sighed, her face somewhat sad. He grabbed her by the arm.

"You hear me?"

"Yes, I hear you. Loud and clear," she said, trying to be cold as possible.

She began to sweep again the broken glass into little piles. He put out his cigarette nervously.

"I don't suppose you had any Asian women on or off the base," she declared with intended inquiry.

"Yes, I did. But I loved you."

Enid paused sweeping the glass.

"Then who are you to judge me?"

"You're a woman."

"Oh. And women aren't supposed to get any pleasures out of life, is that it?"

Ted began to pace around the room in spots with no broken glass.

"It's not that…"

"What was she like? Give you baths all the time? Serve you rice wine? Walk around on your back? Rub your tired, aching GI muscles?" she asked, now that he was equally on trial.

"All right. I've only got a few more days of leave. Why don't we just enjoy ourselves?"

"Is that your way of escape?" she asked, truly resentful of his tactics. "You put the heat on me…always a smugly righteous person who is the prosecuting attorney…and you are the accuser and accused…even before I've finished sweeping this broken glass…" she said with an almost deepening, cynical concern.

"So now you become the accuser, eh? Now who is to judge?" he said.

"Let's forget it. The affair's a shambles. We can't even see through a broken glass darkly."

"I agree. Let us pardon our follies and live for life," he added.

Then he began to help her sweep the broken glass until they could walk barefooted again without fear of cut feet.

As far as Ted was concerned, the relationship was over. The death of innocence is disillusioning and he now continued the relationship on borrowed time and tactics that cut out any future they might have had together. Enid felt awful that Ted had even been unfaithful for promises are whispers on the wind and the wind can carry promises far afield as so many pollen seeds. Their relationship had been a lie. They had lived a lie for many years and perhaps the beauty of wisdom is only possible upon discerning the pervasiveness of human folly. Ted was kept to keep Paris jealous; Enid was kept to make it seem to his buddies on the base that all was going well with his hot love in merry England.

CHAPTER 23

It was an overcast morning at the Paris airport. Kisses planted were only half as sincere as they once were. There was an undercurrent at work. Their words were those that would meet again; their actions were those that said farewell forever.

"Be sure to write," Enid urged as his ticket was processed and his bags weighed.

"Will do. Let's keep in touch," he replied perfunctorily.

"You have a safe trip now. Remember my love for you," she said with emphasis, an emphasis kin to insistence as if to repeat it would make one believe it. Ted smiled as if he would yawn at the same time. The trip, for him, had clarified where he stood. At least he did not have to build her up from far-away places. It was a relief from the burden of distorting and being distorted; they were human after all, capable of playing squash in bed as well as on a wet field.

"Enid, my love, take care," he said in an effort at sincerity. And with that he disappeared beyond the gate to the jet that would return him to military routine. She pressed her face against the glass and waved goodbye. It made her sad to breathe in too many goodbyes for they made her melancholy and yearning. Goodbyes were like peering into an abyss of oneself and feeling a sense of dread that nothing would ever be like it was ever again. And nothing would ever be like it was. But her contracted attention span would save her for as she drove back to her hotel room, her thoughts turned to Paris Brandon whom she had not seen in over two weeks. By this time he should be pretty desperate, she thought. Paris would welcome her with open arms.

She tried his hotel but he was not in. She tried Fleming who was almost overly obvious in his refusal to disclose Paris' whereabouts. Enid was beginning to feel something in the air, a moment when you feel deep down in your bones something is awry yet is impossible to define. In futility, she tried familiar shops, cafés, even parts of the Louvre in her search for him. Things were not going to according to expectations. This prompted a certain feeling of anxiety and frustration. In the Tuileries Gardens she sat watching passersby and gazed at a little boy sailing his sailboat. As soon as the wind shifted, it would capsize. It seemed the boat was not prepared for winds that blew a certain way. Neither was she.

Then across the way, next to a soda stand, as couples passed with their walking dogs and red balloons and made up faces, her eyes lighted on a man who let out a blue haze of pipe smoke. His back was to her. But she recognized him but not the willowy blond at his side. Could it be? No. As he turned, she recognized him then disbelieved, then recognized him, then disbelieved her own eyes. It was. It truly was. No, it couldn't be. How in heaven's name, she thought. Paris it was. With a girl. A blond no less. And there welled inside her a resentment, an anger, and a purple-eyed monster-head with bulging jealous eyes. How could he? It has only been a couple of weeks. That thankless philosopher! That monster of deceit who makes promises and loving whispers. The ingratitude of it all. Oh, life is not the way she thought it was at all! Her expectation-bubbles popped with the force of blown tires. Men are so cruel, heartless, insensitive, she wailed melodramatically on stage before her audience, namely herself. A blond, no less! Enid's world was just about to collapse. What to do? She watched for a moment while she boiled inside. They were so happy and carefree. And all of a sudden she despised their happiness and felt hate and anger with every ounce of her body. Her thoughts were assassin thoughts directed at Paris then herself. No, she must not let him know of her presence. Oh, how she would love to pull the hair out by the roots, those blond roots. Ugh! But she would wait. There were ways more subtle in which she could get the message across. There was more than one way to avenge the basic inhumanity of men.

Ducking out of their view, she strolled on toward a bridge that crossed the Seine. She boiled every step of the way. The toy shelves, cardboard walls, the synthetic fabric of mass-produced surfaced assurance of her doll house was about to collapse. The anxiety began to eat her alive. There would be another philosopher, a more mature man that would make her happy for things certainly must get better and better. Were there any philosophers for sale? She would find one and then security, happiness, and a Mercedes Benz would be hers, forever and ever. She could be anybody's mistress as long as their promises were roses, buttercups, and lusty lays all her days. There must be a man who would give her security back to her, who would marry, or at least live with her and then happiness would be hers. Enid followed this delusion consistently and her consistency must have seemed virtuous to one so tormented by seeing Paris with another woman.

Once on the bridge, about midpoint, she paused and gazed at the currents. The Seine was not still enough for her to see herself. Traffic zoomed behind her and she stood between the two banks and watched life throb on either side. And then she turned and leaned against the wall and watched people pass from one side to the other. Some laughing, some sad—passing over the bridge. Her anger subsided into hurt and she wept and a tear or two rolled down her face that was as light and airy as any angel's could be. Enid was so human and so very lovely. It was the games that made her what she was and she was so vulnerable and so lovely at the same time. No wonder Paris preferred this woman to philosophy. For philosophy did not have the face of an angel. For all her calculating, she was still beautiful. If that is a sickness, then all men attracted by beauty must be sick.

Before she knew it, someone was beside her. A heavy wine smell lingered on his breath but his cheek was soft as he rubbed it against hers. She was almost afraid to look. But at that moment, Enid panicked and quick as a fox, she ran as far away from him as she could and soon she was out of sight.

The next day she saw Paris. He smiled and so did she. He had not seen anyone, especially any blond. Only gradually did she realize the accusing mind and the guilty mind are two angles of same scene. So badly had she needed a picture to justify her rage that she created one. Her guilt was absorbed in the passion play of the moment.

The waiter brought to them hot-buttered rolls and a pot of tea. It was a clear morning in Paris. She had bought an apple and a pear from an outdoor market and gave the apple to Paris.

"Ted gone?"

"Sure is," she replied.

"Still love him?"

Her eyes met his, then flew to the ground.

"Love doesn't die all that easily."

Paris smiled faintly.

"What game now?"

She threatened to leave.

"Please stay. One should never leave in the middle of a meal," he said. "The tea gets cold. I wish to marry you," he said, intending to shock her.

"But we haven't even gone to Spain yet."

Paris did a double take.

"What does Spain have to do with it?" he asked rhetorically.

He was used to her evasions. Everything had to be utterly certain, utterly secure before she could do anything. Nothing was ever absolutely secure. That is why it was an evasion, like allowing a fish enough line so that it could fight a little longer and perhaps jump the hook. His questions, though serious in intention, were treated as trivial for the trivial is a safe evasion through which we can learn to love our illusions even more. And, besides, it isn't much fun being serious all the time.

"Well, we must wait until I've visited Spain to know for sure."

"That's a crock—"

"Paris, you don't have to be gross. After all, you are a philosopher you know."

"That has nothing to do with your current game. Humans are masters of self-deception sometimes. You have mastered yours. Besides most philosophers I know are obnoxious."

"I just want to see Spain. Then I'll know whether it's Ted or you."

Paris shook his head.

"Do you have to absolutely certain to believe anything? Do you have to be absolutely secure to risk anything in life? Are you afraid of decision? Or are you afraid of the dead selves you must tread over in the wake of choice? No one can be all his possible selves…unless in dreams and symbols. Is it fear or courage, timidity or bravery? Or are you just a guilty mirror of what people will think of the choice you make for your life?"

Then he paused with a deep sigh.

"I'm sorry. I myself am in a quandary as to decision."

Such a consideration was just what Enid wanted. He was too dispassionate to mete out an unjust judgment. He was so fair-minded he was wishy-washy. Here was her out:

"So you shouldn't judge me when you should judge yourself."

Chances are, in this area, Paris needed a firmer spinal column. Men are best made by their own exaggerations; it's the truth of their gait that reveals them most.

"That's true but it's the principle of the thing. I mean it's an evasion to make one's love contingent on a trip. What does Spain have to do with what you can choose now? Why wait? Maybe after Spain we'll have to wait till the Acropolis to find out more and more."

"You said it. I didn't," she replied with a fickle bounce to her hair. Paris just smirked. It was like bureaucratic buck-passing from one extension to another.

"You like some tea?" she asked as the perfect hostess.

"Not now," he replied, frustrated. Many cynical remarks came to his head: "Time and trouble: that's women for you. The game players: women at home and downtown. Evasions for sale: free to the highest stupidity. Women, the fools' choice: the price is your sanity."

But such cynical thoughts were transitory even if edifying. Ambivalence best described him. He knew he loved her but one can only love in a delusion when game-playing is the only rule of order.

"Why do you play games?"

"Because I'm good at them," she replied. This bolted him.

"But why?" he repeated.

"There is no 'why' to game-playing. It's just fun. Besides, it's a woman's prerogative."

"I've never heard such crap," he said with contempt and disgust.

"Have it as you like it. Life goes on, Paris. Life goes on."

"Christ. I've got to take a walk."

"Can I come along?"

"No. I wish to be alone. To be alone, by myself."

"Have it as you will."

"I will," he said as he strolled off into the streets.

CHAPTER 24

It was a slow but gradual realization that Blythe was not totally engaged to Fleming. One day while out eating peanuts and careless tossing away the shells, Fleming watched the river currents as they mirrored his life. Along with the ones that flowed seaward were also eddies that coiled about one another and did not leave each other alone. They went against the grain. And Blythe did as well. He wondered where she had been all those hours she was supposedly shopping. In fact, her shopping was for an extra lover. The hot, tempestuous hours were fading from her relationship with Fleming and Elaine was a charming French girl of fifteen with roseate cheeks and bright red lips that kissed her with such ecstasy that Fleming, the love of her heart, was forgotten. It was not that she did not love Fleming; only the passions had cooled. When the volcanic fires cooled, boredom set in with that dull, semi-conscious ache it can often bring.

Elaine had been shopping one day and had been trying on several suits in the department store window. Her legs were slender but firm and her breasts were also firm and inviting. She had finished the lycée or high school only recently and was ready to continue her education with a little less learning. Blythe at first admired her from across the room and smiled. She was bolder: she invited her to lunch. She pressed her hand tenderly as they went to a café. This aroused Elaine who was slowly growing aware of her attraction to the older woman. They spent all afternoon together. Lunch, then a stroll through a park, then coffee. It was not too many afternoons later that they made love with all the delight and ecstasy of two long-time lovers. What was sad was the Fleming began to notice his relationship drifting apart like two rafts that, no longer moored to each other, drift apart with time and distance. More and more, he would walk by himself since she always had an excuse to be gone. And as they let the waters flow between them, for everything that is lovely lives to perish, there emerges a dozen possible selves never heard of or imagined. Like a butterfly, even humans undergo metamorphoses and become the dreams only dreams dream. But Fleming was tolerant. He met Cher only days later and traveled with her to Spain. He had imbibed enough philosophy to be wise but not enough to become a nit-picky scholar. By contrast, Paris was still floundering in footnotes. His awareness was dimmed by details…and, of course, Enid Brown.

Blythe later re-fell in love with Fleming and chased him to Spain. But timing as well as rhythm is part of the dance of life and when they met at a café in San Sebastian, it was a memento mori to a moribund relationship.

She first saw him buying a large basket of fruit and she engaged his attention. They went to a café and she smoked half a dozen cigarettes and began to wheeze with an asthma attack.

"Stop smoking all those weeds, Blythe. You know it's bad for you," he said during a lull in her wheezing. Blythe was high-strung and nervous. Her anxiety was the face of the age. Fleming peeled an orange.

"Want a piece?"

She took a slice after the wheezing had subsided.

"Not bad," she said. She was feeling insecure so many of her perceptions were distorted in some way.

"How's Cher?"

Fleming looked up at the question.

"She's fine."

"You love her?"

"No, love is elusive. You don't find it. You become it. Then it is as elusive as oneself. It takes time to learn to love. Like a good wine. It ages in the vat. Whether it's a concord or muscatel grape. Age, not just longevity of association. That's love. This affair is in transit. All affairs are. Since they are not aged, they are in transit."

"A fine sermonette, Herr Doktor," she replied in the fashion of a friendly fräulein.

He bit into an apple. A lost look welled into her eyes.

"I miss you, Fleming."

"You do, eh? The past few weeks say otherwise."

A sad mouth and sad eyes were her offering.

"All right. We drifted apart. But that was in France."

Fleming's brows rose and he paused eating his apple.

"What does that have to do with it?"

"Nothing I guess. My words shift with boundaries. I thought…"

"Nothing doing, Blythe. You don't just leave someone you profess to love, that is, unless all your professions are merely lies."

He finished the apple and tossed the core away.

"You won't take me back?"

Fleming shook his head. Blythe rose to leave with purse in hand.

"What will you do?" he asked.

"Oh, nothing much. Get bored and go into politics," she replied, hiding hurt. And with that she left.

CHAPTER 25

I t is possible to view oneself as always in transit since it is often difficult for a person to convince himself he has arrived. Often selves thought to be dormant, are like Plato's forms, awaiting recollection. Such was Blythe after her heart had devoured itself in tears over her broken romance. Though time is the thief of love, one can live to love all over again. At first she thought of Elaine and Yolanda. But distance, linear time, cooled the passions.

She had returned to France, leaving Fleming in Spain. In Paris, as she awaited a train, she met a ruggedly handsome priest with cold black hair and large blue eyes. Her acquaintance with religion was scant, even a conventional education, and it both fascinated and scared her that the situation should be so. Her eyes twinkled as they talked and his tanned face contrasted with the white collar and gold crucifix tucked into his shirt.

So fascinated was she that she forgot her train to Calais. There she was with all her baggage captivated by a priest who attracted her in spite of her somewhat negative religious sentiments. They strolled to a café and sat and talked and drank tea.

"What work do you do?"

"I do what is necessary," he replied with a low sonorous voice.

"Like what?"

"I sniff out the smelly socio-economic structures that are the prisons of the mind, of poverty and then try to change them if possible."

"Isn't that out of the ordinary? I mean priests are in the church."

"The church is the world, my friend. Boundaries are artificial lines used as nets to catch us. If the world is seen as a problem, revolution on some level is the solution."

"Revolution?"

"Yes," said the priest, now deadly serious.

"You mean violence?"

"If necessary."

"You mean guerilla tactics?"

"If you want to call it that. It is the only rational solution. Revolution."

"I went through that. Revolution I mean. It was all a show. My own vanity at stake," she said with a sigh as she gazed off into the distance.

"Maybe you are right. But that makes revolution impossible," countered the priest.

"I don't know. Maybe all ideals and ideologies are futile," she declared, obviously reminiscing over her past political activities.

"All I know is then tyranny exists, it is a sacred act to oppose it. My father, you see, was murdered by the Gestapo for his underground church activities. They used him as long as they could in the concentration camps then poof. Executed. Our whole family was spied on, threatened, and persecuted by the Nazis. I hate tyranny in any form whether it's from a Hitler or a Stalin."

She listened intently as she drank her tea and studied his cheek bones, determined mouth, and soft lips. He fascinated her so much as she had difficulty not appearing to stare.

"So you see, as long as those in power want to dehumanize and desensitize man, either by imperialist aggression or the acquisitiveness that preys on man's capacity to estrange himself from his fellow in the name of this or that, I must be a revolutionary. The body of Christ in action. The peoples' liberation. Must we watch the exploitation of underdeveloped countries of the world? Must we continue to increase the walls that divide nations and peoples? No. Anything less than sanity, anything less than the beauty of earth and life is unacceptable to me as a human being first and a priest second."

Then he paused.

"Excuse me. It wasn't a speech I had in mind."

"Oh, please go on," she urged.

"No, let's talk of other things."

"It's getting late," she said as she looked at her watch. "I've missed my train. I can't believe it. I've actually missed my train."

"There's probably another one tomorrow. The trains leave on schedule everyday," he said.

"By the way," she said, "do you have a place to stay?"

"Not really. I could find a place with other members of the order but I'm not up for theological debates."

"We could find a place together," she suggested, filling her eyes with his being.

"Suits me fine," replied the priest.

"You would?" she asked somewhat timidly.

"What's wrong with two people staying together?" he asked somewhat sharply.

"Nothing…I guess," she said as her stereotype began to collapse.

"They checked in at a hotel. The desk clerk's brows rose as he saw the priest with her. When the clerk's look became irresistibly inquisitive, Father Zack, said with a wink:

"She wants a *prolonged* confession."

"Oh, I see," said the clerk, completely disarmed and left in suspended animation.

Once in their room, they began to unpack their bags.

"Have you ever slept with a woman before?" she asked out of the blue.

"No. Just the pretty ones," said the priest.

"To be honest, I've never even been this close to a priest before."

"We're pretty good guys. What else would you like to confess?"

"Well I do have some questions."

"Fire away," he replied as he sat himself comfortably on the bed with his head cupped in his hands, almost amused.

"Well isn't it immoral to sleep with a woman? I mean a priest to sleep with a woman?"

"Why should it be immoral unless I went on the assumption that sex is somehow bad. Exploitative sex is bad. Non-exploitative sex can be magnificent. Sex is beauty in divine intent. How can one be a doctor of the soul without knowing the body first, eh? And what about a priest with a woman? Do you think priests are idols? Plastic playthings who dress in straightjacket societal expectations make them wear? That is true, to an extent, of almost any vocation in organized society. But priests have sexual desires too, my dear. We are poets in the cloth. Whoever said sex is dirty is a liar. There have been those in the church who have said sex *was* dirty. But I, your priest, am not bound by conditioning from the past. The flesh is divine. Cherish it."

By this time Blythe was blown out.

"But doesn't this conflict with your beliefs?"

"My dear, beliefs are prisons of the mind. Little boxes. Faith is wide open. Faith is the eternal now. If we live not in faith, we die in beliefs and that's what causes all the conflicts, all the oppressive governments and churches and schools."

"I never thought of it that way. That's really far out," she said as she lit a cigarette and lay down next to him. A long pause ensued.

"You're very different..." she said in a few minutes. "I mean you know I just didn't think you were...*that* different. Guess I haven't been to church is so long."

The priest said nothing but stared out at the setting sun-tinted sky.

"Tell me," she began, "why do we jump to conclusions? I mean I had you all wrong. You're not the way I thought."

The priest smiled.

"Society defines roles; people play them. It is sad, in a way, because expectations are set up which dictate our directions, our feelings, our images of ourselves. And that is...a lot of baggage to cart around. A priest is a poet of the sacred here and now. Too often we let the definitions get in the way. And then you can't be real. Then it's fake. You have to pretend you're someone you're not. And we get hedged in…and slowly die. We get dogmatic on one point or another; we get exclusive and think we're the chosen few. But the world is full of surprises. And then you realize, in some solitudinous moment, that you have the Buddha and the Christ within you, that all humanity is one fabric, and that only foolishness thinks well of itself to the exclusion of other possibilities. In other words, you get your head on straight. You act. And then you want to embrace everyone, the stars, the trees, the clouds, and the sea and the moon. Then you realize how really beautiful each divine occasion is in its perpetual perishing. And you see the divine in each face and you learn to love beyond the confines of your particular reckonings. Then, only then, will you know what I am talking about. And that includes the naked body and sexual love. End of my tenth homily."

Blythe put out her cigarette. She rolled over for a longish second and peered into his eyes that twinkled continuously.

"You're a beautiful man and I want to make love to you," she said softly. They said nothing as they kissed passionately. Soon their bodies were almost indistinguishable. Her body scintillated with ecstasy. She held him ever so tightly. Passionate kisses rained on her cheeks and thighs; to her this was most revolutionary. Never had she been with a man of such consuming passion, a passion for life, love's fire. With him love was anytime and anywhere. That is why the Song of Solomon was his favorite book. And that, too, was revolutionary. The warmth, the touch, and the passion, impressed her. How much she had longed for such a passion! Desire consumed them, pressed them, and their world loved even in a tiny portion of space. One sometimes discovers love in silent spaces. She wanted all of the world to love. Passion and fever and beauty— all were one. Her body heat matched his. Their loving, as man and woman, was an essay in self-integration, of loving bodies loving. Blythe was topsy-turvy; everything melted and she discovered she was vulnerable, had explored finitude, and found that loving was a sacrifice where act and thought were one. Father Zack was full of fire and life; he was real, flesh and bone, not a stereotype, but human, neither the illusion of self-sufficiency nor the illusion of excessive dependency. Their loving act was a long look for each was a child of each with nature as their tutor and history as the space where one learned to be aware, timelessly aware.

CHAPTER 26

The morning came and birds sang and a peace dwelled in them. There was the joy of passion, the love of lovers. Blythe lay awake and her eyes floated across him from the curls of his black hair to his toes. Next to the bed she spied his valise. She had not seen him open it the night before so curiosity compelled her to open it and see for herself. For a brief moment the zipper stuck but soon it opened, revealing a submachine gun and a stack of papers that resembled government documents. Never did she suspect him to be carrying a machine gun. She did not know whether he was a devil or a saint or some hybrid of the two. Printed on one of the papers in bold letters was the inscription: Top Secret. Underneath it in handwriting was "Revolution: the Rational Solution. Revolution: now or never. Throw off the chains of communist and imperialist and economic aggrandizement even in the forms of organized crime!"

A snort from him caused her to quickly re-zip the valise and lay back as if to pose as a relaxed semi-sleeper.

In a moment, just as the sounds of birds amid traffic assumed a high-fevered intensity, Father Zack opened one eye then another, blinked several times, and then focused his big blue eyes on her.

"To be awakened by beauty is a blessing. How are you this morning?"

She rolled over and kissed him.

"Does that answer your question?"

"Actions can be best answers. Your lips are wine presses. Can one refute love in act? Never! Beauty's her own argument." And he kissed her long.

"Looks like a beautiful day out. The sun's out," she said.

Father Zack seemed serious as if he had something on his mind.

"What're you thinking?" she asked.

"About where I must go."

"Where must you go?"

"Nowhere that you would know about. Let's just say it is a matter of politics."

"Do you know where you are going?"

"Yes, but it's a secret. Behind closed doors."

"Are you a government agent?"

"No, governments are walls. My job as priest is to break walls and out-economize economies."

"You sure are a different kind of priest. And handsome, too."

"You haven't heard a word I've said," he replied with a sardonic grin.

"That's because I'm confused about you. It's been awhile since I've slept with a father."

Father Zack laughed. Then those blue-stallion eyes became serious again.

"I must leave you today."

"Why?"

"Because it's time to go. I have a date."

"A date?"

"No. An appointment. Let's put it like that. I have a revolution to go to."

"A revolution?"

"Yes, guerilla warfare. Holy wars. The crusades."

"Crusades?"

"Yes, to abolish the law of labor. Labor law. The organized castration. Women's work. To take inventory is blasphemy. The refusal of orgasm. Do you understand? To prevent the sale of labor, the exploitation of people already schizoid. Tragic and comic masks: managerial psychology. The promotions, the pay raises are prolonged exploitation. There are many revolutions to see the pure light," he said in passionate but iridescent tones.

"These are the crusades?" she asked.

"The holy wars, wars of love," he replied softly.

"Wow," she said slowly to herself. "I want to go. Please take me, I beg you."

Father Zack thought a moment.

"Too dangerous. Not for you."

She frowned but understood. She would never see him again.

CHAPTER 27

I t was nine-thirty. The sun shone. They waved farewell to Fleming and Cher who remained in San Sebastian. The train strained, pulled forward, stopped, then strained again until it crawled, lazily, out into the bright sun, leaving San Sebastian behind. Paris, Sparky, and Jocko sat alone in the first class cabins. Behind them trailed the third class or peasant class cabins with dark brown skinned Spaniards hanging out the windows. One held a large rooster by the feet and watched its wings flap back and forth. Another held a large jug of wine and waved gaily.

"I knew we should have taken third class," remarked Jocko. "It ain't no fun here. No women. No drink."

"I agree," said Sparky. "We're the only ones here."

Paris said nothing, but, like the other two, gazed at the fun and frolic in the third class cabins.

"Whose idea was it to go first class?" asked Sparky.

"Mine," murmured Jocko with regret, "mine."

The train traveled about ten miles then stopped.

"What's happening?" asked Jocko.

"I don't know."

They had stopped out in the middle of nowhere. There was no station in either direction or on either side of the train. Jocko leaned his head out the window and the peasants let up a roar in Spanish, waving their arms wildly and the rooster just as wildly.

"No station in sight," declared Sparky who could not understand why the train stopped. A couple of cows grazed not far away and a tiny farm could be seen in the distance. The forests were thick with contrasting shade and the Pyrenees provided a ruggedness for remembrance. The scenery was picturesque, a different Spain in the north. Twenty minutes passed and the train grunted, strained, and lurched forward and began to crawl at a slow pace. The sun was bright and hot. The peasants were partying, the women dancing to shouts of "olé!" A door opened suddenly. A tall, dark mustachioed Spaniard dressed in a conductor's uniform passed through, paused, and stared at the three, suspiciously, then passed into the rear cabin. Thirty-three minutes passed. The train stopped again. The three were hot, sweaty, and beginning to get hungry. They had money but had not brought along any food since they had planned on eating in Madrid in early afternoon.

"What the hell's wrong with this train?" snapped Jocko.

"Beats me," Sparky replied.

Paris just shook his head. "I've never been on a train like this," he said. "They can't be refueling. We haven't gone far enough to need fuel."

"This reminds me of the buses in the States. They stop at every railroad crossing. But this train don't stop except at the cattle crossings," barked Jocko whose impatience was already felt by the other two.

"God, no wonder the peasants bring booze and women and song. They are the only smart ones," said Jocko who observed the peasants make their own merriment on a tedious train ride.

"They sure are," agreed Sparky who opened two or three windows as it was getting hotter at high noon.

"There are some cows," said Paris.

"Hamburger. Look at that hamburger. Makes me hungry," said Sparky.

"Let's ask that conductor what's wrong when he comes through again."

Just at that moment the train lurched forward again.

"Here we go again!" exclaimed Jocko. "I can't believe it."

The train began to go faster and soon the scenery passed like a blur in slow motion. Paris watched as the forests and meadows passed.

Not too many minutes later the steady clicking of the train began to slowdown again.

"Don't tell me we're stopping. It can't be," remarked Sparky.

"It is," Jocko replied. "It is. We're stopping again. Probably to wait for the shadows to cross the tracks. I know we're stopping to see if the train can start again. The conductor's on grass and the peasants are on wine and we're on nothing. Just great."

"We're not even on," replied Paris who had loosened his shirt collar.

"We could've walked to Madrid at this pace," remarked Sparky.

Sure enough, the train had stopped again.

At that moment, the conductor came through again. Jocko asked him in broken Spanish what was wrong with the train.

"No comprendo, Señor," was all he said in reply.

Jocko asked him again.

"Habla usted Ingles?"

"No habla Ingles y no habla Español," he replied, shaking his head.

Jocko asked him what was wrong again.

"No comprendo. No habla," the conductor repeated.

Jocko asked Sparky and Paris:

"Can either of you speak better Spanish? I've tried."

The conductor stood there smoothing his mustache. Paris eyed him suspiciously, gave him an askance look from head to toe.

"You know this is a strange train ride. So many stops and starts. Makes you stop and think. I've never been on a train like this. Have you?" asked Sparky.

"No, I haven't," replied Paris.

"I sure haven't. I'm hungry and tired. Three hours since we left San Sebastian. We've stopped at every cattle crossing in the last fifty miles. I don't understand it."

"It is strange," said Paris, beginning to reflect as was his wont. The train began moving again.

"I see Paris has begun a train of thought," said Jocko who eyed him with impatience. Paris smiled, self-conscious.

"How in heaven's name did we ever get on this train?" asked Sparky with a rhetorical flourish.

"We wanted to see the terrain, didn't we?" said Paris, reflecting as he was wont to do. "Remember that lovely line: 'The rain in Spain falls mainly on the plain.'"

"Good time to bring it up, Paris. Maybe if I just don't think about it, don't see all that scenery out there, it will vanish," suggested Sparky.

"Perish the thought," replied Paris.

"Yes, and I'll forget women and wine and live on borrowed time," said Jocko stoically.

"And every time I open my eyes…the world's out there all right. It's hard to close the old eyes and forget misery sometimes," said Sparky, stroking his hair.

"Maybe that's why misery lasts," suggested Paris.

Sparky nodded as he watched the trees through the window.

"Yet if I had know it would take this long, I would never had come," said Jocko. "You like at least a preface before you get into the book," he added.

Paris closed his eyes and thanked God for the day. The trinity was quite miserable for the time being.

"The peasants…they know where it's at," said Jocko, watching the fiesta in the third class cabin.

Paris opened his eyes and looked puzzled. He shot a stare at Sparky who, sensing the stare, stared back at Paris. Jocko opened his eyes again and stoically listened to the other two.

"Are you thinking what I'm thinking," Paris said to Sparky.

"How can I think what you're thinking? I'm not you," Sparky replied with an irritation that only superficially covered up his curiosity.

Paris almost laughed out loud.

"That is true literally. I meant figuratively."

"How can two people by figuratively thinking be thinking the same thing?" asked Sparky quizzically. "Paris, you've been doing philosophy too long."

"Knock it off Sparky," snapped Paris.

"Two people can be on the same wavelength…if they concentrate… the vibrations are untold revelations. Anyway, I was just thinking…I thought you may have been as well."

"Well I was thinking because I am conscious. You must be conscious to think," said Sparky still impatient with Paris.

"I agree but what I wanted to tell you is that—"

Suddenly they heard a large crash as if plates and cups had fallen from a high shelf.

"What was that?" demanded Jocko. "This is very strange," he added. Just then the conductor came through, wearing a white dinner jacket.

"Señor, señor," Jocko called.

The conductor halted, turned toward him sideways, and raised his brows.

"Pasta, vino, por favor," asked Jocko.

"No habla, no comprendo," replied the conductor.

The conductor smiled faintly, a knowing smile, a smile not unacquainted with the joys and sorrows of the world.

"Porque usted no habla," asked Paris, quickly. Paris stared at him with his large, blue eyes.

"No comprendo," replied the conductor with a frown.

"Porque usted no comprendo, señor," asked Paris.

"No habla," replied the conductor with a deeper frown.

"Como esta usted?" asked Jocko, following Paris' train.

"Yo soy muy bien. Muchos gracias," replied the conductor as if he was a child first learning to name his own sensations.

"Parlez-vous français?" asked Paris.

"No habla français," he replied with difficulty.

"Sprechen Sie Deutsch?" Paris asked again.

The conductor looked sad. "Nein, monsieur, Ich spreche nicht Deutsch, señor."

"Warum sprechen Sie nicht Deutsch?"

"Ich weiss nicht, monsieur," the conductor replied.

"Wem sind Sie?" asked Paris.

"Ich weiss nicht," replied the conductor with a frown. With that he waved goodbye and in two shakes of an April wind, he was gone. Paris sat back in disbelief.

"Extraordinary," he said as he packed his pipe, thinking.

"What were you guys talking about?" asked Sparky.

"We asked him if he spoke English, Spanish, French, German," began Jocko.

"Go on," asked Sparky, utterly curious.

"No, no. You don't hear anything, remember," said Paris, kidding him.

"C'mon, Paris."

"You're the one who said the world did not exist..."

"Okay, okay. So at least I'm not a skeptic twenty-four hours a day," confessed Sparky. "Please tell me what all went on."

"He kept telling us he did not speak nor understand any language we suggested to him. But he knows them or at least some of them because he could speak some words in Spanish and German though he had difficulty pronouncing the words..."

"You think something's wrong with him?" asked Jocko.

"I don't know. I asked him who he is in German and he said he didn't know..."

"It's hard to know who you are in any language sometimes...and especially to know yourself," said Paris.

"Weird," said Sparky.

There was a quiet as they watched the scenery outside the window, the sun-baked passes, desert land, dry, bright-colored, and glaring. After sixty-six minutes the train stopped again.

"Oh, no. Guess what fellas. We're stopping," said Jocko.

"I am starved. I know. Why don't we get some wine from the peasants," suggested Sparky.

"Not a bad idea," said Jocko. They got up to open the door to the next cabin.

"It's locked. Didn't the conductor just go through here?"

"He sure did," replied Paris. The only sound was the hissing of steam from the wheels and the singing and merriment of the peasants.

"What can we do?" asked Sparky. Paris rose.

"I'll go forward and ask the engineer what's happening."

He strolled through the aisle to the cabin door. It, too, was locked. Paris began to wonder. What kind of train is this? Why was there no one on this part of the train? Who was this conductor who mysteriously came to and fro from cabin to cabin? He walked back to the other two.

"It's locked," he said.

"Well, all we can do is wait. Our time will endure," said Jocko.

"I don't like this situation," remarked Sparky with a resigned cynicism that provides the heart of any skeptical reaction.

"Neither do I. There are too many unanswered questions. Who is that guy anyway? I'll tell you what…let's stall him. Jocko, if he starts to run, grab him. You, too, Sparky. Three against one. We have a right to know where we are and what we are doing on this train."

So they waited. And waited. Twelve minutes later, the train pulled its heavy grey body forward, faster and faster until the rhythmical clack, huff and puff, resounded familiarly in their ears. Paris smoked his pipe casually. Sparky read from a book. Jocko just looked resigned out the window at the scenery and the peasants he would see whenever the train curved snake-like through north central Spain. A fairly strong wind had come up and it felt cool on their faces. Some of Sparky's papers flew up in little circles in the cabin; then he held them with a paperweight. Out of the blue Jocko asked:

"You believe in God?"

Paris coughed and almost choked on the question.

"I think so. I try to. But it is hard," confessed Paris.

"I don't," replied Jocko.

"Why don't you?" asked Paris.

"I don't know. It just doesn't mean anything to me. I guess there's a certain something though," he said. This enticed Sparky who was listening as he looked up from his book.

"You guys are just dreamers. There is no such thing as God. You should know that by now. You're old enough. Why even ask the question?"

"How are you so sure there is no God?" asked Paris.

"I'm not sure but it's all so irrelevant."

"What *is* relevant then?" asked Paris.

Sparky was only mildly interested in the question but knew he was dealing with Paris' inquisitive mind and, feeling challenged, felt compelled to engage and be engaged by him.

"Security. Money. The good things of life like education, a good job, prestige. Good food. A good woman. Good health. Those *are* relevant to me," said Sparky. Paris nodded as his fire went out.

"Maybe you are right," said Paris thoughtfully. "Those things are important. But you know, I can't help but feel there is something more to life than just satisfaction of needs and goals...I mean...don't you think or believe life has a significance that...shall we say puts it into perspective?"

Sparky shook his head. Jocko listened, absorbed. Paris struck a match.

"No. It may have significance but I am more interested in money and security than anything else. Good health. I think that's quite relevant. Cash value. Dividends now," Sparky replied.

Paris felt sympathetic to what Sparky was saying and yet he himself saw such things as an obstacle to an awareness that for all its fragility and fleeting moments made life whole.

Sparky did not like such questions and felt a bit uneasy because of Paris' insistent questions. Sparky was a pragmatist, one for whom practical everyday affairs had the most meaning. He was not interested in Paris' high-sounding philosophizing. Paris, he thought, needed more of the earth than heaven.

Jocko piped up: "I agree with you both. I like the money, the security, and I'd like to think there is a purpose to it all. A center. A whole. But I must confess I love the flesh of woman more than metaphysics. Wine is my sunset. Beer my dawn."

"Eloquent, my dear Jocko. Eloquent," said Paris with a smile.

Just then the door latch moved abruptly. Their words melted and flew back into a primordial silence, lost.

They waited. Three minutes passed. Nine minutes passed. Their hearts beat like three brush strokes in the Chinese character for "heart."

All of a sudden, when their throats were dry by now, the door flew open. There stood the conductor who eyed them for a long moment then smirked. Cautiously he stepped into the cabin. He cocked his head as if to hear a word but nothing was spoken. Just then Paris said:

"Señor, where are we?"

"No comprendo," the conductor replied.

Like three panthers, they jumped him. The conductor tried to get through the door but Sparky and Jocko pulled him back. Paris locked the door. Then he broke from them and raced forward through the cabin. Jocko pulled his coattails which ripped. Sparky grabbed a leg. Paris got him in a strangle hold and pulled tightly, cutting his breath.

"Where's the key to that door?" demanded Jocko.

"What door?" he replied in plain English.

"Cut it out," said Jocko who was kicked in the leg. He punched the conductor in the mouth. The conductor flipped Paris into a seat. He got up, lunged at the conductor and climbed on his back, pulling his hair and shouting. Jocko pummeled him in the stomach. Sparky clutched both his legs so they could not move. This finally toppled him combined with Jocko's punches and Paris' weight.

Once on the aisle floor, the conductor was outnumbered. They searched him. Sure enough there was a key, presumably to each cabin. The conductor fought wildly when Jocko took the key as the conductor writhed under the combined weight of Paris and Sparky.

"No, no, señor. That is mine!" he kept shouting.

"I'll tell you what. You guys hold him. I'm going to unlock the cabin door."

Jocko tried to unlock the cabin door; it was locked.

"Didn't he just come through this door? Yet this key does not unlock it."

"Don't ask me how that happens," said Paris.

"I'm going into the engine car and talk to the engineer."

After a minute, he saw and spoke to the engineer.

"When will we get to Madrid?" he asked.

"In about two hours," said the engineer.

"How come it has taken so long?"

"This is a Spanish train. We're not in Switzerland."

"Two hours? Yes, but we have to stop by a convent for a few minutes. After that, we'll go nonstop to Madrid."

"By the way, why is the conductor such a jerk?"

"He thinks being a conductor is below his rank in life for he is a blue blood. So he acts like an ass," said the engineer in good English.

"Okay, thank you," said Jocko who returned to the first class cabin.

"You can let him up now. Two more hours and we'll be in Madrid."

The conductor got up, wiped himself off, cursed them under his breath, and disappeared into the next cabin.

The train trip went on for awhile longer with one stop at a convent long after the moon had gone down over the often poverty-ridden landscape until dawn had risen and dispersed the anonymous dark of night and finally pulled into the station in Madrid. The peasants who had slept off their merry-making through the night, were ready for anything that came their way as they flocked off the third class cabins in their brightly colored shirts with yellow and red neckties and long, drooping mustaches and large wine jugs under their arms.

The train began filling with new passengers and the three stood with their bags gazing at the train that had provided them with an unusual experience.

As they made their way toward a cab station, Paris turned around and gazed long at the train. He paused, looked again, and rubbed his eyes in disbelief.

"Hey look," he said, touching Jocko on the arm. Both Jocko and Sparky turned and peered curiously in the direction Paris gazed.

"What?" said Sparky, who, when he turned saw a broad grin on Paris' face.

"On the engine." They looked in vain at the engine.

"Is there something we're supposed to see?" asked Jocko who also noticed the big grin on Paris' face.

"On the engine," repeated Paris. "Look what's written."

They gazed at the words yet nothing registered.

"So," said Sparky, a bit annoyed at Paris.

"'Dialéctica'. What does that mean?" asked Jocko. By now, Paris was beginning to laugh for it had just dawned that the train itself was just another coil in the Hegelian dialectic called history.

"History talking in one long train," he said with a laughter that peeled and finally fell into an icy silence.

"That's why the stops and starts for that is part of it all." And with that Paris laughed long and hard. Tears came to his eyes.

"History's a jester. The jokes have been on us," he said as he began to laugh again.

"I'm glad you found it amusing," snapped Jocko as they got a cab to the Hotel Grand Via.

CHAPTER 28

M adrid was sunny and warm and busy. Sunlight filtered through the blinds as they unpacked.

"I'll never forget that trip," said Sparky who stretched out on his bed.

"Me too," said Jocko who had bought some wine, poured it into his bota bag, and was squirting some into his mouth. Paris lit his pipe and put some clothes in a drawer. They had traveled with one bag a piece. All three had cameras of one sort or another. They stretched, yawned, and relaxed. A pair of old white-washed doors opened out over the city; a curtain separated them from the windows. The water ran very slowly in the faucets and the room in general was not plush but adequate. Their room was the only one on that side of the floor; a staircase wound its way down to the hotel manager's desk which was right in the middle of everything. They soon came to know all too well the hotel manager who was a little man with thick glasses. He stood about five feet four inches tall and wore a watch too large for his arm. As it turned out, he was everything, from pimp to gadfly to thief all wrapped up in one. Often he could be seen emerging from a back room with a señorita as he zipped up his pants with a conspicuousness that was audacious, at least according to the trinity from England.

"That wine's good," said Jocko, wiping some from his chin.

"Let me try some," asked Paris. Jocko gave him the bota bag and Paris squirted a long stream into his mouth.

"It is good," he said, returning to his pipe and relighting it.

"So good to stretch," sighed Sparky. "I'll never take the trains in Spain again."

"You have no appreciation of dialectic, Sparky," said Paris tauntingly.

Sparky just smirked at Paris. He knew Paris was just joking. Some more time passed with nothing said in particular as the afternoon deepened into sunset and they began to get hungry. They soon got some apples, salami, bologna, cheese, bread and tiny seafood delicacies to go with their wine. A table sat in the middle of the room and they put the food on it and sat down. They cut the salami, bologna, cheese into strips and made sandwiches and drank wine. Jocko loved the raw oysters and scallops; Sparky preferred the strips of pickled herring; and Paris went to work on the jumbo prawns.

"I think we ought to tie one on tonight," said Jocko popping an oyster into his mouth and washing it down with blood-red wine.

"Can't you relax the first night, Jocko?" asked Paris.

"I didn't come here to mess around with books," he said with a dig at Paris who thought of nothing better than an evening with Shelly and Keats.

"Live it up, Paris," said Sparky. "You only live once, you know."

"Maybe so," said Paris, "at least in this way."

Jocko glanced at Sparky with disgusted looks.

"Okay, we live more than once," said Jocko. "Can't we live this one to the fullest? And if there's a next one, live that one when it comes."

Paris smiled.

"You guys go ahead. I'm too tired."

"Don't be a party pooper," said Jocko.

"No, I want the evening to relax and unwind my bones. Read some poetry."

Jocko and Sparky eyes each other demurely.

"Have it your way. To me it's a whole waste of time to sit around reading."

Jocko was not one to worry too much about Paris' decisions but he did feel Paris tended to be a bit too bookish at times and that tended to irritate him.

"Books are just ways of preferring another's experience to your own," suggested Jocko. Sparky's brows raised in anticipation as he looked at Paris.

"That's true," said Paris, mildly curious at what Jocko was saying.

"Why not live your own experience?" asked Jocko, honestly.

"Right now I'm too tired. And besides, I don't mind another's experience as long as I don't have to live it fully, embodied. Anyway I'm sure I'll not read that long. I plan to get a good night's sleep."

Jocko glanced at Sparky with a "at least we tried" look.

Not long after, Jocko and Sparky left and went five blocks away to a bar across the street from the Café Madrid. They got a table on this warm night and ordered drinks and cigarettes.

A trumpet, guitar, piano, accordion, and bass quintet played softly inside below mirrors that reflected their instruments in the lights. Several other couples occupied tables outdoors although they were only shadows set against the dying dusk. There was a quiet steady hum of voices at various levels of intensity and such voices, muted, streamed like black magic to the night. Across the street an orange neon sign blinked, skipped, blinked on and off. It read: *Café Madrid*. Sparky and Jocko sat, smoked, and drank for awhile, feeling lighter as the dark deepened. Jocko puffed and said:

"Paris is going to be a dead weight."

"It looks that way," agreed Sparky.

"I didn't come here to read and go to museums. I came for wine, women, and song. I mean to get me a nice woman and make love," said Jocko.

"Not easy with these women being escorted by their mothers," Sparky said as a dark señorita strolled by with her chaperone on her arm.

"I like the Basque women…the Castilians too," Jocko declared.

"I just like women," said Sparky. "I tell you I'm so horny, it feels like I've grown antlers."

"You probably have," replied Jocko who began to feel the air around Sparky's head. "By George you do."

They laughed.

"What do two young Americans do in Madrid?"

"They get laid," declared Jocko. "Now we've got to find a way to get laid for sure. There's gotta be some women who are horny here."

"We'll find them. Don't worry," said Sparky as he drank his third gin and tonic.

"I wonder what Paris is doing?" asked Sparky after awhile, now nearly glassy-eyed and gazing at the Café Madrid sign.

"Probably reading Hegel or Keats by now."

"Yeah. I'll tell you. If he doesn't want to get laid, I'll never trust another philosopher again."

"There's got to be more interesting things to do than solve the mind-body problem," averred Jocko.

"I tell you…when I'm in bed with a woman…why they h'aint no mind-body problem," said Sparky with a hillbilly twang like he was fresh out of ye olde cabbage patch.

"God let's hope not…I would think the only problem at that point would be the angle of entry," replied Jocko with a professional air. They both laughed again.

"So what's between Paris and Enid?"

"As far as I know, she stayed in France. That's why he came with us."

"Are they together or split?"

"Split. I don't know how permanently."

"I think I'd screw Enid if she were here," said Sparky.

"Shut up, Sparky. I'm getting horny just listening to you. Naw, I don't know how much is going on between them. He said they had a blow-up in Paris. She cancelled her trip to Spain. He came anyway. She is unsure about a lot of things."

The evening drifted on with the piano's melody alternating with an accordion and waves of music drifted into the late evening. A few couples left and strolled down several blocks to the main streets of Madrid; others just passed into the shadows, one or two pausing to kiss in the shadows out of moonlight. They drank on. Soon the moon crossed into the western sky and Jocko and Sparky were still drinking and had been eating peanuts for about an hour.

"What do you sha…I mean say…about getting home. I-I'm feeling dizzy," said Jocko with his head unsteadily propped on his arm.

"Sh-ure…I tell 'ya I'm utterly and surely shitfaced, as they say in the military," said Sparky, his head rolling slightly as he spoke.

"Well, let's go," he said as he laid money on the table and tipped the waiter. At that point a dark and sultry señorita passed by their table in the direction of their hotel. Instinctively, though with a slight weave to their gait, they followed her right to the gate leading to the hotel. In fact, she strolled in and ascended the stairs.

"Did you see what I saw?" asked Sparky.

"I sh-sure did," said Jocko, leaning on Sparky for support.

At that moment, Sparky fell onto the grass and Jocko fell on top of him.

"Get offa me," said Sparky who could not hold up his body; he was barely holding his drinks.

They struggled to their feet and weaved their way up the stairs. The señorita's room was on the floor below their room. They paused at her door.

"Hey wait. I'm dizzy again," said Jocko, "it's hot in here. Very hot. I swear I hear music."

"So do I. When you're drunk, you hear music everywhere," instructed Sparky who was leaning on the balustrade with a precarious look on his face.

"I guess-so," agreed Jocko, who was now becoming slightly pale and a bit sweaty. Finally they reached their room and could not find the key; this tickled Sparky who began laughing convulsively. Jocko found the key but couldn't find the keyhole.

"Damn it Jocko. You know half of life is finding the right hole. I swear you look like a virgin trying to screw a virgin. You gotta find the right hole."

Finally Jocko found the keyhole and in they lumbered. Only a small night light was on. Paris was sound asleep.

Outside, there came the sound of guitars.

"I swear I hear music," said Jocko again looking more and more pale.

"It's coming from the windows," whispered Sparky who went to the window, pulled back the curtain, and down below were a group of guitar-strumming mariachis.

"I'll be damned," Sparky exclaimed in a whisper.

"You probably will," whispered Jocko who was both dizzy and pale.

"Come here," Sparky said, motioning him to come to the window.

Jocko came and leaned over the window; they both hung out right over the mariachis who were softly serenading the señorita one floor below them. In fact, the pretty señorita stood right below them with a shawl on.

Just then Jocko began to vomit. Up came the half-chewed peanuts, his meat and cheese all flew out indiscriminately. Some landed on the señorita who gasped, thinking at first it might have been the droppings from an overly-large seagull. One could hear the splat of Jocko's vomit on her bare shoulder after she had taken off her shawl to examine it. One whiff and she knew. As she turned her face toward them, swearing in Spanish with several "Pendejos" on her breath, Jocko vomited again, landing right on her face. She was furious and ducked into her room and out of sight. Jocko was having fun. Then the smell of Jocko's vomit nauseated Sparky and he, too, began vomiting. Some landed right on the lead guitarist and he, too, began shaking his fist at the two gringos. Jocko's landed on the castanet player who, as one might imagine, began shaking his fists and swearing. Their vomit had ruined the señorita's evening as well as a serenade by the adoring mariachis. Both Jocko and Sparky hung over their windows sick as dogs. Soon, understandably, the mariachis began to throw rocks and just about anything they could get their hands on.

"Cut it you bastards. Can't you see we're just defenseless Army brats?" exclaimed Sparky. They, too, ducked inside and made it to the bathroom where they cleaned up and tried to vomit some more. Soon the mariachis left. Amazingly Paris slept right through these events.

"What a night," said Jocko with a pained grimace on his face. They both somehow made their way to their beds and fell into them after a night's exhaustion.

CHAPTER 29

Next morning they awoke. Paris was already up and shaving. Jocko's head hurt. So did Sparky's but not to the extent of Jocko's headache.

"That was a rough night. Boy do I feel like cracked crab that's been cracked all night in the jaws of whatever."

"I just want something to eat. And some coffee. Strong coffee. Guess I'll go down and ask the manager where we can get some food. I'm not used to continental breakfasts."

He descended the staircase and came upon the hotel manager, Julios Bonita. After having told Sparky where to get some food, he added:

"Mucho señoritas. Baestra Street," he said, making a large bosom with his hands. Every time he would say the word "mucho" the breasts he imitated with hands grew larger and larger.

"Where are they?" Sparky asked with a gradually increasing coherence, especially since his hormones did not care whether it was day or night.

"Mu-u-u-cho señoritas. Baestra Street," repeated Bonita with a laugh and a grin, holding up his huge watch.

"Time for you gringos to sample the meat, eh?" he said in the best English he could muster.

"I guesso," replied Sparky almost naively. "Almost any meat will do at this point," he added.

"Mucho señoritas," replied Bonita, again making breasts with his hands.

"Yes. Si. Mucho señoritas," replied Sparky, imitating the large breasts as well.

Bonita laughed and held up his watch again with a devilish smile and a lecherous laugh. Sparky got some food and they ate salami, apples, oranges and drank coffee they had bought.

"I gotta get me a woman," said Jocko, downing the rest of his coffee.

"Well, I know right where we can get one," said Sparky.

"Where?"

"Baestra Street. At least according to this dude for a hotel manager we have. He keeps saying 'mucho senoritas' this morning."

"We'll have to find out. I'm almost as horny as you are Sparky."

"That's pretty darn horny. Welcome to the 'Come blow your own horn club.'"

In his thoughts, Paris was a million miles away. He was thinking of Enid and their relationship as a whole.

"You wanna come, Paris?"

"No, that's not my line. A whore you mean?"

"I guesso."

"No, not for me."

"Why not?"

"I dunno. I'm a prude I guess."

"That's close. You and Enid are not prudes."

"That's different," Paris said, a bit on the defensive.

"How so?"

"I love Enid. I wouldn't love a whore."

Jocko and Sparky gave each other knowing looks with just a thin trace of smiles.

"You have to love someone to ball them?" asked Jocko. Sparky listened intently, tasting an apple.

"I do. Maybe you don't."

"Come off it! You've balled women you never loved and you know it."

Paris sat pensively, watching the sunlight peep through the curtains.

"Maybe so. I just don't want to."

"Have it your way," said Jocko with a shrug of his shoulders.

"You don't mind if we do…" said Jocko, again feeling ever so carefully how far he could approach the subject with Paris.

"No, you go ahead. I can be on my own here. You all have a good time."

"Well, we feel we're leaving you out."

"No, you're not. I'm leaving myself out. It's my choice."

"As you like it," said Jocko, then added as an afterthought:

"Paris, we missed you last night. We feel we're not altogether in this in that we've split up. I personally don't like it that way. Won't you just come with us tonight? You wouldn't have to do anything. Honest." Paris thought a moment.

"No, I just don't think so," he replied.

CHAPTER 30

They took Bonita's advice and cruised such places as the Bar Americano and the Honolulu Club. Not long after, they returned to the Bar Americano. The two were at the bar, nursing their drinks, when Jocko suddenly felt a hand glide up his thigh. Turning, he met eye to eye a blonde-haired woman about thirty-five years old with a fairly nice figure who spoke with a sultry Spanish accent.

"Jocko, what's she saying?"

Jocko leaned over and she whispered something in his ear. He leaned over to Sparky.

"She wants to know if we want a woman for the night."

"Tell her 'yes,'" shouted Sparky at which point he was touched by a tall brunette who, as it turned out, was working with her blond colleague.

"As her how much," commanded Sparky.

"She says about ten dollars American money for the night. You have enough money?"

Sparky was so excited he almost dropped his wallet looking through it.

"Yes, I have enough," said Sparky.

"Let's go then," suggested Jocko and the frolicsome four strolled outside with their half-drunk drinks still on the bar. They hailed a taxi and drove about eight blocks, stopping in front of a tall apartment building. They paid the driver who had a grin on his face and they entered a swanky apartment building with tropical plants and fish in the waiting room. Up the elevator they went until they came to a three bedroom apartment with two baths, a bidet, and a large living room and kitchen.

"What do you think of this?" asked Sparky.

"Outstanding," said Jocko.

Sparky was so excited he almost wet his pants and by now

was fighting the battle of the bulge.

They all sat down on a spacious sofa, the two señoritas talking in fast Spanish, pausing to give special smiles at Jocko who was obviously the favored one of the two thus far. Sparky did not care who was favored; he just wanted the game to begin. The tall brunette went by the name of Loli and the blond by the name of Estella. Jocko was the interpreter for the group and relished his linguistic privileged access as well as his surging sensations. Loli unzipped her dress as she talked; Estella did the same. They threw their slips onto a tall wall-like partition which had above it a clothesline that held up a curtain. Behind it was a twin-sized bed with black satin sheets on it. Loli had large breasts and very sultry; in fact, Estella was enough to inspire anyone's imagination. Just then Sparky had second thoughts.

"I don't know if I like this," he remarked.

"Now Sparky. Don't be so skeptical. Once you're on, you'll love it."

"But what if I get syphilis?"

"Well, we'll cure it. There's always penicillin."

After a moment or two, Jocko spoke up:

"I'll take Estella. You take Loli. Then we switch off. You got it?"

They then vanished behind closed doors.

CHAPTER 31

⁌————————⁌

The bull trotted into the corrida. Shadows that lined the edge of the bullring were edging slowly, ever slowly toward the station where the matadors with banderillas would wait their turn. In marched the picadors on huge draft horses, their muscles flexing in the rhythm of their gait. They were followed by half a dozen matadors with capes draped over their arms. They were followed by the young matadors, the matadors who were in training, who had many years of fighting to go before they became seasoned matadors and even had a chance at becoming a Juan Monolete or a Luis Dominguin. The bull watched them with a certain curiosity mingled with defiance that expressed itself explicitly when some of the matadors began to twirl their capes—pink and yellow—and arouse the bull and ready him for the fight. He became aroused, hoofed the ground, and charged only to be momentarily lost in the flurry of four or five capes. Repeatedly, he charged them only to gore the air with his long horns. A young matador then stepped out into the middle of the bullring. The bull turned his attention away from the capes and faced the matador squarely and, in a moment, trotted closer. There they stood, motionless, body facing body, each going to try to consume the other, negating the other with their looks, each a subject yet an object for the other, the way humans look at one another when the look becomes a key to the game of alienation and the movement of estrangement. The bull snorted twice; the matador held up his cape at his side, shaking it deliberately. The bull lowered his head, taking aim, hoofed the ground, and charged. Like he spun on glass, the matador swept the cape around and the bull charged past him. The move was greeted with shouts of "olé."

In the sun, high in the stands sat Paris, Sparky, and Jocko. They were all drinking San Miguel beer. Sparky shouted "olé" several times when the crowd sent up a resounding cheer that echoed throughout the entire corrida de toros.

"That bull has horns as long as yours," said Jocko, looking just above Sparky's head at imagined horns.

"Yours weren't exactly trimmed last night either, Jocko," he retorted as he took a swig of warm beer. They laughed as they held the sun at bay with their hands.

Pretty Spanish women sat two rows down. Colorful scarves, bright yellow and red blouses, marked them. Spaniards with bronze skin, close-clipped mustaches, and vivacity expressing their approval or disapproval of the bullfight, marked them. Sparky finished his beer and pulled into his lap a full bota bag. He opened it and held it out and sent a blood red stream of Spanish wine from Pyrenees vineyards into his mouth; when he once missed, it colored his mustache and chin. Jocko then took some as did Paris.

The bull had begun to tire after a series of charges in which the matador had skillfully used his bodily position and cape to avoid the disastrously-sharp horns. Initially full of fight, the bull had begun to tire noticeably.

As he was ready to charge, the bull stood there, motionless, staring at the matador; it was as if he wondered or even realized how doomed he was, a spectacle there, in front of all those who did not mind the sight of his blood or the sport of his flesh, a sport for men who rationalized everyone's suffering but protested their own pains. The bull sensed the game rules and simply stared at the matador who began to shake his cape, to egg on the bull. The matador sensed this in the bull and cocked his head, staring at the bull, at the blood that bathed his flanks from the newly-thrown banderillas, and the matador shivered as a cold, but dimly-perceived thought, gripped him and made him shiver. The bull asked why; the matador now regretted stopping to think for he became sensitive just as he blocked out the noise of the crowd, now with boos in the background. There he stood, life with the sport of victory, cape over sword, hidden, ready for the kill, and the dying, standing there, losing blood and draining energy from the sport. Life and death faced each other, sporting, gamely; the one with a faint smile, the other bleeding.

They loved each other, danced with each other, sacrificed each to the other and time would cut them down one and all.

"You have made me sensitive and now, in agony, I must kill you anyway," the matador said to the bull. The bull stared, half pleading, half enraged, ready to die and angry to live. It was all right if the bull tried to kill him but it was hurting to watch the dying who bravely died with each negation by the other.

"Come on now. Fight like a man I tell you. Fight! Fight! Life is fight! The just is fight!" he muttered to the bull who seemed to sense, in his own way, what was happening. He snorted, scraped the blood-spattered ground with his hoof and charged. His sharp horns barely missed the matador's thigh in the graceful swing of the cape. He turned sharply and charged again, this time cutting into the matador's thigh, at which point the other matadors poured out into the bullring and distracted the bull with their capes. The matador stood there, bleeding, his pink pants turning crimson, glowering with sympathy at the bull. The crowd shouted a wave of boos; they wanted him out of the ring. He was determined to finish off the bull. He ran his fingers along the blade of the muleta. It was razor-sharp; death on edge. Waving the others away, they ceased harassing the bull. There they were again, face to face. The blood lost from the banderillas had weakened the bull yet there was fight in him. The matador glanced at his thigh; it was as crimson as the bull's flanks. He was in great pain; he knew what the bull must be going through. The bull wanted to kill but sensed the cards were already dealt and that it was a certainty that his meat would feed the poor and orphaned in Madrid. The matador held his cape with the muleta just above it and began to shake the cape, daring the bull to charge. The bull did. Suddenly the matador lost his footing. The bull came on. And before he knew it, the sharp horn gored his groin and the matador was thrown high in the air. The bull began pounding hooves at him as the other matadors again distracted the bull with their capes. He refused to leave. The other matadors did not dare approach him unless they wanted to die instantly. Gradually, he edged himself into the ring, picked up his cape; some matadors tried to stop him so he could get medical help but he swung the muleta at their heads. They backed away. They did not want to die the death of the bull. The bull turned his attention to the matador who slowly made his way out again toward the center of the ring. The crowd booed again; Spaniards,

Jocko and Sparky screamed "Señor es loco! Loco!" A siren was heard in the background, outside the multi-storied walls of the corrida.

The young matador shook his cape again. The bull came closer, his nostrils calming, a long strand of saliva dangling from its muzzle, touching the corrida dust. He shook his cape again. The weakened bull was becoming aroused. He dug his hoof into the dust as if to make a grave. Then he charged and gored the young matador again. But this time the matador did not miss. Into the firm flesh between the shoulders of the huge bull, he ran the length of the muleta. Instantly the bull lurched, wobbled, tottered, and with an angry yet despairing snort and with a look of defiance as surrender, of hate and of love, slumped forward on his haunches and with his gigantic pink tongue, now spotted with fresh blood, of the dying into life, lay his massive head on his front legs and died. In plunging the muleta deep into the bull for the kill, the young matador himself fell with his full weight onto the sharp horn that rammed itself deep into him. He later died at a local hospital. But the bull had been killed. It was then that the crowd cried "olé."

CHAPTER 32

Several days passed in which Paris visited the magnificent Prado Museum in Madrid. Paris learned to appreciate the pleasantly plump models of Peter Paul Rubens and the sheer power of the paintings by Goya such as "The Third of May, 1808" and "The Nude Maja." But time to return to England was imminent. Sparky, Jocko, and Paris flew to Barcelona for an overnight stay then sat drinking San Miguel beer at an outdoor café. Their train was going to leave in awhile for Paris and they were drinking goodbye to Spain.

"Barcelona has been fun, hasn't it?" commented Paris.

"What we've seen of it. We should've come earlier," suggested Jocko.

"Maybe. But I enjoyed Madrid the best. You can't beat a good woman," said Sparky.

"Horny again, Sparky?" asked Jocko, slowly turning his beer.

"Always on the loose. I tell you there's nothing better than a good woman," he said.

As usual, Paris was slightly pensive, even a bit high. Sparky noticed it.

"What's on the philosopher's mind, pray tell," he asked with all the flourish he could muster.

"Not much. Just thinking."

"That's all you ever do," said Sparky. Paris just shrugged.

Sparky leaned back in his chair then looked at his watch.

"Train will be leaving in five minutes. We ought to go."

At that they rose, bought tickets, and boarded. They found a compartment by themselves and in a matter of moments the train lurched forward and soon a large funnel of smoke trailed the engine, graying the air as it rumbled through northeastern Spain soon to be in the Pyrenees.

"I hope this train doesn't stop at every cow pasture," remarked Sparky.

"Let us pray it doesn't," said Paris.

This train was not like the one they had taken to Madrid; this one stopped every once in awhile to pick up passengers and was on its way. The train sped its way from Barcelona and around twilight it rumbled through the soft-sloped, purpled vineyards of the Pyrenees. Paris stood long gazing out the window. Sparky read a book on how to consult the *I Ching*; although weary, Jocko too gazed out the window. Paris sat next to Jocko.

"Some of the best wines are from those vineyards," observed Paris.

"Oh," muttered Jocko.

"Beaujolais," said Paris. Jocko did not respond. He was getting tired.

"I'm going to retire," he said as twilight deepened. With that he climbed into the overhead bed, opened the blanket, and pulled it over him and laid down to pleasant dreams. Soon Sparky closed his book and put his coins away. It was getting too dark to formulate questions, toss coins, and draw hexagrams. Besides, he was tired. So he climbed up into the other overhead bed and soon pulled the blanket over him. Paris wondered if those beds belonged to someone else who had reserved them. He did not wonder long for he, too, began to nod drowsily even though he opened his eyes every once in a while. The vineyards were now behind them and the train increased its speed out of the mountains. They had almost dozed when the door was slid open with a loud shot. None of them peered at the door. It closed again with a bang.

"What was that?" asked Jocko in a loud whisper.

"I think the conductor. He's inspecting how many sleepers there are in each compartment," replied Paris in a loud whisper.

"Let's just fake it," suggested Sparky. "He doesn't know this isn't ours."

"Fine with me," said Jocko. Pulling up his cover, it was almost over his head. Sparky, too, rolled back to his original position, facing the wall so that his face would not be seen. Paris put his head on the sidearm of the long, lounge-like compartment chair. He, too, turned his face away from the light from the passenger corridor that beamed in when the conductor opened the door. Soon the train decreased speed and the clacking rhythm slowed until the clacks were further apart. Finally the train stopped. Voices and footsteps were heard. The door again flew open.

"Cette salle, est-il pour vous?"

"Non. Je ne sais pas. Nous pouvons rester dans l'autre salle," replied the man and his wife. The door closed. With a lurch that nearly flipped Jocko and Sparky, the train bolted its way into the night. Sparky was laughing his hips off.

"That's one way to do it! Just sleep your way into heaven. I sure needed this rest," he said, laughing again. Jocko, too, was enthusiastic about their claimed compartment. Paris was indifferent. He just knew it would be a long night and that he would be glad to see Blythe and Fleming again. Another two hours passed. Twice the door flew open and stayed open for several minutes. Each time they just froze; Sparky almost giggled outright but managed to muffle his laughter in the pillow. It was around five-twenty that the train stopped again. This time many people boarded. Sparky peered groggily over at Jocko.

"Something tells me this is the end. Our time's up."

Jocko did not respond. Only Paris was awake, although he had catnapped.

"Yes, I agree. This is too long a stop. Our compartment is about to be taken."

"Let's fake it as long as we can," said Sparky. Suddenly the latch raised and the door was slid open with an even louder bang than previously.

Sparky plunged his head into his pillow. Paris closed his eyes as the light flooded the compartment. Sparky felt a hand on his leg.

"Monsieur, monsieur," exclaimed the conductor.

Sparky did not move. Then the conductor began to shake his leg. Sparky did not move. When the conductor hauled off and hit him, Sparky rose like a jack in the box.

"What're you trying to do? Rape me? You French frog!"

He doubled his fist and the conductor moved toward the doorway.

"Non monsieur. Ne fait ça pas. Les peuples ici—cette leure compartement!" A whistle blew. There was the sound of running feet.

"Hey Jocko, let's get up. This might be trouble."

Jocko roused and was out of bed in a minute and jumped down to the chairs below. Paris sat up and leaned his head against the window. Jocko and Sparky sat opposite him. Just then the people who had reserved the compartment came in and climbed into bed. As well, two other couples filled the lounge chairs so that none of the three would have a place to sleep all the way to Paris.

As the train rolled on it was only another two hours to Paris. About forty miles outside of Paris, the dawn peeked through the trees as the train rolled by. Paris loved this for it was his favorite hour of the day as little farms and villages and tall groves of trees gave the sun's ascent a strobe light effect. Soon they reached Paris fairly well rested.

CHAPTER 33

The train arrived in Paris. Sparky, Jocko, and Paris stepped off at the Gare de Paris. Steam curled and hissed from the wheels of other trains about to embark for distant points. They went Metro Underground to the Latin Quarter. After winding up the stairs, they knocked on the door. In his pajamas, Fleming opened it. "Welcome back," he said. They went in, sat down and chatted for awhile. It was the day they planned to return to England. September had oozed over them like red wine. The winds were even gusty as they gazed out over the cobbled streets down below. That afternoon they flew Air France to England and it was not until they reached the Manor after about four hours in the air and on train that they began to unwind.

"It's great to be back," said Jocko as the taxi pulled out of the graveled bullring.

"I already miss Spain," waxed Sparky who lifted his bag with a strain.

"This side door ought to be open," said Paris. Sure enough, it was. No one seemed to be back yet.

"Don't tell me we're the first back," complained Sparky as the cage-like elevator took them to the third floor. Out they came, down the hall, and into their room. The manor was quiet for the most part that late September. Evenings were late in coming; the sun remained as if to defy its own setting. Pigeons cooed in the trees by the cricket field. It was peaceful there. A silence pervaded the gaudy testimony to early Victorian opulence. Its halls creaked; the elevator or lift grunted under student-teacher weight; and the only sound came from the kitchen below where the clanging of silverware echoed the hallowed and British Empire nostalgia-filled halls with a peculiar emphasis.

"Boy was that a mistake," said Jocko from his cubicle.

"What?"

"Getting back so early. Why I bet Zee is still in Africa," he replied, unpacking his clothes as they all were.

"Still, it is great to be back," sighed Paris. "Maybe there will be some peace and quiet around here and I can read some more Plato."

Fleming was quiet; he had grown a beard; he had had a long day and it was relaxing to be home. He strolled into Paris' cubicle. Sparky and Jocko soon left to hunt for any other returned students. Paris was filling his drawers with pants, shirts, and socks.

"Well, how was it in Spain?" asked Fleming.

"Fine. No complaints. Went to the Prado and saw a bullfight. Met some whores and had a good time," he said.

"I did as well in Paris. Nothing like French whores," said Fleming.

Paris cleaned his bed, lit his pipe and sat back and unwound.

"I thought you weren't into that," Paris said, flipping the pages of *The Republic* of Plato.

"I missed Blythe and was horny as hell."

"Hell is horny," replied Paris. Then he added: "You haven't seen her?"

"No. Last time I heard she was in Spain…with some priest," Fleming replied almost wistfully.

"She was with a priest?"

"That's what I heard."

Then after a long pause.

"You still care, don't you?" Paris asked, pausing to push the tobacco down.

"Not sure," he said, stroking his beard.

There was a long, healthy silence.

"You know...one night...I was walking along the Seine so very sad. Depressed. And I longed to find out why I was sad..." began Fleming, staring at the floor then at Paris.

"Did you find out?" Paris asked, ever curious.

"No. But I fell down to the bottom of life, utter despair. I went and drank some wine and tried to drown everything. My life, my education. Everything. So I walked along the Seine and sat down you know, like we used to, and watched the moonlight bounce off the ripples. Then somewhere a guitar played. Softly. And as I sat and listened with nothing at all to do in the universe except just to sit there..."

"Go on," said Paris, anticipating.

"Well, I sat there and saw the moon in a still portion of the river..."

"Go on, man," urged Paris who was not aware his light had gone out but who puffed anyway.

"Anyway, the moon began to seem as if it were smiling, even laughing."

"The moon?" asked Paris with a chuckle.

"The moon."

"The moon laughed," reiterated Paris.

"Seemed to."

"Well?"

"Well, the moon smiled and laughed. And it was as if everything was light. Harmonious. Peaceful. And I was lifted with that moment by something, I know not what, that made me feel as if everything was all right, kind of like the dream I told you about, that all would be well even if..."

"Even if?"

"Even if everything did not seem to work out the way I wanted."

"What on earth do you mean?"

"It's like this. You go down, down, down to the devil and you keep on going. Down so low you have even forgotten what was and who you were. And then the moon smiles and even laughs. And then like that night when the guitar played, just sitting there it all happened. I mean just sitting there. Doing nothing."

Paris relit his pipe.

"Sounds to me like the grace of God."

"Yes," replied Fleming.

"Realization that we make waves without consulting the moon. But the moon's still there."

"And beauty flowed into me like sugar into corn at dawn."

Paris again said nothing.

"You know a couple of us, in spite of all this, may just have grown up a bit in the time over here," commented Paris. "I know you've changed a helluva lot."

Fleming smiled vaguely, his smile increasing as he contemplated the words. Then he said:

"You know, this has been quite an education."

"So much to learn, so little time to do it in," Paris said softly.

"One thing must be known above all else."

"And what is that?"

"The self," replied Fleming. "Did not Socrates say the unexamined life is not worth living?"

"That's right. Unfortunately we don't examine life today in philosophy; we are merely blinded by propositional analysis. But this time is almost over. Philosophy will recover. It must."

Paris put out his ashes and laid his pipe on the edge of a suitcase he used as a nightstand. Fleming stared into space.

"One must do as the Indian philosopher Nagarjana said," he remarked as he shot a glance at Fleming who seemed lost in his own thought.

"Oh—and what was that?"

"In his treatise on prajna or wisdom, he says one must learn the swan's art of extracting milk from the water."

Fleming smiled. Just then the door opened and they could hear Sparky and Jocko cursing as they came in the door. Jocko came to the cubicle curtain and stood there:

"Blythe's back," he said to Fleming.

"She is? How do you know?"

"I just saw her downstairs. She's with the cook staff."

Fleming was delighted and dismayed at once.

"Who else is here?"

"Ev and Luwanna so far," Jocko replied. He came into the cubicle and stood next to the bureau drawers. "You guys been shooting the bull?"

"Yes, we shot some bull," replied Paris.

"So Blythe's here, eh?" said Fleming. Jocko nodded.

"There gonna be dinner?"

"Probably not," Jocko replied. "They, the cook staff, say it's not officially time for them to begin to serve meals. Most faculty and students are gone."

"Do they need an official time to serve meals?"

"Apparently."

Paris shook his head.

"I guess we should go and have the lot for five shillings six pence at Tony's Truck Stop."

Then added to Fleming: "You hungry?"

"Not really. They serve too many beans with the lot."

"You can buy something else."

"Okay. We ought to go. I want to get back and get a good night's sleep. Let me get some money and another shirt on," he said, leaving.

They left in Sparky's minivan and ate a hearty meal. Later that evening, they returned. The manor was dark with few lights on. By now, Paris was anxious to see Enid again, although he was conflicted by such a contemplated encounter. The others went to the commons room and began to play music. Paris strolled to the elevator, got in, and pressed the button. With its characteristic strain, the elevator lurched and then

291

quietly delivered him to the top floor. He got out and went to her door and peered down the long corridor to where her bed was. A lamp was lit. He knocked. No answer. He knocked again. The sound of bed springs careened down the wood paneling. A shadow appeared on the opposite wall then a head appeared at the corner of the wall. It was Enid.

"Come in," she said. Down the corridor he strode with a gait that faintly suggested a shoot out.

"Why Paris..." she said.

"Yes?" he said with a slight rise in his voice.

"Come in. Come in," she said as she put down a book on the burial rites of the Kwakiutl Indians. He came in and sat down on her roommate's bed.

"It's been a long time," she said. "How was Spain?"

"Oh, fine. Good times," he said.

There was a long awkward silence as if words could not be found for former lovers who have come together once again.

Then Paris said: "How was France?"

"So-so," she said with a shrug. "Met some interesting people."

Then Enid grew serious.

"I've missed you, Paris. I've thought about you a lot."

Paris smiled faintly.

"Same here," he replied.

"I think you should know that Ted and I are over."

There was no expression Paris' face but if one inspected closely, a softening could be detected around his mouth.

"I'm not surprised."

For a moment she lost her composure and dabbed a handkerchief around her eyes. In a few minutes, her composure returned.

"Why don't we go for a walk," he said.

"Yes, a walk would do us good."

They took their heaviest coats and went downstairs to the very front room of the manor. By the door there was a statue of St. George slaying the dragon and just opposite that was a stone urn with figures from Greek antiquity in bas-relief all around it. Paris, like Fleming in his more guileless moments, was a lover of art. For Paris art, like the varieties of logic, seemed to go with philosophy. Such an urn would catch his eye and send him into a forgetfulness that only remembrance would relish. They stopped at the bottom of the staircase.

"I've never noticed that before," he said, pointing to the urn.

"A work of art. The figures…lovers in pursuit. See this one here. He's after the maiden who flees into the safety of the forest."

"Come, let's go, Paris."

"I can't help but think of those lines from Keats:

> *'She cannot fade, though thou hast not thy bliss*
> *Forever wilt thou love, and she be fair!'*

he said, pointing to the two lovers on the sides of the urn.

Since she was a lover of literature, Enid was quite moved by Paris' remembrance of those exquisite lines.

"Art is a sounding to another life," commented Paris as they strolled out into the evening lit by a harvest moon.

Shadows engulfed them until they were almost at the center of the bullring. The long shadows of the manor house made an almost gothic silhouette, almost eerie in the quietude of the night. Sometimes such a large place, such as Erehwon Manor, was so quiet it was scary. Into the shadows cast by the side wall of the courtyard, they disappeared. Just then the bells tolled. Nine o'clock. On occasion the light grasped them, fondled them with a playfulness that romance best becomes. Moonlight had soft, changing fingers and the tiny features of human life it touched had an almost primitive magic about it. Moonlight was for meditation.

"Look how bright it is. You can see the cricket field from here," with a lilt to her inflection.

"Yes, it is. So bright. An autumn evening. The full moon," replied Paris, who paused and knocked the ashes out of his bowl.

"I remember when I was a kid, we used to run in our birthday suits whenever a moon was out…"

"Really? Why?"

"I don't know. But it was fun. It really was," she continued.

They strolled until they reached the bridge and paused.

"It's so quiet I'm almost embarrassed to make a sound," he said, leaning over the bridge as he stared at the quiet waters.

"Come on. Come on. Let's take out a boat," she said, almost dragging him to a path that led to six boats there for use by the students.

The water was like glass, smooth with a sheen. Paris dipped the oar in and paddled.

"How peaceful," he said.

"Yes, and all to ourselves," she replied.

Just then a bullfrog leaped off a rock and splashed into the water. Enid almost jumped out of the boat.

"God that scared me," she said with a gasp.

"Just a frog," he said, paddling on.

"Look at the moon. Doesn't it make you drunk just to gaze at it?" she said after awhile. She sat back on the stern.

"Yes, if you look at it long enough, you can forget you're on the earth," Paris replied. He would paddle, let the boat glide, then paddle it again. Sometimes he would not paddle at all, just let the boat drift where it would. He, too, sat back to admire the moon. The boat edged its way down toward a group of trees that partially hid the moon.

"Let's get out of these shadows," she said.

He paddled the boat again into the moonlight, then let it drift again.

"You keep letting this boat drift…"

"So?"

"We'll end up in the shadows each time. Look at all the trees here," she said, pointing to two large elms as well as several willows.

"Don't worry, we can always return," he said.

A long silence ensued. The boat drifted further.

"I hear something. Shhh," she said.

Paris perked his ears and listened toward the water.

"Sounds like some ducks. I'd say about a hundred yards down. Let's go."

Quietly, deftly, he picked up the paddle and dipped it firmly into the water. The boat glided with hardly a sound through tree shadows then light patches again. They said nothing. They just watched as a group of ducks and geese appeared on a little island. Paris edged the boat into the shadows of a stately elm. The island had one weeping willow under which the ducks and geese slept. Paris held onto a root that jutted from the bank. This way the boat would not continue to drift. In a low whisper he said:

"Those two are Toulouse geese," he said, pointing to a large gray goose and gander.

"Those are Peking ducks. The white ones. The females are the ones we heard. Drakes don't make that much sound."

Enid nodded.

"What are those?" she said, pointing. Paris strained his eyes. It was hard to see in the moonlight.

"Those look like Mandarin ducks from China."

"Ducks from China?" she whispered.

"Oh, yes. Much smaller. At least they're shaped like Mandarins. Hard to keep in captivity I've heard," he added.

Just then one of the ducks quacked loudly, piercing the air, as the others began quacking.

"Females again. They're the loudest and the ugliest."

"I resent that Paris Brandon," said Enid, louder than a whisper.

"Shhh. I wasn't referring to you," he said.

"Well…I don't like what you imply by such statements. I'm a female and I'm not loud. Nor am I ugly," she insisted with an almost childish abandon.

"I didn't say anything about you. Don't be so touchy. You don't have to be on edge all the time."

Having now heard them, the ducks were themselves on edge. They did not particularly like intruders, especially at nights when they could not see into the shadows. After all, neither goose nor gander, nor duck nor drake was prepared for this interruption of their island paradise. Imagine such! The gander hissed in their direction, his long neck curved s-like. The drakes did not say much; they figured the hens had already quacked so much before, they would not compete with them for the air waves now. The goose hens honked loudly to see who might honk the loudest then they would pause to gossip and chit chat about whose honk really was the loudest.

"You see...you disturbed their little island. Now they know we're here."

Enid stared incredulously at him.

"The poor little ducks and geese are now disturbed," she said, mimicking a false sympathy.

Enid was quite disgusted.

"I just don't like your characterizations of females," she said.

"All right. All right. They are neither loud nor ugly. Does that suit you?"

"No, not at all," she replied, trying to extract at least three more pounds of flesh.

"I won't play your games anymore. Let's go back. We've intruded on another world and given the geese our own sideshow," he countered.

"No, I want to stay," she said, pouting.

"We're going," Paris said fiercely and with authority.

"We're staying."

"No, we're going," he said, reaching for the paddle the same instant she did.

"Give it here," she demanded.

"No, I'll paddle," he commanded. They both fought for the paddle.

"Cut it out!" he said. "You're going to tip the boat!"

"I don't care."

"You're rocking the boat, Enid," he said, fiercely.

She grabbed the paddle and took a swing at him; he ducked. As they fought, the old gander leaned down to his hen and said:

"Those silly geese. Look at those humans. Utter folly. Sure would like to decode their language sometime. But I can guess at what they're saying."

His hen did not duck a reply.

"Well, George, we've had our spats too, you know," she said as her brown eyes winked at him. She continued to cut several blades of grass with her orange beak as she listened to the late adolescent movie across the way in the boat. "They're acting childish, don't you think so George," clucked the hen again as she chewed a luscious blade of grass.

"Of course they are. You know we animals are not supposed to be talking since humans, the human animals, cannot fancy themselves being rational and enlightened if they for one moment thought that dumb animals could talk. Well, let them be rational and enlightened. I still enjoy talking to you as I always have, Martha," as he pecked lice off her back feathers.

"And I enjoy talking to you, George. What's good for the gander is also good for the goose," she said, rubbing her long neck against his left wing.

Over on the boat, Enid held onto the paddle as Paris had grabbed it again.

"Don't you dare," he screamed.

"I dare," she cried, defiantly.

"Don't rock the boat," he commanded.

"To hell with the boat," she screamed.

Just then they both tried to get the paddle, turning in the same direction and the boat turned, plunging them into the water.

"Now look what you've done."

"Me? You're just as much at fault. Don't blame me."

Enid was spitting water and treading water. Paris tried to climb back into the boat but Enid kept pulling his leg.

"Let go, Enid. My God. What're you trying to do?"

"That's my business," she countered.

By now the ducks were quacking up a storm; the geese were honking gaily. It was truly a show to behold.

Soon Paris climbed the bank, pulled the boat in, turned it over and let the water out; Enid waded to the bank. Paris was angry.

"You want to paddle with me down there or not?"

"All right," she said. They pushed the boat, climbed in and were off. As they glided to the middle, Enid began to rock the boat again.

"Enid, don't," he warned.

"Don't what?" she said as if dumb.

"Don't rock the boat. My God, women are here to torture us," he said, lifting his arm toward the moon.

"And men are here to torture *us*," she said, tauntingly.

For several moments he concentrated on paddling, hoping she would not rock their globe around. But she did.

"Enid," he said as water splashed in his face. "Cut it out!"

On the opposite shore, the geese and ducks shook their heads as they watched them ever so slowly paddle back up the river. She rocked the boat again. Exasperated, Paris exclaimed: "Woman is hell." To which she replied:

"What is good for the goose…"

"Thank you, Enid, for your asininity this evening. We've all…been charmed by the delights, seductive and otherwise, of womanhood. Now will you just go to hell!" he yelled.

Enid decided to rock the boat again.

"My God, why did you put this wench on earth to torture me for?" he said, pleading skyward.

Enid swatted his buttocks with the other paddle.

"Ow!"

"Don't call me wench, Paris Brandon. If you do, I'll knock your head off," she commanded, holding the paddle in a swinging position.

He glanced over his shoulder, and after seeing the paddle raised high in her hands, he decided to keep his mouth shut. Soon they arrived at the place where all the other boats were lodged. It was inconspicuous, a shady place which shielded the boat from the cars that passed over the bridge to and from the manor.

"Let's get out of these wet clothes," she said as she stripped.

"Why do that?" he said, irritated.

"I don't like wearing wet clothes," she said, with a note of defiance.

They picked up their heavy coats that they had left on the bank until they returned.

Paris sighed with a shrug.

"Have it your way, woman," he said, disgustedly.

They climbed up to the bridge and re-crossed it in the direction of the manor. To the right was a long field that, save for a road that led to a small farm and nearby church, ran all the way to the outer courtyard of the manor. It was this field, part grass, part tall hay, they now entered beneath the moon. They walked and wandered for a fairly long while without saying anything. Much was thus said. He, too, had taken off his wet clothes and walked along as did she in the heavy coats they had brought along in case the weather cooled.

"I'm sorry for all that," she said, holding her wet clothes in her hand.

Paris did not reply.

Another silence passed.

"I *am*," she said.

"Am what," he growled like a bear.

"Sorry."

"Hrrrmp," he said, boiling. He was thinking how right Fleming had been to see that Enid was simply making a fool of him, that her games were well-structured and well-executed. Fleming was right; all that stuff about having to wait until after the visit to Spain to decide who she loved was sheer stupidity. How he looked forward to talking to Fleming!

"Paris?"

"Hmm?"

"You love me?"

He kept walking.

"What?"

"You love me?"

"Of course when autumn dust swirls in your angelic hair, when…" he replied, half mocking.

"Do you?" she interrupted.

He stopped as she did.

"Is this another game?"

"No," she said. There was a note of sincerity in her voice. Paris started to walk, but she grabbed his arm. He paused.

"I mean it."

There was a slight smirk on his face.

"What do you say?" she asked, almost entreating him.

"What can I say after you act like tonight?" he asked.

"A woman has a right to raise hell sometimes…even if it's with someone she loves," Enid said with an uncharacteristically deliberate manner.

He began to leave again but she touched his arm.

"Paris, I do love you," she said.

"Woman, how many follies are spoken with the word 'love,'" he replied.

"With this folly," she said as she hugged him close to her.

Paris was moved. After a long while, he said:

"If love be folly, as the moon is my witness, let it be," he said, as he returned the hug and kissed her with all the passion of a Catullus for a Lesbia.

The hay was yet warm from the sun. Enid just poured kisses all over him. Then they continued their walk to the manor.

CHAPTER 34

Next morning the sun slowly peeked through the clouds and broke out into the sky to burn with all it was worth.

"Nice day out," said Jocko who put on his pants by the window then peeked into Sparky's cubicle. Sparky sat on his bed pulling on his socks.

"Morning," he said sleepily.

"Let's go, Sparky. Breakfast is on."

"Be right with you. Get this sock on," he said, as the sock only reluctantly eased over his heel. Jocko peered into Fleming's cubicle. He was sound asleep. He went to Paris' cubicle: sound asleep.

"What a bunch of dead heads," he muttered, "Here it is nearly nine-thirty. Dead bodies."

"That means all the more food for us," said Sparky, licking his chops.

"You're getting as bad as Ev," Jocko said low. "Hurry Sparky. Comb your hair later." Sparky combed his hair.

They soon departed. Only Peter, Paris and Fleming remained in their cubicles. Zee was not yet back from Africa. Hardly anyone else was either. Fleming woke, yawned, and stared at the light from the window that opened out on the Midlands through the circle of trees that formed part of the bullring. He rose. Looking in his mirror, he thought:

"I must have aged during the night. I look so old now. And I'm still an undergraduate," he said, rubbing his beard. To the window he strolled and breathed the fresh air that tingled his nose. Today, they will all be back, he thought. This is the day of the great return to the home far away from home. Funny how home was thought as being away from where one was. But home was where you were, he thought. Musing on this idle tidbit, he pulled back Sparky's curtain. Seeing no one, he proceeded to Paris' cubicle and pulled open the curtain. Paris was staring right at him as his head poked in.

"Aha! A mummy come back to life! Good morning," he said.

"Good morning and how are you?"

"Just fine," replied Fleming. "You have a good time?"

"Last night?"

"No, last Halloween."

Paris smiled. "Oh, sure."

"How was Enid?"

"Light as a frost, as moon-swept as a deep forest, a lovely field of poppies, circular like the eye of a hawk circling," replied Paris.

"A moon can do that I'm told. It must've been quite a night."

"Feathers were made not as light, bears have no teeth long enough," Paris said again.

Fleming shook his head, half-dazed, half-amazed.

"Must have been tea and biscuits," he said with a wink.

"Tea and biscuits: the twins: now and forever," replied Paris with a wink.

They both roared like tigers.

"Tea and biscuits, eh?"

"Sun and moon last night united," replied Paris.

"Sun and moon?"

"In one body," he replied with a deep breath.

"Sacred silence plays fountains and in the noise only the silence keeps," said Fleming.

They both laughed with a roar that almost split the window panes.

CHAPTER 35

That afternoon most of the students returned. Unpacking, giggling, story-swapping, all took place with a refreshing merriment. The faculty as well returned with stories to tell about the warm waters off Mozambique, the flight to Morocco, the Carlsberg brewery in Copenhagen and the rest.

In the weeks that followed Enid and Paris grew closer together. This was, in part, facilitated by Ted being out of the picture altogether. Fleming and Blythe remained on speaking terms; she had left her priest to his revolutionary activities and flew to Paris and then on to London. She did not say much about that relationship until one day she came into the front study that opened through tall windows onto the courtyard green below where several were playing soccer. Paris was studying when the tall, mahogany door opened and Blythe poked her head in.

"You busy?"

"Just studying," he replied.

"Can we talk?"

"Sure," he replied. He left his books on the table and went into a larger parlor where the daily *London Telegraph* was deposited. They sat in big chairs.

"What's on your mind?"

"Fleming," she said, lighting a cigarette, her long legs crossed.

"What about him?" Paris asked, stroking his mustache.

"I still care."

Paris smiled faintly.

Outside, Fleming stood and watched the soccer game. Soon bored, he strolled up the steps that led to the cricket field. At that instant, clouds parted and the sun shone. He cut along the edge of the cricket field and mounted more steps until he was confronted by a swamp. At one end was a statue of some saint who solemnly stared at the swamp. He then cut left and embarked upon a half-shaded woodland trail. In trees above him pigeons cooed. This was one of Paris' favorite haunts. As the sun moved farther west, its hue cast a reddish tint to the wild roots and tree trunks. He had sat for some time and watched the sun shafts illumine the particles of dust that danced with abandon. Somewhere far off in the bushes the murmur of flies could be heard. Soon he got up and moved to a white bench and sat staring at the rolling fields of Lincolnshire and clouds in the distance. Every once in a while he heard yells from the soccer game. He must have catnapped for the next thing he knew someone was shaking him.

"Fleming. Wake up. Fleming," the voice repeated.

He sat up groggy-eyed.

"What is it? Oh, Paris. I must have been asleep."

"Yes, you were," Paris replied as he sat next to him.

"How long?"

"I don't know," replied Paris.

Fleming wiped his face until his head began to clear.

"How are things?"

"Pretty much usual. Saw Zee. He's back from Zaire. Saw Joan. She's back from Stockholm. Saw Blythe."

"Oh?"

"She's still in love with you."

"Kid's stuff," scoffed Fleming. "You know…"

"Fleming," interrupted Paris.

"What?"

"Listen to my words, glue your eyes to my mouth."

"Talk then," said Fleming, almost pretending not to care about what has gone before.

"She wants to see you again."

"Now?"

"Now."

"I'm beyond that. I just don't want to be with her now," he said.

"Why?"

"I don't know why."

"Because of the pregnancy?"

"It's not that," he scowled.

"You sure?"

Fleming rose and paced the country path on the east side of the bench, occasionally pausing to gaze at the waving hay of Lincolnshire fields.

"That's not it."

Paris eyed him like a hawk.

"If that's not, what're you pacing around for?"

"Paris, you're a good man, wide in understanding, wiser than most, but this is something you don't understand."

"Perhaps," replied Paris, "but it's been you who has projected the fetus size and made it larger and further along than it really is. Why just now she doesn't even show that much. And you've been seeing a five month or seven month pregnant woman when it has only been a few short weeks."

"How do you know all this?"

"I've listened to you. You always talk as if she were eight months pregnant. You've made a fertilized egg into an infant. It's you who, defending yourself from yourself, has made it larger than it really is. Is it not your fear, your guilt that has done this?"

Fleming paused in his pacing. Long and hard he thought.

"I think you're right," he said slowly. "But even if this right be admitted, still it doesn't mean that understanding even oneself is enough."

"Of course not. Being self-aware, though painful and full of suffering, is not enough. But it does mean that you don't have to lay on her anymore than she can bear."

"What do you mean by that?"

"No one is forcing you to do anything. She just still loves you."

Fleming, who had turned his back on Paris, whirled around:

"But that implies quite a bit. Yes, you are subtly forcing me to…see her again."

"No, not necessarily. If you don't, don't. If you do, go ahead."

"Oh, you damn philosophers! Uttering tautologies."

"Don't deflect it, Fleming. I'm only saying that she does still care and that you have laid on her all kinds of your own feelings that are an injustice both to yourself and her."

Paris lit his pipe but it went out. His yellow shirt with red flowers shifted in color as the sun swung into and out of the clouds.

"Maybe so. Maybe so," he said as he stared off into the distance.

There was a long silence, primordial, profound.

Paris, too, gazed into the distant Lincolnshire fields. The tinkling of sheep bells added an impressionistic glow all about.

"It is a pain to see her sometimes," said Fleming as if there had been no conversation break.

"And a pleasure to see Joan?"

Fleming nodded in reply. He strolled over to buttercups that grew in bunches along the woodland path.

"Like this flower, I close when the pain of nightfall approaches…"

"And open when Joan opens her petals…"

A faint but acknowledging grin came on his face.

"Yes. I don't like pain and suffering."

"No one does," replied Paris who was now bending down beside the buttercup.

"Then why bother with it? I know I can't handle it. The eye of suffering does not close but remains...vigilant."

"A good question. But first ask yourself which is more painful to bear? Your guilt or the chance that it might be your baby?"

"My guilt. The suffering is too much."

"But suffering teaches, whether it is chosen or not. And have you not learned a joyful wisdom even here?"

"I don't know what you are hunting for in this web of conceits, Paris..."

"Hyssop on turtles, marjoram on hares, oregano for the evening, and sage for eternity."

"What?" Fleming sharply replied.

"Spice deepens the flavor of finest food. Grow carrots and radishes if you wish. But reconciliation is a hard lesson and we despise it. So, my friend, with compassion you can afford even Blythe."

"These words you already knew. They just keep closest to the breast and only breathe in the silence."

"Maybe so. You know, I think you're a crazy philosopher," Fleming said as he, too, stared at the buttercup.

"As Emily Dickinson said: 'In much madness is much sense.' The capacity to divine things. To feel their petals, their texture, and give the evening proverbs to live by. One cannot discern the heart with logic on the breath. "

A big grin came on Fleming's face and he shook his head as his fingers touched the delicate stem and then the petals of the buttercup.

"So fragile our thoughts are," Fleming mused, "and such liars..."

"So fragile the spirit," mused Paris. "One must go deeper than the behaviorists and the statisticians for wisdom. "

"You cryptic bastard," Fleming said. "I thought philosophy taught you to be clear."

"Clarity only obscures...the refined strings...on our guitars..."

Fleming grinned broadly. Paris stared at the sun for a moment.

"It's time to eat," he said. "Time to celebrate sundry comforts of the sun."

"Yes, it's time," replied Fleming as they left the buttercups on the woodland path.

CHAPTER 36

S upper was just over. The clatter of dishes echoed throughout the long eating hall interrupted now and then by Skip's barks and the giggling of the kitchen staff. Luwanna made her usual rounds of the tables, gathering as many bananas that had been left in the fruit bowls as she could. Fleming eyed her with interest. When she came to his table, he said:

"Haven't you got enough bananas already, my dear?"

Luwanna was slightly flustered and began to smile her painful smile, careful not to arouse Fleming for she had heard that he was wild with women.

"No, I really like bananas," she said in a quickly flippant manner.

"You certainly must," Fleming said, winking at Sparky who ate the rest of his beef curry on his plate.

"Fleming, I don't like your sarcasm," she said, flatly, as she reached in the fruit bowl for another banana.

"Me? You must be kidding. Why would I be sarcastic with you, my sweet?"

"You're making fun of my love for the potassium in bananas," she said, becoming a bit hot under the blouse. "You're just monkeying around with me."

"I'm not trying to make a monkey of you. I just want to know why you take so many bananas."

"I told you I like to eat them," she said, smiling with a painful smile. She started to go.

"Wait. Why do you like to eat them?"

"I dunno. All I know is that they feel good going down," she said.

Fleming eyed Sparky who returned the eye, grinning.

"They really must…for you to eat so many," Fleming replied.

Again she began to go.

"Tell me, have you a boy friend?" asked Fleming.

"I don't like men at all," she said, beginning to peel one of the bananas.

"Why not? You too good for them?" Fleming asked.

Sparky was keeping his head down as he ate to avoid a certain impulse to laugh.

"No, it's not that. Men are just bores. I have a lot of other things going. I'm really quite busy."

Sparky could hardly contain both himself and the curry. Quickly he washed it down with milk.

"I can well imagine," Fleming replied. "You must be very busy indeed. You're an 'A' student. On the honor council. And you're pre-med. You've got a great career ahead of you."

"You see, I'm a busy woman," she said.

Painfully, she smiled again as her accomplishments were listed. With that, she went off to Ev's table. But, as usual, Ev's bowl was empty. To avoid Luwanna's rounds, he made it a practice to eat all the bananas before eating dessert. That way he could eat it all. Sparky began on his dessert.

"Very busy girl indeed," he said with a smirk. Fleming smiled.

"Indeed. I'm sure those bananas give her…the energy to remain busy, too," he said. As his head turned, he saw Blythe at another table across the hall talking to her friend, Susan Sullivan.

"See you upstairs," he said as he got up. Sparky nodded as he watched Fleming stroll across the hall to Blythe's table. Her eyes rested on his as he approached. She was casually smoking a long cigarette, one that exuded a stylish sophistication. Susan was Irish pride, a poetic mouth, a sacred heart, with endearing freckles and a loveliness no words could say. Fleming came and sat opposite Blythe. Suz, her nickname, seeing they may want to talk privately, moved back her chair.

Blythe said: "Don't go."

But Suz said: "I really must. You two talk. I must go water my roses."

"Roses?"

"The ones in my window." She up and left with all the lightness of foot she could muster. She was a bit shy and equally quiet but was strong in her own way.

As the kitchen help began clearing tables, giggling, and Skip's bark became louder, Fleming said: "Let's go."

They rose and went out into the courtyard. Just then the bell rang seven times. The Union Jack had been lowered.

"How've you been doing?"

"Fine," she said without expression.

Her blue dress shone even darker as the light faded in the dying of the light. They walked past the Duke of Earl's limousine toward the main gate that led down the road to the main road leading to Grantham. Fleming was barefooted so he walked more on the grass than usual.

"How is…" he said, indicating her abdomen with his eyes.

"All systems go," she said with a slight curl of her lips. Her tone was that of a submarine commander ordering a dive to five hundred feet.

"You're still going…to bear it?"

She nodded with a cursory glance at him. Much there was that was not being said and much in not being said, was said.

"Till death do us part," she said, cynically, sarcastically.

"That's one way to bear a life," he replied, with a lightning smile as they arrived at the gate. Smile she did not.

"A large gate…even in autumn," he said, deflecting the punch.

"Yes. One way heaven, one way hell. A gate of hell," she said in a tone of resignation.

"An autumn gate full of choice marigolds and well-worn mandelas…"

"Fleming!" she exclaimed.

There was a silence as the iceberg pierced the poetry.

"A cold shot," he remarked.

"Colder it will get if…"

"If?"

"If you don't get on with it. You're wobbling. Get on center. Square with me," she said, her hands demanding, lovely, menacingly on her hips.

"Get on with what?" he asked quizzically with a faint yet genuine naïveté.

"What's on your mind?"

"I just wanted to talk…"

"Well, then talk brother…" she replied, impatient.

"Let's walk further," he said.

A car passed them with one headlight out. It was Foo Ki's minivan. He resided in one of the smaller rooms one floor below Room 33. He always sped into the bullring to test his brakes and frighten anyone who might be watching. He was a chemistry major and quite proud of his van.

Fleming smiled as he listened to Foo Ki's van scatter gravel all over the bullring, but Enid was not smiling.

"Well?" she said, hands on hips.

"Oh, yes, as I was about to say…"

Fleming suddenly did not know what to say. It was hard to talk as friends once love had been in the game.

"Fleming…shall I forget it? Shall I forget you?"

"Every forgetting is remembering by another name," he said, low.

They continued walking.

"I honestly don't know whether to forget you or remember our loving times together," she said with a tenderness that made her even lovelier in the dying light. There was a silence and only the wind and his footsteps could be heard.

"So much to forget, so much to remember," he said, after a few minutes.

Then his attention drifted: in a way, he knew he loved her and always would but there was so much ill-feeling in the past weeks that he could not concede to her demands for affection. He then quoted:

"in time of all sweet things beyond
whatever mind may comprehend,
remember seek (forgetting find)
and in a mystery to be
(when time from time shall set us free)
forgetting me, remember me"

She was silent for a long while. The wind shifted.

"It's not an either/or proposition, then…" she said, finally.

"No. Either/or propositions are convenient fictions for decision-making of the human mind. Just verbalizations. Forgetting and remembering flow into each other."

"That's painful," she replied.

"Maybe, but you must realize the who you are in love with today is buried, to be able to love the who of tomorrow. We cannot help but forget in our remembering. The injustice is to remember only the way those we love were. That's our habitual, partial vision," he said, "we tend to forget all the nuances, tones, rhythms that make a developing life."

"Yes, but we cannot remember the future," she protested.

"Yes, but that would be a most just memory," he countered.

"No man has that memory."

"No, that's true…and that's a shame," he said. "Maybe only God has that."

There was a pensive silence.

"Well, do you love me?" she asked, piercing the silence like a blackbird call.

"Not the way you want," he said.

"But I do love and care for you, Fleming...I want you to know that..." she said, with an almost a light weeping tone to her voice. She sniffled and fell into his arms. They hugged and then walked along in silence.

CHAPTER 37

T he train flew like a pitch-black ball through the night. Only faint lights of villages popped into view in the dusk of the French countryside not far from Geneva. So long the trip had been. Then it was discovered that the train would re-route and go to Milan rather than Florence since flood waters had engulfed the citadel of the once-powerful Medici family. Groans rose like carnival balloons when the re-routing was announced but pretty soon the weary had forgotten the longer route across the northern portion of the Italian peninsula and settled into talking and drinking to kill the time. Ev was drinking a lot then periodically hitting the bathroom; Sparky and Jocko were perched on top of one of the bunks sharing a fifth of Scotch and joking and laughing. Fleming sat next to Joan who was flattered by his attention; Paris stood at the window watching the night go down as Turin was just ahead. Cassandra Pappas came up to him and said:

"You look sad, Paris," said in her bright red dress.

Paris was a thousand miles away.

"Huh?" he said, dumbly.

"I said you look sad," repeated Cassie who was often snapping her fingers and swaying her hips to music no one else heard.

"Oh, no. Just thinking," he said to make conversation.

"You think too much. You're always thinking," she said, shaking her head.

"No crime in that…" he began.

"That's not the point," she said, "you never have time for fun in life. Isn't that a form of madness or a lack of courage?" she suggested almost as if she had not said it.

"Maybe," he replied.

"I hate to see you sad…or thinking. You've been in philosophy too long. You need to dance, to sing, to feel rhythm in your bones, not sit around thinking all the time. I tell you what…why don't you dance with me right now."

"Right now?" asked Paris, annoyed at such a suggestion.

"Right now. No time is like right now," she said, snapping her fingers. After being accustomed to the over-turning moments of dialectic, Paris felt this was a condescension to the masses, or, if you prefer, the vulgar. Such was sometimes a prejudice of philosophers in that if you were intelligent enough to be a thinker you must not divulge your secret opinions to the masses but forever despise them for not being thinkers, especially in the nocturnal observations of one's journal.

"No, Cassie, this is not the proper place for dancing."

"Where is the proper place, my dear Apollo of the dialectical circuit?"

"In a dance hall. That's what it's there for."

At that she burst out laughing. The more she laughed, the more embarrassed he became. He began to scan the corridor to see if anyone else had heard or observed them. No one had.

"What's got into you? You drunk?" he asked, anxiously hoping no one would see them.

Cassie laughed and laughed.

"Drunk with joy. That's so funny. And so…proper at that," she said with a deliberateness that he did not tolerate well.

"What's wrong with a dance hall?"

"Nothing," she laughed, "but it's so stupid. If I didn't know you Paris, I'd say you were either a logician or a lawyer. No one…I mean no one thinks that stupidly or properly highly of one's thought as you do," she said as she bent over laughing until tears began to flow down her cheeks.

Paris smirked. He thought and thought of the best way to exit but something also curiously attracted him to her. Not knowing what it was, he lingered dumbly.

Finally her laughter subsided. One look at him and she began to giggle again. With effort, she finally learned to control herself.

"Come on. Dance with me, won't you?"

"Cassie, you must be drunk."

"I'm as sober as a trial judge who has out thought the law," she said with a giggle. Her arms seemed somehow longer than most; in fact, both she and Joan had very long arms as in the paintings of El Greco.

"Won't you dance with me," she repeated.

Paris smirked. He reached for his pipe but it was not in his pocket, his usual place, and that began to annoy him.

"Cassie, why are you bothering me in this way?"

"I am not. I just asked if you would dance with me. And you've given me nothing but excuses. You live and die in words, Paris. But your words do not impress however much you use them as masks. So won't you dance with me?"

Paris heaved a heavy, heavy sigh.

"There's no music," he said with exhaustion. He was impressed with how strange she was talking and behaving.

"Ah, there's where you're wrong," she said, bending her ear with her finger as if to hear more deeply. "Can't you hear it? I can."

Paris listened but heard nothing.

"No, nothing," he said, glancing at her distrustfully.

"Ah, then you hear nothing..."

"That's right."

"I knew you had good ears. Nothing is the sweetest music. So let's dance."

Paris was puzzled and showed it. His brows rose. She took his hand and began to sway to the music of sweet nothing. Self-conscious, Paris swallowed hard and to humor her and himself, he went along for the dance. Nobody ever believed her view that anyone could dance to music that no one could hear. As they danced and danced, the sound of the train became an orchestra of sounds unnoticed before. She smiled as she swayed and in the light seemed like a moonlight madonna. My eyes must be playing tricks, he thought. But after awhile he did not think anymore of it or anything because he was absorbed, as was she, in the dance. The music that could not be heard was heard loud and clear. Funny how it was that only a short time before he was asking to hear such music or to dance in a dance hall only. But it was not that any longer. Her smile beamed and he, too, found a smile even on his usually thoughtful face. Her long arms enabled her to reach farther out and from a place or so away, she tenderly touched his cheek. The music was even sweeter. He felt as if he had climbed in his mother's womb, died and found moonlight to play in: such was one road to heaven, the music of dream. After a long while, she said:

"Now we're one. You and me," she said, her arms like a dozen serpents, swaying and coiling.

"It is fun...to be one," he replied, almost in heaven such that angel's wings could be heard above his ears. He had never been here before, in the lightness, such that he felt as if he had lost himself. And one could indeed do such in one's mother's womb. Cassie changed colors in the light; now green, now blue, then pink, then back to the color of flesh again.

"You see," she said, arms coiling, "there is much magic in dancing. You feel it? Manna from heaven?"

"Yes, but must we paint ourselves that way?"

"Oh, sure that's how we call you you and me me."

"With paint?"

"Yes, until the music melts it into magic and masks," she said.

"Oh, well, what is it?" he said, tilting his head toward a mask.

"Oh, just a god. Just another god."

"Another god?"

"Yes. God is never taken in by masks. Not even his own. But this fellow...why the theater is still for him...you might call it the persona review."

At that she began to laugh as she had previously although it sounded as if it were coming from some mask. The music had become quite loud.

"Well, all I can say is…that this train hasn't burned too many masks…"

"Don't worry," she said, "it will."

Paris laughed. So did Cassie.

"That was funny," he said.

"Yes. Not worthy of any explanation," she replied.

"We are one. Two in the moon's sun," she said.

"But are we?" he said and suddenly he fell against the window pane and wondered what he was doing with cold sweat on his forehead.

"Now, don't tell me…" she said.

"What?"

"Has the music stopped for you?"

"Yes, no more music," he replied.

"Why did you have to doubt…that we were one?"

"I did, didn't I," he said, as she still swayed magically to the music he no longer heard. "I am sorry."

"Oh, well…put your mask back on if you wish…"

"But I don't…wish to," he said.

"The music stops whenever you doubt you and me are one," she said. "I have no doubts…so the music is lovely."

"A honeymoon. Paradise. I've heard it. The crossing-over…why I did not know masks were that heavy," he said, wiping sweat off his forehead.

"Of course, it's oracular to know this," she replied. "I must be going now, Paris. I do hope you hear sweet nothings again sometime," she said, waving to him as she stepped out the door into the next car.

Just then Enid came out to go to the bathroom.

"Paris, where've you been," she asked.

"Out of this world," he replied.

"You been drinking? You're sweating," she said, wiping his forehead.

319

"No. No," he said.

"It's certainly been a different trip than expected, isn't it?"

"Indeed," said Paris, glancing around the train to see anything move.

"We've been re-routed and that's what has taken so long," she said as she held his hand.

"We can learn much in being re-routed," he said.

Paris was keenly aware of having stepped into whatever it takes to emerge again into everyday consciousness.

"Have you been mad that we've had to go another route?"

"No, but there are many routes but we must only take one at a time," he said as he began to hunt for his pipe and yet he was not hunting for his pipe at all. Without warning, he held her close and kissed her long. Enid was not only surprised but disturbed. She liked things planned in advance (unless they were in a boat on the river back at the manor) and only when things were expected did she enjoy them.

"Paris, what is going on?"

"I'll tell you later. Sometime later," he said as his voice drifted off.

Next day at Falconari, they stopped and passengers bought small bottles of wine, salami, chunks of cheese, and bread. As they ate, waves of the Adriatic Sea crested and broke into white mustaches on the rock-lined shore.

"Sure is a long way to Rome," she said.

"Yes, it is," Paris replied as he made a salami and cheese sandwich to eat with his wine.

CHAPTER 38

S unlight still penetrated the closed blinds. Fleming turned over after swearing several times. Paris lay still, very still. The light did not bother him as much as it did Fleming.

"Too bright," he muttered. He got up and pulled over the cream-colored curtain to blot out the light even more. Fleming was becoming angrier. He tried to go back to sleep but it was too bright. He got up and stood on a chair and tried to pull the blinds closer to the window sill.

Paris woke. Out of his eye, he watched Fleming's endeavor to darken the light. Without warning the entire blinds fell, crashing to the floor.

"This damn place," he shouted in the brilliance of the sunlight that flooded the room. Paris was giggling, trying not to draw attention to himself. Fleming was pissed off. He picked up the whole blind apparatus again, and, cursing, tried to fasten the blinds to the window top. One end was fastened. Just as he was about to snap in the other end, the whole thing fell again with a resounding crash.

"Shit," he shouted. Quickly he turned toward Paris' bed. Paris was still.

"My God, are you dead or something? I've been shouting and you haven't even budged."

He went to Paris' bed. Not a movement could be discerned.

"That's unbelievable. You can sleep through anything Paris."

Paris raised up and yawned and played ignorant. It was much more fun to play ignorant.

"Hmmm?"

"Don't hmmm me. You heard all my shouting."

"No, I didn't. What were you shouting for?"

"Can't you see?" he said, pointing to the blind.

"Oh. Oh, let the sunshine in," he said.

"Yeah, well, I can't sleep with the sun right here in the room with me," Fleming retorted. He was miserable without enough sleep.

Just then, a knock at the door. Paris quickly put on his robe. Fleming put on his pants and a shirt. It was a maid. Smiling, she came in and saw the blinds on the floor.

"I bring back some help," she said in broken English. She was a delightful figure and Fleming began howling like a coyote as soon as she went down the hall.

Paris smiled at him.

"Oh, that's so sweet. We ought to break blinds every morning."

In a minute, two maids came in, both good looking, with trim figures and enough magnetism to induce some muffled howls. One maid turned and said:

"Is there dog in here?"

"Oh, no. You hear dogs?" asked Fleming.

"I thought so. Must be wrong," she said, as they both pushed the blinds up and snapped them in place.

Fleming was almost foaming at the mouth, chaffing at the bit. He was ready for this Italian pasta in a blue dress. He howled again. In fact, he sounded more and more like a coyote. As they had finished, the maids smiled wisely at the Americans.

"You know something?" said one with big brown eyes.

"No. What?" said Fleming almost panting.

"Your fly is open," she giggled. Fleming turned red.

"That certainly let the cat out of the bag," he blushed.

They both giggled.

"Oh, by the way, lunch will be served soon. In twenty minutes in the cafeteria," she said, her brown eyes beautifully twinkling."

"What will be served," asked Paris.

"Pasta."

"I'm sure he'll be hungry," Paris replied, indicating Fleming with his head.

"It sounds as though he is already," said the one who spoke better English.

Paris laughed. Fleming was embarrassed. The two maids left.

CHAPTER 39

But bear in mind your lover's wage
Is what your looking-glass can show.

—Yeats

They gazed up at the Sistine Chapel ceiling. Muscular Adam lounging, almost carelessly extending his arm to God portrayed as a bearded patriarch. Thin, frightened, apprehensive, curious Eve gazed at Adam. She had never witnessed such Greek proportions undressed in biblical theme. It had been two hours and the group still studied the panel long after a professor of Art at the University of Rome had described the narration with all the fluency and carefulness of an artist.

"My neck hurts," complained Fleming.

"Your neck always hurts," retorted Paris.

"That is beautiful," appreciated Cassie.

"When is dinner?" queried Ev.

"For you, twenty-four hours a day," snapped Jocko.

St. Peter laughed and again stared wondrously at the panel.

"What's he going to do to her?" asked Luwanna.

"Rape her," barked Fleming.

Apprehensive lest anyone get any ideas, she adjuster her knife which she kept in her bra. At night she kept it under her pillow for safe-keeping.

"It's just another representation, art as representation, another illusion," declared Sparky in his olive green sport coat, khaki pants, and open-collar shirt.

"Oh, Sparky, you always make the world illusory," suggested Blythe who had quietly moved closer to Fleming, trying not to be obvious.

Enid stood next to Paris and talked low to him. John Diamond was ready to kiss Daphne Fox's hand with relish.

"Why don't we move down to the Last Judgment. I'm hungry," repeated Ev, who was searching around for something to eat.

"We'll eat at the hotel in awhile, Ev. You just had three plates of spaghetti at the hotel just two hours ago. Can't you wait?"

"I dunno. I'm just hungry," replied Ev who really lived to eat and was not happy that no one else packed away thousands of calories a day as he did.

"Why don't you do something with your body instead of just filling it with food all this time?" asked Sparky who was irritated at Ev's continuous demand for succulent cuisine.

"I exercise," sulked Ev.

"Yes. Getting the fork to your mouth exercises your arm," snapped Sparky.

"Shut up, Sparky, or I'll sit on you," replied Ev, who was becoming hungrier by the minute and angrier at Sparky's hyper-attention to the details of Creation.

"Full of wonder in the beginning," remarked Paris.

"Yes, when Adam and Eve were one. God was them. Creator-created. One," remarked Fleming.

"Together yet one," said Blythe whose body was near enough to breathe their musings. Fleming turned to her and looked strangely at her then resumed gazing at the Creation.

"Does God always wear a beard?" piped Luwanna, who did not like beards.

"No, that's just an image, a representation," replied Sparky who well knew the limits of human finitude face to face with what cannot be imaged.

"I'm hungry," said Ev again.

"Then feed on the air," replied Fleming.

"Gee, that's not very filling," replied Ev who unbuckled his belt to tighten it one notch further.

"Everything is food, Ev, so eat the air," replied Fleming who was becoming irritated at Everette's insistence.

"You don't understand. I need to eat."

"No, you don't," replied Fleming as they had subtly moved on until they were under the Fall.

"You see Eve couldn't say no to food and neither can Ev," remarked Fleming. "That's when all the shit flew and we began to rock the garden and hate the Father, a blood sacrifice. Rock the garden and you devour Father and Mother," he said.

"You're crazy, Fleming. That's not me. I'm male. That's Eve," replied Ev.

"You also have an extra 'e' somewhere. But that is to confuse with names. Everyone has an extra 'e' somewhere."

Much of the crowd had left the chapel and somewhere just dimly perceptible above those remaining a chant arose:

"Come and taste and see how good the Lord is…" It was as if an order of monks was holding service.

"There you go, Ev. Go eat the Lord," suggested Sparky.

"I'm afraid the Lord is not very filling," replied Ev.

"And who would want to eat God anyway?" asked Jocko who had been listening. "What a vulgar thing to do."

Ev laughed at that.

"Sure doesn't beat pasta."

"Maybe that's not what is meant," suggested Blythe.

Two dozen eyes turned her way, half-surprised, half-annoyed.

"What do *you* think," asked Fleming.

"It can be very filling."

"How?"

"Not physically," she replied, becoming a bit self-conscious as if a spotlight landed on her.

"How?" insisted Fleming.

"You know how," she said. Like a dentist's patient not wanting a tooth pulled, she resisted his effort to pull the word out of her.

"That's all just bullshit," negated Jocko who thought such talk was at best nonsense.

"Before you nix everything, let Blythe speak if she wants to," suggested Paris.

Jocko pushed his hair back over his eye and shrugged his shoulders.

"You can be filled if you so desire...on nothing."

At this Jocko laughed. So did Ev whose stomach was growling like one dozen bears just out of hibernation.

"Right. On air, I presume," snapped Jocko who loved to mock in the name of a naïve empiricism.

Blythe did not say anything else.

"What she means, or I take her to mean, is that one can be filled spiritually," said Paris who was not too happy with Jocko's mockery.

"Now what exactly does that mean?" asked Jocko imitating G.E. Moore.

"It means that consumption is to incorporate ourselves projected as other. You feed on victims of your mockery. But your victims are the banished selves you resist, the snakes that curl under the rug of your dreams."

"It is not too clear. Sounds like poetry to me," he scoffed as he looked to Ev for propositional support.

"What you want is death by literalism: linguistic philosophy. The clear definition is a boundary that obscures. That is why roses must bargain for the right to breathe, why swans must defend themselves in court for being long-necked, why hawks must petition for the right to hunt, why wolves must steal when they can. Legalism-literalism-as-castration."

"Bah! That's nothing but poetry. No true propositions there," scowled Jocko who was beginning to feel a tiny bit uncomfortable jousting with Paris.

"Whether it is or not according to your definition, what Blythe says is true. If Ev would make room in himself, become empty, he might be filled."

"That's ridiculous, Paris. How dare you call yourself a philosopher."

"Why? Because I repudiate narrowness."

"No. No. Because spiritual filling is impossible. Food is first."

"Yes, yes. I agree. The material basis of consciousness but that does not rule out the spiritual dimension of consciousness."

"Okay, okay," conceded Jocko, "I'll grant you that. But being filled on air, on nothing, is patently absurd and self-contradictory," countered Jocko.

"Not really. Think about it. Everyone is food. To eat is to be available to be eaten. If so, then to eat is to accept the victims of yourself, the victims of your mockery. That is why you secretly love them so much, a part of you that you cannot accept."

Scowling, Jocko muttered a few under the breath comments. "Ok, ok. It's poetry but I'm beginning to get some idea of what you're saying. But the fact remains that Ev is hungry and so am I," reiterated Jocko.

"Looks like we won't get to the Last Judgment today, eh Blythe?"

Paris winked at Fleming. Enid put her arm in his and they strolled back to the Casa Palotti for a late lunch.

Chapter 40

That evening when the last faint traces of daylight cut into sky, Paris and Enid stood beside Trevi Fountain. Paris was impressed by Enid calming down in recent weeks. Usually hyperactive with a sometimes minimum attention span, Enid was very much singular in her affections. There was none or little talk of owning a Mercedes Benz as the ideal of life and a more ready acceptance of herself as well as another in such an impractical but foundational subject as philosophy. But Paris was cautious. He was not taken in by moods of the moment although he knew them well. He valued their creativity but was interested in a long-term application. Paris, too, was beginning to change, if not mature. There just might be something to such a relation, he thought as he watched the water fall into the fountain.

"You've been relaxed lately. How come?" he asked.

"I don't know. Meditation I guess. Been doing yoga," she replied.

"Really now. What got you into that?"

"Was going in circles on the way to nowhere. Never time for anything. The merry go round was going too fast," she said, gently squeezing his hand.

There was a long silence except for the drops that continuously merged with the fountain's water. Several tourists were there throwing coins into the fountain.

Then Paris spoke:

"I've noticed you're much more relaxed. Still think a Mercedes-Benz is the only thing in the world?"

She peered into his depths.

"No."

"How about wealth?"

"No."

"Reputation?"

"No."

"Pleasure?"

"No."

"Pain?"

"No." With that, Paris was amazed.

"Why?"

"No need for them."

"Really?"

"Really."

"Why?"

"I don't know." Then she paused: "Yes, I do."

"What?"

"The good of Spinoza."

Paris grinned.

"The intellectual love of God?"

"Of course."

"You've been reading Spinoza and doing yoga. What a combination! God as eternal substance and yoga to get you beyond it. Hmmm. Sounds like you've been around me too long, Enid," he said, "you must not do too much. Women are not good philosophers."

"That's a lie and you know it. Women are the secret and sometimes not-so-secret philosophers."

"I won't argue," replied Paris with a shrug.

"Let's go to the Coliseum," she suggested as they strolled through the nocturnal sounds and lights of the eternal city. Tiny cars buzzed by them; trucks groaned with loads from Naples, Bologna, and Milan. Into the Coliseum shadows they vanished.

"No lights," she complained.

"But look at the stars. Sky's as clear as crystal."

"Just think. Romans used to have gladiatorial fights in here. Christians thrown to the lions. Slaves that were but puppets to the wishes of an egomaniac emperor," observed Paris.

"Look. What are those blocks of cement?"

"I don't know. I thought it would be open space in here."

"Grass growing. Wow. Time is plastic. It has been stretched ever since I've been here. The U.S. is an infant in history."

"Only white man's history. Our imperialism is of recent vintage. The Native Americans had ancient civilizations. America's an old land. It's just our history, we think, that counts. We are only self-deceived," replied Paris.

"That's right. It is as if America is only European. Amazing how brainwashed we are," she replied, gazing at the stars.

"Yes, we are. But it was our manifest destiny to move west and slaughter. We have so much to offer, so we think, that we think we are gods with technology. We are truly self-deceived. Self-deceived," he repeated.

They strolled out of the Coliseum along the whirring rush of traffic.

"I love Rome," she said quietly as they strolled arm-in-arm.

"Why is that?"

"I don't know. I think I could live here. I like the climate."

"Yes. The sunny south. Wine filled to the brim. I like it too," he said.

Paris was aware of how deeply he cared for her but he was not trusting enough to throw himself onto her with zeal or devotion, at least not yet. He was, however, enamored of her, although he did not show his feelings as he had formerly when Ted was definitely in the picture. Social life was a masquerade: the question was which mask to wear and when.

Such was the way he hid his feelings. More time was needed if through the clouds he was to discern the stars of her eyes and the sun of her intent.

"Would you ever want to marry me?" she said in such a matter of fact way that he was taken aback by both question and manner.

"What makes you ask that?" he asked as they turned into a quieter street.

"Just curious," she said as she peered into the direction of his eyes.

But Paris would not look her in the eyes. Instead, he pulled her closer.

"I don't know. Why don't we see what happens?" he suggested.

Suddenly she halted and gazed into his eyes.

"I cannot wait forever. I'm not getting any younger," she said, flatly.

Paris frowned and bore a hole in her eyes with eyes that could penetrate even veils of illusion.

"So are you anxious to know?"

"Frankly, yes," she said with an urgency to her voice that he did not like.

"Why? You're still young. You're only in your twenties. You're sounding like you're in your forties. Why the panic? You're not even graduating."

"I don't like your tone, Paris. You sound doubtful about us. Is there any future?" she said with a slight lilt of demand to her voice. She stopped holding his hand.

"Enid, what has gotten into you? Must I decide right here and now?" he asked.

Enid began to sulk and was moody enough to make a scene which he hoped she would not do.

"Paris," she began. "I'm sick of it all…the indecision…"

"But think now," he began.

"I don't want to think. I want to get married," she said.

"Oh, come on. Don't make this into…"

"I'm not! I just want an answer," she said as tears filled her eyes.

Paris was becoming angrier by the moment.

"Look, it was you who said you had to go to Spain to find out if we were right for each other. Remember?"

Enid frowned and pursed her lips and a tear wound its way down her beautiful, smooth cheek, for she was very lovely even when she cried.

"So I did," she said, monotone. She searched for a hanky in her pocketbook.

"This is a two-way street. Love's a sport, the contest of wills. So…"

"I see. So it's only a sport to you, eh? Well…it's (sniff) not a sport to me. I love you, Paris. I really do," she repeated as the hanky dried her eyes. They strolled through some grass and sat on a bench. A glow hovered over the city from all the lights and the magic that was Rome. Paris was becoming disgusted.

"Enid, we're not high schoolers anymore. Gone are hamburgers, French fries, and milkshakes all the time. We're in college. This is a serious decision," he said with a slight laugh in his voice which dismayed her even more.

"Paris Brandon…" she began but frustration burned her words.

"Let time take its course," he suggested. This made her furious.

"Let time take its course," she mimicked, "Is that all a philosopher can do?"

He laughed and laughed. At that point, she darted from the bench and marched in the direction of the Casa Palotti.

At first he rose to chase her, but declined. Above him was a statue of Caesar Augustus. Paris eyed it for a long while then stood next to the statue and had an imaginary conversation:

"What would you do, oh Emperor?"

"I'd haul ass after her, you fool," replied the statue.

"Women aren't made to conquer, are they?"

"Of course. A man brings out the woman in woman. Always," said Caesar.

"You know you're not a bad emperor for a statue," said Paris.

"You're not a bad philosopher for a student," replied Caesar, almost caustically. Fascinated, Paris asked:

"Am I dreaming or dreaming that I am not dreaming?"

"Anything you wish. I'm not an oracle, you know," replied Caesar with a slightly caustic air.

"I did not know dead matter could talk," he continued.

Caesar narrowed his eyes at Paris almost in disbelief.

"All nature is organic. All nature, you fool. And you dare call yourself a philosopher! The human race has gone to the dogs. No more esprit, delicatezza. No more Latin rhythms. Instead fools who think all nature is not alive. Schelling thought nature is alive. So can you. I'm a panpsychist at heart, you know."

Paris grinned. "Indeed. Indeed," he said.

"So be a man and chase your woman. Believe me, that's what she wants. Every Jesuit and Zen master knows so. At least the ones I've met."

"Okay, Caesar. I'll chase her. You've really helped me in this."

He bade farewell to Caesar Augustus and dashed in the direction of the Casa Palotti that overlooked the slow-moving Tiber River.

CHAPTER 41

Only moments before the pope on his red velvet throne had said: "If you would be old enough to remain young enough, be one with God. Grace is a gift, o lovers, in valleys of mist and meditations in moonlight. May you realize true community, be a church on this earth for all, the social infinite. May you become masters of peace baptized with holy fire for Christ. Amen."

As orders of priests and nuns, soldiers, sailor, students, tourists, ardent Catholic and Protestant laity filed out of the long, majestic halls of St. Peter's Basilica into the long Via de Consiliazione, Paris said to Enid who walked ahead of him:

"Enid. Enid."

She did not turn around.

He called again.

She did not answer.

He then ran ahead until they were shoulder to shoulder.

"How about a walk along the river?" he suggested.

Hesitantly she thought; reluctantly she replied.

"What for?" she said, finally.

"A talk."

"We've talked too much already," she replied coolly. Sadness mapped her face for it was one of sorrow.

He grabbed her by the arm and pulled her to one side as most of the crowd filed out the doors, leaving them with relative quiet.

"Last night…"

"Didn't you say enough last night?" she interrupted, not giving him her eyes. Her blond hair and clear skin were a delight, angelic, even when sorrow was written on it. Her lips were not sensuous so much as cherishable. Her breasts were not large, not like Joan's but small, firm, aesthetically pleasing.

"No," he said as she turned to follow the crowd.

"Look. Here's the Pietà," he said, to attract her attention and change the subject at the same time. Smirking, she let him show her the Pietà.

"Look at Mary's mouth. Her dying son. Her pity. Even marble can speak a face."

Enid curled her lips, dully pretending to listen.

"The greatest work of pity in all of Rome."

"I pity you, Paris," she said, a bit irritated.

"But look. Look at the dying Jesus."

"I'm looking at a dying Paris," she commented, smartly.

"No. No. My dying time is 'not yet,'" he replied. "But look at those lines, those scars on our Lord. It is as if he is saying 'Thou art a soul in bliss but I am bound upon a wheel of fire…'"

"You're not getting anywhere with me, Paris," she interruptedly affirmed as resolutely as she could.

"Let's go for a walk then," he said as he squeezed her breast, playfully.

A faint, but quickly vanishing, smile came on her pretty lips.

"I'll listen. But when your words become too much, I'll shut it off," she said as if giving a promise. Off they walked, talking.

CHAPTER 42

Fleming had glued his eyes to Joan's body all during the papal speech. Now he walked with her along the brownish waters of the Tiber. Leaves fell as they walked along: gold, honey, red, yellow, purple. They paused and watched as a leaf curled and swirled lightly until it landed ever so gently on the river surface.

"Fall is really here," she said, musing.

"Leaves are going. Time's up," he said.

"You know something," she said. "I hate getting older."

"You're quite young to worry about getting older," he replied as their eyes watched the leaf flow with the current far down river.

"Yes. But I am…" she said. "I feel that I have not arrived anywhere, dedicated myself to anything except merely having a good time all the time," she replied as they strolled on.

"Dedicated?"

"Yes, like those nuns back there. They're doing something with their lives. They're dedicated…"

"But you're dedicated to an education. Isn't that enough for now?" he asked, somewhat puzzled.

Her eyelashes were elegant and one area among others Fleming continually filled his eyes with.

"But not in the same way. I want my life to be meaningful, to have a meaning…" she began. Then her voice drifted off.

"It doesn't now?"

"Yes. To some extent. I don't know. I just feel restless..."

"Everyone gets restless sometime," he said, still not figuring out where her currents were leading.

"Yes, that's true but...I don't know what it is...the same old routine... writing papers...reading tons of books...having a good sex life..."

"And a beautiful body," Fleming chimed in, gazing at her shapely breasts and curvaceous hips; he was licking his chops, much like one can taste a steak just by smell. She smiled her appreciation.

"A good sex life, eh?"

She gave him a sensitive glance.

"Who's the lucky one? Tom? Harold? Mickey? Pete? Why don't we get it on sometime, Joan. I dig sex," he said, becoming aroused.

"No, Fleming...you're like a brother to me..." At that point, his face fell almost half a mile.

"Oh, that's nice to know, Joan. Well, you know what they say... incest is best," he suggested with a laugh that went over like buzzards at a watermelon feed.

"No. No, Fleming. You've already gone too far," she said. "Besides, Pete is unbeatable."

"Oh, I bet he is, madam," retorted Fleming with a certain twinkle in his eye. She laughed.

"Peter comes several times a night," she said, naively bragging. She paused to pull her bra higher, prouder.

"What does he do, work for a pump company?"

"No. He manufactures tennis balls."

"I hope he brings new ones for each match."

She laughed again at his smutty puns for she admired the Shakespeare in him.

"Yes, he doesn't like to play with old balls," she replied.

"Those old balls don't go very far," he remarked.

"No, I'll stick with the young balls for now. They have a zesty bounce to them," she added with a grin.

"Yeah, they have a testy bounce to them," he replied, casually.

"That *was* bad, Fleming," she said, cutely and quietly amused by such talk.

Silence wound its way about them as they strolled along. After awhile, she said: "I'm thinking of becoming a nun, Fleming."

His eyes almost fell out.

"What?" he said in utter astonishment. "You? A nun? Oh God save us from such a disaster," he said, gesturing heavenward.

"Fleming, don't," she said, adjusting her bra again.

"Oh, please don't go," he pleaded with a half-comical spirit.

"What's wrong with it?" she asked, becoming disgusted at his antics.

"Nothing's wrong. It's just…not a place for you. You don't belong in a convent. You're much too beautiful."

"Very weak reasons, Fleming. Very weak," she declared as she observed the river.

"Yes. But I urge you to stay. Don't go. It's so isolated," he argued as he stroked his beard, through which his teeth shone in a smile as he studied her voluptuous body.

"Fleming, I thought I could talk to you. But I was wrong. You don't believe in anything, do you?"

"Well…sure. Yes I do."

"What?"

"Sex."

A big smile came on her face.

"That novelty goes quickly. Even in foursomes. I've done it. I've done everything for pleasure and she is a fickle goddess, an addiction. But it is fleeting. Lovely but fleeting," she declared, pushing her hair out of those deep blue eyes that were poetically sensitive.

"But you haven't done it with me," he pleaded.

"Fleming, you don't understand. Pleasure gets old. Old and sterile. Mechanical. You whisper love but you don't even mean it. It's just another in a long succession of faces. It all becomes empty. Empty," she stressed.

They walked along for a long while even past an old stone bridge, the Ponte Mezzio.

"One thing I don't understand," said Fleming after they had crossed the Tiber.

"What?"

"How can you exude sex and be contemplating such an action?"

"Well, it's this way. There are certain things you have to do sometime. I learned early I could get what I wanted from men by a little touch here, a little lick there. But after awhile they become putty in your hands. It's a game. A life-long game. Sex is…well a mask that we wear…sometimes… to hide many things. Mine was my fear of not being attractive, of a failure in the great man chase…as if the goal of life was some such stupid result…some stupid statistic. So by wearing such I never had to give myself at all. My body spoke too eloquently for that."

"Go on."

"Well, there comes a time when you grow up. Or at least you think you do. And once all that other stuff is out of your system…then you can and have to be…sooner or later…real with yourself…and as far as possible…in spite of the masks you still must wear…to carry on social life… to be yourself…to be attuned to yourself as unique in what you are…"

"But who *are* you?"

"Me. Just another mask but closer to the core. The onion almost peeled down to nothing. That is when I'll have arrived. When I get to the nothing where no labels apply…I'll know. A somebody, a nobody. Light and shadow. Hard to find someone who's not gaming around until you cease gaming around."

Fleming was without words. Joan Bradshaw was more than shapely breasts, curvaceous hips, and long legs. She was beyond description.

CHAPTER 43

D ays later after tours through the Vatican Gallery, the Roman catacombs, the Roman forum, Sparky and Jocko were awaiting the noon meal, each lying on the bed as sunlight streamed into the room they shared with Fleming and Paris.

"Can you imagine the poor bastard who ends up with Joan?" asked Jocko in a typical playful mood. A journalism major, he adored hot facts, especially if they were distorted by words.

"Can you imagine it," said Sparky dumbly gazing at the crucifix above the wash basin.

"I can just see it now. At the community meeting her husband stands around, chatting, and one by one, her lovers come by to express their gratitude," declared Jocko.

"How do you mean," asked Sparky, half-curious.

"Oh, let's see. Imagine some guy saying: "Hi, I'm your local lawyer… I just let your wife into my briefs.""

At that Sparky howled. In his laughter even the crucifix was funny.

"Can you imagine the look on her poor husband's face?" Jocko was tickled. At that Sparky laughed again.

"Hi, I'm your local doctor…I just gave your wife a free pelvic exam," suggested Jocko.

Pretty soon Sparky's imagination caught fire.

"Hi, I'm your local paper manufacturer…I just gave your wife a ream."

Jocko almost fell out of bed with laughter.

"Hi, I'm your local gardener…I just seeded your wife."

Sparky laughed so hard the walls shook.

"Hi, I'm your local fireman…I just hosed down your wife."

Jocko was beside himself. Tears began to flow.

"Hi, I'm your local policeman…I just let your wife play with my pistol."

Sparky was clubbing his pillow he was laughing so hard.

"Hi, I'm your local architect…I have designs on your wife."

Jocko was rolling over.

"Hi, I'm your local novelist…I just concluded with your wife."

Sparky was up to his arm pits with laughter.

Jocko was finally becoming somewhat controlled to think up more.

"Hi, I'm your local baker…I just popped a few dozen in your wife's oven."

At that point Sparky almost died laughing.

"Hi, I'm your local electrician…I just plugged your wife."

Jocko was in tears again with a red face.

"Hi, I'm your local milkman…I just left your wife a pint of cream."

Sparky was kicking the foot of the bed and pounding on the pillow as well.

By now, Jocko was nearly hysterical, but it was pleasurable pain for his laughter came not from the throat, but from the belly.

"Hi, I'm your local TV repairman…I just gave your wife a new tube."

Sparky kicked the bed, pounded the pillow, and rolled over several times.

Jocko gradually regained control of himself for it was his turn.

"Hi, I'm your local pharmacist…I've just given your wife one every two hours."

Sparky curled over and assumed the fetal position.

"Hi, I'm your local cigar salesman…I just gave your wife my largest Havana." Jocko was in tears again.

"Hi, I'm your local plumber. I just drained your wife."

Sparky was shaking his head with laughter.

"Hi, I'm your local rancher. Your wife has a fine spread."

Jocko was howling and could barely see the room.

"Hi, I'm your local psychiatrist…I just freely associated with your wife."

Sparky almost flipped over.

"Hi, I'm your local electrician…I just hot-wired your wife."

Jocko's sheets were now wet.

Sparky was howling at the top of his lungs when Fleming and Paris came in. This did not stop the laughter. They both looked at one another, puzzled. Paris shrugged his shoulders at Fleming who was bewildered.

"What's so funny you guys?" asked Fleming, stroking his beard and sitting with his feet on the desk. Paris sat on his bed. And from the pandemonium, it gradually quieted down. When Jocko and Sparky ceased giggling, Paris asked:

"What was that all about?"

This sent Sparky into a peal of laughter again. Jocko grinned but did not laugh. He just pushed his red hair back with his hand and sat in his print shirt with ukeles on it and blue jeans.

"Well, we were just imagining that the town's men would say to the poor bastard whoever married Joan at a town meeting of sorts. Stuff like: 'Hi, I'm your local paper manufacturer. I just gave your wife a ream,' explained Jocko rather proud of such an invention. Fleming frowned.

"We were wondering when we came up here…what all the laughing was about…" said Paris whose pipe hung down from the corner of his mouth.

"We had nothing else to do…" explained Sparky who was now a bit, but not much, more sober. The hawk on his shirt wrinkled with his every move and his tanned face and short brown hair gave him a more solid figure than he was.

Paris noticed Fleming frowning.

"What's wrong?"

"Nothing. It's just that Joan is more sensitive than that…"

"In bed you mean," taunted Sparky.

"You ought to get to know her. It's true. She screws like a bunny. But she's really very sensitive…"

"You don't believe that crap, do you?" queried skeptical Sparky.

"I have no reason to doubt her."

"Ah, hogwash. The woman doesn't know when to stop," scowled Sparky. "Besides, you've screwed her, haven't you?"

Fleming shook his head.

"That's bullshit. I saw you sleep with her many a night," charged Jocko.

"So?"

"So you screwed her, right?"

"No. Never have. Slept with her though," he said.

Just then a dark-complexioned girl announced lunch.

CHAPTER 44

"Wear me as a seal upon your heart…
For love is strong as death."

—Song of Solomon 8:6

Overcast, so much so, the gulls almost blended into sky. The journey was trying down the Appian Way although the bus driver had told many jokes along the way. He was a fat man with large puffy jowls, dark red hair, and a large wart on the tip of his nose. His stomach rolled around whenever he laughed. His voice was deep, an ocean swell, jovial, affable enough to give dreariness a much-needed rest.

Once in Naples, their boat's engines slowly turned over. They climbed aboard and looked forward to the Isle of Capri where the Roman emperor Claudius spent much of his time at the Villa Jovis and a proletarian university in 1909 had operated from Maxim Gorky's home. Capri's beauty, romance, color was well-advertised in the travel agency's brochures. But weather conditions were ominous. A storm was brewing in Sicily. Naples might get it. But now was a moment of calm.

As usual, Paris packed his pipe. Blythe gazed at Naples as the boat snorted, growled, and slowly plowed seaward. Fleming faked playing guitar on a pillow of red roses in the cabin below, where a bar had been laid out. Joan wore tight pants and an even tighter sweater which outlined her breasts with a startling pointedness. Jocko watched her carefully as she poured everyone a tall mug of beer. Sparky preferred wine. Enid shared a beer with Paris. She was so lovely, her complexion clear, her hair a homage to the Norwegian sun. Antonio, who lived on the third floor, and who also smoked grass most of the time, curled in a corner of the leather-pleated lounge chair and lit up a joint, inhaled, held his breath, then ever so slowly let it out. Most of his college education had been one long high. Enjoying a high was his way of life. He hoped most of those opposed to grass might try it first before condemning it. It has an amazing ability to alleviate pain in patients with certain life-threatening diseases. St. Peter and Fleming, along with Sparky, occasionally were the only ones from the golden hogs of Room 33 who ever shared a joint with Antonio. St. Peter often reacted with a food trip called the "munchies" and usually cleaned out the kitchen refrigerator. But St. Peter was not always stoned. Neither was Sparky. But they both thought life was worth a high now and then.

After awhile, Paris and Enid ascend the stairs to the lookout deck. Their boat ever so slowly passed the sleek white Italian liner, the Leonardo da Vinci, and soon began to pass a long line of the U.S. Navy ships, destroyers, small tankers, a light cruiser or two. Paris gazed at the lengthy liner:

"Gorgeous, isn't she," he said.

"So long, so luxurious," she remarked.

"I'm part Norwegian, you know. I've got sea mysticism in my veins. I adore ships. I love the sea…the smell of salt spray…the restless murmur of the wind… would have loved to sail Viking ships…set out from Oslo…I tell you God's song is in the sea winds…"

Enid listened with amazement at the rapture of his love.

"My father was a builder of ships, did you know that?" he asked as he finished the last sip in his beer.

"No," she replied, her eyes glued to his every inflection.

"Well, my father used to construct hulls like that liner…or those navy ships. Used to tell me how a hull was judged beautiful by how she angled in from the prow before expanding to her widest girth…like the USS Missouri battleship…truly gorgeous," he said, gazing at the liner. "There is something about the sea…that awakens in me a deep longing… a desire to lose myself in the sea…"

"To lose yourself?" Enid asked, curious.

"Yes. To find yourself...to lose yourself...in the swell and rhythm of the tide..."

"Why would you want to lose yourself in the sea?" she asked as she pusher her hair from her face.

"I don't know...I often have dreams of the sea...of the mysterious... of something mightier than my own little concerns..." he said as his voice drifted off.

They had not noticed how swiftly the winds arose much like the winds that rose out of nowhere to send the Greek fleet of Agamemnon in the direction of Troy. The wind whipped the sea and made its waves lash against the boat which tossed like a tiny tea cup in the now roaring waters of the Bay of Naples. One lurch sent Paris' beer mug sliding across the deck. Soon the boat was rocking even more violently than before, a miniature squall. It seemed as if its tiny engines would not be able to make it through the choppy waters out to Capri. Paris and Enid held on to one another and to the rail as they grew dizzier staring as the engine's wake churned now at half speed as their stomachs churned and rolled in the up and down motion of the sea.

In minutes, Paris was hanging over the rail, feeding the fish. The winds blew violently. Down below, as Fleming stood to lay the guitar on a leather seat a jolting chop of the sea sent him flying and turning through the air as if he was shot from a cannon only to land miraculously upright in a chair. Chairs slid across the floor. Hands held onto wall fixtures and everyone, including Sparky, believed this was the end of it all.

"Carumba!" shouted Antonio. "What a high. This is almost the highest I've been. What a time to roll joints."

Blythe sat in her chair between a wall and a table that slid periodically. One of the last mugs of beer flew off the table and crashed against the storeroom door. Joan held her feet against a cabinet to press herself against the seat cushion. Sparky, Jocko, and Fleming rocked with the boat and did not get hurt. St. Peter somehow made his way to the bathroom where he sat and watched the floor come all the way up to his nose and fall down again. His face was as green as his sport coat. He was high, sick, and nauseated all at once. He did not know whether to confess his sins or vomit. He felt horrible.

Topside Paris hung over the rail like an old drunk. Enid as well fed the fish her lunch. Somewhat cynically she mused and hoped that the fish in the Bay of Naples enjoyed pasta as well, however half-digested it was. Both were pale as the wind relentlessly poured its fury on them, with gusts that tossed the tiny tour boat to and fro.

"God I wish this would stop," yelled Paris. Enid wiped her mouth on her sleeve.

"Yes. I'm sick as a pregnant beagle."

"Eloquent at such times, aren't you?"

She laughed, even giggled at the folly of trying to outshout the wind. If they had taken any steps without the railing, they would have been thrown across the deck or up against the cabin. There was little footing on deck.

After twenty minutes of this, the winds began to diminish their velocity, enough so that the boat began to make headway. Soon the island appeared before them. They could not believe it. A wind-protected harbor opened its arms to the little craft as it sped across the turquoise waters. Once docked, they disembarked and walked to a waiting bus. Antonio had to be helped aboard. St. Peter's green was becoming pale. The nausea of their time had faded. Up the long, circling slopes of Capri the bus wound. Vineyards well-blasted by the rain held their heavy grapes with a refreshed solemnity. Once at the top, Anacapri, trees yet danced in the wind. From their vantage point, they could see the cream-colored walls of villas overlooking Capri. Offshore, two large rocks jutted from the turquoise-colored Mediterranean. They were battered again and again by the restless tide. Enid stared long at the white dance of foam that tumbled down the sides of the rocks. The sea was yet wild on that side of the island—so different from the calm waters of the harbor.

Lunch at the Hotel San Miguel was exquisite. It offered a stunning view over the multi-blue shaded waters near the Blue Grotto, and a large rock with a wind-weathered hole in the center that peered into the fathomless blues of the sea— all these combined to make eating a seafood delight, even though St. Peter, Enid, and Paris were understandably not as eager to eat as the others.

Jocko kept trying to hustle Joan who repeatedly warded off his advances, all to the amusement of Fleming who smiled and winked knowingly at Joan. But it was, of all of them, a close time for Paris and Enid. They had weathered the worst and sun began its ascent into their lives. Capri was a poem of romance. It brought out the lovely blue of her eyes. It brought out the seriousness in Paris that he could only dimly understand. Paris was growing deeper, layer by layer, into love. It was a happening at the wind-swept ends of heart and mind. The curious thing was that, for the first time, she, too, felt secure in the relationship and once it had taken root, love grew wiser and deeper. Paris had become an empty chalice exquisitely filled and renewed daily by the shimmer love painted in their eyes and on their cheeks.

Most had gone to the tourist shops. But they remained as the winds died and sun pierced the steel-gray clouds. Arm in arm they walked.

"You know...I had given you up for dead...during the Spain trip... you were such a bitch that day," he said as they strolled along.

"I was a bitch...a bitchy bitch...you've seen all of me...or the dimensions I care to show, that is. You still love me?"

Paris grinned showing his teeth with extra verve.

"I guesso. I've loved you from the start. You know that."

At that, she reached up and kissed him with a genuineness that made him feel good all over.

"You turn my prose into poems... I cannot love anyone more deeply than I do you..."

They kissed again. A glow shimmered on their faces. This was it. It was evident that things had coalesced unlike any previous time. There was a feeling if rightness about it, a stability, a harbor into which each had gone. Love had been growing all the time, through the fights, regrets, and fears. Then one fine moment love happened. What had been only dimly perceptible now became increasingly clear. They felt they were meant to be together. After all the uncertainties, they soon would be. To that extent Paris was again only dimly aware. But Enid, uncluttered by the usual cataracts of reason and logic, saw quite clearly into what was occurring. Right now she just smiled to herself and remained in the warmth of his arms.

CHAPTER 45

R ome had been fun. Only weeks ago Rome had warmed them. They
had learned about art, people, themselves. Even the unforgettable episode of Jocko dancing nude on the train just north of Florence
in an endeavor to attract Joan's attentions had faded somewhat into
the comical burlesque rather than the comical seriousness that Jocko
intended. Even his wildness a week later when raging around the manor,
he had begun dancing on the roof, no one, including Joan, high as she
was on Newcastle-on-Tyne Brown Ale, was particularly impressed. The
Roman toga party was a success with the music of *Mourning Sickness*,
a rock band from Liverpool. Term papers were typed to the unsteady
rhythms of weekends in Wales or the Isle of Wight. St. Peter finished
his in the library of the University of Nottingham after which he spent
the day rowing two young British girls, Sheila and Diane, up and down
the Trent River in a rented rowboat. Zee Ferguston, always efficient,
punctual, had his papers done so early he could afford to play cricket
with Antonio who was stoned enough to be consistently defeated with
ease. Luwanna even learned to laugh as spontaneously as Duci one night
when the Baliol players from Oxford presented a satire on British foreign
policy in Rhodesia. She laughed at these lines of their song:

> Rule Rhodesia
> That's what we've got to do
> So if you're black, brown, or yellow
> Sucks to you!

This song was sung to the melody of the British national anthem for weeks afterward in the men's shower room. Ev still packed away the potatoes and became obscenely obese. Sparky and Jean Pense formed an alliance with the dubious merit of sleeping together for a mutual avoidance of boredom. Fleming and Blythe were one speaking terms but only as friends. Joan was entertaining men, so much so that the thoughts of becoming a nun were increasingly remote.

Autumn winds came. Their time in Britain was nearing its end. Some were sad at parting; others were glad to be going home. One of their final field trips was to Stratford-on-Avon to learn more about Shakespeare and attend at least one performance of his plays at the Royal Shakespeare Theater.

CHAPTER 46

Fleming and Paris left the Chaucer Head Bookshop and strolled in the direction of Clopton Bridge that crossed the gentle currents of the Avon. Next to the Royal Shakespeare Theater, they stopped and talked as the swans marched by seeking tidbits or pieces of bread.

"So you're getting married?" asked Fleming with a faint disgust as well as awe on his burgundy-bearded face that shifted red shades in the autumn sunlight.

"Yes. This is it," replied Paris, packing his pipe, smiling at the swans with black feet.

"I still can't believe it. Just a couple of months ago, you two were fighting like alley cats," replied Fleming, who, unlike his friend, was skeptical.

Paris smiled as orange glowed wildly in his pipe bowl.

"Well...it's been different. War then peace," replied Paris. "Who can say what a woman will do or think tomorrow? I trust her anyway."

Fleming took some bread from his pocket and tossed it to the long necks awaiting it.

"It's still hard to believe that you would even consider marriage...I mean after all the philosophy you've had."

Paris almost choked on his laughter.

"Philosophy does not exclude marriage, you fool. It might even make a philosopher mellow. You never know," Paris said with a smile.

"She's put you through it before...I just hope she doesn't walk on you again like she did with Ted hanging around. Boy, I'll never forget that," declared Fleming with a finality inappropriate to the situation.

"Maybe you ought to forget it. If I get myself into hot water, that's my fault. If I have made a mistake, I take the consequences," declared Paris who was now teasing a swan with an extraordinarily elongated neck.

"But I've seen so many failures," protested Fleming who, when he was not looking, had a piece of cracker snatched from his fingers.

"If it's a failure, so what? Do the stars cease to shine?"

"No," replied Fleming after a longish moment, a pause that reflected. "You're right. I'm just fearful I guess."

Paris smiled and puffed his pipe and fed the long-necked swan.

"Fear's a strange event."

"Why?" asked Fleming who cocked his head and stared at Paris' bright eyes.

"It prevents daring to venture. Only when we want to keep and hold...do we fear that loss..."

"You mean I fear loss?"

"In a sense. Altered relation. Lifestyle. But this is all in passing... undergrads...beer...parties...wine, women."

"Parting in every meeting...joy in every sorrow..."

Suddenly a broad smile unraveled on Fleming's face.

"Anxiety about the future is only wasted energy...the future is seeing into the present..."

And they both began to laugh so loudly some of the swans became embarrassed and left to stroke on to less loud passersby.

CHAPTER 47

The sun slanted through late afternoon haze. Enid casually observed crew members rowing rhythmically on the mirror-still waters of the Avon. Behind them was Holy Trinity Church and off to both sides was its graveyard. They had spent the day shopping and had purchased, among other things, blue sweaters made of Scottish wool. The way sunlight hit the stones of the church and the gravestones was somehow momentous and memorable. It was a time in their lives that flowed together in a mutual harmony prompted by love. Joy outlined their faces. Their world glowed since this day was a day *for* them. There was a charm and a warmth in the air that animated them with reverie.

"The sun sits well..." offered Paris, musing.

"Yes. Even the gravestones appear peculiar...an iridescence...there's something serene about this place..." she said. "I love Stratford. A little village nestled in the Cotswolds. The voice may turn poetic here. A splendor, an exposure to the open air, swans, late afternoons, and the lazy buzz of flies. Philosophy can be in tune with poetry here. Prose dances with castanets. A marriage to sky and wood: the poet's hour, a twilight unmasking, unasked for, a wooded cask of vintage metaphor and sweet sounds of easy Avon currents to the sublime strokes of dozens of swans in summer ease or winter's rage. No wonder Shakespeare's pen glided so easily over psychic globes and unbrushed characters. Here rhythm fills in the blanks, verse tender, tragic, pathetic, and outrageously comical. Such are the luxuriant tones of song unheard here in the spoken evensongs of Warwickshire."

Into the vestibule of Holy Trinity Church they walked. They were the only ones there. Eventide service would not begin for another three hours.

"God, it's silent here," whispered Paris as he scanned the altar.

"It sure is," choked Enid.

"The silence here is so strong...I can almost hear music," declared Paris who was quite impressed by the solemnity.

"It's like time has reached zero..." said Enid after awhile as their curiosity scanned the literature at the rear of the church.

"Yes. Infinity in a flower. The clear light."

Enid now sat on a large, wooden pew.

"The slightest movement here says much."

Paris could hear her scratch her arm; it sounded like a busy street corner in Brooklyn or Buenos Aires.

"Can you imagine it being so quiet...that you can listen to your heart?"

"Yes, one can do that when close to God," Enid replied.

"In touch with oneself...when one sneeze is like smashing the sound barrier...God in stillness...the way light filters over there..."he said, pointing to a corner where light fell on the deep wooden pews.

"Shakespeare's remains have been here for centuries..."

"Yes. His voice is quite loud..." he said.

"I could not worship here...at least not with words..."

"Only breathing...like a yogi...would really dig this place. Think of the weddings that go on here when no one is around. Bliss. The highest bliss. Cosmic consciousness."

"Yes, yes, yes," she replied in a quiet, creative ecstasy.

After lingering a few minutes more, they went outside as Enid put her arm in his as they strolled through the graves, here and there, pausing to read the dates on them.

"*Hamlet* was superb last night," he said after a friendly silence.

"Much better than *Winter's Tale* the other night. Somehow I still find Lear much more to my liking," Enid replied as they strolled down another path of graves.

"Oh? Why Lear? Paris asked.

"Because Lear has to die several deaths...and even become a fool...to suffer so much to realize..." she said as her words floated like butterflies on the Warwickshire wind. Paris paused and peered into Enid's lovely blue eyes that appeared green in the bright sunshine.

"What?"

"To realize...that love in a certain way can never be put into words..."

"You mean when he asks his daughters how much they love him?" asked Paris.

"Yes. And the one who truly loves him says 'I love you according to my bond, no more, no less.'"

"What are you trying to say?"

"That no words can ever...speak as loudly...as the silence of the embrace...of the arms that reach out...of the eyes who conduct weddings of the soul...and those lips that in uttering sweets utter nothing...the profundity of the nothing amid the sweets..."

"Your voice is a lovely lute..." he said, tapping ashes out of his bowl onto a grave.

"Love that embraces silently is often love that *is*. That is Lear's mistake. He assumes words have the final say. Not at all. Can you ever exhaust love in words?"

"No," said Paris in a forceful voice. "Never."

Enid smiled.

"So it is. Lear has to become more foolish than his fool...in order to learn that little forgetfulness. One can go to sleep between birth and death by not realizing what cannot be put into words. That is a wasted life, in a sense."

"Maybe so. But lovers still must use words however painful, however corralled..." offered Paris, fiddling with his pipe.

"This place is a breath of the eternal," he said as they strolled to the altar. A wreath of azaleas lay on Shakespeare's tomb.

"Anne Hathaway, Dr. Hall..." Enid said almost in a whisper. Her blond curls contrasted with her blue knit sweater; her eyes wide with curiosity in blue.

"So quiet you almost hate to speak...the silence says it all."

There followed a quietude, a reverence that amazed their minds and freed their imaginings. It was all a release, a wedding rehearsal, man and woman, together and found. They felt a stillness that wound its way to the older, primordial, pre-logical awareness of mind that plunged them deeper into the recesses of touch and expanded them beyond the reaches of their horizons. They were in stillness at the center, a touch of the divine. Out of such Arcadian springs there bubbled an awareness of how words shoot across surfaces and do not dive to the depths. As their awareness deepened, there they found bliss as clear as blue sky on a summer's day. This was their first wedding, the wedding beneath the words, the body's wedding.

After such, they left the church and strolled through book and dress shops with a smile on their faces.

CHAPTER 48

"I can't believe it, Fleming. You're dressed up," said Daphne as Fleming straightened his tie in the hall mirror outside the chapel.

"Once in a lifetime, my dear. Once is enough," he said with a cavalier twinkle in his eyes.

Everyone was dressed for the occasion. The giant chandelier in the chapel was light; its radiance mellowed the sharp faces of monsters and saints carved in wood on the walls next to each pew.

Only minutes before, Father Noel had parked his motorcycle and with his ponytail flopping strode through the hall to put on his clerical robe. Fleming was best man; Blythe, her pregnancy not quite obvious, was the maid of honor. The student body as a whole was dressed, excited, and felt this event was the peak of their time in Britain, a time about to end in two weeks. Ev was busy relishing the cookies and cakes on a table outside the sanctuary.

Paris was nervously fidgeting with his cumberbun in front of the mirror. Father Noel stood next to him, taking off his long leather motorcycle boots. Other students periodically came in and out to check their appearance or to chat with the groom.

"Don't be nervous," said Noel as he took off his leather-fringed pants.

"Now, Father," began Paris quite self-absorbed.

Father Noel smiled. "You know I'm the primal mother, Paris," he said with a hearty laugh. Puzzled, Paris asked:

"With whom did you study theology?"

"A Professor Nietzsche, my favorite professor of theology. Fritz Nietzsche."

"Most clergy don't talk about a primal mother. I was just wondering. I met him once at a pub in Edinburgh."

"That's him," smiled Father Noel. "Isn't he insightful?"

"Indeed he is," said Paris.

But even this did not calm Paris down.

"How can you be so calm?" Paris asked, combing his hair.

Father Noel began to take off his jade necklace, his turquoise Navajo-made beads from New Mexico, his Gemini necklace with the yin-yang twins made of gold carved on it set against the Green Dragon of spring and the White Tiger of autumn.

"It's just natural. Flow with the tide, Paris. We've talked about this before. God is always there. Forever. Where every breath is…" Noel said with a smile. His face was deeply tanned, his ponytail down to his mid-back, a tiny turquoise earring accentuated his ruddy ear lobe, his arms were quite muscular as were his shoulders.

"What if it's not for me?" asked Paris with uncharacteristic anxiety. Father Noel took off his shirt, baring a well-tanned chest.

"Then it is not for you," said Father Noel calmly as he put on his pants and gazed with a faint grin at Paris' perplexities in the mirror. Seeing Paris still troubled, he said:

"Put your worries away. Stay still. Let the stream clear. Then flow with the way of life. You're making worries too large. Faith and risk are one breath. God is a lover, my friend, and whether personal or impersonal, God is there. God changes masks between acts and revelation. Be at rest and divinity will be with you all your days. But you know all this, Paris," said Father Noel, combing his long hair with smooth, unhesitating strokes, searching Paris' face.

Paris smiled.

"I'm just nervous. I've never been married before."

Father Noel put his hair in a ponytail, put on his clerical shirt and collar, which could not be too clearly seen beneath his well-trimmed beard.

"You will do fine," he said, calmly. "Enid's as nervous as you are... and besides you love her. That helps. Hard work to keep that going but it's worth a life. Just don't sit around on a mountain of self-doubts and you just might regain a glimpse of paradise. That is truly a wedding to celebrate...when people have their heads together. By the way, I hope you have rehearsed your poem of love. It individualizes the services...and for Christ's sake...I hope you used some imagination. God will dance at your wedding. Let's go. Time's a-wasting," he said with a grin as he danced his way into the chapel.

Paris began nervously adjusting his watch. Jocko, in a rare moment, when he too, had dressed up as an usher, shuffled up next to Paris.

"So you're going through with it, eh? You poor bastard. I thought philosophers never married."

"This one is," said Paris with extra emphasis.

"Don't worry, you're on time. The chapel's right around the corner," he said, eyeing Paris' nervous playing with his timepiece.

"I know. I know," he replied.

"I hate to see a good man bite the dust. This marriage thing is for the birds. I just like screwing women. No marriage for me," said Jocko, combing his red locks with a certain cynical abandon.

"I'm not biting the dust," declared Paris.

"Sure, Paris, sure," replied Jocko with a mock assurance.

Paris frowned.

"Jocko, you're a good man but—"

"But what?"

"But sometimes your attitude is..."

"What?"

"Diseased. That's what."

"Well, I hate to see a good philosopher go to hell..."

"Jock, that's enough. Keep your cynicism to yourself. Someday even you might find it in yourself, if you expand your concerns beyond playing musical beds, you might actually grow close to someone...and really, I mean really, love them. And maybe you don't think you can or ever will—and you are already scoffing at me with your laughter—but it is the most wonderful event in all the world. It doesn't have to be gushy, sentimental, romantic, although those elements are there. It doesn't have to be super-realistic as if it all consisted of fights over who cooks, who left the toothpaste top off, who didn't let the dog out. But there is a glow about it all. You just want to be with that person come sorrow and joy. Maybe you will someday, Jock."

"I doubt that. Marriage kills love and you know it. It's a lot of hogwash for the priests and the lawyers. I avoid it like the plague," said Jocko quite proudly.

Paris smiled: "Maybe you are right. Maybe marriage kills love. But I'm willing to gamble that love can last through an entire married life together. So" he said, "see you at the celebration.

"Yes. I'll see you," said Jocko who now pondered things in a thoughtful silence.

Paris left and soon the procession was to begin. At the altar stood Father Noel with a serene face. Paris and Enid slowly strolled down the aisle. Next came Fleming and Blythe and they were followed by the ushers and bridesmaids. An organist sat silently to one side of the altar. Once having reached the altar, Enid and Paris stood, hands entwined.

Father Noel said: "Dearly beloved, we are gathered here in the sight of God and in the face of this company to join this man and this woman in holy matrimony, to allow one another to be available for the birth of Christ in the soul, and to grow with one another in sickness and in health and to minister each to each and to trust in the Lord forever."

Father Noel stepped closer to them. Jocko kept eyeing Joan Bradshaw; Blythe could not take her eyes off Fleming who studied his friend's expression in the ceremony.

"Paris Lee Brandon will you have this woman as your wedded wife? Will you love her the way a woman is to be loved? Comfort, honor, not to possess her in sickness and in health as long as you grow the same path together?"

"I will," Paris said, peering into Enid's eyes.

"Enid Linda Brown, will you have this man to be your wedded husband and to live together in the holy event of matrimony? Will you love him the way a man is to be loved—the art of love, comfort, honor, and not posses him in sickness and in health as long as you grow the same way together?"

"I will," answered Enid.

"Paris, how do you find this woman?" asked Father Noel.

Paris responded with a wedding poem's lines:

"Like a branch of white jasmine
Is you, my love, among the willows"

"Enid, how do you find this man?" asked Father Noel.

"My love has adorned
My pillow and my lips
Are red from loving."

Father Noel intoned:

"May you be at peace
In winter's suns
And warm summer rains...

Observe the ethical and
Let the seas of life
Wash between you.

Be far enough away
To be ever close;

May you find and experience
God beyond God where words fail;

These are the weddings of the soul
Not paper but spirit: such is
Love between man and wife."

Then they exchanged rings, saying:

"With this ring, we are wed: in the name of the Father and the Son, and of the Holy Spirit: all as one."

They knelt and Father Noel touched with one hand both their shoulders and said:

"For as much as Paris Lee Brandon and Enid Linda Brown have consented together in being wed and have witnessed the same before God and saints, and the underlying rhythms of cosmic consciousness, and have pledged their spirits and given rings, I pronounce them man and wife, in the name of the Father, and of the Son, and of the Holy Spirit. Amen."

Paris and Enid rose.

"Ladies and gentlemen, I present to you Mr. and Mrs. Paris Lee Brandon." All those in attendance clapped for the newlyweds. "

"Paris and Enid, congratulations," said Father Noel. "Open the wine and champagne. Let celebration spin this world."

At that point the organist began to play "Holy, Holy, Holy" as champagne and wine bottles were uncorked. Everyone congratulated the newlyweds. Then everyone danced and enjoyed the festivities long into the night.

CHAPTER 49

Next morning Father Noel awoke. Sunlight streamed through the large stained glass windows that dramatically silhouetted the heads of saints carved in the deep mahogany pew ends. The pew was not particular hard; there just had not been much room to turn over. His head felt a bit sour. Weddings had a way of doing him in, especially when he drank champagne and then followed it with wine. He had to return to his parish, Eternity's Sunrise, before four o'clock. He sat up and held his head for a long moment.

"What a night," he muttered. Rousing his strength, he rose and went into the kitchen to get some coffee to sober up and the cook gave him some dried meat and cheese. He then returned to the room to secure his street clothes.

In minutes he had put on his leather outfit and his beads, his long leather boots. Just then Paris came in.

"I hoped to find you here," he said.

Father Noel parted his hair in the middle so he resembled an Apache.

"I want to thank you," Paris said, extending his hand.

They shook hands.

"Don't mention it."

"Enid and I—we loved it. Everything. It said everything we hoped a wedding might say. They're usually so traditional, stuffy, and unreal."

Father Noel smiled as he put a head band on to hold his hair in place.

"You look like Geronimo," suggested Paris.

Father Noel just laughed.

"Oh, by the way, Father, once one is married, what does one do with it? I mean to keep it going…"

Noel gave him a disconcerted but well-knowing look.

"Are you fighting?"

"No."

"Then why do you ask?" he said, brushing his hair in long, even strokes.

"Just for…my own knowledge."

Father Noel nodded quietly.

"Keep it free, open and easy. Don't push. Grow together. Know your weak points but don't make a point of them. Learn from them. That's all I know. The rest you have to decide as situations arise."

"Thank you for that," Paris said, thinking over what he had said.

"I must go. Must be at Eternity's Sunrise in a couple of hours. My best to you both. God be with you," he said as he tied his clerical garb to his motorcycle. He pumped it and it began to hum smoothly.

"Paris, come see me sometime." Then he stuck up his thumb to the wind-currents and said with a smile: "All systems go." And off he rode to Eternity's Sunrise.

Paris watched him disappear in the distance. As he turned, a figure caught his eye's corner. It was Fleming. Paris smiled. Fleming extended his hand; Paris shook it.

"Deeply moving. Last night," declared Fleming.

"You liked it, eh?"

Fleming nodded.

"I must admit it was moving. A priest from Eternity's Sunrise. And a poet and philosopher. I guess this means a parting of the ways," suggested Fleming.

"The way is not parted," replied Paris, concerned for his friend's concern.

"How do you mean?"

"Certainly there has been a change. I'm married now. But why must friendship not go on?" said Paris, eyeing him with care.

"Oh, it can, I suppose. But can it in the same way?" asked Fleming with his hands on his hips.

"If it were the same way…that presupposes no change has occurred. Don't worry, Fleming. Lay your heart down. Friends will be sooner or later. Let things be. And we'll be," said Paris, touching him lightly on the shoulder in a gesture of friendship.

Fleming smiled faintly.

"All right. All right," was all Fleming said. After a pause of a moment's reflection, he said:

"How's Enid?"

"Lovelier than sky on infinity's morning."

Fleming smiled broadly.

"Someday, my friend, we will all be decoded. Our cryptic remarks are not favored by clarity and precision-loving philosophers."

"Ah, but clarity is only another obscurity…this time in the name of simplicity. You know that, Fleming," Paris said, smiling even more broadly than Fleming. Together, arm-in-arm, they strolled into the manor.

CHAPTER 50

Except for one guitarist who was born in Swansea, Wales, all of The *Well-Born Dead* were born in Liverpool. Two guitarists, a drummer, one bassist, one pianist: they played mostly hard rock, country western with swing, even cool jazz. Their music blared through the manor so loudly that some of the painted angels on the ceilings were visibly moved, assumed such noise heralded the last judgment or at least the four horsemen of the apocalypse. Everyone came to this last big event of the year, the Shakespeare Ball. Paris came as Macbeth; Enid as Lady Macbeth; Fleming came as Anne Hathaway; Blythe came as Othello; Jocko came as Richard II; Sparky as Owen Glendower; St Peter as Mistress Overdone; Zee as Friar Lodowick. Others were Cassandra Pappas as King Lear; Jean Pense came as Puck; Joan as William Shakespeare; Antonio as Caliban, to mention only a few. Outside the ballroom was a corridor in which one could escape some of the noise. Inside, a long bar was opened and Worthington Ale, Sweet Stout, Lunatic Brew, Lucky Madness were served.

The dance floor was filled with dancing, swaying, and sensual bodies. Anne Hathaway at first danced with Puck; Richard II with Mistress Overdone; Macbeth kissed his wife with tenderness between dances. Foxy on guitar played solo for one dance; Rafael on bass accompanied Moon Sun on piano. Body Beautiful did a drum solo; Mystic East dazzled minds on another guitar in a duet with Foxy. They swayed with grace and a full moon outside.

This time Body Beautiful and Mystic East did a duet and the music swayed. But soon it was time for a break. The *Well-Born Dead* stopped playing and eagerly sought bottles of Lucky Madness or Sweet Stout and the cooler air outside. Everyone stood around chatting.

Anne said to Will: "You've left me with twins, Hamnet and Judith. Why don't you come back, Will?"

"Nay, madam, on the banks we loved to the Avon's song; and before you knew it, we had to put on the banns. Once with you, I had to leave you, though you did eventually get my second best bed."

"Your will is too meaty for me, a ghost in Elsinore, an estate of broadly-told imaginings. But I loved you with everything I could."

"Aye, you did. But I had to play with my globe and spin the sphere around. Like a sweet-mellowed swan, I had to make my strokes bold and clear for every character written."

They laughed and passed drinks around.

Puck said: "Where there's a Will, Anne Hath a way."

They all laughed.

Lear said: "Puck shall be my fool."

Puck said: "No one can be more foolish than you, Lear."

Lear replied: "Nay, seems madam, I know not seems. It is. You are my true fool, Puck. Jest for me, fool."

Puck became angry and stomped off to the other end of the punch table.

"This is a fun masquerade. What is this game called?" asked Mistress Overdone from the Boar's Head, holding her sultry hips with holy abandon.

"Masks," replied Friar Lodowick, disguised as himself.

"The price?" asked Richard II with garden looks and herbal crosses.

"Jealousy," replied Othello, masking blanched cupidity.

"No, screwing your courage to the sticking deodorant," replied Lady Macbeth with daggers in her lovely Scottish eyes.

"No, the price is the play…the ego-drama," injected Shakespeare with his characters smoothly brushed and well made up.

"And what happens when you pay that price?"

"You find that you are bound…upon a wheel of fire…" replied Caliban who spooked each individual's island with a mirror of himself.

Just then a huge room-wide chandelier which hung in the ballroom gently lowered itself until it spun in a circle all around them. This intermission was sponsored by the *Well-Born Dead*. A break between acts was a smoking revelation. The more they drank, the faster the mirrors spun around them: mirrors of all sizes and shapes. Some magnified their heads; others shrunk their bodies; others just mirrored body parts such as eyes, noses, ears, arms, mouths.

"An eye as big as your nose, Mistress Overdone," said Macbeth.

"What a large phallus you have Lady Macbeth," shouted Lear, who was now on his own heath, the winds, rains of himself, about to burn up.

"Yes, a tripartite division: a mouth, arm, and leg: my universe," announced Glendower. "I told you that at my birth, the heavens shook, the skies full of flaming selves, all colors, complexions, textures of mind: reverend wonders. A gentle embrace: one love potion. Puck, on my eyelids paint them smoke color. God my eyes are big mirrors, colors all—"

"Something is rotten in the state…" asserted Richard.

"Isn't it wonderful," replied Caliban. "How wonderful, prosperous, that your identity had to be paid for in words, poetic snatches down by the river. Yes, something is rotten in the state…"

"Of our disunion address," inserted Friar Lodowick. "What faces, hands, bodies we have, fragmented mirrors all in one ballroom."

"Wherein we each shake a speare. Here. I'll unzip mine and play with my globe again," said Will.

"By the way, Will, I've heard there's nothing good in your globes but a good will," said Othello, turning white.

"See how large my eye is…ah, there it goes…when I take a survey of all the world, time must have a stop," replied Will, downing his fourth Lucky Madness.

"Split selves in one whole, entire, complete globe. The king's men know we have not been practicing active non-action," replied Macbeth. "Ever since, my prayers have stuck in my throat."

Caliban had had twelve lunatic brews, one for each month. He held high his lucky thirteenth:

"Here's to a universe of mirrors: may our bodies rise from the *Well-Born Dead* and touch us live and help us play with words as we play..." he said, swallowing hard.

Mistress Overdone had had enough: "It's time, ladies. You know it's time...to turn over. On your bodies, now. Baptisms are free."

They all changed their positions as they drank and mirrors swirled, gyrated on unseen axes."

"So you want to join the play, do you?" asked Shakespeare, twitching his auburn mustache and beard.

"Yes, my love," replied Anne, pregnant with twins.

They found a circle within the circular play of mirrors, ever circulating, in motion but as they did so, they noticed a door open into their mirrored circle. In danced other characters such as Bardolph, Dogberry, Petruchio, Queen Elinor, and Prospero: they whirled like dervishes into becoming, being, and ongoing destruction. They were like huge cultural eyes that dilated with the times. They seldom danced alone for they always held hands; they were joined by silk threads.

"I'll be..." muttered Macbeth as the trinity danced to the rhythms of the swirling mirrors in the circle of well-brushed characters.

"I'm getting dizzy," said Mistress Overdone, flailing her arms in self-degeneration. And they could hear the whirl of the mirrors' increasing velocity.

"So you want to join the play, do you?" said Shakespeare.

"I do," replied Lady Macbeth as her eyes rolled out to the end of time and rolled back with love.

"Aren't you somewhat out of character, Will?" asked Glendower.

"Never. I'm always in character," replied Shakespeare.

"You know Will is never out of character," asserted Puck. "Why that would mean he lost himself tomorrow. And you know he just lost himself today."

"Heavy, heavy. Don't get too heavy," sang Lear, still hunting for his fool, until Richard pointed out his garden below his belt.

"And you? Haven't you had enough of old death in your austere versions?" said Shakespeare to Macbeth who grinned and sang:

"Being is my toenail; becoming is my rump. We know when the light goes out. Hahaha. Tralalalalala."

"So you want more dying on your characters? Oh, a sprinkling of becoming, please. Add marjoram for melody; sage for eternal delight. Sit on the heads of the two Gentlemen of Verona if you must. We must get the lie in motion, the wheel of suns, your final incarnation. Touch earth and I will make you a large kingdom for a little grave."

Two tablespoons of becoming later, the mirror whirled so fast that noses, eyes, mouths, all blended into a oneness, a mass for mirrored eyes, a requiem for lost lines and the old differences in a previous light.

Once drunk, they were one and had died already many, many times.

"I'm lost," cried Mistress Overdone.

"It's about time. Let's see…nine past eternity. It's about time," replied Will.

"Yes, it's about time," said the merchant of Venice, wiping the sweat from his Fu Manchu.

"Three faces of illusion," shouted Julius Caesar. "Look how graceful Pericles' arms are. You made us be true, Cymbeline."

"Thank you. You see, folks, you get only one for the price of three. So laugh and begin to die again. Such is your mirror."

All three spoke from the same mouth with equal grace in their sameness.

"Okay. The show cannot go on. No more. We will no longer learn only from our eyes. From then until now."

"No more plays?" asked Othello.

"No, no, no the show must cease," said Will.

And with that, the mirrors ascended and they returned to only names and words and arguments: the rocking sound of the *Well-Born Dead.*

CHAPTER 51

I t was unusually quiet on departure day. Memories filled the air and what mattered, what was valued, was retraced throughout the last breakfast. Homecoming was an event that spawned a variety of reactions as varied as personalities. Some were anxious to leave; others were afraid to leave and clung to their friends and memories; still others had made a home away from home during their stay and thoughts of return appalled and repulsed them.

Ev packed away ten pancakes; Skip still barked with vigor as he added several tail hairs to the custard pie, presumably as a farewell gesture; John Diamond had courted and was still courting Daphne Fox on the cedar staircase; Professor Arsse had finished his lecture on irrelevance in education which caught everyone unaware; Foo Key was still doing alchemical experiments in his third floor room; Fleming was still on a movement away from Blythe. Through her suffering, Blythe had become even more sensitive, and had already given birth to untold dimensions of her poetic self; in her relationship with Fleming, she had become uncalculatingly serene and she would soon be a mother. Joan had successfully outmaneuvered Jocko; Sparky still slept with Jean Pense; St. Peter yet watched his clock; newlyweds Paris and Enid were getting along well and looking forward to the wedding reception at their parents' home; Judith got special permission to leave school and move to Paris to be with Yolanda; Zee was awarded a renewed scholarship; Duci still giggled through it all.

Through their time in Britain, they had learned quite a bit from life but there was always much to learn. The two hours by bus passed quickly and after they had gone through customs at the London airport and were sitting there, awaiting their boarding, Fleming reminded Paris of a moment they had shared:

"This is the day," said Fleming, casually.

"Yes. Returning. Coming and going," replied Paris, as Enid listened next to him.

"You remember that day in Stratford?"

"Which one?"

"The day of the swans?"

"Oh, yes."

"Remember how just as we were not wanting to leave…"

"Oh, yes. I remember."

"Remember how the swan with the longest neck…was really nice and long and black," said Fleming, stroking his beard.

"Yes. That swan had a necklace on its neck…" remembered Paris.

"Remember…it was so friendly…it got out of the Avon and came to us…very tame…and it gave you a necklace of Cowrie shells."

"Yes, I remember. It gave them to me."

"And remember what you said?"

"No, what'd I say?"

"You said 'Every departure is a returning with necklaces of remembrance.'"

Paris smiled and said:

"God you have a good memory."

"This is a good time to remember…before you forget," said Fleming with a twitch to his beard.

Paris lit his pipe and smiled. That was what he did before every departure.

THE END

CPSIA information can be obtained
at www.ICGtesting.com
Printed in the USA
FSOW01n1825051217
41824FS